Winner of the spur award for best Western Historical Novel

"[Captures] with grace and passion that agonizing point in history when the opening of the Western frontier spelled demise for the Indian civilization. Cooke deftly weaves its many layers around births, deaths, love affairs, visions awaited, dreams interpreted, battles avoided and begun . . . a lovely chronicle of a changing world."

—*The Philadelphia Inquirer*

"*The Snowblind Moon* can justly be called an epic tale of the struggle between the Indians and whites for control of the Plains in the 1870s. Cooke's prose can be lyrically beautiful . . . And his research is comprehensive . . . an admirable drama."

—*Los Angeles Times*

"Engaging . . . informative . . . The battle scenes are vivid, and everday life is depicted in authentic, fascinating detail."

—*The New York Times Book Review*

"The grandeur of vision, the sweep of history, the inevitable clash of race and time . . . *The Snowblind Moon*, in fact, delivers all that and more."

—*New York Daily News*

"A giant-sized record of the 'civilizing' of the West."
—*Library Journal*

"Rich narration . . . highly believable . . . a gem."
—*St. Louis Post-Dispatch*

THE SNOWBLIND MOON by John Byrne Cooke

BETWEEN THE WORLDS

THE SNOWBLIND MOON

JOHN BYRNE COOKE

TOR

A TOM DOHERTY ASSOCIATES BOOK

THE SNOWBLIND MOON PART ONE:
BETWEEN THE WORLDS

Reprinted by arrangement with Simon and Schuster

First TOR printing: July 1986

A TOR Book

Published by Tom Doherty Associates
49 West 24 Street
New York, N.Y. 10010

ISBN: 0-812-58150-4
CAN. ED.: 0-812-58151-2

Library of Congress Catalog Card Number: 84-14009

Printed in the United States of America

0 9 8 7 6 5 4 3 2 1

For my father, who helped to instill in me a love of books, which was easy, and of history, which took somewhat longer.

When I was a boy the Sioux owned the world; the sun rose and set in their lands; they sent ten thousand horsemen to battle. Where are the warriors today? Who slew them? Where are our lands? Who owns them?
—SITTING BULL

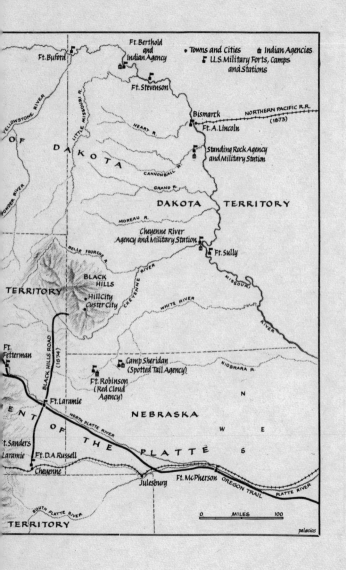

• Towns and Cities   ⚑ Indian Agencies
⚑ U.S. Military Forts, Camps and Stations

Ft. Buford

Ft. Berthold and Indian Agency

Ft. Stevenson

YELLOWSTONE RIVER

LITTLE MISSOURI R.

HEART R.

Bismarck

NORTHERN PACIFIC R.R. (1873)

Ft. A. Lincoln

OF

DAKOTA

CANNONBALL

Standing Rock Agency and Military Station

POWDER RIVER

GRAND R.

DAKOTA TERRITORY

MOREAU R.

Cheyenne River Agency and Military Station

BELLE FOURCHE R.

BLACK HILLS

Hill City
Custer City

CHEYENNE RIVER

Ft. Sully

MISSOURI

TERRITORY

WHITE RIVER

RIVER

BLACK HILLS ROAD (1874)

Ft. Fetterman

Camp Sheridan (Spotted Tail Agency)

NIOBRARA R.

Ft. Robinson (Red Cloud Agency)

N

Ft. Laramie

NEBRASKA

ENT OF THE

NORTH PLATTE RIVER

W

E

t. Sanders
Laramie

Ft. D.A. Russell

PLATTE

S

Cheyenne

Julesburg

Ft. McPherson

OREGON TRAIL

PLATTE RIVER

SOUTH PLATTE RIVER

TERRITORY

0   MILES   100

palacios

Department of Interior
Washington, December 3, 1875

Hon. E. P. Smith
Commissioner Indian Affairs
Washington, D.C.

Sir,

Referring to our communication of the 27th ultimo,
relative to the status of certain Sioux Indians
residing without the bounds of their reservation and
their continued hostile attitude toward the whites,
I have to request that you direct the Indian Agents
at all Sioux Agencies in Dakota and at Fort Peck,
Montana, to notify said Indians that unless they
shall remove within the bounds of their
reservation (and remain there) before the thirty-first
of January next, they shall be deemed hostile and
treated accordingly by the military force.

Very respectfully,
your obedient servant,

Z. Chandler
Secretary

Prologue

For the moment, he was content. The wind gusted snow in Hardeman's face and he could hear the hard flakes striking the skeleton branches of the willows that stood around him in the valley bottom. On either side of the narrowing valley, snowy hillsides wooded with lodgepole pine and naked aspens rose into the soft layer of cloud that obscured the ridgetops. Saddle leather creaked as the horse shifted its weight to one hind leg and crooked the other hoof up on its toe. The sounds were clean and sharp in the cold air. Hardeman could make out the noise of two branches rubbing together twenty yards away and the rush of water over a rock in the small open patch of river nearby. For the most part the river was still snowbound, but the water flowed with a swollen urgency that spoke of spring. Even the river had been fooled by the chinook wind that had warmed the plains for two weeks, luring young boys in the settlements out of doors to play in the mud.

The horse rubbed its head against Hardeman's back, trying to slip the bit from its mouth.

"Go on, now." Hardeman pushed the animal's head away. The roan was tough and compact, born wild on the plains, obtained in trade for Hardeman's big chestnut before he and Johnny Smoker had left Kansas. He hoped he would never again have use for a horse that needed grain to survive. This one would make it through the winter on cottonwood bark if need be. He tethered the horse to a stout willow branch and stood looking about him at the falling snow. He felt as if a layer of deadening callus, carelessly acquired during years of neglect, had suddenly slipped away from him, allowing him to see and hear properly for the first time in a long while.

He was alone in the river bottom, a man in his forties, strong and compact, standing near middle height. The eyes set deep beneath his brow were a color for which there was no proper name, verging from brown toward green, or perhaps blue, depending on the light. They seemed to look on the world from a secret redoubt. A small scar stood out over his left cheekbone, pale against the skin. The hair of his close-trimmed beard was flecked with gray, as were the curls that covered his neck and ears between his hat and the upturned collar of his slicker. The hat showed none of the wide-brimmed Texas influence that was moving steadily northward with the southern cowhands. It was made of silver-gray beaver, now gone brownish from years of dust and sun. Except for its age and the ringed sweat stain above the simple horsehair band, it would not have been out of place on the streets of Philadelphia or New York.

Stock-still in the wind and snow, Hardeman was comfortably warm. His winter longjohns and high wool socks, kersey-wool pants and wool shirt and buckskin jacket and St. Paul canvas slicker with its heavy blanket lining guarded him well. In the bottoms of his high army field boots were carefully cut pieces of mountain sheepskin with the wool still on. Today the oilskin was unbuttoned and the cardigan he sometimes wore beneath the jacket was stowed away in a saddlebag. When he and Johnny left Kansas even the St. Paul coat had been rolled up and tied behind his saddle, but the thaw had ended when they reached Cheyenne. The chinook had died away and a new wind had come from the northwest, returning an honest winter chill to the plains and blowing straight in the faces of the two riders as they made their way from Cheyenne to Fort Fetterman and beyond.

He had been gone from these regions for eighteen years.

During that time the Union had been tested by rebellion and held together by the will of a brooding country lawyer from Illinois, dead these ten years and more. Now the nation was strengthened by a band of iron rails spanning the continent. Since the war, Wyoming and Montana territories had been hewn from Dakota and Idaho and Utah; Kansas and Nebraska had become states; Colorado was to enter the Union this year, on the nation's one hundredth birthday. The frontier, that invisible line said by those who lived behind it to separate civilization from what they called "wilderness," had moved west across the plains from the Missouri settlements and now threaded its way among the peaks of the Rockies. Everywhere new towns were growing and the buffalo grass was turned under by plowshares; but the land north of the old Oregon road, from Fort Laramie and the Black Hills west to the Big Horns, in whose southern flanks Hardeman now stood, had changed not at all. It still belonged to the Sioux.

His contentment vanished abruptly at the thought. He turned to contemplate the two rifles, a model 1873 Winchester and a Sharps buffalo gun, that hung in scabbards on either side of his saddle. From the agencies in Dakota there was word that the Indians there were slipping away to the west in small groups, to the Powder River country, to join the wild bands. Two days before, Hardeman and Johnny had passed through Fort Fetterman, but since then they had seen no sign of man nor a single pony track. The hostile Sioux were keeping well away from the old emigrant trails.

Hardeman took the Winchester, leaving the thunderous Sharps behind. There was no sense waking the dead just to get a little meat. He set off through the willows on foot, glancing from time to time at the wooded slope on his right, calculating where a deer might come down to drink. If he found an elk he would have to get close with the Winchester, but he thought it unlikely that he would see an elk. There was precious little sign in these hills and not even a rabbit track so far this morning in the new snow that was still falling.

As he moved silently along the riverbank his eyes sought every swirl in the wind-packed snow, each blade of dead grass left over from summer, every broken twig. These were the signposts of the mountains, telling the man who could read them that one animal or another, four-footed or two-footed, had passed this way, or that no creature had passed here at all. Knowing the signs could mean the difference between eating and going hungry, between living and dying. The mountains were not generous with information, but they provided enough for those willing to learn how to find it. Hardeman had learned. Remembrance flooded through him and he felt once again in touch with this world.

He had been seventeen when he first came to what was now the Wyoming Territory, a Philadelphia youth determined not to waste precious time behind the desks of a boys' academy or a university while other men opened up a continent. His father's urgings had kept him in the academy until his studies there were done, but within a week of receiving his diploma he had left Philadelphia to make his way across Pennsylvania on foot, and when he tossed his bedroll to the Negro deckhand and jumped aboard the riverboat at Pittsburgh, he knew only that he was going west. That summer of 1851 the Oregon Trail was crowded with wagons hurrying to the gold fields of California, but when young Chris Hardeman made his way across what was then known as the Great American Desert, already an apprentice scout on his first passage west, he had gazed in awe at the Big Horn Mountains looming to the north and the Wind Rivers standing sharp against the western horizon, and even before he carved his name deep into the weathered sandstone of Independence Rock he knew that no faint promise of gold flakes in the bottom of a pan could keep him long from these sights.

He had been as green a youth as ever set foot in new country, but he had learned quickly. Seven years a wagon scout on the Oregon road and by the end of that time one of the best; just twenty-five years old when he left off guiding wagons to explore other parts of the West, first for government survey parties and later for the army. Fortune had delivered him into the enterprise for which he was perfectly suited, from which he derived the most satisfaction. He had left home to take part in a great adventure, to make his mark on the frontier, and from the first it seemed that other men welcomed him and made room for him to set his shoulder next to theirs, where they pushed along the great wheel of progress. Wagon-masters and generals and common people cut from every cloth had depended on him and he had taken constant pleasure in leading the way, a man at home in what most thought of as wilderness. He had been happy at the thought of living out his days as a scout, certain with the sureness of youth that the need for such men would continue through his lifetime.

If he had followed the path his father had staked out for him, he might have become a lawyer, like his father, like the Illinois rail-splitter, but he had jumped that fence. And before he had found time to go home for a visit, to tell his parents of the life he had found, the typhoid had taken them. The news reached him six months after the fact, convincing him, in the midst of his grief, that the law was not proof against the twists of fate that inevitably changed the lives of men in ways that could not be foreseen. In the western mountains a different kind of law held sway, one not made by men and not subject to their lapses in enforcement. It was just, and truly blind, and Harde-man was comfortable under its rule.

He paused and looked around at the wooded slopes. He felt deep within himself a calm he had not known for a long time, and he realized as if it were a new notion how much he loved this high country of the Rocky Mountains. He wondered whatever could have kept him away for so long.

Pain stirred in an old wound. He shifted the rifle to his left hand and rolled his right shoulder slowly, giving an invisible nod to a God he rarely addressed. It was fitting that the shoulder should trouble him now, to remind him of how much had changed seven winters before, on the Washita River down in the Indian Territory. On a cold November morning two bullets had brought a sudden end to his scouting and had created in a moment a relationship of wounds between him and the boy called Johnny Smoker, a bond in blood as strong in most ways as any between father and son, he guessed, although he had no children of his own. He and the boy were seven years older now, Johnny nearing twenty, most likely, although neither one knew just when Johnny had been born. Johnny was downstream in the night camp, waiting for Hardeman to return with fresh meat.

He started off again along the riverbank, picking his way silently among the clumps of willow. He felt the emptiness in his stomach and wished he had stopped to have a bite of jerky or a cup of coffee before leaving the camp. He had come awake an hour ago, leaving sleep behind in a moment, as a man should in the mountains. Looking about in the dull blue light of predawn he had discovered Johnny building a sweat lodge. It was not large but was perfectly made in the plains style, four slender willow poles on a side, all bent down and tied together and covered with the blankets from the boy's bedroll. And there was Johnny in his longjohns and boots, hunkered in the snow, warming rocks on a small fire in front of the lodge as patiently . . . as an Indian. Hardeman had grown suddenly and irrationally angry and had saddled up and ridden off without a word to get fresh meat if he could find it. In those first wakeful moments, seeing something so unexpected, he had suddenly doubted for the first time his reasons for coming here.

How could he doubt leaving the settlements, where he had never wished to be? How could he doubt returning to these mountains, standing so real and comforting around him? The doubts seemed unfamiliar now, dreamlike, a memory from before waking, not after.

His roving eyes found the signs they were seeking —a depression in the new snow betrayed a pathway worn in the old snow beneath; tufts of hair were caught in the brush along the narrow trail through the willows. Close at hand the water tumbled over a fall of rocks, moving fast enough to keep the drinking place open in all but the deepest winter cold. He shut the other thoughts from his mind and concentrated on the hunt. They were half a day's ride from Putnam's Park and he wanted to arrive there with a full belly and meat tied behind his saddle. It didn't pay to be beholden to anyone when you were bringing bad news.

He turned his head, feeling the wind on his cheek, and backed away to a thicket of willows downwind where he would be hidden from all sides and still have a clear view of the pathway to the water. He hunkered slowly in the brush, cocking the Winchester and testing once the single motion that would bring it from his knees to his shoulder. He grunted softly at the pain that sprang from the old wound. It bothered him more these days, especially in the cold.

I'm getting old, he thought, and laughed aloud, surprising himself. He looked quickly around, but the nearest game was still somewhere else. "You want to see meat today, you best keep shut," he told the willows and the snow, and fell silent. Not too long before, he had seen a Kansas judge sentence a mule thief to ten years in prison. As the man was taken away he had called out to the judge, begging for a reduction in sentence on account of his advanced age. The thief was forty years old. It had struck Hardeman that a man could give up and grow old any time he pleased, but he didn't figure to let that happen to him. He had his mind half made up to see the new century come in before he died—if a horse didn't fall on him or if he didn't get taken by some sickness that lurked wherever there were too many people. If he didn't let the wrong man provoke him to anger. If he lived out the month, which was perhaps least likely of all.

He drew the collar of the oilskin close about his neck and settled himself for a long wait, glad for the moment to be alone with the stream and the mountains. He passed his mind back over the half mile he had covered since leaving his horse, and found that although part of his attention had been occupied with other things, he could remember every fallen log, each clump of willow, every turn of the creek. He could find this place at night if he had to. He was pleased by the thoroughness of his recollection and was glad he had not fallen on careless ways. This was not safe country for fools. A man could not predict what weather a wind or a cloud might bring in any month of the year, nor what else might befall him unexpectedly in the mountains. All he could do was to be ready for whatever came. There was no certainty here, and Hardeman grinned at the awareness, a familiar feeling he had once known daily and had left behind like a worn-out shirt.

A breath of wind twisted through the willows, whisking the snow off the branches and depositing it in a cloud over the squat form of the man. Hardeman did not move. He willed himself to be a part of the mountains, like a rock or a stump. A measure of his earlier contentment returned and he recognized now the feeling that had comforted him so. He felt at home. Perhaps the settlements had not dulled him as much as he had feared. He would need all his old cunning, for he had returned to scouting after seven long years, determined once more to lead the way. At his own request, and in violation of a silent oath he had sworn that bloody morning at the Washita, he was scouting for the army again, and the army was going to war.

BETWEEN
THE
WORLDS

CHAPTER ONE

In a sheltered upland valley, circled by ridges and accessible in winter only through a cut in the hills where the river flowed between a low cliff on one side and a wagon track cut into a steep hillside on the other, the smell of woodsmoke hung in the air. Up against the wooded foothills at the north end of the valley the wagon road ended among the buildings of a small settlement dominated by a two-story log building that for more than twenty years had been the largest private dwelling and public house between the Black Hills to the east and South Pass far to the west, at the foot of the Wind River Mountains. Behind the building stood a large barn, a chicken coop and a pigpen, and a scattering of sheds and outbuildings. Closer to the creek, standing against the woods, was a tipi of northern plains design, painted in the style of the Sioux. From the peak of the tipi and from two rear chimneys of the main building, smoke drifted away to disperse in the winds that occasionally gusted a plume of snow from the long front porch of the big house.

In the snow-covered meadow below the settlement a tall black man and a teenaged boy tossed hay from a large sled drawn by two draft horses. Strung out behind the sled were fifty or sixty mixed-breed cattle browsing on the hay, a few horses and mules among them. The two men pitched the hay in even lines on either side of the sled, careful to spread it out so the less aggressive feeders in the bunch would have room to get enough.

"That's about the last of it," said Julius Ingram. Hutch nodded. Julius said the same thing every morning. Every morning they loaded the big sled with hay and hauled it to the bawling cattle in the meadow and every morning when the hay was almost gone Julius would say "That's about the last of it," and Hutch would nod, saying nothing.

At first he hadn't said much because he'd never worked for a nigger boss before. Not for a lady boss either, for that matter, although he was used to both of them now, to his own surprise.

"Whoa." Julius spoke no louder than if he were talking to Hutch, and the two Belgians stopped in the traces. The short hair that curled beneath the flat brim of the Negro's hat was gray. His mahogany skin lay smooth over every bone and muscle in his face; the effortless movements of his broad shoulders as he cleaned the last of the hay off the sled suggested reserves of strength untapped by the morning's work. He wore a new corduroy coat, and wool pants that had once been light blue but were now so faded and stained and patched that they could not be said to have any distinct color.

At seventeen, Hutch had attained nearly his full height and still he was a good head shorter than Julius. Unlike the tall black man, who appeared lean despite his strength, Hutch's form was stocky and heavily muscled, his movements short and economical. He took off his wool knit cap and stuffed it in a pocket of his old blanket-lined canvas jacket, enjoying the feeling as his scalp cooled in the wind. The thaw that had lasted for nearly two weeks was over and done with but the day was tolerable even so, nothing like the bitter cold days of midwinter. The snow that had been falling since before dawn was thinning now, and for the first time that morning he could see across the creek and the broad expanse of willow marsh to the far side of the valley. He breathed in deeply and noticed, not for the first time, how the smell of smoke from the stoves in the main house stayed in the air on a day like this when the clouds were low.

"When the chimney smoke's on the rise, you'll see clear skies," his mother had told him. "When the smoke hangs low, it's bound to snow." But the rhyme hadn't explained how low-hanging smoke in the hot Kansas summertime back home had foretold the coming of black thunderheads and sudden violent wind squalls and crackling lightning that you could see walking all around you on the endless plains. Hutch wondered if it was the same here in the mountains in the summer.

He had come upon the little mountain park with the first snow in autumn, getting plenty anxious about where he was going to spend his first winter away from home, looking for some cattle spread that didn't already have all the winter hands it needed. All the outfits along the Front Range in Colorado said they couldn't use another hand and if they could they'd hire on some man who had worked for them before, or a man anyway, not some runaway kid from Kansas so green he wouldn't catch light in the midst of a prairie fire. So Hutch kept heading north and west, toward the new ranges opening up in the Wyoming

Territory, hoping he wouldn't have to go all the way to Montana to find work. But in Wyoming the story was the same—Sorry, boy, you best try farther on, up Virginia City way, mebbe, but stay west of the Big Horns if'n you reckon to hang on to your hair. He never would have come on the Putnam place at all if he hadn't gone wrong at the fork, mistaking the Putnam Cutoff for the old Oregon road. Not long before he rode into the valley and saw the big house he had realized he was lost, and heading deeper into Sioux country. The farther west he had come on his travels the more talk he had heard about new trouble with the Sioux, and he had been considerably relieved to see a white man's outfit and a welcoming face at the door, even if that face had been the dark visage of Julius Ingram. Hutch hadn't felt too particular about a man's color just then, so long as it wasn't red and decorated with war paint.

Miss Putnam had taken him on, wanting to know only if he was willing to work hard. "Yes, ma'am," he had said. "Everyone calls me Lisa," she said, but it went against Hutch's upbringing to call a white woman twice his age by her first name, so he settled for Miss Lisa and after a while she had settled for that too.

She had asked him another question that first day. It had seemed a strange one to Hutch and for a moment he had wondered if it were a condition of his employment—she asked if he could play the guitar or banjo. When he said he played the banjo a little she had fetched an old banjo from the attic. It was in good repair, only in need of tuning. He began to play a little tune his uncle had taught him and he didn't even notice when the tall darky named Julius reached up and took a fiddle off the wall. Before he knew it the fiddle had joined in as pretty as you please and for the first time Hutch suspected he had found not just a place to spend the winter, but a place where he might be happy into the bargain. It seemed a considerable deal, and more than he had hoped for.

The music appeared to mean a lot to Miss Lisa and the others. Hutch found that Julius knew a few hundred tunes of his own, white man's songs from the southern mountains as well as Negro dance tunes. Hutch and Julius traded songs, and with their music they had warmed the kitchen in the Big House on many an evening while winter got down to business outside. It was only later that Hutch was told the banjo he played had belonged to Lisa's father, who had died back in the fall.

That there was a painful gap in the ranks here had been as obvious to Hutch from the start as the empty chair at the head of the table and the fresh grave on the knoll behind the main house. It was too early for the people here to talk much of Jedediah Putnam, but Hutch gathered that a man was gone whose kind passed this way all too rarely. In bits and pieces Hutch had learned more about the former mountain man from the almost mythical company of Jim Bridger and Kit Carson, Joe Meek and Jedediah Smith, until Jed Putnam had assumed in Hutch's imagination the stature of a giant, almost a living presence, or perhaps more a sort of benevolent ghost, still protecting and presiding over Putnam's Park.

"Zeke!" Julius' voice was sharp. The lead horse had been slacking in his harness, letting his partner, Zeus, do the work. Now Zeke leaned into the collar and the sled jerked forward. The two Belgians were half of a team of four. The two pairs served alternate duty, and the full team was used every few days, for breaking new trails. The feed lines were moved regularly so the manure the cattle produced in winter would be spread across the hay meadows by spring and just need a pass with a tooth harrow to break it up so the grass would grow under the dried-up pies. During the recent thaw, all four horses had been used often, and even so there had been days when feeding took all morning, what with getting the sled unstuck three or four times.

Hutch liked the daily ride back up the valley to the barn after the hard, sustained work of loading the rack from one hay crib or another and feeding the cattle. On the cutting cold days, of which there had been many, he and Julius sat on the sled with their backs against the plank front, sheltered from the wind. On warmer days like today, Hutch stood in the middle of the rack and looked at the hills and the valley bottom and the settlement so perfectly situated at the head of the park. Keeping his balance against the uncertain motion of the sled was a game he played with himself, adding to his enjoyment. Today he had timed his reaction to Zeke's lunge perfectly, and he smiled. The work here was hard, as Miss Lisa had said it would be, but Hutch didn't mind hard work. He had quickly learned that Julius was a fair man, and worked half again as hard as Hutch could on his best day. At home, Hutch had been the strongest in the family, his father included, but he couldn't stay ahead of Julius. Before long, Hutch had stopped thinking of Julius as a nigger.

He was beginning to feel at home here, even if it wasn't much of an outfit. The beef herd was small, and the cattle were some kind of Longhorn-Shorthorn cross that Jed Putnam had been experimenting with, not the familiar Texas Longhorns Hutch had known in Kansas. The Texas cattle didn't require any such coddling as winter feeding. Just turn 'em loose and they'd fend for themselves all right. A Longhorn thrived on neglect. He would grow fat on range a lizard would shun for lack of cover. He would walk all day without water and gain weight on the trail. Or so the Texas drovers claimed. But he took four years to grow to market weight.

The notion that this was a fault had come as a surprise to Hutch when Julius first pointed it out. Hutch had seen the first huge herds of Longhorns driven past his pa's place when he was just eight, and as he stood there goggle-eyed and drop-jawed he had decided in that moment that as soon as he was old enough he would become one of the youths folks were already calling "cow-boys." Without giving it much thought, he had accepted the commonly held idea that the Longhorn was the very paragon of bovine development. But it was strange how a new notion could make an old one seem to fade, where once it had shone so brightly. When he thought about it, it made good sense that a steer that gained weight faster than a Longhorn was a better deal from a stockman's point of view, and Hutch had begun to look with new interest at Jed Putnam's mixed-breed cattle and to ask questions about them. He had been surprised to learn that steers he had taken for three-year-olds were not yet two.

Old man Putnam had only been running cattle for a handful of years, Julius said. After the fur trade gave out he had been a wagon guide for a time, leading

emigrants to Oregon and California, and then in the
fifties he had turned to road ranching, which was to
say he ran a kind of a cross between a trading post
and a hotel, the way Hutch understood it. He had
pioneered the Putnam Cutoff and built his outfit here
in what came to be called Putnam's Park, providing a
place where the westbound emigrants could restock
with supplies and rest their weary draft animals.
Hutch thought it odd that Putnam had picked a place
so out of the way up here in the Big Horns. He had
seen other road ranches on his travels, pretty tumble-
down affairs, most of them, and most were abandoned now, but at least they were right there on the
road where a person didn't have to take a detour just
to find them. Of course, there weren't so many wagons on the old trails now anyway, what with the
railroad. By the look of things, old Jed had turned to
raising cattle in the nick of time.

To Hutch, the days of road ranching and prairie
schooners on the western trails and the even more
remote years of the mountain men and the beaver
trade were only slightly more real than the fairy tales
his mother had read to him. By the time he saddled
his mule and lit out on his own, the settlement of the
western territories was no longer in question, and the
struggles and deeds that had achieved that certainty
were known to Hutch only in the broadest outlines as
part of the folklore of the times. Like any sensible
youngster, his eyes were firmly fixed on what lay
ahead, not on the past. What had drawn him west in
his own turn were the new tales of the growing boom
in beef cattle that now reached beyond the Kansas
trailheads up into the northern plains, where there
were opportunities born every minute for a young

man who wasn't afraid of hard work. When the snow melted he would move on to the kind of big spread he dreamed of, where he could become top hand by the time he was twenty-five and raise as much hell as he liked in town on Saturday night, once they built a town close enough so he could get to it. Miss Lisa and Julius talked of building up the herd in Putnam's Park, but this would never be the kind of place Hutch saw in his mind's eye. He'd have his pick of any ranch on the north plains when his reputation was made, and someday maybe even marry the boss's daughter. It unsettled him somewhat that on this place here the boss's daughter was the boss, and she was as old as his own mother, who was thirty-four and already had five children of which he was the eldest. Lisa Putnam had none, and no husband either, if it came to that, which Hutch thought was strange considering that she wasn't half bad-looking for an older woman, but that was her business. It was enough that her place was a good place to winter, a place where Hutch could learn the rudiments of cow-boying without making a fool of himself in front of a lot of other boys his own age. Come spring he'd move on, but for now he was content. He still didn't say much, but it was no longer because he felt like a stranger. A lot of talk just wasn't in his nature.

Once they reached the yard the horses knew the way without guidance and they picked up the pace, anticipating their daily ration of oats. The sled skimmed along, the rack creaking and the pitchforks wagging back and forth like drunken lookouts, held upright by the iron ring Harry Wo had bolted to the frame of the rack, their butts resting in an old bucket nailed in place below the ring.

"Whoa." Julius stopped the team beside the corral fence. As he moved around the Belgians, unbuckling the harness from their steaming flanks, he enjoyed the practiced ease in Hutch's movements and his familiarity with the complicated tack. Even that morning back in December when they had gone off to feed the cattle for the first time, it had been obvious that the boy knew horses. He could get milk from a cow too; right from the start he had taken to helping Harry with the milking before breakfast. But it was plain when Lisa signed him on that young Hutch didn't know straight up about beef cattle. He was learning, though. Julius guessed that the boy was from a farm back in Kansas. He spoke of Kansas now and again, but he hadn't offered the story of his short life and a man didn't ask that kind of question without some kind of invitation. Julius appreciated that aspect of frontier custom more than most, although he had nothing in his past to hide. It was just that he was used to his freedom now and guarded the right to keep his past to himself. What and where he had been was his own concern.

He felt the defensive anger rising in him without cause and he caught himself. There was no need to get his back up. Nobody here had ever pried into his past. Lisa knew his story because what old Jed hadn't told her Julius had told her himself. She enjoyed hearing him talk about the Southwest and his years on the Texas cattle trails, although to Julius his own stories had always seemed pale in comparison with the fables old Jed had liked to spin around the glory days of the fur trade back in the twenties and thirties, when he and Bridger and Meek and the rest had roamed the Rocky Mountains as free trappers. The

barest hint that you would like to hear one of those
tales could set old Jed or his brother Bat going for
hours. It was a wonder to Julius that the mountain men
had found any time to catch beaver, judging by the
way they liked to sit and jaw. He smiled at the
memory of Jed Putnam.

"Something funny?" Hutch asked. They had turned
the horses into the corral and poured a measure of
grain onto the packed snow and put away the harness, all without a word said between them. There
was no need for constant talk when two men had
worked together for three months doing the same job
each morning, just the way there was no need for too
much conversation when they all sat down together at
mealtimes. Some days they would go through three
meals without much more than "Please pass the
salt" or "I'll have that last piece of pie if nobody
wants it," and some days they would sit around the
kitchen table after the noon meal, drinking coffee and
laughing and talking until finally Julius stood up and
said they'd better get to work before it was too dark
to do anything but mend harness. People in close
quarters either fit together or they didn't. Julius's
father had taught him that, before he was sold upriver
to Macon. Folks had to fit together and make life
bearable, either that or somebody had to go. Hutch
was good company. He'd make a good hand if he
stayed on.

"I was thinking about old Jed."

"He was something more than just an ordinary
man, I guess."

Julius shrugged, unwilling to deny the common
humanity that Jed Putnam had possessed in such

uncommon measure. "You look close at his brother
Bat. He's cut from the same cloth."

As they left the barn they heard a woman's scolding voice issue from the buffalo-hide tipi that stood
alone near the woods. Julius put out a hand to stop
Hutch and together they watched the tipi, grinning in
anticipation. The dependable frequency with which
this scene repeated itself was a comfort to them.

A mongrel dog leaped through the entrance flap,
followed by a white man, gray bearded and gaunt,
dressed in the buckskins of a mountain man. He wore
a skunk-fur cap and a hooded blanket capote that
hung from his shoulders and flapped about his leggings. The hood of the capote was thrown back
despite the falling snow; the plaits of hair that hung
on either side of the man's head were greased with
animal fat and wrapped in otter skin. In one hand he
held a long percussion rifle. Without looking back he
set off for the main house, his thin legs making long
strides on the narrow path beaten in the snow. Behind him a short Indian woman stepped out of the
tipi, still scolding in her native tongue. She was
Hunkpapa Sioux. The women of her people were not
afraid to tell a husband his responsibilities when he
shirked them, or to make clear what he should do to
put things right, but they would never scold a man to
his face, least of all in front of others. The woman
bent to pick up a few sticks of firewood from a small
pile near the tipi's entrance, as if that were her only
purpose in coming outside, but she continued to speak
to the world at large, to the sky and the trees and the
snow, glancing at the man just once and raising her
voice when she saw that he was making for the
house. Perhaps her husband thought that the deer and

elk walked right up to the lodge and lay down to be butchered, she suggested. Perhaps he only left his lodge now because it was so full of meat that there was no room in it for him.

The old man marched ahead, never pausing or looking back. The woman made more observations, equally as pointed, but at last she fell silent. Once a man was set on a course of action, a good woman held her tongue.

Julius had understood some of what the woman had said, enough to grasp the nature of her complaint, and he was shaking with silent laughter. Hutch knew none of her words, but he knew perfectly well what was going on, and he too was laughing.

"Good huntin' lately, Bat?" Julius inquired innocently.

The mountaineer stopped in his tracks and glared at Julius and Hutch, whom he had not noticed until now. They were still laughing as they entered the door to the kitchen of the main house.

"Wagh!" Bat Putnam let out a grizzly bear's snort, the fur trapper's all-purpose interjection of surprise, pleasure, disgust or general exclamation. It was poor doings for a man to be forced out of his own lodge without so much as a bite of *wasná* by a wife who says if he's grown too old or lazy to hunt, he'd best get used to going hungry; it was worse yet to be mocked in front of his wife by a good-for-nothing darky and a bantam rooster too young to crow for real. The two of them put together didn't amount to a heap of goat shit. Well, they'd get no more satisfaction out of John Batson Putnam, not this day. With a cup of Lisa's coffee to warm him, he'd show those

two that this coon could still raise sign in whatever
weather God in his considerable humor decided to
ply the mountains with.

He resumed his march toward the house.

CHAPTER TWO

It seemed to Lieutenant Whitcomb that he was entering a land where the Creation was incomplete. He
had imagined the western country as gently rolling
and covered with grass, perhaps looking from afar
somewhat like the rolling swells of the Atlantic on a
peaceful day, as he had often seen it from the beaches
of Cape Henry. Around Cheyenne the pleasant grasslands had met his expectations, but here the countryside was broken, unfinished, as if God had deemed it
unworthy of any further effort. To the south and west
a range of mountains cloaked blue-black in evergreens rose into the gray clouds that stretched flat
and featureless in all directions, but near at hand the
land was unclothed. What few stalks of grass there
were had clustered together for comfort, and the
landscape was devoid of trees except for a few stunted
specimens on the low buttes and a ribbon of tall
cottonwoods hidden down in the bottomland of the
North Platte, which hereabouts flowed in a shallow
canyon a half mile off to Whitcomb's right. Even the
brownish-yellow soil that served as the earth's poor
flesh in these regions was insufficient, for on every

slope and low summit the rocks—the bones of the planet—showed through.

The alien surroundings heightened Whitcomb's sense of loneliness. Overhead the twin strands of telegraph wire picked up the hum of the wind and he wondered if they were also carrying other messages, more comforting and friendly. He had only to follow the wires to reach Fort Fetterman, for they ended there, but as he topped each rise he saw only the telegraph poles marching onward and no glimpse of the fort. For a day and a half he had seen no living soul and had no company save for his horse, and so when he spied another rider approaching the wagon road from his left flank he greeted the sight with a surge of profound gratitude.

A glance was enough to identify the man as white. By his appearance Whitcomb took him for a wandering mountaineer or perhaps a scout for Crook's command returning to the fort from a reconnaissance of the surrounding country. The man was cloaked from neck to stirrup in a long fur coat and he kept his seat with perfect ease as the horse covered the rough ground at a steady trot. A rifle rested across the rider's lap and the body of an animal—Whitcomb guessed it was an antelope—was tied behind the saddle. A black-and-white border collie trotted behind the horse, content to let the larger animal break a path through a shallow drift of old snow. When horse and rider reached an expanse of bare ground, the dog trotted ahead.

Earlier that morning Whitcomb had led his own horse on foot for more than an hour, trying to walk off the cold that had chilled him to the bone ever since the clouds had covered the sun scarcely an hour after it rose, but he had remounted some time ago, anxious to keep up his pace. Now he touched his spurs to the tired animal, urging him into a faster walk in order to intercept the other rider as he reached the road. The man would know how much farther it was to the fort and some talk would be welcome— anything to forget the cold and wind. He pulled the collar of his dark blue greatcoat higher about his neck.

Second Lieutenant Hamilton Whitcomb was twenty-two and knew that he looked younger. His sandy hair and hazel eyes and open, unlined face contributed to an impression of untried youth. But he was wiry and he had endurance. "You have the build of a cavalryman," his father had said, certain that the family tradition of military service had been doomed to extinction by the surrender of the South. Whitcomb was conscious of the heavy gold West Point ring on his left hand. He was the only one of the Virginia Whitcombs presently in uniform and his father could not forget that the uniform he wore was that of the South's conquerors.

He had traveled alone from Fort Laramie, eighty barren miles to the southeast along the old Oregon Trail. From Cheyenne to Laramie he had ridden with a dozen replacement troopers whom he had escorted west on the train from department headquarters in Omaha. The road was choked with gold seekers hurrying north toward the Black Hills of Dakota, and everywhere along the way the small contingent of troops had been greeted alternately with shouts of encouragement in their task of quelling the Indians and jeers for having failed to do so thus far. The numbers of the argonauts had astonished Whitcomb and he had hurried his little troop along, all the more anxious to join General Crook.

Six months had passed since the latest peace commission had failed to negotiate a successful purchase of the hills from the Sioux. Smarting from the many promises that had been made and quickly broken by the whites during the course of their successive encroachments into Indian lands, the Sioux had demanded staggering sums for the Black Hills, which they revered as the "sacred center" of their nation. The amounts named by the various chiefs had ranged upward from thirty million dollars. The peace commissioners had offered six million, which the Sioux promptly refused, but the country needed new capital to speed its recovery from the financial panic of '73, and from Washington City the rights of the Sioux appeared small compared with the hunger for gold that pervaded the halls of the Capitol. Two years before, General George Custer had conducted a military reconnaissance of the hills and had reported the presence of gold "from the grass roots down," in the words of his exuberant dispatch. Since then, troops had struggled halfheartedly to root out white miners who slipped into the hills past the army roadblocks. With the failure of the peace commission the troops had been withdrawn and thousands of prospectors flooded into the hills. Throughout the winter they had scrabbled for gold with one hand while fighting off the angry warriors of Crazy Horse with the other. As spring drew near, the matter was still unresolved and new hordes poured daily into the diggings. The presence of the miners served as a goad to remind the Sioux that the advance of the white race could not be denied, while the planned military campaign, which

Whitcomb was to join, would round up the last of the hostile bands in the Powder River country west of the Black Hills and complete the containment of the nomadic warriors on the Dakota reservation. With the spirit of resistance broken, a final settlement of the Black Hills dispute would quickly follow.

Whitcomb felt his pulse quicken at the thought of the coming campaign. He had feared during his years at West Point that the Indian wars would end before he could take part, denying him what might be his only chance to win recognition on the battlefield, and until a week ago he had despaired of obtaining field duty on the frontier. But then his orders had arrived, unexpected and electrifying: a three-pronged assault was about to be launched against the hostile Sioux, with General Custer leading the Seventh Cavalry from Fort Abraham Lincoln in Dakota Territory, Colonel John Gibbon moving southeast from Fort Shaw in Montana, and General George Crook, commander of the Department of the Platte, advancing northward from Fort Fetterman; if Whitcomb could reach Fetterman in time he could join Crook's force and take part in the campaign. The fact that Crook, whose command comprised Utah and Wyoming Territories and the state of Nebraska as well, had chosen to lead the expedition himself attested to its importance, and within an hour of receiving the message, Whitcomb was packed and on his way. In a handful of days he had crossed two-thirds of the continent, but when he reached Fort Laramie it seemed that his haste might have been in vain. The company to which he was assigned, E Troop, Third Cavalry, had already gone on to Fetterman, and the post adjutant at Laramie, to whom Whitcomb delivered the replacement troopers, informed him that Crook was reportedly impatient to be off and would certainly set out as soon as the last elements of his command reached him.

"But I have to get there before he leaves!" Whitcomb had protested desperately. "What arrangements have been made for my travel to Fetterman?"

"Arrangements?" The post adjutant had looked perplexed. "Why none, I'm afraid. Departmental orders state that no one shall travel alone west of Laramie, and I can't spare an escort. We've got the Black Hills road to police, you know, and you've seen what a job that is." He saw the disappointment on Whitcomb's face and he looked the young lieutenant up and down thoughtfully. "Of course I'm a pretty busy fellow," he said. "I can't be expected to bring every new shavetail up to date on all the standing orders." And with that he had returned to the papers on his desk, ignoring Whitcomb completely.

It had taken Whitcomb only a moment to see the opportunity the post adjutant had offered him. Somewhat taken aback by his own audacity, he had tiptoed silently from the adjutant's office and left Fort Laramie alone. He had made ten miles before seeking shelter at dusk in one of the countless ravines that cut the desolate red-clay countryside; there he had built a small fire of scrub cedar, hoping that the warming glow would not be seen by unfriendly eyes, and he had managed to get some sleep in the buffalo robe he had bought from the post trader at Laramie. That had been the night before last. Yesterday he had covered fifty miles under a brilliant sun, following the wagon tracks that paralleled the North Platte. Bunchgrass grew in the ruts now where twenty years before the emigrant wagons had often traveled ten abreast.

The other rider was drawing near and Whitcomb was about to call out a greeting when he crested a low ridge and saw Fort Fetterman before him, less than two miles away, its buildings grouped along the edge of a plateau overlooking a section of the Platte where the bottomland stretched out broad and wide. He could easily make out a beef herd foraging under guard near the fort and a much larger horse herd farther away. Plainly, a large force was in the garrison. The dozens of wagons grouped by the road would belong to the expedition's supply train.

Whitcomb felt his heart pounding in his chest. Crook was still at Fetterman and his lonely journey had been worth all the risks.

"Good morning, Lieutenant," the rider said as he gained the road. He's a scout, Whitcomb thought, or he wouldn't be able to read my rank so easily. As the fur-coated rider slowed his horse to a walk, Whitcomb drew himself up in the saddle, eager to make a good impression no matter who the man might be, although it was with some difficulty that he contained his excitement. He was proud of himself and his new field uniform, and glad that he presented a neat and relatively clean appearance despite the rigors of his journey.

"Good morning. It's a splendid day."

The man nodded politely. He was in his late forties, Whitcomb judged. He wore brown corduroy trousers beneath his bearskin greatcoat, and scuffed army boots. The bottoms of the corduroys were burned, as was the brim of the man's felt Kossuth hat, which was faded from black to a sun-bleached brown. There was a dark patch on the crown where an insignia had been torn away. It was a cast-off hat, no doubt given

him by a generous officer, and had probably been
used to beat out many a campfire. The man's blondish
beard was unkempt, but his blue-gray eyes were calm
and level and something about him conveyed an
innate dignity.

"It could be that a change in the weather is coming," the rider observed, seemingly unaware of
Whitcomb's scrutiny. His speech was that of an educated man, but that was not so surprising. Men of
every sort came west, Whitcomb knew, and educated
men could be found in any occupation. He regarded
the low clouds for several moments, feeling the northeast wind on his cheek, trying to decide how to
respond. A few flakes of snow were in the air now
and it did seem warmer than the day before, in spite
of the wind and clouds, but he decided to be cautious; if there was one thing the scout would know, it
was the weather.

"I'm not familiar with the plains," he offered.
"Until a week ago I had never been west of the
Alleghenies."

"You are from the South, I believe. Virginia?"

Whitcomb stiffened involuntarily. The number of
Southerners at West Point had increased steadily in
recent years, and by the time Whitcomb graduated,
there were almost as many Southern cadets at the
academy as there had been before the war. The
Northerners had grown accustomed to hearing Southern accents and Whitcomb had almost forgotten that
there were men who might form certain opinions of
him on the basis of his speech alone. But he had
nothing to hide.

"Petersburg," he said, confirming the man's guess
and leaving unsaid everything that name meant to

anyone who had lived through the last year of the war. While Grant had kept Lee and his army bottled up at Petersburg, Sherman had made his devastating sweep through Georgia, and after nine agonizing months of siege, Lee had been forced to withdraw from Petersburg in defeat. A week later he had stepped into the McLean farmhouse at Appomattox Court House to surrender his army, and the last hope of the Confederacy.

"You are too young to have fought in the Rebellion," the scout said. It was not a question.

Whitcomb felt the blood rise to his face. The man was offering him a chance to disassociate himself from the Rebel cause. "My father fought with Jeb Stuart until the general's death," he said firmly. "Both of my uncles served with the Army of Northern Virginia." The scout was a Yankee, that was certain. No Southerner spoke of the Rebellion. Ham Whitcomb's father and uncles called it the War Between the States, or the War for the Southern Confederacy, or the War for States' Rights, but only a Yankee would call it the Rebellion. A rebellion implied a revolt against a legitimate government and the South had denied the legitimacy of an unbreakable Union. But Ham's father and uncles had fought their war and they had lost. He had no wish to revive the struggle, but neither would he allow a stranger to cast doubt on his family's honor.

The scout merely nodded in a way that implied no judgment and they rode for a time in silence while Whitcomb's anger cooled.

"I imagine you have come from Fort Laramie."

It was Whitcomb's turn to nod calmly, as if riding alone across eighty miles of frozen plains was something he did without a second thought. Too late he realized that he would have preferred to invent a different route by which he had arrived at Fetterman. If the scout should mention a young lieutenant riding alone from Laramie, things could go hard for Ham Whitcomb.

"They sent you on without an escort?"

"My regiment has been ordered into the field," Whitcomb replied, deliberately avoiding the question. It was an army tradition that an officer whose regiment was ordered into the field in his absence would cut short his leave and go to any lengths to join his men.

"I imagine we must all cast a blind eye at regulations now and then," the scout said.

So he knew of the standing orders. Well, there could be no going back now. " 'Pity the warrior who is content to crawl about in the beggardom of rules,' " Whitcomb said. "That's from Clausewitz. I don't imagine you have read him. But don't misunderstand me. I only disobeyed a rule that was keeping me from my duty."

The scout nodded, seeming to accept this. "Was there any sign of Indians along the way?" he asked.

"I saw no one, red or white." Whitcomb was glad of the change in topic and some of his former excitement returned. "Frankly, I've heard that the danger may be overrated. At Laramie they say there are only five hundred hostiles outside the reservation."

The scout smiled fleetingly. "Oh, there may be a few more than that. Still, with a little luck we may have them on the run before long."

"You're going on the expedition?"

The scout nodded.

"I think you're right, about having them on the run, I mean. With Crook and Terry and Gibbon all in the field, we should bring the hostiles to bay."

Whitcomb was surprised to see no reaction from the scout, only another nod of acknowledgment, but then he remembered the telegraph. Fort Fetterman must have been notified that General Alfred Terry instead of Custer would lead the column from Fort Abraham Lincoln. The news had reached Fort Laramie only hours before Whitcomb and his troopers arrived at the post, and it had been the topic on every lip. After a winter's leave, during which he had been lionized by Washington and New York society matrons, Custer had returned to his regiment a week ago only to be summoned back to Washington at once by a House committee that was investigating corruption in the handling of Indian affairs. Custer had requested that he be allowed to testify by deposition, but the House was controlled by Democrats who wanted to miss no opportunity to embarrass President Grant, and they had insisted that Custer should appear in person. The "Boy General"—a nickname that had stuck with Custer since the war, when he had been promoted brevet major general at the age of twenty-six—was widely known, and he would bring much attention to the hearings. In Custer's absence, General Terry, the commander of the Department of Dakota, had assumed direct command of Custer's regiment.

That Custer had been summoned to appear had come as no surprise to Whitcomb. For four years at West Point he had prepared himself for duty on the frontier by learning all he could both about the native peoples there and the officers that now sought to

quell their warlike ways, and he knew that despite
their very different temperaments, both Generals Crook
and Custer abhorred any underhanded dealings on the
part of Indian agents, not only for the practical reason that such thievery aroused justified resentment on
the part of the savages, but also because it offended
each man's sense of honor and fair play. Crook's
success in taming the fierce Apaches with his scrupu-
lous fairness was well known, and Custer had spoken
loudly on the subject of Indian Bureau corruption
more than once, frequently offering his written opinions to the newspapers. Such attention on Indian
affairs only served to emphasize the failure of Grant's
Indian policy, which had been intended to end the
corruption and assure the Indians a secure future in
American society.

As the white race pushed steadily westward both
before and after the Civil War, successive tribes had
been persuaded to accept small reservations in place
of their formerly limitless homelands in exchange for
payments of money and the long-term delivery of
annuity goods, so called because they were usually
delivered on an annual basis. The budget of the
Indian Bureau expanded rapidly to provide for the
goods, and the opportunities for corruption increased
in direct proportion. The position of Indian agent
paid just fifteen hundred dollars a year, but it was
widely charged that an agent could retire comfortably
in three years on the graft that would virtually be
thrust upon him. Contracts were bought with bribes,
the agents pocketed first-class payments while obtaining tenth-rate goods, and some supplies were privately sold to white citizens instead of being disbursed
on the reservations. Even as these practices became

widespread, some government officials, both military men and civilians, urged a policy of outright extermination of the Indians, saying that they were sub-human brutes who could never have a place among civilized people. In his first inaugural address, Grant had attempted to lay such talk to rest. He spoke of the Indians as "the original occupants of this land," and expressed his sincere hope that they could indeed be civilized and in time become citizens who were equal in all respects to their white brothers. His first Commissioner of Indian Affairs was Ely S. Parker, a full-blooded Seneca Indian. Together they attempted to institute policies that would treat the Indians fairly and begin the process of educating them in civilized ways. To stop the rampant corruption, Grant passed control of the reservations to the various religious denominations, in the hope that men of God would have as their first concern the welfare of the Indians' souls rather than filling their own pockets with the government's gold. But now, as Grant's second term drew to a close, it was apparent that human frailty had proved more than a match for the President's dreams. Most of the schools promised for the reservations had never been built; annuity goods were often late or insufficient, or they simply did not appear at all while greedy men grew fat on Indian hunger.

As Whitcomb had learned these painful facts, he had found himself agreeing with those who proposed that the Indian Bureau be returned to the War Department from the Department of the Interior, whose minions sat in their offices in Washington City and remained almost wholly ignorant about the distant lands they administered. His learning was as yet untried, but now, seeing this foreign landscape for the first time, it seemed to Whitcomb that the politics of Washington City and the conflicting proposals of groups both in and out of government were forces so remote from these vast regions that they could have no relevance here, a hundred miles from the nearest railroad and centuries in time from the marble columns of the nation's capital. Surely, trying to administer the Indians and their lands from Washington City was an enterprise with no greater chance of success than attempting to warm the chill winds by the application of Greek philosophy.

He looked around him and wondered what sort of men the Indians were, to choose this place for their home.

Custer's appearance before the House committee might bring matters to a head, and if Crook's campaign succeeded, perhaps that would convince the Congress that the officers of the frontier army were the men best suited to deal with the Indian problem.

The scout had made no reply to Whitcomb's expression of hope about bringing the hostiles to bay and Whitcomb decided to elaborate on it a bit. He was confident that he could hold his own on matters of tactics and strategy, no matter how much experience the scout might have on the plains.

"Even if there are a thousand or more on the loose, the capture of a single village should break their spirit. That's Sheridan's plan."

The scout's border collie spotted a jack rabbit in the brush and bolted suddenly across the road in hot pursuit. Whitcomb's horse shied, but he controlled the animal in an instant without moving his hands on the reins, using only a slight tightening of his knees.

Horsemanship was something else he wouldn't concede to the scout.

"You agree with General Sheridan?" The scout regarded him calmly.

"Yes, I do." General Philip H. Sheridan was commander of the army's Division of the Missouri, within which General Crook's Department of the Platte was situated. It was Sheridan who had instigated winter campaigns against the hostiles in late 1868 on the southern plains. In that winter George Custer had obtained a signal victory over some Cheyenne camped on the Washita River in Indian Territory. Despite a lingering controversy over whether or not the Cheyenne had actually been hostile, Custer's success had proved the virtue of Sheridan's tactics.

"In summer the Indians have a tactical advantage over us, one of mobility," Whitcomb explained. "They can live off the country and move about quickly, while we're tied down by our supply trains. Even with several columns converging from different points we can't make them fight unless they want to. If they don't like the odds they just slip away. But in winter the advantage is ours. The Indian horses are too weak for prolonged reconnaissance and the warriors stay close to the villages. If we surprise one camp and take the savages under guard to Dakota, it may convince the rest that resistance is useless." He realized that much of what he had said would be known to the scout as a matter of common sense, if not as strategy, and he added, "At least that's the way I understand it. I'm sure you know more about this than I do."

"I'm always glad to hear some fresh thinking on the subject."

Whitcomb didn't feel that he had added any thoughts

that were remotely fresh, and he realized that he would do well to keep his opinions to himself from now on. There was a cold reception awaiting young lieutenants fresh out of West Point who sought to educate their superior officers. It occurred to him belatedly that anything he told the scout might be reported to those same officers, and he wished he had been more guarded in his speech.

"I see you have been hunting," he said, hoping to shift the conversation to safer ground. He would let the other man do the talking for a while. Scouts were notorious storytellers, and it wouldn't hurt him to hear some tales of these wild lands that were so new to him.

"The officers enjoy some wild game now and again," the scout said. "Have you had antelope?"

"I'm afraid not."

"You will have it tonight." The scout lapsed into silence.

Disappointed to find the man so taciturn, Whitcomb was nonetheless cheered by the thought of hot food. Since leaving Fort Laramie he had eaten nothing but hardtack and jerky. He had been in the saddle before dawn that morning in the hope of reaching Fetterman in time for the noon meal.

They were nearing the first of the fort's outbuildings now, passing by a large corral where a stable sergeant was supervising the installation of a new water trough. Whitcomb returned the sergeant's salute as the scout waved a greeting. Not far away two companies of cavalry were firing at makeshift targets. Whitcomb took this as evidence of the thoroughness with which the troops were being prepared for the campaign. Target practice was not a regular feature of the soldiers' training, and on the frontier, where ammunition was scarce, it was virtually unknown.

Like many another frontier post, Fetterman had been a fortified bastion during the constant Indian troubles of the middle sixties, but the high plank fence that had once enclosed the headquarters building, barracks and parade ground had mostly been taken down since then, leaving only a tall log gateway, where three guards stood at ease, and a few sections of fencing behind the barracks. The stables were half a mile to the east of the main buildings, together with shops where blacksmiths, wheelwrights and saddlers practiced their crafts. Between the stables and the rest of the fort a ravine descended to the river plain, some hundred feet below the level of the plateau, and as the two riders rode past the ravine Whitcomb saw parallel lines of army tents on the bottomland. There were twelve companies in Crook's command, ten of cavalry and two of infantry, and by the look of it the entire force was encamped on the river plain. Beyond the neat rows of canvas tents stood a cluster of what appeared to be Indian tipis.

"Are our men using captured Indian tents?" Whitcomb inquired of the scout.

"Those are real Indians, Lieutenant. Thirty-six lodges of Arapaho. The Indians know we're up to something and the Arapaho are going in to the agencies. If there's to be trouble, they want to be well out of it. The chief of this group is named Black Crow. He is one of the reasons we expect to find a good many hostiles up north. He calls all Sioux 'Minneconjous,' and he says there are plenty of them up toward the Yellowstone. 'Heap plenty Minneconjous,' he told me. 'Makeum tired countum.' "

"I see." Whitcomb absorbed this sobering information with interest, but much of his attention was on the fort and its surroundings. Here and there among the buildings he spied a figure in dress and sunbonnet—an officer's wife or laundress—but the women were all but lost in a sea of men; everywhere about the plateau, squads were drilling on foot and horseback; packers moved among the wagons and worked over the rows of mule packs spread on the ground near the supply train; there were no idlers and nothing out of place. The scene confirmed everything Whitcomb knew about General George Crook, who was reported to concern himself with the workings of his command down to the smallest detail, and to have no patience for carelessness or neglect. He was also said to take a great interest in the welfare of his men, and Whitcomb hoped he might have a chance to meet the general during the course of the campaign, but he was careful to keep his expectations within reason. Even General Crook would have little time to chat with junior lieutenants.

The bugle notes of recall-from-drill sounded from the parade ground, and the squads began to disperse and make for the mess halls and kitchens on the far side of the large quadrangle. Whitcomb smiled. He had made dinner with fifteen minutes to spare.

"Just in time," the scout echoed Whitcomb's thoughts. He quickened the pace of his mount slightly. The collie ran ahead through the gate and paused to look over his shoulder, waiting for his master.

Whitcomb liked the scout. He found himself inventing a history for the man. Perhaps he was a gentleman of good family, one who had failed in life through some misfortune and come west in middle age. Men of every description had done so, some taking new names to give themselves a fresh start or to avoid the law, which might reach even into the territories if the crime was serious enough, but Whitcomb felt sure the man was not a criminal.

"It's been a pleasure riding with you," he said as they approached the gateposts. "I'm Lieutenant Whitcomb. I would be pleased to know your name."

The guards came to attention. Whitcomb returned the salutes, surprised to notice that the scout did so as well.

"Velcome back, Herr General." The German corporal of the guard pronounced "general," with a hard *g*.

"Thank you, Corporal," said Whitcomb's companion.

Ham Whitcomb felt a soft pounding begin in his ears as the blood rose to his face and banished the last trace of chill from his ears.

"General! I see you had good hunting, sir." A lieutenant a few years older than Whitcomb strode rapidly toward them. He was solidly built and round-faced, of medium height. His mustache had been allowed to grow long until it nearly covered his mouth.

"Only fair, Mr. Bourke," said the "scout" as he reined his horse to a halt and returned the lieutenant's salute. "There were two of them. I missed the other. Lieutenant Whitcomb, this is Lieutenant Bourke. Lieutenant Whitcomb is joining our little expedition, Mr. Bourke."

Whitcomb thought the pounding in his ears would deafen him. He knew his normally ruddy cheeks were flushing crimson with embarrassment, but he

could do nothing except sit rigidly in his saddle,
wishing the ground would open beneath him and
swallow horse and rider whole. How could he have
failed to recognize Crook? He had seen photographs!
But in the photographs Crook's beard, which had a
tendency to fork naturally in the middle, was neatly
combed into two precise points, while he would certainly not bother to comb his beard before setting out
to hunt by himself, as he was well known to do!

"Pleased to have you along, Lieutenant," Bourke
said, smiling at Whitcomb. "To what troop are you
assigned?"

"Company E, Third Cavalry," Whitcomb managed to say in something resembling his normal tone
of voice. He chose to use the formal designation
"Company" in the general's presence, although the
practice of referring to cavalry companies as "troops"
was common usage throughout the army. "Naturally,
I will report to the post adjutant as soon as possible,"
he added quickly.

"I can save you the trouble," Bourke offered. "I'll
be seeing him right after dinner and I'll tell him you've
arrived. Your troop commander is Major Corwin.
You can report directly to him."

"As you wish, Mr. Bourke. Thank you."

"Colonel Stanton informs me his scouts believe a
change in the weather is coming," Bourke said to
Crook. "They say it will snow tonight."

"What does Grouard say?"

"The same thing, sir."

"And Pourier? Garnier?"

Bourke smiled. "I believe for once the scouts are
unanimous in their opinions."

Crook gave a short grunt that might have been a

laugh. "It could only happen on the twenty-ninth of February. Please tell Colonel Stanton I agree with his scouts and ask him to report to me this evening after supper. Convey my respects to General Reynolds and ask him to see me at his convenience this afternoon."

Bourke saluted and withdrew, leaving Whitcomb alone with the general.

"The worse it gets, the better," Crook said. "I prefer to hunt Indians in bad weather. It's the only way you can surprise them." He dismounted stiffly. The dog flopped down at his feet, looking perfectly at home. "I hope you will forgive me for not introducing myself, Mr. Whitcomb. I like to know my officers and to hear them speak frankly. Unfortunately, frank talk is not all that common when general officers are on hand. I meant no deception."

"Yes, sir. I understand, sir." Whitcomb sat at attention in the saddle, looking straight ahead.

"Your father is Colonel Cleland Whitcomb, I believe."

Whitcomb looked at Crook now and saw that the general was regarding him kindly. "Yes, sir," he replied.

"He is a gallant officer. He was at the Point when I was there. A year or two ahead of me, as I recall. I hope he is well."

The officers and men passing by on their way to dinner glanced at the pair, alone on the parade ground, but the general spoke in a conversational tone that did not carry.

"He has been in failing health, I'm afraid, sir," said Whitcomb, feeling the hurt again. Cleland Whitcomb had returned from the war a broken man, bitter and unforgiving, and his health had declined rapidly until he was little more than an invalid. He had not spoken a word to his only son since Ham's appointment to West Point had arrived in the mail. Ham's mother and his uncle Reuben came to his graduation ceremony, but there had been no word from his father. Feeling unwelcome at home and having nowhere else to go, Ham had refused the leave that was customary for newly graduated cadets, and he had been assigned to staff duty at the headquarters of the Department of the Platte in Omaha until a field post could be found. But then before Ham could entrain for the West, his father had taken a turn for the worse and Ham had gone on leave after all, at first spending the quiet autumn days in a deathwatch over the comatose elder Whitcomb, and then, when his father regained consciousness and Ham was banished from the sickroom, wandering the wooded hills with his dog and his shotgun as he had done in his boyhood. In time he had accepted garrison duty at one of the posts near Petersburg, and when it seemed likely that his father would live for months or years rather than just days, he had once again requested transfer to the frontier. Providentially, some of the companies being assembled for General Crook's campaign against the hostiles were short of officers and Ham was offered one of the vacancies. He had taken the next westbound train after a final visit to his father during which he had received only a cold stare in reply to his expressions of farewell.

"I am very sorry to hear that he is not well," Crook said, and Whitcomb heard the sincerity in his voice. "Well, I enjoyed our ride, Mr. Whitcomb. I am glad to have you in my command."

"Yes, sir. That is, thank you, sir." Whitcomb

came even more stiffly to attention in the saddle and gave the general a perfect salute, his eyes fixed straight ahead on an icicle dripping from the eaves of the telegraph office fifty yards distant.

Crook returned the salute and led his horse away, the tattered bearskin coat flapping about his ankles, the dog following behind.

Whitcomb dismounted slowly, his limbs weak from the cold. He held on to the saddle for a moment to steady himself, conscious of the many glances directed his way.

"Oh, Mr. Whitcomb." The general had paused and turned to call out to him.

"Sir?"

"You had better find some proper clothing."

LISA PUTNAM'S JOURNAL

Tuesday, February 29th. 10:30 a.m.

It is mild this morning, twenty-five degrees when I went in to put on the kettle and rising nearly to freezing as it began to snow just before first light.

Six months ago today, on the day after my father's stroke, I began to keep this journal. I have grown used to the daily ritual of writing. It helps me to order my thoughts and to view my own life with some dispassion. I am glad that I decided to continue this family tradition. At least one Putnam in each of the last seven generations has kept a journal that has been placed, after the author's death, in the family library in Boston. I believe I am the first of my sex to take on the task.

I have put off my writing until mid-morning today

in order that I may have a bit more time to myself. This seems to be a day for looking back, a habit my father did not encourage unless it enabled one to go forward with renewed determination. It is in that spirit that I have looked back on his life to see what lessons it may provide.

The pain I felt upon his death has diminished with time, and in looking back now, the first thing I feel is anger—anger at myself for not seeing while he was alive just how remarkable a man he really was. I loved him very much, but I took him for granted. To me he was just a father, which is to say a great deal: disciplinarian, taskmaster, comforter and friend. But it has only been during the months just past, when I tried to diminish my loss by getting to know more about him through his journals and letters, that I have come to see his full height.

He summed himself up quite well, without realizing that he did so, in a letter he wrote my mother in the summer of 1851. It was written in the Sink of the Humboldt River, in what is now Nevada Territory, and posted some weeks later in Sacramento. It came to us around the Horn. "I have a good deal of time to think, ranging out in front of my train," he wrote. "I am beginning to get the makings of an idea. I believe a fellow could make a living by helping the emigrants; not by guiding them but by helping them along their way from the trailside. Old Gabe—you recall how often I spoke of him—is situated on Black's Fork of the Green and is doing well for himself. He ferries folks across the river and sells them whatever they need. It's a life I think we could take to, if I find the right place. I was a pretty fair trapper and I intend to be pretty fair at what I do next, and this road-ranching business, as they call it, tickles my fancy. Of course, the migration won't last forever, but it may offer a way to live in the mountains and a way to pass the time until we see what is coming along next. The fly in the ointment is that there's not a spot right handy to the Oregon road where I would ask you to live, but I have a notion about that too. Do you suppose these good people would do us the kindness of going a little out of their way? I don't mean to tease you, but I won't say what I'm thinking until I'm sure of myself.''

As this reveals, he dedicated himself to changing successfully with the times, and I believe that to be his greatest achievement. It was no mean accomplishment for a man born in the year of the Louisiana Purchase. Like the majority of men, my father never by his own hand guided the course of the nation at some turning point in history, but unlike the majority he had an inclination of mind that allowed him to see those turning points as they passed by and to adapt himself accordingly, and in the end I believe he survived the changing fortunes of the frontier better than most of his contemporaries.

As a young man he left the home his ancestors had established in Boston and came west to lands that were then marked on the best French maps as <u>terre inconnue</u>. He helped to make them known and he had a hand in the great expansion and prosperity of the fur trade. He came for three years and stayed for fifteen, and when the trade declined he viewed that decline with regret but moved on willingly to other things, first back in New England and on voyages abroad; before long he returned to the West to assist the great migration that has now largely accom-

plished its purpose: to extend the Union across the continent. And yet even as he took part in events that had significance far beyond his own life, even as he saw and understood the historical forces at work around him, he lived a life of true independence, seeking a freedom few men are willing to shoulder. He chose to place his home far beyond the reaches of what we call "civilization," and here he found his greatest happiness. And then, near the end of his life, he undertook what he believed to be the enterprise of the future, establishing beef cattle in the northern territories. He charted this new course with as much confidence as any of his sea-merchant forebears when they set sail on the trackless oceans.

And yet this recounting of my father's life omits the one accomplishment he would like other men to notice. He wanted it known that by his presence here and his good relations with Sun Horse's band over so many trying years, together they have shown that it is possible for the red men and white to live side by side in peace, without either one being compelled to give up his way of life. He hoped they might serve as an example to others, and to some extent his hope has been justifed, as long as peace prevails over the region. But he wished no praise for this success, nor for the others. "A man's got a duty to live right, like his Maker intended," he used to say. "He does that, he don't need no pats on the back from them that ain't up to it."

And so he leaves a twofold lesson: first, one must choose a way of life that has some part in the larger scheme of things; and second, no matter what enterprise one chooses, one must live "right," as he put it so simply. I will try to follow his example. The immediate challenge at hand is to build up the herd with the new stock and make a go of raising beef.

That seems like more than enough to keep me (and Julius, and the small crew we have assembled here) busy for the foreseeable future.

Julius and Hutch will be in soon. I must help Ling with dinner. She was in the kitchen before me again today and had the fire going, even though I have begged her to rest in her bed in the morning. She is in her eighth month now, perhaps her ninth. We are not certain. I worry for her, but she tells me not to. Chinese women, like Indian women, are accustomed to work right to the beginning of labor, and I believe this habit would benefit Caucasian "ladies" as well. Surely none of us is more frail than little Ling. Harry says nothing about his wife's condition, but I think he would be glad to have a doctor in attendance at the delivery. (There is no chance of that, I am afraid.) In this wish as in so many other things, Harry has adopted the thinking of his new land.

There have been no white travelers through the park for more than three months now. The last were the two Mormons who shared our Thanksgiving dinner on their way to the Salt Lake. I have welcomed the solitude, but now I look forward to spring.

CHAPTER THREE

Lisa heard the men open the outer door to the small entryway off the kitchen, laughing and stamping the snow from their boots. She touched the huge enameled coffeepot on the back of the stove and jerked her hand away with a sharp intake of breath, more startled than hurt. The pot was unexpectedly hot.

Ling Wo turned, anxious. She was a short and delicate Chinese, beautiful by the standards of the Orient and pleasing to Western eyes as well.

"You hurt?" The small woman took Lisa's hand and examined it closely before letting go. "Okay. You be careful." She turned away, her huge pregnant belly preceding her as she returned to the bread dough she was kneading on the broad wooden counter.

Lisa touched a finger to the chunk of butter on the sideboard and rubbed a little on the burned finger. She had inherited her mother's fine-boned patrician beauty along with her father's more rugged constitution, yet she dressed in a way that accentuated neither. Her hair, which shone from patient brushing, was piled loosely on top of her head and held in place with a simple whalebone comb, the single ornament she permitted herself for daily wear. Her long dress of indigo-dyed wool was bought from a catalogue, with nothing to distinguish it from countless other simple woolen dresses to be found in countless outposts of the West. But she had her father's cool blue eyes, and like him she had something in her look and manner that commanded attention. Those who shared her life in Putnam's Park were rarely unaware of her presence, and none was more solicitous of her welfare than Ling Wo.

The Chinese woman's predominance in the Big House had increased following Jed Putnam's death, as Lisa's attentions were drawn more urgently to the larger concerns of the ranch, and it was from the kitchen that Ling administered her bailiwick. The big room had pots and pans, and stovetop and counter space sufficient to prepare meals for a hundred, and the pump by the galvanized sink was a time-saving convenience, making it unnecessary to go outside for water. Years had passed since the facilities had been put fully to the test, but for Ling, disuse was no cause for neglect. The spare cookware and china was kept spotless, neatly stacked in cupboards and on shelves, as if she expected a train of wagons to appear on the river road at any time. The second cookstove was seasoned and blackened, free of rust, even though it had not felt the warmth of a fire in many years. The long plank counters were scrubbed clean between meals and the gingham curtains on the windows were kept washed and pressed. The heavy kitchen table that could seat a dozen hands at haying time always bore a vase of fresh flowers in the center, so long as flowers bloomed in the park or in the beds that Lisa's mother had planted around the Big House. In winter the same vase contained delicate arrangements of dried grasses and leaves that Ling picked in the fall and carefully preserved for the winter months. Yet in spite of Ling's loving efforts to make the kitchen and the rest of the house welcoming and cheerful, Lisa couldn't escape a feeling that some essential element of life had gone from the house years before and would never return, leaving the quiet hallways and empty bedrooms somehow incomplete and superfluous. She was glad when mealtimes brought some gaiety at least to this one room. She wrapped her hand in her apron and lifted the coffeepot, marveling at the way Ling treated her sometimes like a child with no sense of her own.

It's because I'm not married, Lisa thought. She thinks there is something deficient about a woman thirty-three years old and not married. Perhaps there is. If I had lived somewhere else, where I could have met some men other than emigrants and drummers and miners. . . . But that wasn't the reason she hadn't married, and she knew it.

Lisa had been just ten when Jed Putnam sent for his wife and child to join him in the house he was building beyond the Missouri in the Big Horn Mountains. Eleanor Putnam had groaned inwardly when she first saw the huge structure of logs, but Jed was sensitive to his wife's civilized background and he had already begun furnishing the house with certain comforts he had had shipped and hauled all the way from Massachusetts—carpets and paintings and some small items of furniture—and more he had bought at exorbitant prices in St. Louis and St. Joe. Eleanor had taken a deep breath and then she pitched in to help, and she had made the house a true home. In later years she wouldn't have traded Putnam House, which they simply called "the Big House" within the family, for the finest mansions of the Cabots or the Lowells.

From the outset, Lisa had taken to life in the park the way a beaver took to water. She was the first to spy incoming wagons on the river trail and she rode out to meet them in every kind of weather as she grew from a flaxen-haired girl to a willowy sapling no longer a girl, to the striking young woman she had become when she returned in the war years from the fancy school back in Massachusetts where she had been sent at her mother's insistence. Her hair darkened as she grew until it was the color of a fine bay horse. The sunlight seemed to shine along each individual hair and linger there, flashing with a light of its own in the lampglow or firelight of evening. More than one bachelor emigrant had forsaken the conventions of courtship and had asked her, after knowing her for less than a day, to go with him and become his wife in the promised land of California, but she had sent these impulsive supplicants on their way without regret. Often she had accompanied departing wagons to the crest of the West Pass just for the pleasure she took in riding back alone into the comforting embrace of the small valley.

She had cast her lot with Putnam's Park.

Unbidden, an image arose from her memory of a summer day in the park and a troop of soldiers riding up the wagon road. She had been twenty-four that year. At the head of the column rode a young officer whose eyes belonged to an older man. He was a veteran of the war and when he met Lisa something in him had become suddenly open and vulnerable. . . .

"What's the matter with you today? You feel okay?" Ling asked, concerned anew.

"I'm all right." Lisa set aside her dangerous thoughts of the past and put out two cups as Julius and Hutch entered the kitchen, leaving their overboots and coats behind them in the entryway.

Beneath the stove there was a small movement as a large orange cat shifted position in his blanket-lined sleeping basket. He looked at the newcomers blearily and closed his eyes again. His name was Rufus, and he had been picked from a litter of barn kittens by Ling six years before, shortly after she and Harry came to Putnam's Park. He was the only animal permitted in the house. He was long-haired and massive, and Lisa liked to imagine that he belonged to some small, rare species of bear, because he adopted a state of virtual hibernation throughout the winter months, usually venturing from his basket only to eat and answer the other requirements of nature.

"That bad-eye cow's gonna calve first," Julius said. "Another week or two."

"How is her eye?" Lisa poured the coffee, knowing the answer to her question. The cow's cancer could not be cured. She was a good mother who raised fat and healthy calves. This one would be her last.

"Getting worse." Julius moved to the washbasin to clean his hands.

"The brindle cow might win out."

"Two bits on Bad Eye." Julius brightened, taking the bait.

"Done," said Lisa. Lord, if my mother knew I gambled, she would turn over in her grave. But Julius was smiling. Lisa knew the moods of her crew as well as she knew the weather in Putnam's Park. A moment of discouragement at the wrong time could sour a whole day and today she didn't want that to happen. Whether she and the others could fulfill her father's vision of a cattle ranch in Putnam's Park was very much in doubt, but this was no time to linger over uncertainties. She planned a lively noontime to raise the spirits of her crew and turn their thoughts to the future. Every job on the ranch had but one purpose—to assure the survival and good health of the calves, and the start of calving was the first sign of spring, the renewal of the annual cycle. Each season had its jobs and the shifting from one to the next marked the passage of time more certainly than the changing pages of the Currier and Ives calendar that hung on the wall by the entryway door. Even now there were fences to mend, work that should already have been done before the demands of calving grew too great. As soon as calving was over, the calves would be branded and then driven with their mothers out of the park onto the surrounding mountainsides, where they would wander higher as the green grass advanced up the slopes. In the park the meadows would be dragged with harrows to disperse the manure left during the winter, the irrigation ditches would be inspected for badger or gopher holes that could cause sudden washouts, and the irrigation system would be extended a little, claiming more land from the sage and bunchgrass as the feeder ditches were lengthened by Harry and his plow. As the days grew longer Lisa and Julius and Hutch would walk the ditches, raising the water level with planks and stones and lumps of sod, forcing the water over the banks to trickle everywhere among the green shoots. Irrigation was a job that continued through the summer, and Lisa enjoyed the peaceful quiet of days spent walking in rubber boots with a shovel over her shoulder. Then, when she and Julius agreed that the grass was mature, the water was cut off and haying began, and when the cribs were full and the meadows reduced to golden stubble, the cattle were gathered and driven back to the park, where the herd was culled of old cows and poor mothers. These, together with the mature steers, were driven to the railroad in Rawlins, and if the first snow had not fallen before Lisa and the drovers returned, it would fall soon, heralding the arrival of yet another winter, to be followed by another spring and another crop of calves. It was a stately progression of events, a continuity from which Lisa derived much pleasure, but this year she looked forward to the arrival of the first calf with a special anticipation. She needed the living proof of rebirth and new life as a sign that this particular winter and her time of mourning were done.

She was about to say something more to keep up the talk of calving and its attendant chores when the entryway door opened again and her uncle Bat stepped into the kitchen.

The mountain man nodded to the room at large, leaving his long rifle in the corner of the little entrance hall so the heat of the kitchen wouldn't sweat out moisture inside the barrel where it might foul the charge of powder just when he finally had meat in his sights. He shut the door behind him and glanced at the cup warming Hutch's hands. "Lisa, you got a cup of java for a poor feller's been pitched out'n his own home?"

Lisa smiled. "There's plenty of coffee, Uncle Bat. What have you done now?" She handed him the steaming cup she had poured for herself.

"Penelope says don't come back without I fetch some meat. Didn't put it in so many words, but she made herself plain. Meat, she says, to the feller that's kept her fed since Cain was a pup. This child knows sign, and that's the truth, but I ain't made a raise since afore Christmas. Ain't no man set eyes on more'n a scrawny doe or two since then, and them scarce as horns on a duck."

"You can have some beef, I imagine," Julius said, expressionless.

"Beef! She won't have none of it! *Pte gleshka*, she says. White man's buffalo! No good, she says. Got no heart." He smote his chest with a fist. "No sir, this child's got some cold trackin' to do 'fore he gets fed."

For more than thirty years Bat Putnam had lived with a small band of Sioux now led by Sun Horse, the aging Hunkpapa peace man. Bat and his wife, Otter Skin, whom he called Penelope for reasons he had never explained, had arrived in Putnam's Park in October, a month after his brother Jed's death, having been notified by an Oglala hunting party that someone had died here. The Oglalas had chanced to pass by the park on the day of the burial and they had observed it unseen from the shelter of a wooded ridge. When they encountered Sun Horse and his band near the Yellowstone on their fall hunt, they had passed on the troubling news, for they knew that the band wintered near the white settlement. Bat and Penelope had arrived as soon as they could, and not long after that the Sun Band, as Sun Horse's people were called, had gone into winter camp in their own valley seven miles to the north. Bat and Penelope had stayed in the settlement through the winter months and Lisa had been comforted by their presence.

Bat turned to Hutch now, his eye carefully noting the steaming pots on the stove behind the boy. "How you gettin' by, Hutch? This old nigger workin' you to death?"

"Not too bad." Hutch grinned. He was used to the trading of insults between these two. At first he had expected one or the other of them to be dead within days, if not hours, judging by the reckless claims each made about the other's character and ancestry, but before long Hutch had perceived that the gibes old Bat and Julius hurled so freely were just their way of letting the other one know that while he was clearly worth no more than a long-dead horse, he had a friend in this world.

Lisa moved to set the table, smiling inwardly. Winter doldrums were quickly banished at the hands of her uncle's often merciless good humor. No one else could have referred to Julius in such a manner and received a smile in return, but Julius knew very well that in the trappers' *patois,* "coon" and "nigger," "critter" and "child" were applied to oneself or a companion without rancor and with no regard for color. Lisa's father had clung to the mountain man's way of talking until his death, although he, like Bat, could drop its mannerisms if he wished. For the Putnam brothers it was not just a style of speech but a way of thinking, a way of living, as well. Its usage kept alive memories of grand adventures and "shining times" long past.

Lisa opened a drawer and began to gather silverware. "You better eat something before you go out into that," she said to her uncle, nodding toward the window. Outside, it had begun to snow again.

Bat sipped his coffee, trying to count the forks in Lisa's hand to see if she had already got one for him or if she was waiting for the stalking game to go a few steps further. She kept the silver hidden from him. "I dunno." He shrugged. "A man don't cut trail too good on a full belly. Takes the keen eye of hunger to make a good tracker."

"Good thing," Julius said, grinning as he dried his hands on a ragged muslin towel. "I don't set to table with white trash, 'specially not with no squaw man too feeble to lift a gun."

Bat snorted, ignoring Julius as if such a comment from that quarter was worth no notice at all. He watched attentively as Ling lifted the lid of an iron cauldron that had already filled the kitchen with smells of slow and careful cooking.

"Good dinner today," said the small Chinese, stirring the pot. She too had her part to play in this ritual. "Beef stew, beans, biscuits, dry-apple pie."

Bat thought of the way Ling laced her dried-apple pie with molasses and a touch of salt, and he felt the juices start to run inside his mouth. He winked at Hutch. "Oh, well, long's you ain't makin' that heathen Chinee food."

"You like Chinese food!" Ling stamped her foot. "I make *Kung Pao* beef, you eat it all! Don't leave none for Julius!"

Bat grinned. Here was a child whose goat could be got every time, rain or shine. Pass a remark about her cooking and Hannah, bar the door. "Was that Chinee food?" He feigned surprise. "I figgered it for Mexican. So hot it like to tore me a new throat."

"You know it is Chinese food!" Ling shook her large wooden spoon at him. "Mexicans don't know nothing about hot food. Chinese people make hot food two thousand years before Mexicans! Mexicans probably send some old fool like you to learn how to cook. Marco Polo come to China, he bring your grandfather. Old fool die on the way home, nobody remember how to cook right so Mexicans throw everything in pot, hope it come out okay." Ling turned back to the stove, muttering in Cantonese.

Bat was struck momentarily speechless by the chronology and geography of this pronouncement, and before he could frame a reply the kitchen door opened again and Harry Wo entered, bowing slightly to Lisa, who bowed in return. Harry was only a few inches taller than his wife but he was nearly three times as wide, even in Ling's pregnancy, and so solid that when he was standing still he seemed to be rooted where he stood as firmly as a tree trunk. His years as a railroad worker and blacksmith since coming to America had merely reinforced an already formidable strength, and in all the time he and Ling had been in Putnam's Park, no man had bested Harry Wo in arm wrestling, that most frequent physical contest of the western territories, which was conducted with every emotion from good-natured horseplay to mortal determination. He glanced around the kitchen now, noticing the smiles on every face except that of his wife, who was still muttering as she ladled stew into a heavy earthenware serving dish. Harry addressed her briefly in Cantonese.

Ling replied with a few short words and gestured with the ladle in Bat's direction. Bat grinned and Harry suppressed a smile as he took his place at the table, his stout body moving with an unnatural grace. His shirt and trousers were western, but his hair was braided in the traditional queue of his homeland. What had once been a mark of servitude to the Manchu overlords in China had become in America a badge of stubborn pride for Harry; it had pleased him to discover that the horse-riding Indians so feared by most Americans also wore their hair long and sometimes tied at the back.

Lisa carried the first serving dish to the table and in clearing a place for it she almost accidentally rearranged a few things she had concealed behind the breadbasket. When she moved away, Hutch saw that an extra place setting had suddenly appeared. Try as he might, he couldn't keep a grin off his face. The whole thing puzzled him almost as much as it pleased him. Whenever Miss Lisa's uncle had a fight with his Sioux wife or just got tired of eating jerky and pem-

mican and dog stew, he'd walk down to the house
and pretend he didn't want to stay to the meal he'd
come just in time for. There would be a little talk that
didn't lead anywhere and never got around to old Bat
accepting the invitation outright, and pretty soon they
would all sit down and Bat would sit right along with
them. How it made them all feel so good, Hutch
didn't know, but it made him feel good too. It was
kind of like watching a pickaninny do a perfect little
dance step to somebody playing the mouth harp; a
simple thing, but it made a person glad to see it.

As if it were no more than his birthright, Bat
Putnam sat down at the table. Ling was at the sink
now, washing a few carrots in a pan of clear water,
and it struck Hutch that sticks of raw carrot were one
of Bat's favorite additions to a meal. Ling was doing
her best to look serious and annoyed, but there seemed
to be the beginnings of a smile playing around her
mouth. Julius saw that he couldn't throw his wash
water into the sink and so he turned to the door,
preparing to pitch it out into the snow instead, and he
too was smiling, glancing back over his shoulder. He
opened the door and turned to step into the entryway,
and he found himself face to face with a gray-haired,
blanket-wrapped Indian, who grinned and gave a
loud whoop, shaking his feathered lance in Julius's
face. Julius took an involuntary step backward, spill-
ing some of the wash water on his boots and wool
trousers.

"*Hau, kola,*" the Indian said solemnly.

Hutch found it necessary to sit in a convenient
chair. If the whole episode between Bat and Ling Wo
had been planned, it couldn't have been better preparation for the Indian's arrival. Hutch too had been

startled at first, and a little afraid, but when he recognized Hears Twice he gave himself up to laughter at Julius's expense along with the others in the kitchen, who made no effort to conceal their delight at his surprise and discomfort. There was something about spending long winter months cooped up with a handful of people that led to outbreaks of practical joking. More than once, Hutch had suffered a similar fate at Julius's hand. He laughed until he choked and then he laughed some more as Bat pounded him on the back to stop the choking.

Julius looked the Indian up and down. "Some friend," he snorted. "You creep around like that, some day I'm gonna shoot first and see who it is later. You do better to walk right up and knock like a white man." He brushed past the old Indian and opened the outer door. A gust of cold air and snow swirled into the entryway and kitchen as he tossed the panful of water into the snow. A horse was tethered at the hitching rail close outside the back door. Julius slammed the door against the wind and stepped back into the kitchen. It serves me right, he thought, letting someone get that close to the house without being seen or heard.

"Well, just don't stand there," he said. "Come in and get warm if you've a mind to." Hears Twice was a frequent visitor to the settlement. He had initiated his own participation in the winter games on a day years before, when he had shaken hands with Julius and left the astonished black man holding the hand and forearm of a recently deceased Crow warrior, which Hears Twice had concealed under his robe. An invisible score sheet was kept, on which the old Sioux had just drawn even, making up for the time

Julius had put salt in the sugar bowl before offering
him a cup of coffee.

The Indian set his lance aside and stepped into the
kitchen.

"What you got there?" Julius demanded. Ever
since he had opened the door, Hears Twice had kept
one hand behind his back.

The old man brought out two dead rabbits and laid
them on the countertop. "*Le mashtínchala lila
washtepi, Julius. Lila chépapi. Aghúyap'na tehmugha
tunkché wachín.*" These rabbits are very good, Julius, very fat. I want bread and molasses for them.

Like Bat's wife, Hears Twice spoke Lakota, the
tongue of the western Sioux, using simple words and
phrases but always testing the black man's rudimen-
tary grasp of the language by using a few words he
might not know. As he spoke, the old Indian moved
his hands gracefully as an aid to understanding, indi-
cating the rabbits, pointing at the bread now rising in
covered pans, crossing his forefingers to indicate the
exchange of goods.

"I'll trade you bread for 'em," Julius said, choosing to conduct the bargaining in English today. "I
cain't trade no molasses, not till we get more. We're
about out."

"*Tehmugha tunkché,*" the Indian insisted. "Mola-
say."

"No molasses." Julius was indifferent, in control
now. He knew how much Hears Twice loved fresh
bread. "The bread'll be ready after dinner. Think of
it all hot and crusty. Fresh bread. *Aghúyapi lila
washté.*"

Julius picked up one of the rabbits and felt the
frozen corpse to judge how much meat lay beneath

the thick winter coat. He was careful to conduct his dealings with Hears Twice with the imperturbable dignity that was expected, always observing each formality in turn. If the Indian ever took it into his head that he could get the better of Julius in trade, there would be no end of trouble.

Finally he nodded his satisfaction and set the rabbits on the counter. "You want some coffee? It's hot. *Pezhuta sapa, washté?*"

The Indian's face broke into a broad, gap-toothed grin. *"Hau, Julius! Pezhuta sapa na mitákola sapa, lila washtéyelo!"* Yes, Julius! The black medicine and my black friend are both very good! *Wakályapi* was the proper word for brewed coffee, whereas *pezhuta sapa* referred to the beans or dry ground coffee, but Hears Twice did not correct the black man, preferring to make the play on words. He laughed softly, well satisfied with the trade. He would ride home later with fresh bread wrapped in his blanket and he would take home the other three rabbits that he had found in his trapline this morning. He was an old man, but still he brought home food when he could. His daughter Mist would be pleased. Her husband had urged her once, in the quiet of the night, to put the old man out in the cold. He is useless, said Little Hand, but Mist had said that as long as there was food in her lodge she would share it with her father. He was a man of power, a man whom Little Hand would do well to respect, as Sun Horse respected him. Neither one knew that Hears Twice had overheard.

Hears Twice moved around the kitchen now, smiling and shaking hands with everyone in turn. Shaking hands was one of the whiteman's few good customs. Show that you hold no weapon; clasp the stranger's hand with your own, each feeling the other's strength. The practice had caught on quickly among the people of the plains and mountains. A whiteman welcomed to a large village could find himself shaking hands with everyone in camp until his own was sore from the effort.

When he reached Bat Putnam, Hears Twice made a few quick motions with his hands.

"Pretty good, Hears Twice," Bat responded. "How's yourself?"

Hears Twice answered with more signs, his hands weaving rapid patterns in the air, each gesture of one or both hands conveying a word or phrase graphically and with surprising speed: the edge of a hand passed across the belly to show the cutting pain of real hunger; a slight fluttering of the hand to signify uncertainty or a question; both hands raised beside the head with index fingers curving upward to evoke the horns of a buffalo.

Bat grew more serious, switching entirely to the sign language now, his own hands moving quickly.

Julius tried to follow what was said. He had first encountered the silent language of the hands when he was with the cavalry in Texas and Arizona. It was known throughout most of the continent, enabling tribes whose spoken languages were more different than English and Chinese to conduct trade or arrange a treaty, or just to exchange insults or declare war. Good sign talkers could carry on a conversation more rapidly than two people could speak any tongue, white or Indian, losing no subtlety or nuance in the process. Hears Twice used the gestures often, for he spoke very little, and Bat was his equal in fluency.

Julius missed half of the signs, but he could gather the meaning. Sun Horse's people were experiencing poor hunting, and hunger had entered the village.

Hutch didn't see how anyone could make out the individual signs, but he knew it was possible. Maybe he would ask Julius or old Bat to teach him the sign talk. It might not be a bad thing to know how to parley with Indians. He had seen the signs used by the Kickapoos and the Sac and Fox Indians in eastern Kansas and he already knew a few of the most basic gestures.

"How come he won't talk out loud to nobody but Julius?" The question had been bothering Hutch all winter and he realized that there was no longer a reason not to ask it. He felt enough at home now to ask something that was really none of his business.

"Talkin's bad for his medicine," Bat said. "He's called Hears Twice on account of he hears everything twice, once afore it happens and again when it happens. He claims he hears better if he don't talk much."

"But he talks to Julius." Hutch was watching the old Indian warily, half suspecting that Bat was pulling his leg and half fearing that what the mountain man said was true.

"Julius speak good Lakota," said Hears Twice. He gave Hutch a wink and chuckled as if this were some kind of private joke.

CHAPTER FOUR

"Wagh!" Bat leaned forward, his eyes ablaze. "Them Injuns come out'n that gully like ants stirred up by a stick, and only four of us, so we put out for tall timber, but old Meek's mule, she wouldn't budge." His hooded capote was put aside now and his buckskins gave off an odor of smoke and old grease that was discernible among the other kitchen smells.

In a pause between the stew and the pie, they were all caught up in his tale. The meal was one at which everyone had had something to say as the stew and beans and biscuits were consumed in prodigious amounts, but as the comfort of a satisfying meal began to sink in and the conversation lagged, Lisa had prompted her uncle to recall the adventures of his youth, and he had needed little urging. Bat catalogued his past with stories, remembering battles and discoveries and deaths and high times in the words by which a friend had later told the tale, or as he liked to tell it himself. This was one of his own, and he told it with broad gestures, often half rising from his seat to imitate an action he was describing, sometimes slapping a hand for emphasis on the heavy pine planks of the table, which were aged a rich and mottled brown by years of hot dishes and spills and wiping with linseed oil. As usual, Hutch was spellbound.

"He's a-poundin' on that critter's head 'n' kickin' her ribs, but there she stands, just as ca'm as ca'm. Meek, he sees the Blackfeet comin' for him and he reckons he'd like some company to help fend 'em off, so he hollers 'Hold on, boys! Thar ain't but a few of 'em! Let's stop and fight!' Well sir, I was coverin' ground pretty good about then. Passed a herd of antelopes and made such a wind it tore the hides plumb off their backs." He paused and looked closely at Hutch to see how much the boy would swallow. Hutch was grinning hugely. "Well, maybe it just ruffled their hair a mite, but I was goin' *some*, and that's truth. But I says to myself, 'Hoss,' I says, 'Meek's in trouble and Meek's your friend,' so I yanks my cayuse 'round and starts back and the other boys they come too, but just about then that mule of his caught her first whiff of Bug's Boys, and if there was one thing like to give that mule a fit, it were to catch the scent o' Blackfoot. She took out for the Yellowstone, and afore you could say 'I'm a nigger,' Meek was leadin' the pack of us and I'm bringin' up the rear, Blackfeet close enough to hit with a stick, and they was a passel of 'em and that's truth. The boys, they holler at Meek, 'Hold on, Meek! Let's stop and fight!' But Meek warn't lonesome no more, ner hankerin' to fight a hunnert Blackfeet neither, so he hollers back, 'Run for yer lives, boys! There's a thousand of 'em! They'll kill us all!' Fact was, that mule had the bit in her teeth and he never did turn her till he got clear 'cross the Yellowstone. We didn't set eyes on him for a week."

Bat sat back in his chair, looking anywhere but at Hutch.

"But how'd you get away from the Blackfeet?" Hutch wanted to know.

Julius had heard the same story a few dozen times over the years and it was a marvel to him the way the one greenhorn in a room would always walk into such a simple trap with his eyes wide open.

"Never did," said Bat, as solemn as a judge. "My horse went down and they was all over me like wolves on a lame buffler."

"But you—" Hutch saw his error too late, and now the laugh was on him. That was the trouble with Julius and Bat, you couldn't stay ahead of them for a minute. But he had to admit that the rules of the winter jokes were fair: each was made the butt in his turn, and there was no malice.

As the conversation resumed, Hutch plunged back into it, the others drawing him along and being so attentive until he felt proud enough to bust that he had been allowed to give them a good laugh at his expense.

Only Bat stayed withdrawn from the renewed gaiety, once he'd had his laugh, choosing instead to remain for a while in a backwash of memories, reliving in his mind the happy times of fifty years before, when an impulse of his father's curiosity had launched him and his brother Jed into the short-lived society of the mountain men, the freest and most exhilarating life Bat had ever known.

Jed had been the eldest of Joseph Putnam's three sons, and he had come west first, in the spring of '22. It was only by a blink in the eye of Fate that he, and Bat after him, had avoided being sent to sea instead. The Putnams were a Boston family of seafaring merchants, and it was a family tradition that those who were later to run the business should learn firsthand how its lifeblood was sustained; upon reaching eighteen years of age, the male offspring were berthed for three years on a Putnam ship, there to be tested and toughened, and, it was hoped, to grow into the kind of men the family or one of its ships might be glad to have at the helm. But Joseph Putnam was a man of some foresight and not inextricably wed to blind tradition. There were stirrings on the American frontier a dozen years after the epic explorations of Lewis and Clark; the elder Putnam suspected that new opportunities would arise in the vast domain beyond the Mississippi and he wanted to miss none that might profit J. Putnam & Sons. In 1821, the year his son Jed turned eighteen, Joseph Putnam was interested in rumors that American investors were about to enter the fur trade again after some tentative failures in recent years. The manufacture of gentlemen's hats and gloves guaranteed a never-ending market for beaver plews, as the hides were called; beaver had been the fur of choice used in making fine felt for hundreds of years, and showed no signs of falling from grace. It was said that the lands near the headwaters of the Missouri River were a fur kingdom of unparalleled wealth, but many wild tales were told of those unknown regions; Joseph Putnam was a prudent man and he wanted reports from someone he trusted. And so Jedediah had received on his eighteenth birthday, when his brother John Batson was just ten years old, an unexpected choice: spend the traditional three years at sea or three years instead on the western reaches of American territory, beyond the broad waters of the Mississippi. Young Jed had already felt within him the stirrings of a wanderlust that he suspected would not be satisfied by coursing over salt swells that stretched from one horizon to the other; he chose the frontier, and in April of 1822 he made his way up the Missouri with a brigade of trappers launched by William Ashley and Andrew Henry, the first Americans to enter the fur trade for keeps. Their one hundred and fifty men were to employ the river highways of the Missouri and its tributaries, traveling by keelboat and wintering in forts they built on the rivers, as the French and English had trapped the northern waterways of the continent for more than a century. But the enterprise was thwarted in its infancy by the implacable hatred of the Blackfoot Confederacy, which sat astride the Missouri's upper reaches.

The Blackfeet showed uncommon tenacity in bearing a grudge. Two of their number had been killed by the Lewis and Clark expedition in a half-baked mêlée set off by some petty thievery on the part of the redskins. The Blackfeet viewed the deaths as an inexcusable overreaction. In retaliation, they declared perpetual open season on whites, who thereafter found themselves treated as fit subjects for stealing from, shooting at, or inflicting slow death upon whenever the slightest opportunity permitted. The trappers came to regard the Blackfeet as the Devil's children; ''Bug's Boys'' they called them, with a mixture of respect and defiance.

Denied the upper Missouri, the Ashley-Henry men turned inland, moving westward across the Great Divide into the valley of the Green River and beyond. There they found the promised fur kingdom and something else besides, something that in the end was more cherished by the trappers than the pelts they sought, for it was here that the trapping profession grew to full size. Freed from dependence on the Missouri for transportation and resupply, the trappers soon abandoned the habit of wintering back in a company fort. They stayed in the mountains year-round, learning the streams and backwaters and all the ways of the country until they belonged no longer to the rivers and forts and keelboats, but only to the mountains.

They were supplied at an annual *rendezvous* held in the trapping country, where Jed Putnam and the others gathered by the hundreds to trade the season's take for Galena lead and Du Pont powder and sharp Green River knives made in Massachusetts and transported in gross lots as far as St. Louis by J. Putnam & Sons, along with blankets and trinkets and all manner of foofaraw to trade with the Indians who flocked to the Rendezvous in the thousands. The elder Putnam was waiting for the moment when he could take a hand in the fur trade itself with some degree of safety. Three years came and went, but the uncertainties in the trade remained constant, and Jed gladly obeyed a suggestion that he stay on in the mountains he had come to love. He kept his father apprised of developments by means of discerning, enthusiastic letters that often took six months or more to reach Boston, where they were read to the assembled family in the drawing room after dinner; Jed's news was absorbed by young John Batson like water in sandy soil.

At the Rendezvous of '27, held at Bear Lake, Jed was astonished to see Bat among those arriving with the supply train. The younger Putnam was grinning from ear to ear, unfazed by the thunderous mock attack the trappers and Indians launched in waves on the pack train. Bat had jumped the gun a bit, coming west at age sixteen and without benefit of parental consent, but Jed's letters had fired his imagination until he could stand the waiting no longer. The middle brother, Jacob, had duly gone to sea upon reaching eighteen two years after Jed. He was back now and had taken his place in the business, proving himself as sober and industrious as his father. The truth was that although Jed and Bat were separated by eight years of age they had always been of much the same spirit and neither one particularly liked Jacob, who was cast from a different mold. The present arrangement suited them perfectly.

Jed took Bat under his wing when the Bear Lake Rendezvous broke up and they traveled together. They were among the first to turn free trapper, owing allegiance to no company, taking orders from no *bourgeois,* or booshway, as the Americans called the men who led the brigades. They lived as unfettered as the hawks, traveling the length of the mountain chain and out to the Columbia bar, wintering in Taos with the *señoritas* or in the Bitterroots with the bighorn sheep, returning in summer to the Rendezvous, where they sold their plews to the first company to reach the appointed gathering place with whiskey and supplies.

Bat became aware that the talk in the kitchen still concerned the days of the mountain men, and the joy Lisa's father had taken in that life.

"I'd of like to known him then," Julius was saying. "Strong as he was when I knew him, he must of been something when he was young."

"Strong?" Bat interrupted. "He could hunt bear

with a switch. Liked to hop on the back of a grizzly and make him buck.'' He winked at Hutch. ''Wasn't a man in the mountains could outshine my brother Jed. 'Ceptin' me.'' He grinned, remembering the look of Jed astride his horse, Hawken rifle across his saddle, always laughing at some foolishness or other.

''That's what Pop always said about you,'' Lisa said, smiling.

Bat didn't rise to the bait. He just nodded and said, ''We was *some* then,'' the vigor leaving his voice as he felt the loss again. He thought of telling Hutch the story of the dancing bear to keep his own spirits up, but he never told it as well as Meek did, and before he could decide whether or not to start in on it the conversation had passed him by and turned to the weather and the snowpack in the mountains and the chance for a good hay crop. That was all right for them, he guessed. This cattle business might turn out all right, the way Jed had said it would, but such things held little interest for the mountain man. The warmth and the food had made him drowsy, and he had lost any desire to trek through the cold in search of some contrary beast that was almost certainly far away and headed in the wrong direction. Hunting could wait for a while. Just now he wasn't done remembering.

His first year in the mountains hadn't been without its hardships for a sixteen-year-old boy, and as if the natural challenges weren't enough, he had had to suffer the constant gibes and pranks the trappers directed at every greenhorn, until one morning when he and Jed and a few others were camped on Pryor's Fork and a grizzly shambled into camp before anyone was awake. Bat was aroused from his dreams by a soft grunting close at hand and he looked up to see the great bear lifting a youngster named Toussaint right up in the air by the shoulders, bedroll and all. Toussaint was too petrified even to cry out. Almost without thinking, Bat lifted his rifle from his blankets, where it rested at night to keep the powder dry, and let fly at the bear, creasing its brain and waking the rest of the camp just in time for them to see the bear stagger about in a drunken waltz for several moments, still holding the tongue-tied boy, until it keeled over stone dead into the fire pit. "Well, sir, poor Toussaint reckoned old Bat had missed him clean," Joe Meek said later in one of his many recountings of the story, as he imitated the bear's dying waltz. "Wagh! Old Bat cain't miss! He'll make 'em come or I'm a nigger! Toussaint, he figgered his only chance war to give that b'ar a dance, if'n that's what he come fer. Well, sir, he just begun to get the hang of the footwork when down goes old Ephraim, deader'n a hammer. Old Bat he says, 'Thar's b'ar fer breakfast, boys,' and lays back in his blankets, ca'm as ca'm."

Old Bat had been all of seventeen when that took place but from then on he was one of the boys, and for the first time in his life he had felt that he was standing on his own two feet, out from under the shadow of his older brothers. "Hooraw fer the mountains!" he would let out occasionally for no apparent reason, and nobody looked twice because they had all felt the same at one time or another.

Bat smiled at the memory, but the smile turned to a frown. The trappers' life had been one a man could glory in and he and Jed had lived that glory to the hilt, never dreaming that their livelihood had been dealt a mortal blow by a humble worm that lived halfway around the world. But Jed had seen the signs, and so had John Jacob Astor.

Bat gave a snort of disgust, which caused Julius and the others to look in his direction, but he paid them no mind.

He held Astor personally responsible for the death of the beaver trade even though he knew there was no truth to support such a grudge. He harbored it because it pleased him to get back in that way for all the trouble Astor had caused Ashley and Henry and the free trappers, but he blamed Astor mostly for his perfidious abandonment of such a splendid life merely because he suspected it would no longer afford him a profit.

Astor had been one of the first Americans to test the waters of the fur trade, long before Ashley and Henry. In 1811 he had sent an expedition to the mouth of the Columbia to establish a post there and challenge the dominance of the Hudson's Bay Company in what was then still British America. The post was called Astoria and its inhabitants Astorians. Astor was a man who did not intend to be forgotten. Astoria was abandoned during the war of 1812, but Astor re-entered the trade with a vengeance a few years after Ashley and Henry. His American Fur Company prospered, and in time he absorbed almost all of the original Ashley-Henry men. But in 1832, when the trade was near its peak, Astor had seen a new kind of top hat on the streets of London during a visit there, one made of silk. He guessed that this product of the China trade was the coming thing, and within a few years he had sold his holdings in American Fur and retired from the trade. The trappers

scoffed at his caution, even in the face of falling
prices, but Jed Putnam had nodded quietly and started
thinking about what he would do next. A man didn't
have to look to the streets of London or Boston to see
trouble for the fur trade, he said. Right there in the
mountains anyone but a fool could see that the best
beaver grounds were trapped out and new grounds
were as hard to find as virgins at Rendezvous. "Beaver's bound to rise," the others said, but it didn't,
and the popularity of silk hats continued to grow.

At the Rendezvous of '37 Jed had bought no supplies, and when the gathering disbanded he had turned
his horse toward South Pass. There he had taken a
last look back to the Green River and the mountains
beyond, where the remaining mountain men, Bat
Putnam among them, walked streams in which the
old beaver dams now went mostly unrepaired. He
knew that some of his friends would linger there for
years and some would die there, joining all those
who had already gone under at the hands of bears and
Blackfeet, winter cold and plain carelessness. He
didn't begrudge them that choice, but clinging to the
dead past just was not in his makeup, and so he had
spurred his horse eastward, hoping to find something
to do with the rest of his life that would give him just
a small portion of the satisfaction he had felt during
his years in the mountains.

"Poor doin's," Bat muttered. He had no liking for
the memory of Jed's departure and the demise of the
beaver kingdom, but a man needed reminding now
and again that the world was something more than
dry powder and fat cow.

Realizing he had spoken aloud, Bat looked up to
find Hears Twice gazing at him. Bat made signs that

said *I am thinking of long ago,* and the Indian nodded. He knew that what lived in memory was just as
real as what a man did today. Bat could savor his
deeds and pleasures of the past simply by remembering them faithfully or by telling his stories to a
friend, just as the Sioux kept their history alive by
continual telling and retelling of the great deeds. If
the memories died, the past would be gone, for they
did not write things down. Only in the winter count
did they preserve the barest framework of that living
history. The count was kept by the band's remem-
berer, the historian, on a specially prepared elk or
deerhide. He chose a single picture to represent the
most significant event of each passing year and drew
that picture on the hide. But the winter count was
like the poles of a lodge, useless without the memories of the people to cloak it and contain therein the
past life of the band. Bat smiled at Hears Twice. The
old man knew what it was to remember the past.

Hears Twice had eaten with the others and for the
most part he had been content to follow the conversation with his eyes, as was his custom on such occasions. No one was sure just how much English the
old Sioux understood, but he laughed along with the
rest when something funny was said, and if he didn't
it was just as likely that what he had heard didn't fit
in with the Sioux notion of what was funny rather
than because he hadn't understood. Now and then he
made a few signs of his own when the talk turned to
something that concerned the Sun Band as well as the
settlement in Putnam's Park, such as the sudden
snowstorm or the scarcity of game or the passing of
the recent thaw. He repeated what he had told Bat
earlier—hunters from Sun Horse's village had had

little success in the recent moons, bringing in scarcely enough meat to supplement the small resources of jerky and *wasná* from the fall hunt, now almost gone. The Lakota—for so the western Sioux called themselves as well as their language—were hungry. He conveyed the news matter-of-factly, not wishing to dwell on his people's misfortune. The Sun Band lived in the old ways of the Lakota, scorning the domesticated Sioux who lived near the Indian agencies in Dakota and subsisted on handouts of beef and wormy flour from the government. Ridicule would be heaped on any of the Sun Band who lowered himself, even in times of hardship, by begging from the whites. Hears Twice came to visit today because he could bring something to trade; it was only proper that he stayed for a meal when visiting a neighbor's lodge. When the apple pie was served he nodded his thanks with dignity and contained his secret delight.

As the dishes were cleared Julius took his fiddle from its peg on the wall and tuned the strings. Hutch lost no time in reaching for the old banjo. If Julius was content to let the little ranch take care of itself for a while, he would get no argument from Hutch.

Harry Wo finished the last of his coffee and got to his feet. He had grown accustomed to the strange flowing melodies played by the black man and the boy, but he had work to do. The others could stay in the kitchen all afternoon if they wanted. When the snow melted they would want shoes for the horses and sound wheels on the wagons and Harry preferred to set those things in order now at his own steady pace, making a little headway each day on the never-ending list of blacksmithing and carpentry chores he performed so well.

Hears Twice rose as Harry moved to the door, and motioned him to wait. Since their first encounter Harry had instinctively accorded the Indian the deference one properly showed an elderly and wise man and now he waited patiently as Hears Twice stepped to the entryway. He returned with his lance and Harry saw that the blade, which some Indian had made from a large blacksmith's rasp, was bent. Hears Twice handed the lance to Harry and made a few signs in Bat's direction.

"He says straighten the blade and make it hard again with white man's magic."

Harry grunted. "You tell him Harry Wo ain't no white man. I got my own magic. Tell him he must pay." He would temper the blade so the old Indian could split the shoulder bone of a buffalo bull with it, if he had the strength.

Without waiting for a translation from Bat, Hears Twice made signs.

Bat grinned. "He says he already heard how much it'll be. He'll fetch you a couple of rabbits in a day or two."

Harry nodded, and favored Hears Twice with a trace of a smile as he slipped into his canvas coolie's jacket. He liked the trappers' rabbit fricassee that Jed Putnam had taught Ling to make. It was a welcome respite from a diet heavy in beef. Taking the lance with him, he stepped out into the snow.

To Harry, Hears Twice's ability to understand English and his refusal to speak it, except rarely, were unremarkable. Harry too had learned English fairly quickly, at least the understanding of it when it was spoken. But his pride, so insulted by the universal disdain expressed for the natives by the English bar-

barians who dominated foreign trade with China, absolutely prevented him from speaking in a manner that would encourage feelings of superiority in white listeners. He had shunned the pidgin English used by the British in China, and always chose his words with care. In America he had avoided the ingrown settlements of Orientals, where the prejudice of the surrounding white communities was strongest. He moved in this strange land in his own way, at his own pace, finding places for himself and Ling where they could observe, rather than be observed. It was easy for Harry to respect Hears Twice's silence.

The forge in the blacksmith's shed needed only a little stoking and a few puffs of the bellows Harry had made himself, and soon the fire was glowing warmly. He took off his jacket and threw back the heavy tarpaulin that served to protect the open side of the shed against the worst weather. When it was clear and truly cold, Harry could work in his shirt sleeves with the tarp down, but today the temperature was near freezing and he liked to watch the falling snow as he worked. It took a considerable effort on the part of the weather to make Harry Wo feel a chill. After the winter he had spent in the Sierra Nevada Mountains driving spikes for the Central Pacific Railroad, he regarded any lesser weather with quiet disdain.

In a short time he had the lance blade glowing as he prepared it for the anvil. Outside the shed the flurries thickened and thinned, sometimes revealing the full length of the valley floor down to the cut in the hills where the river trail passed through to the foothills and the plains beyond. Harry was from the mountains of eastern Szechwan province and, despite all the peculiarities of this foreign land, when he was alone with his work and the falling snow he felt at home. He raised his eyes often from his work, appreciating the infinite variety of motion the wind imparted to the white flakes that flew as gracefully as birds, and he was the first to spy the riders approaching on the wagon road.

In the kitchen, the fiddle and banjo sustained the festive mood of the noonday meal. Lisa paused in the washing up to enjoy the rhythms of the music, much as she might have stopped to rest in the penetrating warmth of the first summer's day. She felt a serenity that seemed to have its origins not just in the peaceful atmosphere in the room but outside the house, in the valley beyond, as if the whole of Putnam's Park were wrapped in a mood of tranquillity. She was pleased by the success of her dinnertime conversation. If anything, Julius seemed even more ready than she to get on with the work that lay ahead, and for the first time she felt a growing confidence that they would succeed in fulfilling her father's vision.

The tune came to a close and Julius smiled. Hutch's banjo playing had improved tenfold with almost daily practice during the winter and he now wove the melody so skillfully into his style of playing—"drop-thumb," he called it—that Julius often took a harmony line and left the melody to Hutch.

"Is it true that Hears Twice can hear things before they happen?" Hutch glanced at the Indian. He had been thinking about it as they played.

"You mean like them rabbits he promised Harry?" Hutch nodded. Julius smiled and shook his head.

"He was funnin' with Harry. He always pays him rabbits when he needs something done."

"Now and again he'll give you a start," Bat put

in. "Injuns ain't like white folks. A bird'll look at 'em crosseyed and they'll take it as a sign. Old Hears Twice, he gets his signs afore the rest of 'em now and again."

"You'll fill the boys' head with notions," Lisa chided.

Hears Twice had enjoyed the music, occasionally sipping from a last cup of heavily sweetened coffee, but now his mood grew serious as the men looked in his direction. He had observed the formalities of his visit, making his trade, accepting food when it was offered, discussing matters of interest to all; it was time to state his real reason for coming. He caught Bat's eye and began to make signs.

Bat grew suddenly interested. "He says he heard somethin' last night; that's why he come down today, for a look-see. Somebody's comin', he says. Visitors. They'll be along pretty soon, he says."

"At this time of year?" Lisa found herself growing apprehensive. No casual travelers would be abroad in this region, not for another month or two, and not even then if the rumors of an Indian outbreak persisted.

Bat looked carefully at Hears Twice, seeking an indication that this was a joke springing from some impenetrable area of Lakota humor, but the old Indian met his gaze solemnly.

Julius got to his feet and started for the door that led to the dining hall and saloon. Lisa moved to follow him.

"You let me see who it is," he cautioned her, and he passed through the door, followed by the other men.

The large L-shaped room they entered could seat seventy or more at its long wooden tables and benches.

It was dusty from disuse and so cold that the men's breath hung in small trailing clouds behind them. A long bar ran the length of the back wall; in the shorter leg of the L was a small general store whose shelves were now mostly empty. Antlers and horns and stuffed heads hung from the walls, and an immense potbellied stove dominated the middle of the room. Like the great hall of some medieval castle, which it resembled in function if not in construction and scale, the saloon had been used as a banquet room, trading post, dance hall and makeshift theater over the years; but perhaps because of the way the bar confronted anyone who entered through the main door from the porch, or in acknowledgment of the smiling woman who reclined in the obligatory oil painting behind the bar, the room had come to be called simply "the saloon." In deference to the well-bred sensibilities of Lisa's mother, the lady in question was thoroughly draped in a garment that revealed her curves but only hinted at charms that were more freely displayed in similar portraits to be found in countless cowtown taprooms.

The men crossed the cold room to the windows, Hears Twice close on Julius's heels and Hutch trailing along out of curiosity. Outside the snow was falling lightly and they could see halfway down the valley, past the first hay crib, past the clump of pines where the road made its last turn and ran straight for the settlement. Except for the cattle, still searching the feed lines for a mouthful of hay, the valley was deserted.

Julius glared at Hears Twice.

"*Úpelo*, Julius," the Indian said softly. "*Wana úpelo.*" They are coming now.

Bat watched the cattle for a time. They accepted snow or sleet, rain or shine, passively. Unless spooked by some real or imagined danger, they never showed excitement. What was the use of a life like that?

He turned back to the saloon. He had always regarded the cavernous room as a monument to his brother's optimism, but the cattle might serve just as well. The saloon entombed a past that was dead and gone, while the pregnant cows represented Jed's hope for the future.

Jed's ability to accept the dying of one good way of life and then another had always been a source of wonder to Bat. Even when the fur trade, the grandest life a man could wish for, showed signs of turning moribund, Jed had accepted that calamity without complaint and had looked to the future with his eyes full of hope.

At the time, Bat had wondered if Jed might not be something of a fool. Hadn't Jed been Bat's teacher, conveying to his younger brother all his own love and understanding for the mountain life? How could a sensible man turn his back on it all and ride away, never again to see the long crystals of ice forming on a still mountain lake, of an autumn morning?

Well, of course Jed had come back. After a dozen years spent lollygagging about back in the States and riding Putnam-owned ships as far away as China and England, he had heard the mountains' call and he had returned, first to guide the emigrants and then to settle here for good, in Putnam's Park, however unlikely a place it had seemed to set up road ranching.

Jim Bridger had been the first to choose the life, and he had asked Bat to go in with him, but Bat had turned him down. Old Gabe had a right to go soft in the head if he liked, but Bat would have none of it, then or later. Gabe had set himself up on Black's Fork of the Green, back in '42, plunking himself smack next to the Oregon road, where he was subjected to the full force of the human river that flowed westward on the trail. It had been just a trickle at first, meandering to the green valleys of the Oregon country. Politicians had urged the settlement of Oregon for the greater glory of the United States, but most men thought more of self than nation, and it took the cry of "Gold!" to get them going. Then the trickle became a flood of men, scrambling for the diggings in California, and Gabe had had to suffer every nitwit in the bunch, each fool who stood in the light of the setting sun and asked which way was west. Gabe had answered them all and pointed out the road, and he'd done all right too, until the Mormons drove him off in '53.

At least Jed had been sensible enough to realize that he had no wish to weary himself answering foolish questions; what he wanted was someplace to raise a family and live out his days in contentment. And so he picked a place up off the flat, in country that had some shape to it, where there were trees to soothe the eyes and cooling breezes in summer. Nearby was an old Indian trail and a pass through the mountains by which travelers could return to the plains and pick up the Oregon road at South Pass, where it crossed the Divide. The Putnam Cutoff drifted more than sixty miles north from the main trail, and the detour cost a few extra days, but at certain times of the year its advantages were clear to any man with a grain of sense. Four or five days weren't such a price to pay in a journey of four months or more. Not when it meant you could reach the halfway point with stock well fed and feeling fresh.

Bat smiled. Jed was a crafty son of a bitch and nobody's fool; Bat had come to see that in time. Jed had chosen this valley because it suited him, and because in wintertime Bat and Sun Horse were just a couple of hours' ride over the next ridge. He had blazed his cutoff and pointed the way, kind of like laying out bait. But of course what he had really done was pose a challenge for his fellow men, to see what they were made of, and for the most part they had lacked the gumption to pick it up. Taking his cutoff required some courage and wisdom, and Jed was thus protected from the worst fools on the Oregon road, who were in plentiful supply. Take a long way 'round? Nossir, not me. Their business was to get to California, and quick about it. Greed drove a man faster than a whip.

Those that did take the cutoff found no trap at the end of the bait trail. More like the pot of gold lit by the rainbow of promise. When the land along the main trail was grazed bare in midsummer, the experienced scouts and wagon bosses knew they would find good pasture in the broad bottomlands of Putnam's Park and they knew the condition of the stock was paramount. While the horses and mules and oxen browsed placidly on the rich grass, the emigrants ate Eleanor Putnam's cooking, as much of it as they could pay for, conserving their own supplies for the journey ahead. Here, six weeks or more from St. Joe, they knew the demands of the trail all too well, and they could set right mistakes they had made at the start. They might buy some items they were short of or lacked altogether, or unburden themselves of something useless in exchange for what they needed. Before long, Jed had added a small wing to Putnam House, providing a handful of extra beds where the more genteel among the travelers could spend a night away from the cold ground and hard beds of their Murphy wagons. The rooms were clean and free of insect life, the food was good and the company lively, in welcome contrast to the miserable shacks and pigsty conditions that characterized most of the ranches that hovered along the emigrant roads like buzzards waiting to filch the traveler's savings in exchange for a bellyache from bad food, a swollen head from bad whiskey and a host of new reasons to scratch under his longjohns.

In the judgment of those experienced on the trails, Putnam's Park was the best road ranch in the West, if not the most convenient. Those who came here to rest and regather their strength declared it the preferred haven between the jumping-off places in Missouri and the myriad trails' ends where the individual hopes, dreams and greed of the emigrants led them.

Even so, the saloon had been full to capacity only a few dozen times over the years, and not once since the early sixties, but those rare occasions had been enough to satisfy Jed, convincing him that he had done right to build a room big enough to contain high spirits and high jinks without busting at the seams. He had received his guests with an almost baronial propriety, basking in the talk, laughter and many-tongued altercations of the emigrants, who had been glad of the chance to sit with their feet up to the big stove on a cool mountain evening, listening to Jed's tales of a time just twenty or so years before when there were only twelve hundred white men north of

Taos, and every one of them a better man than any
stuck-in-the-mud hog farmer or city dweller back in
the States, sure as God made the beaver swim and
the water run clear in the Rocky Mountains.

Bat looked about the saloon, trying to imagine it
warm and full of life once more. Nearby, Julius
stood with folded arms, looking out a window, "Ca'm
as ca'm," Meek would say, waiting for what would
come. Hears Twice and Hutch stood beside him, the
boy shifting about and peering through the glass
panes. The snow had thinned somewhat. From where
he stood, Bat could make out the outline of the
western ridge.

He had to give it to Jed: he'd picked a good spot
and done all right, even if Bat had never thought
much of road ranching.

To give himself something to do he ambled the
length of the room, counting his paces. Too short for
a shooting contest, but broad enough for a person to
do a proper job of kicking up his heels to music, as
Bat knew from experience. He missed the dancing.

He hadn't set foot in the saloon three times during
the winter. He disliked places that were haunted by
voices of the past. It seemed to him that the logs and
planks sometimes whispered echoes of all they had
heard over the years. Bat looked at the broad plank
floor that had been trod by so many feet clad in all
manner of boots and shoes—and moccasins—every
pair of them, save those that belonged to Indians or
the people who lived in the park, in that unrelenting
hurry to get somewhere else that only a white man
with ambition seemed able to muster. Today the
planks guarded their tales under the fine mantle of
dust that had sifted down since Ling Wo last swept

the floor. Just when Bat was ready to confront what the ghosts had to tell him, they fell silent. It irritated him but did not surprise him; he had long ago come to accept the perverse nature of things in general, in the material and spirit worlds alike. Besides, the ghosts held no secrets from him. He knew the sort of men who had passed through this room and why they came no more. They had been noble and base and everything in between, men as different as honest farmers just looking for a chance to start anew and gold seekers hoping to strike it rich without dirtying their hands. Oh, yes, there had been gold seekers. Fortune had played a small joke on Jed Putnam. With the discovery of gold in the Idaho country in 1860 and in Montana three years later, some of the fortune hunters turned north from the Oregon road and Jed found himself playing host to the very same greed-driven men he had come here to escape. They were packers, a lot of them, riding horses and leading mules, able to get over the West Pass earlier in the spring and later in the fall than wagons could. As usual, Jed took the turn of events with good grace and did what he could for them; by then he had more pressing worries than the avoidance of fools. The miners moved to the new gold fields by two roads, one laid out by John Bozeman along the eastern flank of the Big Horns, his route following the Putnam Cutoff for the first seventy miles or more, and the other up the Big Horn River valley to the west, blazed by Jim Bridger, who had returned once again to scouting. Jed advised all and sundry to take Bridger's route. It lay in the country of the friendly Shoshoni, and by then there was trouble with the Sioux.

In the summer of '51, when Jed was still guiding

wagons, Bat and Sun Horse had been at Fort Laramie
for the great peace council, the first one between the
whites and the tribes of the northern plains. The fort
had only recently been purchased by the army; before
that it had been a trading post under several names,
and numerous bands of Sioux had wintered there for
twenty years, trading with their white friends. "Loaf-
Around-the-Forts" the other Lakotas called them. At
the council the white men had sat in chairs and the
Indians had sat on the ground—Lakota and Cheyenne, Crow and Blackfoot and Arapaho and Shoshoni, friend and enemy alike—and together they had
agreed that the whites could have a single road through
the country to get them where they were going. "The
Holy Road," the Indians called it, because while on
the road the whites could not be touched, not even a
few horses run off for sport. Even then some of the
tribesmen had felt the first stirrings of concern as
they watched the endless procession of whites across
their lands, looking for all the world like a column of
ants when seen from the distant buttes, all trudging
westward, the whole vast tribe moving from the old
nest to a new one for reasons known only to themselves. One Shoshoni orator had suggested that his
people might move east to the lands the whites were
vacating.

Bat shook his head. Fancy notions they all had. It
seemed like a long time ago. One road for the whites
and everything else for the red men. Sun Horse
wasn't even called Sun Horse yet, and the band was
led by his father, Branched Horn. They were of the
northern bands, those who kept to themselves and
scorned the too-easy life of the Loafers. The mountains still held out a high-flown dream and a golden

promise to Bat and his Lakota brothers, and it was two more years before Jed started building in Putnam's Park.

And then, after the house was built and the Putnam Cutoff was blazed, even as the first adventurous wagons rolled gratefully into the cool green bottom of the little park—especially grateful then, for the year was dry—Fate had reached out a cold finger and touched the Holy Road and after that nothing was the same.

Down at Fort Laramie a Mormon's cow had wandered away from a party of emigrants. Some said the cow was on her last legs and purposely abandoned, but whatever her condition she had seemed attractive enough to some Sioux camped a few miles from the fort. The animal was taken in hand and butchered, and the Mormon, perhaps seeing a chance to gain more than the cow was worth, reported the loss to the post commander and said the animal had been stolen. The commander designated a young lieutenant to take a squad of men and seize the offending Indians, and it was here that Fate played her malevolent part. The officer chosen for this detail was named Grattan, and he had often expressed a confidence that with thirty men he could cut a swath through the whole Sioux nation. Now he had his chance. Taking his thirty men and all his mammoth ignorance of Indians with him, he went to the heart of the Sioux encampment and demanded the surrender of the thieves. The great Brulé headman Conquering Bear met with Grattan and protested that the warriors who had seized the cow were Minneconjou visiting the camp; guests in camp were inviolate, he explained; no one could lay a hand on them. This custom had the force of law among the Sioux. Let our friend, the agent at Laramie, handle the matter, Conquering Bear asked. Grattan refused. The headman then offered a good mule in exchange for the cow, but again the officer refused, and he was fast growing impatient. The Lakotas who understood the white man's talk knew that the interpreter was not translating properly, but before this could be explained to the officer, he made a move toward Conquering Bear, his soldiers leveled their rifles, and from somewhere a shot sounded.

Conquering Bear fell. And then a great noise rose over the encampment, with more shooting, and when the dust blew away on the warm summer winds, Grattan and his thirty men had followed Conquering Bear in death. The Indians struck their lodges and fled.

Thus the fire was lit. At first it had only smoldered, flaring briefly here and there as one side and then the other perpetuated a cycle of misunderstanding, violence and revenge. In time the conflict had burst into full-scale war. The troubles had forced the emigrants to take roads farther to the south, away from the old trails along the North Platte. The telegraph was moved, and when the rails came they too followed the new route. And although it remained where it had always been, Jed's road ranch in Putnam's Park had gradually receded from the narrow thread of civilization that linked the Pacific coast with the eastern states until it was little more than a forgotten outpost. Well before the end of the sixties, the stream of visitors had dwindled until a cannon could have been fired across the saloon in midsummer without endangering a living soul. When new peace treaties pacified the Sioux, the wagons did not return. For almost eight years now, a tentative peace had rested uneasily on the Powder River country, but the few wagons that still followed the western trails found enough fodder along the main road, and only the foolhardy would think of venturing into the last hunting grounds of the Sioux.

And just as he had accepted the death of the fur trade, Jed had accepted the end of his road ranching with equanimity, and he had turned to the future. Bat looked out on that future now. The flakes were falling thick and heavy, fluttering to earth in a dead calm, but he could still make out a few cows plodding through the snow, sniffing for a few bits of hay. And then something else caught his eye.

"Wana hípelo," Hears Twice said. They are here.

Bat nodded. "Two of 'em." He glanced at the old Indian and saw that he was smiling. It did not surprise Bat that the prophet was right; he had come to expect it.

The door from the kitchen opened and Lisa stepped into the saloon, wrapped in her wintertime riding coat of mountain goatskin, made with the thick white fur turned in.

"Well?" she asked as she joined those at the windows.

"They're comin' now," Bat said.

"I don't see anything," she said, but she stepped back, moving closer to her uncle. He put his arm around her, feeling her apprehension, the fear of approaching danger. It wouldn't have been so in the old days, before the Indian troubles, he thought. The fear had arisen in recent years as if it had sprung out of the ground. But the seeds had been planted long ago, and the crop had been nourished by the blood of two races.

He separated himself from Lisa and moved closer to the windows, putting all his attention on the dim figures in the snow. He had whiled away much of the day with memories of times long gone. Now it was time to pay mind to the strangers, whoever they might be. Strangers riding into camp brought a change, for good or naught, but they always brought a change.

"I don't see nothing either." Hutch scratched at a pane that was frosted over by his breath. He moved down to the next window, as if moving ten feet to one side might give him a line of sight past the falling snow.

"You ain't been long enough in the mountains," Julius said. "Snow catches your eye. You got to look through it like it wasn't there."

The flurry thinned a little, and now Julius too could see the riders as they appeared like men coming out of a mist on a river bottom. They were white men. The bearded one had a rifle in a boot under his right leg and the butt of another gun showed briefly on the other side. Loaded for bear, that one. A buffalo hunter, maybe. But what was he doing here?

The other rider was clean-shaven and younger.

Julius felt a sudden resentment at this intrusion into the isolation of the park. There was healing going on here, slow work that needed more time. Lisa was getting over the loss of her father, but she was only now ready to look ahead. If old Jed had lasted a few more years, or if Lisa had married and her man had come to live here and take a hand in things, then the loss of Jed Putnam might not have struck so hard. But there was no use iffing. Jed had died when he did and things had to go on without him. Julius had been planning on steering Lisa's thinking toward the days to come and he had made a start at the noon meal, but he wanted more time for slow talk warmed by the kitchen stove, the way Julius's mother and maiden aunt had talked, sitting by the small stove in the cabin when he was a boy. Minutes would pass without either woman saying a word. Then one would break the silence and for a time the soft flow of conversation would reach Julius where he lay in his bed, trying to stay awake. The gentle talk of those two women had been his lullaby, comforting him as it drifted past his bed the way the big river drifted past the plantation wharves. He needed that kind of talk with Lisa while the park was still sealed off from the world by winter, but he had waited too long.

The riders were drawing closer, and Julius made out the carcass of a deer behind the bearded man's saddle. The brim of the younger man's hat was curled slightly in a Texas roll, and a rope hung from the horn of his saddle, which was also Texas-style, made for work, not show. Perhaps they were just a pair of drovers who had kept going north after a drive up the Kansas trails. Their comfort in the saddle, their indifference to the weather, the steady pace of their horses—these things spoke of men at home out of doors. But then Julius noticed how the younger man rode a pace or two behind his companion, glancing constantly from side to side. There was no mistaking it—he was covering the bearded man's rear. Between the two of them they would miss nothing that happened on any side. Julius grew uneasy. If they were only a couple of drovers, what were they doing here in the middle

of winter? Visitors, Hears Twice had called them.
The old Sioux was right. The riders had a sense
of purpose about them. They had the bearing of men
set on a destination, and everything about them said
it would take more than a half-baked mountain storm
to make them seek shelter. Whatever their purpose, it
had brought them here.

Julius motioned the others back from the windows
and he reached for the double-barreled Richards shotgun that hung above the front door of the saloon.

CHAPTER FIVE

Hardeman's eyes roamed the settlement, taking in the
dormant garden fenced with chicken wire to keep out
the deer and rabbits, the chicken coop and icehouse
and the woodpile stacked high with split wood even
as spring drew near. He saw the lone tipi beyond the
house, noted the smoke from the peak, and felt his
blood quicken. Close to the barn were new corrals, a
pigpen, and three Durham bulls fenced away from
the small herd of cows that were still feeding on this
morning's hay down in the meadow. Four dairy cows
were kept away from the bulls too, in their own
paddock. The house and barn were well placed for
shelter from the north winds, set on higher ground up
away from the creek to avoid the coldest air that
hung along the valley floor. A small spring house
stood by the stream, where half a dozen geese were

paddling about in the water. The little ranch lacked for nothing. It was just what Jed Putnam had seen in his mind's eye when the place was only a dream.

The cattle in the meadow had caught Hardeman's attention as he and Johnny rode past. The cows were a crossbreed, Durham and Longhorn he guessed, confirmed now by the presence of the Durham bulls by the barn. With the cows were three or four mature steers, kept back to provide meat for the settlement, but the herd had been culled in autumn, there was no mistaking that. It was a seed herd with all the pure Longhorn blood weeded out and the proportion of Durham blood about to be raised another step. The bulls were being kept off the cows until summer so no calves would be born during the coldest months of winter. Taken all together, it smacked not of some helter-skelter outfit trying its hand at raising tough and chewy beef, but of a thoughtful and controlled exercise in animal husbandry. It seemed that Jed had turned to raising cattle since the source of his road-ranching business had been sent elsewhere by the railroad and the constant threat of the Indian wars. Like so many others, he had apparently decided that raising beef was the occupation best suited to the Great American Desert.

A rhythmic clanging came from a shed built against the barn, but Hardeman was prepared for the sound; he had seen movement in the shed as he and Johnny rounded the clump of pines at the last turn in the road. Whoever it was had had more than one chance to see the riders coming, when the flurries thinned to allow a view down the valley. The blacksmith's inaction spoke of a place at peace with itself, unsuspecting, and this suited Hardeman perfectly. By the Indian tipi, a dog sat up and faced the newcomers, but it didn't bark. Near the barn, two cats sat on a stump. They too watched the riders placidly. Not even the animals in Jed Putnam's domain were prone to take alarm at the approach of strangers.

The blacksmith's hammer clanged again, beating a steady rhythm. "He's Chinese," Johnny said. They were the first words he had spoken since the two men left their night camp below the river canyon.

Hardeman moved a knee against his horse and the animal turned toward the shed. Johnny's mount shifted course like a shadow to hold position, and Johnny gave a tug on the lead rope to bring the single pack horse along. The boy's lanky body accommodated the movements of his horse with a naturalness not even Hardeman could match. More than one white man had jokingly remarked that there must be horse blood somewhere in Johnny's ancestry.

Johnny's face was pink from the cold. His straight brown hair was cut short at the top of his collar. His neck was protected by a huge blue bandanna wound twice around and tied snugly. The bandanna was long enough to tie his hat down over his ears in a storm. He wore a hip-length blanket coat and wool pants tucked into boots that came to the tops of his calves. He carried no weapons. The blue eyes beneath the wide-brimmed hat had lost their usual calm; they had become unnaturally alert, like those of an animal turned loose in unfamiliar surroundings. Hardeman hadn't seen that look since their first months together, when a much younger Johnny had first explored the white man's world that was so strange to him. In time the look had left him, and over the years the boy had ridden more than once into the face

of mortal danger with no change of expression or
thought for his own safety, serving as Hardeman's
extra pair of eyes without being asked. It wasn't fear
in his eyes now, any more than it was fear that had
kept him from ever raising a hand against another
man in the seven years they had been together. There
was a change in him, but the reason was locked
somewhere in the boy who never spoke more than a
small part of what was on his mind.

Johnny's unsettled manner puzzled Hardeman, but
the confidence he had felt that morning lingered on
unshaken. He felt the satisfaction in his stomach and
the strength of the deer meat in his body. It was
amazing the confidence a man got from a bellyful of
fresh meat.

He had been waiting for scarcely an hour when the
doe had stepped to the creek to drink, and she had
died cleanly from the first shot. When Hardeman had
returned to camp, Johnny had a cookfire already
made, and there was no trace of the sweat lodge.

"What if I'd missed?" Hardeman had asked.

"You don't miss."

"It could happen."

"Then you would be warm and I'd be hungry,"
Johnny had said with only a hint of a smile. He had
eaten part of the liver raw, seasoned with gall, the
way the Indians ate it. Hardeman had chewed in
silence as the boy tried a few tentative bites before
roasting the rest of the liver over the flames. Johnny
had said only what was necessary as they broke camp
and since then nothing until now.

As they passed the main building Hardeman noted
the unmarked snow on the long porch and the old
paint peeling from faded lettering on the wall. The

words were almost obscured by the lines of snow that clung to the upper surfaces of the gray logs. "Emigrants Rest," they proclaimed, "Saloon & Gen'l Goods," and lower, "Buy & Trade." Over the door in the middle of the porch a sign hanging from an iron bracket swung in the wind, creaking softly, the eyebolts tired from protesting years of westerlies; "Putnam House," it said, and below that an eagle clutched a banner: "We Owe Allegiance to No Crown." The simple statements on the sign and wall, so inadequate a description of Jed Putnam's self-contained mountain hideaway, evoked for Hardeman an image of the man, complete to the puffery of a patriotism that Jed had always kept cloaked in his abundant dry humor. Hardeman suspected that he had hung the sign as much to declare his independence from any pompous government back east as from those on foreign shores. He urged his mount into a trot. The Chinaman would know where the boss might be found.

The riders were even with the end of the porch, about to pass around the corner of the building, when Johnny reined back suddenly. "The door on your right," he said quietly, as a tall Negro stepped onto the porch with a shotgun in his hands.

Hardeman was glad that Johnny had prevented an armed man from approaching behind them unnoticed. He thought to unbutton his buckskin coat as he reined around to face the porch, but the Negro held the shotgun loosely in one hand, the hammers on half cock.

"Howdy," the man called out, and Hardeman decided against any move that might appear hostile; he kept his hands in plain sight on the saddle horn.

The colored man was about fifty, he guessed; strong and unafraid. His walk through the unbroken snow on the porch revealed the rolling hips of someone who had spent years on horseback. A cowhand, maybe; one man in four on the cattle trails up from Texas was black, former slaves moving about the country trying their luck at different jobs, getting the feel of being free men—but then he noticed the man's trousers, tucked into high army field boots like his own. The wool was light blue, or had been, and the faded strips of facing down the outer seam of each leg had once been yellow. They were sergeant's pants, from before the uniform changed in '72. Hardeman could read details on United States Cavalry uniform as plainly as a regimental chaplain read the Bible.

"It's kind of poor weather for traveling." Julius came to a stop at the corner of the porch, looking down at the riders, the shotgun aimed indifferently at the snow in front of the horses.

Hardeman nodded. "The boss around?"

"Could be." Something flicked across the dark face. Hardeman felt he had done something to be judged for, and the judgment had gone against him. The blood rose to his face.

"It could be we'd like to see him," he said, more sharply than he intended. "We're looking for Jed Putnam."

"This is his outfit. You're welcome to step in out of the cold."

"We're obliged." Hardeman swung his horse toward the long hitching rail in front of the saloon, and Johnny followed close behind him. They dismounted and Hardeman busied himself for a few moments with slacking the cinch and removing his St. Paul coat, which he threw over the saddle and the rifles to protect them from the snow. It wouldn't do to be short-tempered now. He was glad the colored man hadn't taken offense at his tone of voice.

Julius lowered the shotgun further. You made strangers welcome whether you wanted to or not; that was a rule of the frontier as important as not prying into a man's business or his past. If they had known old Jed, his suspicions might be wrong.

As they crossed the deserted saloon Julius found that most of his caution was directed now toward the younger man. He was comfortable with the bearded one; that was a man who had seen and done many things that would be revealed slowly, if at all; he would be dangerous if provoked, but he had left his rifles outside and Julius had hung the shotgun back on its pegs before leading the way to the kitchen. The younger man was twenty, maybe twenty-one, and a little taller than the other, but something about him evaded quick understanding. Maybe it was the slight limp, his body moving in a way long accustomed to an old wound or deformity.

It's his walk, Julius thought, but not the limp. The youth wore boots, but he moved across the floor like a man walking barefoot on soft grass. Almost like an Indian.

Julius entered the kitchen first, holding the door open for the two strangers. Only Hutch and Ling were with Lisa now.

"He's looking for the boss," Julius said.

"We're looking for Jed Putnam," said Hardeman.

"He was my father. I'm Lisa Putnam." She offered her hand and the bearded man took it. She had seen the way his eyes swept the kitchen as he entered, pausing in turn on Hutch and Ling before stopping to rest on her. She had met his gaze of frank appraisal longer than he expected, but he did not look away. His hand was strong and warm, recently withdrawn from the glove he held in his other hand.

"Was?" Hardeman was numb, struggling to regain control of his thoughts.

"He died last fall."

"He died?"

"He had a stroke in August. He died a month later." The man was still holding her hand. Lisa withdrew it, feeling an unaccustomed warmth in her face. What was the matter with him? Couldn't he understand a simple thing like that? Her father was dead. For Lisa, the stating of that fact had required an effort of will. Jed Putnam had been felled suddenly on a hot afternoon when the thunderheads stood tall above the mountains; he had lingered for a time, his grip on life tenacious even as an invalid, as he himself remarked. "I'm hanging on," he had whispered to Lisa one day when she asked how he was feeling, never expecting a reply. They were the only words he uttered between his stroke and the day of his death. And throughout that long month Lisa had nursed him and sat with him, watching the remnants of his life ebb steadily away. When the spirit had finally left him, there was no discernible change; his passing was like the fading of the sky at day's end, with no single moment when one could say the light had gone. At the last he had smiled, and the smile had remained when his face grew cold to the touch.

"I'm sorry," Hardeman said, feeling stupid at his inadequacy. He had been on edge ever since entering the warm kitchen. He had glanced briefly at the

Chinawoman and the boy—another hired hand by the look of him—and his eyes had come to rest on the young woman in the simple blue dress who said she was Jed Putnam's daughter. She held a coffee cup in her left hand, and in the first moment Hardeman saw her she had the look of someone caught in a secret act.

He glanced around the kitchen, searching for signs. Six chairs were pushed back from the sturdy wooden table; another was occupied by the young hired hand. Three chairs stood squarely in place. On the table there were wet rings made by half a dozen cups. The plates and serving dishes from the recent meal were in the galvanized sink, half washed; the sideboards were wiped clean. This was not a kitchen where things were left out of place. Even now the China-woman straightened two of the chairs and wiped the table with a damp rag.

The signs led Hardeman to a certain conclusion. There were only four people in the kitchen now, apart from himself and Johnny, but there had been more here just a short time ago.

He looked again at those present. The Chinawoman was at the sink, back at her washing up. The boy, a few years younger than Johnny, sat where he had been ever since the strangers entered, looking from one to the other and then at the colored man and Lisa Putnam, waiting for someone to speak.

Beneath the stove a large orange cat stepped out of its basket and crouched on the floor, ready to move quickly should the occasion demand it. The cat's wariness heightened Hardeman's sense of hidden danger.

None of those here lived in the Sioux tipi outside. Who did, and where was he?

Hardeman moved a little to one side so he could see the room's three doors—one to the saloon, one to the outside, a third that probably led to the back of the house. "I'm sorry," he said again. "I guess that makes you the boss now."

"Julius was my father's partner. Now he is mine."

Hardeman understood at last what had passed across the Negro's face outside. It was anger at being taken for a hired hand just because he was colored. Still, it was a reasonable guess. Christ, he thought, let there be an end to the surprises here. He contained his annoyance with difficulty. The news of Jed's death had caught him unaware. It was a possibility he had never considered; he had always thought of Jed as immortal.

It was Jed Putnam who had taken young Chris Hardeman in hand in the summer of 1851 and taught him the skills of the frontier, and after Jed had left the emigrant trails to set himself up in Putnam's Park, Hardeman had heard news of him over the years. And now he had finally come to see his old friend. The Putnam Cutoff was right where it should be and Jed's mountain park was just as Hardeman had always imagined it; approaching the settlement with Johnny, he had felt Jed's presence in every building and shed, in each of the cows down in the meadow. To find that Jed was dead had put him off-balance. With an effort he steadied himself now. He would need new allies, and there was no telling which one might prove most valuable. He put out his hand to the colored man.

"I guess I left my manners on the trail. My name

is Hardeman; Chris Hardeman. The boy is Johnny Smoker.''

Julius hesitated, but he took the hand and shook it. After all, he had concealed old Jed's death for no reason, just some instinct he still didn't understand. "Julius Ingram," he said. "This here is Hutch. The cook is Ling Wo." He saw Hardeman cover a momentary surprise at being introduced to the small Chinese, who nodded politely before turning back to the dishes.

Johnny Smoker scarcely acknowledged Lisa and the others as they glanced in his direction. He stood apart, too far for a handshake. He had seen Chris shift position and had seen too the sign Chris had made with his hand. It was a small movement known only to the two of them. It said *There may be danger*. From his place by the stove, Johnny could watch the three doors, and everyone in the kitchen. The boy named Hutch was looking at him with open interest now, and his face showed no deception or awareness of danger. Perhaps Chris was wrong. Still Johnny did not relax his guard. He stood waiting for whatever might come, his face calm, but he was not calm within. For seven years he and Chris Hardeman had ridden together, from the dry wastes of the Utah Territory in '69, when Chris had hunted meat for the railroad crews and Johnny had carried water to the thirsty Irishmen, to the cattle trails of Texas and Kansas where Chris had risen quickly to trail boss and Johnny had gained a reputation of his own for his uncanny way with horses. From Chris, Johnny had learned the ways of the people who were moving westward across the land, changing everything as they went, and he could have had no better teacher, for Chris saw men for what they were, with strengths and weaknesses, and he knew that the truth was stronger than any pretense. They had ridden a long way together, Johnny absorbing everything but never truly belonging—except with this man, the one who had raised him and taught him and protected him since the Washita. And then this morning when he awoke among the willows, Johnny had felt a change. The feeling had persisted throughout the day, and although he had tried to speak to Chris about it, he had not found the words. Now as he stood quietly by the huge woodstove, Johnny knew he stood truly alone for the first time in his life.

"You must be hungry," Lisa said. "There's plenty left from dinner. Please sit down." She moved toward the stove to see if the stew was hot, glad of something to do.

"We ate today. We'd be grateful for a cup of coffee." Hardeman unbuttoned his coat, clearing the way to the Colt revolver in his waistband. He moved to the head of the table, choosing a seat where he could face the room. "And some whiskey, if you've got it." He saw the hesitation in Lisa Putnam's movement and the shadow of disapproval that crossed her face, which was as he had intended. It was time these people were put off-balance now, while he collected himself and prepared his move.

Julius was about to protest as Hardeman sat down, but Lisa motioned him to silence and nodded in the direction of the cabinet where the whiskey was kept. No one had sat in her father's chair since his death, but there was much to learn about the visitors and she had no wish to entangle them in her painful memories. She handed a cup of coffee to Johnny Smoker and placed another in front of Hardeman as Julius set a bottle on the table. She seated herself, leaving a vacant chair between her and the bearded man, surprised that he rose partway as she joined him. He waited for her to sit before he settled back in his own seat.

"Did you know my father well?"

"It was a long time ago, Miss Putnam. We rode together on the California road, guiding wagons. We were friends."

"Then his death is your loss as well. I'm sorry."

Hardeman remembered himself at seventeen, lost in the teeming streets of Independence, Missouri. He saw the face of Jed Putnam looking down at him from horseback, sizing him up at a glance; the truth of Lisa Putnam's words struck him and he felt the loss sharply then, accepting for the first time that there was to be no reunion with his friend, a man he hadn't seen in more than twenty years. He poured a dollop of whiskey into his coffee and sipped it, feeling the warmth go straight to his core. He had been at loose ends in the spring of '51, arriving in Independence without money to join a train, without horse, without supplies, and in less than an hour he had met Jed Putnam. The trails blazed by the mountain men had become the highways of a booming westward migration and the skills of the mountain men were once more in demand, this time to keep the legions of greenhorns who straggled across the plains and mountains from dying of sheer ignorance along the way. Jed had already delivered two trains safely to Sacramento, and when he decided to hire young Chris Hardeman, no one had argued. Fortune did not often smile that broadly on a wandering youth. But

Hardeman had let the friendship lie fallow. He had held it in reserve like money in a bank and now it was gone, stolen away without a sound or a warning by the hand of Death.

Lisa Putnam was watching him as he sipped the coffee. Her blue eyes reminded him of Jed's. Was the hair her mother's? He saw how it gleamed, and noticed for the first time the small lines at the corners of her eyes, the furrow of worry between her brows, and the dryness of her lips. The skin on her face showed the effects of the sun. She wore no rings and her hands were marred by half a dozen small cuts and nicks. She spent long hours out of doors doing the work of the ranch, he guessed, caring for the cattle and horses and looking after the smaller livestock too. She was the boss in more than name.

Uncomfortable under his scrutiny, she moistened her lips with the tip of her tongue and looked away, but she couldn't know what he was thinking. She couldn't guess how good a face so plain and natural looked after six months of keeping company with painted saloon girls and the prim wives of proper Kansas citizens. She was in her thirties and showed it. Any woman who lived out of doors on the frontier grew old before her time, and most looked the worse for it, but not this one. Plain wasn't the word to call her by. The mountains had stamped an imprint of strength and character on her; she bore the marks of time like rewards instead of burdens. If you took in the whole woman, the long legs and slender waist and modest bosom, the eyes like Jed Putnam's and the blood rising again to her cheeks, you saw that she was beautiful and felt like a fool for not seeing it at once.

"Your father was wagon boss and chief scout the first trip I took on the Oregon road," he said, forcing himself to smile, needing to disarm her suspicions at the start. "He took me on as assistant scout. I told him I didn't know the first thing about it. He said he liked the cut of my jib. He'd do that sometimes, use seafaring talk."

"His family were shipowners in Boston," said Lisa, relaxing a little, certain now that the man was telling the truth.

Hardeman nodded. "He said if I'd come from Pennsylvania on my own stick, I'd do to cross the mountains with. He gave me a horse." He leaned back, the smile coming more easily now as he remembered the perverse nature of the pinto Jed had innocently offered, knowing the boy would learn much from the hardy Indian pony. He drank again and the warmth began to spread through his body. "He must have looked all over Independence to find a horse that would teach me the most. That one trip was all we made together, that and back through the mountains in the fall. He showed me the beaver country, Horse Creek and Green River and the New Fork Lake. He called it Loch Drummond, after some Scotchman. The next spring he got me a job as chief scout with a big train; they took me on his say-so." In one year with Jed Putnam he had learned more than some men learned in a lifetime, not only about the trail but about the weather and which watering places were dry in spring or fall, and how to talk to the Indians. And then the mountain man had proved himself the best kind of teacher by pushing Chris into the chief scout's job before the youth thought he was ready, making him depend at once on what he had learned and thereby assuring that he would never forget it.

He drained his cup of the last of the coffee and poured it half full of whiskey. Lisa did not entirely disguise her displeasure. Hardeman grew expansive in the telling of his memories. "After that I saw him now and again. Then he quit the road and came up here. I knew about this place before he found it. It's just like he said it would be."

"I'm surprised you never came here, if you were friends."

Hardeman shook his head. "I got my wagons out early in spring, but not too early. Always made good time on the road; no detours. The one year I wanted to take Jed's cutoff the company voted against it." He chuckled. "It was a dry spring and not much grass. I warned them, but they said 'California or bust,' and came pretty near to bust. We lost three animals out of four. They cut their wagons in half in the desert and looked worse'n a bunch of Mormon handcarts rolling into Sacramento, but nobody died." He drank from the cup. "Worst damn bunch of fools I ever rode with." He fell silent, fighting off a surliness that whiskey sometimes brought out in him. This woman disturbed him, looking at him with Jed Putnam's eyes. They had a way of seeming to look past whatever fences you threw up, as if they were saying, "Never mind about that, I know what you are." But she couldn't know the other reason that had kept him from coming by on the trips back from California, when his time was his own and there was no one to vote him down—the notion that he would wait to see Jed until he could measure up to the man and stand beside him as an equal.

For years he had wondered what could give him
the sense of satisfaction felt by a Jed Putnam, a man
who had been there in the beginning, when the mountains were tracked only by moccasins and buffalo.
Scouting had held much promise, and Hardeman had
once been confident that in time his own deeds might
be written in the history of the West below such
names as Jedediah Smith and John Hoback and Kit
Carson and Jim Bridger and Sublette and Hickok and
Jed Putnam. But the Washita had stolen those hopes
away. In the years since then he had been a freight
hauler and a hunter, cowhand, trail boss and lawman,
enough occupations to satisfy most men for a lifetime, but he took little pride in these accomplish-
ments, viewing the list warily as an accounting of
jobs and professions each of which had failed him in
some way or another. Now he was a scout once
again, sure of himself and set on a course. He had
come here to leave his mark on the West in a way
that Jed would approve, he thought, and he had
planned to ask Jed for his help. But Jed was gone,
and there was no longer any measure to meet.

He raised the cup to wet his throat and saw it was
empty. He poured again and looked at Johnny by
the stove. "You getting warm over there, Johnny
Smoker?" A splash of whiskey fell on the table as he
righted the bottle.

Johnny nodded.

"You're welcome, of course," Lisa Putnam said,
sounding somewhat uncertain. "We have more than
enough room nowadays. I'm sorry you came all this
way for nothing."

Hardeman smiled, giving her no warning. "It wasn't
just to see your father, Miss Putnam. You know how

word gets out about one thing and another. We heard, those of us on the trail—back when Jed built this place—we heard he was given the valley by a Sioux chief name of Sun Horse.''

At the mention of the name a chill descended on the kitchen. Johnny Smoker looked from face to face, searching for the reason, but Hardeman kept his gaze on Lisa Putnam and saw that she was afraid.

"What do you want with Sun Horse?" Julius was standing at the foot of the table. He had seen the gun in Hardeman's waistband, knew he was meant to see it, and the knowledge made him angry.

"You know him then." Hardeman's tone made it a fact, not a question.

"Mr. Hardeman didn't say he wanted anything," Lisa said, trying unsuccessfully to keep her voice calm.

"He must be an old man by now," Hardeman said blandly.

"Sure," Hutch explained. "Old Sun Horse, he's just—"

Julius cut him off. "You get on out and mend that harness like I told you."

"You said it'll hold till—"

"You hear what I say?"

Reluctantly, the boy got up and went out, taking his coat from its hook in the entryway. Julius had never spoken to him so sharply before.

In the kitchen no one spoke until Hutch was gone.

"It's true that Sun Horse gave my father the valley." Lisa no longer smoothed the edge in her voice.

"We need to find him, Miss Putnam. We have a message for him from General Crook."

The chill deepened.

Julius sat down at the far end of the table. "Sun Horse is wintering up north this year. On the Tongue, maybe, or the Rosebud."

Hardeman was growing increasingly wary of the deceptions he sensed growing around him. It was time to break the standoff.

"The way I hear it, Sun Horse has spent every winter for more than twenty years in the next valley over from here." He was careful to keep his tone even.

Anger sparked in Julius's eyes. "Are you saying I'm—"

"I'm just saying what I hear," Hardeman interrupted, before the colored man said something that could not be ignored. "He's a peace chief. He stays clear of the hostile bands."

"That's right, he's a peace chief." Lisa took a short breath and gave ground. "You'll have to forgive us if we're cautious, Mr. Hardeman. Sun Horse is an old friend. My uncle lives with him. It's true they winter near here, but we haven't seen them in some time. The hunting has been very bad. They may have gone north in search of game."

Hardeman paused before answering. How much of the truth was she telling him? It wasn't likely Sun Horse would move his people in winter, nor would he be fooled by a February chinook.

"If Sun Horse is a friend, Miss Putnam, you'll help us. We came to warn him. All the Sioux who weren't back on the Dakota reservation by the end of January have been declared hostile."

"Hostile! There has been no trouble here since Red Cloud's War!" Lisa felt a swift anger and a swifter fear, knowing now that the thing she had hoped would never happen had been inevitable, its coming only a matter of time.

Red Cloud's War, so called for the Oglala warrior who had dominated its battles, had ended in 1868 after two years of fighting, a clear victory for the Sioux and their allies, the Cheyenne and Arapaho. As soon as the Civil War was over, the government began negotiating with the Indians for the right to open John Bozeman's road along the east flank of the Big Horns in order to speed the development of the new gold fields in Montana Territory. The government was in debt following the war and the mineral wealth of the western territories was needed to replenish the national treasury. The Indians balked at this invasion of their favorite hunting grounds, and while the negotiations were still going on, troops were dispatched to begin constructing three forts along the Bozeman Trail, ignoring Jim Bridger's safe route west of the mountains. This effrontery brought down on the troops stationed at the new forts Reno, Phil Kearny and C. F. Smith the unbridled fury of the Sioux and their allies. They harassed the soldiers without letup, inflicting heavy casualties, and in the end Washington yielded, unable to supply the forts reliably, let alone provide safe passage along the Montana road. A new treaty concluded at Fort Laramie created the great Sioux Reservation west of the Missouri River in Dakota Territory and recognized the Powder River country—all the land from the Black Hills in the east to the Big Horn summits in the west and from the Oregon Trail in the south to the Yellowstone in the north—as "unceded Indian territory." Most important, it provided that there could be no more cessions of Sioux land unless three-quarters of the adult male Sioux marked their approval on paper.

With the treaty accepted by both sides, witnessed by more than a hundred headmen who came to Fort Laramie to make their marks upon the pact, the troops were withdrawn from the Montana road and the jubilant Indians burned the forts. Since then, the bands that shunned the agencies and the government beef had continued to live west of the reservation, in the Powder River country, and although there had been some skirmishes along its borders, the region had enjoyed an uneasy peace for almost eight years. Lisa's father had warned that it couldn't last forever, not unless the white man changed his ways.

"It's the Black Hills trouble," Hardeman said now. "The government wants all the Sioux on the reservation where it can keep an eye on them. The army sent out riders in December, Indian riders from the agencies, to all the bands in the country here, giving them until the end of January to come in."

"January?" Lisa was appalled. "Who gave an order like that? Do they know how cold it has been this winter?"

"The order came from Washington." Hardeman left unsaid all the distant ignorance that implied. "It could be some of the riders didn't get through, what with the cold. Crook is giving Sun Horse a chance to go in peaceably."

"The riders may not have gotten through because of the cold and they want women and children to travel three hundred miles in January!" She turned away. "They're going to take it all. They're going to take all the land west of Dakota." She looked at Julius. "They are doing exactly what my father said

they would do. The government will move the Sioux
out of the Powder River country and then the settlers
will come in and that will be an end of it. The Sioux
will never get it back." She spun to face Hardeman.
"This is treaty land! Sun Horse has lived at peace in
this country all his life!"

Hardeman drank off the rest of his coffee. The bite
of the whiskey took his breath away and helped him
to keep quiet. Everything she said or suspected was
true. He couldn't oppose her now or she would get
up a head of steam that would vent itself on him and
there would be no help from that quarter, not any
time soon. Let her get her anger out, but don't provoke her or she would argue herself into taking a
stand she couldn't back down from. Jed had taught
him that, about dealing with Indians—"You want a
man to come around to your way of thinking, don't
push him into a corner and don't talk him to death.
You handle him right, he'll come along soon enough
like it was his own idea."

Julius cleared his throat. "I reckon the soldiers
will come when the snow melts."

Hardeman shook his head. "Crook gathered his
troops during the thaw. He's got eight hundred men
at Fetterman right now. He'll be on the move soon, if
he hasn't started already. There will be another column from Fort Abraham Lincoln."

"Damn them!" Lisa rose suddenly. "God damn
them!" She walked to the window, struggling to hold
back her tears of rage. She held herself tightly, her
arms crossed below her breasts as she stared out into
the darkening afternoon. It was snowing in earnest
once more. She could see the glow of a fire in the

tipi by the woods. The wind gusted hard and the tipi vanished in a gray-white cloud.

A log fell in the stove. Ling Wo moved silently to add more wood. She had not understood all that had been said since the two strangers had entered, but she knew that Lisa was worried and afraid, and she sensed that the quiet life she and Harry had enjoyed for almost five years was in danger. She accepted this with an imperceptible shrug. The Western world was mysterious to Ling, who could not fathom the forces that moved it. She trusted in simple things she could experience and believe in. She believed in this kitchen, the most calming room she had found since coming to America. She believed in Lisa and her father, who had taken Ling and Harry in, had shown them the American meaning of the word "friend," for which there was no precise equivalent in the life of their homeland, where the line between friendship and family was a gulf not easily bridged. Here, she and Harry had been accepted as family almost overnight, and to Ling the process had seemed magical. This life had been good to her and she wished it to continue, but if the fate and fortunes of Putnam's Park, all those invisible ruling qualities the Chinese called *joss,* were changing, the change was inevitable and would have to be accepted. Ling did not struggle against the inevitable.

"Sun Horse never raised a hand against a white man." Julius was the first to speak. "He don't allow no one—no other bands—to fight in his country."

"But he turned his back when his young men snuck off to fight in Red Cloud's War." Hardeman had to know where the Negro stood, and Julius's quick anger was his answer.

"He couldn't do nothing else! If you know Injuns, you know that! The chiefs don't give orders like in the white man's army!" Julius sat back in his chair and brought his anger under control, glancing over his shoulder at Lisa, then turning back to glare at Hardeman. "He's been a friend to these folks. He protected them in the war."

Throughout the conflict, Julius had been with the Ninth Cavalry, stationed far away in the Southwest, and had heard only what the army grapevine had to tell about the war. Among the black soldiers of the Ninth, there had been a grim resolve that if they were tested in a similar struggle, they would not add another defeat to the records of the frontier cavalry. But in Putnam's Park he had found attitudes toward the Indians that were new to him. Sun Horse was Jed's friend, and after some initial suspicions, Julius had come to accept the Sun Band, at least, as peaceable neighbors. With Jed gone, he had found himself speaking now as the old mountain man might have replied to inquiries like Hardeman's, sticking up for Sun Horse and concealing his whereabouts, but even as he spoke, Julius wondered at the rightness of his course. If the war should come to Putnam's Park and he were forced to take sides, which would he choose?

"Listen to me, Miss Putnam," Hardeman said. "If Sun Horse goes in to the reservation now it could save the peace. He's Sitting Bull's cousin. The other headmen respect him. It will make them think twice about fighting the army. If they go on fighting, they'll lose, you know that. This is their only hope." The sounds of a recurring dream came to him—cries of triumph and pain, the screams of dying horses . . .

He locked the memories away. He must give all

his attention to the woman or she would see too much. Everything he had said was true, but it was not all of the truth. He had not said what would happen if Sun Horse refused to go in.

He drank again, flushed from the whiskey now. It took an effort to stay alert. He wanted to relax as he might have done among friends, and stop shadow-boxing with the truth. What was it the woman feared? There was something more, beyond the danger to Sun Horse and his people. "Take us to Sun Horse," he said bluntly. "Help us persuade him to go in."

Without turning from the window, Lisa slowly shook her head. When she spoke, her voice was far away.

"His people have no meat. They're not strong enough to travel."

"Crook has a beef herd and supply wagons. If Sun Horse will go peaceably, they'll get beef and blankets and grain; and an escort to the reservation." Lisa turned and Hardeman saw the first flicker of hope in her eyes. His whole hand was on the table now, all except the ace up his sleeve. It was time to play that too. "They can keep their horses. And some guns for hunting. Crook will give his word."

Lisa's mind was racing, trying to summon up everything her father had taught her. Jed Putnam had seen much of the world and he had spent many patient hours passing on what he had learned to his daughter, even when she was a young girl, teaching her with stories instead of lessons, holding her attention with skills he had learned years before around winter campfires where a man's ability to entertain his companions was sometimes as important as his grit in a fight. He had shown her how each great force in the world beyond affected her own life, and during her years in Miss Jameson's School, all the politics and history that her teachers had presented as so many dead facts had fallen into living patterns when seen through her father's eyes. Now, she had recognized at once, even before Hardeman explained, that General Crook wanted to use Sun Horse to persuade the other bands to go peacefully to the Dakota Territory, and she knew that the ways in which the white man wanted to use Sun Horse would not stop there. If his people were allowed to keep their guns and horses while the unrepentant "hostiles" were deprived of theirs, there would be jealousy and dissension among the bands, which would suit perfectly the schemes of the politicians and Indian agents. As long as the headmen were set against one another, suspicious and distrustful, there could be no effective resistance, no concerted outbreak or uprising. They would try to make Sun Horse a white man's Indian, like the once mighty Red Cloud of the Oglala, who had been to Washington and now enjoyed strutting about in a top hat and frock coat. "You see," said the agents, "Red Cloud has learned the white man's ways. He is a good friend to the Great Father in Washington." And in the eyes of his own people the great war leader, who had done so much to win the war for the Bozeman road, had fallen from grace and was no longer trusted. But Lisa knew that Sun Horse was nobody's fool and could resist the white man's blandishments, if he were alive to do it. "How long will it take General Crook to get here?" she asked.

"That depends," Hardeman said. "He'll go on north if I don't find him first. He's after the war chiefs—Sitting Bull and Gall and Crazy Horse. He's giving Sun Horse a chance, Miss Putnam. But if Crook finds another band first and the fighting starts, there will be no beef for Sun Horse and no safe escort. It'll be too late then.''

"Fort Fetterman is less than a hundred miles away," said Lisa. "General Crook's column could be here in a few days."

Hardeman nodded and poured himself more whiskey. He rose and walked to the stove, where he filled the cup with coffee.

Lisa was thinking hard. Crook could be here soon, or he would proceed north, down the Tongue or the Powder. And even then there might be time. If the Indians had their scouts out they would surely see such a large force. Able to strike camp in thirty minutes and to move thirty miles in a day, the Indian villages were like needles in a vast haymow, while the slow-moving soldier columns resembled a field mouse crawling blindly in the stack. The chance of the mouse coming on one of the moving needles was slight. And so there might still be some time even if General Crook passed by Putnam's Park. But Sun Horse must be warned and the matter set before him at once. And he must be made to see that he should not surrender, for that meant losing his home here forever.

But if Hardeman knew where Sun Horse wintered, why had he not gone there directly? Because he had wanted Jed Putnam's help in persuading Sun Horse to surrender, and now he wanted Lisa's. He seemed honestly to believe that the course he proposed was the best one for Sun Horse, and Lisa was just as certain it was wrong. Sun Horse must not go in now;

he must remain free and stay away from the soldiers, and she must find a way to help him do it.

But how? For the moment she did not know. It would take time to find a way, and meanwhile she needed to distract Hardeman from her true intention.

What would my father do? she wondered, and the answer came at once. He would fight. As a trapper he had fought beside his friends against all odds, and on the one occasion when violence had threatened his home in Putnam's Park, he had ridden out alone, ready to die. In the summer of 1865, a time of continuous raiding along the emigrant trails, a war party of Cheyenne had pursued a small wagon train into Putnam's Park. It was the first time trouble had threatened the park, for it was under Sun Horse's protection, and he was a peace man respected not only among the Lakota but among their friends the Cheyenne as well. The sanctuary was known to white travelers, and the knowledge had kept some wagons and pack trains coming despite the Indian raids, particularly those bound for Montana and the gold fields there. Jed Putnam was friendly with the local Indians, everyone said, and they never troubled him. His own brother was married to Otter Skin, daughter of the Sioux Chief Sun Horse, and lived with the heathens. It was said that Sun Horse himself had prepared a potion of herbs and magic that had revived young Lisa Putnam's mother from the fever that struck her not long after Jed brought his wife and child out from Boston to join him, and had restored her to the good health she enjoyed until the day she died some years later of general fragility and a sudden attack of the grippe. Surely there could be no danger in such domesticated savages. Occasionally, the Indians themselves had directed travelers to cross the mountains at this point, by the Putnam Cutoff, or risk their lives if they continued along the eastern slopes.

But on that summer day of 1865 Sun Horse and his people were far to the north on their summer hunt. The Cheyenne had spied the wagons as they entered the river gap and had pursued them into the park, and the travelers had flogged their draft animals while praying with all their might that the tales of sanctuary were true.

After grouping the wagons in the yard between the Big House and the barn and organizing the frightened emigrants for the defense of the settlement, Jed had mounted his horse and ridden out to meet the warriors with his rifle in one hand and the other raised in a sign of peace. The Cheyenne were so impressed with the bravery of the white man who rode down the road alone that they had stopped to hear what he had to say. Lisa had watched the exchange from a second-story window with a trapper's long rifle held steady on the leader of the war party, four hundred yards away.

The Lakota call me the Truthful Whiteman, her father had told them in signs, making the movements broadly so they could be read across the twenty paces that separated him from the Cheyenne. *Sun Horse, the Lakota peace man, gave me this valley. My brother is married to Otter Skin, the daughter of Sun Horse. For twelve winters I have lived here with my family, and in that time there has been no fighting here between red men and white. I first came to the mountains to hunt beaver, and the Shoshoni called me Bear Heart. I fought the Blackfoot and the Crow, the Gros Ventre and the Piegan, and I took their scalps. I have never fought the Cheyenne and I will not be the first to break the peace in this valley, but if you think it is a good day to fight, I will fight. If there must be blood on this ground today, some of that blood will be Cheyenne.*

The warriors had looked at the man who faced them alone, sitting so calmly on his horse. They looked at the settlement and the tight group of wagons, defended by twenty nervous guns, and the Cheyenne leader made signs to Jed. *The Cheyenne respect none more than the true men of peace,* he said. He knew of Sun Horse and the one called the Truthful Whiteman. It was not a good day to fight, not here in this place of peace. The war party had turned and ridden away.

I am my father's only child, Lisa thought, and it is time I learned how to fight for what I believe in.

Hardeman had resumed his seat and was looking at her through the rising steam from the cup in his hands, now blowing gently to cool the coffee. Lisa was suddenly glad he had been drinking. It might dull his perceptions. Let him think that I fight for myself, she thought. A white man understands a selfish motive best of all. If he thinks I am afraid only for myself then he may not see what I can do for Sun Horse.

But what can I do?

"The treaty says that no whites can live here," she said. "Did you know that?"

Hardeman nodded. "Sun Horse gave your father this land before the Laramie treaty was made."

"That's right. He even gave him a deed." Her tone was bitter. "It is a piece of deerskin cut square with a bone knife and written with ink made from berries. Sun Horse wrote the deed in pictures. They are called pictographs, I think, the sort of drawings they use to record the winter count. They say, 'The Sun Band of the Lakota gives the valley of the clear water to the Truthful Whiteman, Jedediah Putnam.' My uncle wrote out my father's name and Sun Horse copied it onto the deed himself. The *P* in Putnam is backwards. The gift was recognized in the treaty of 1868 by letters from the peace commissioners to the Secretary of the Interior. Of course, those commissioners have all retired and the secretary went out of office with President Johnson. Tell me, Mr. Hardeman, will the government recognize that deed when the Sioux are living like beggars on the Dakota reservation?"

"I don't know." Hardeman had not expected this, but he seized on it; it explained the woman's fear and gave him the key to her cooperation. "They might if you help us. Take us to Sun Horse, Miss Putnam, and I'll do what I can about the deed." He found himself wanting to help calm her fears, but he knew the impulse came from the whiskey and he stopped himself from promising anything more. All of his promises would be worthless if events turned against him.

"We came to help Sun Horse," said Johnny Smoker.

Everyone in the kitchen turned to look at the young man who had not spoken since entering the room. There was a slight sound and then a door opened, and from a hallway that led to bedrooms in the back of the house, Bat and Hears Twice stepped into the kitchen.

Hardeman relaxed somewhat, the nagging question of the empty chairs answered at last. The Indian had stayed out of sight until he had a chance to learn something about the strangers. He was as old as a rock, if not a day or two more, and it was plain that he lived in the wild; he had none of the signs of a domesticated Sioux and he showed the self-composure that Hardeman knew as the mark of an Indian who still felt sure of his place in creation. The mountain man would be the uncle Lisa had mentioned and the brother Jed had spoken of now and again, the one who had lived with Sun Horse since the end of the fur trade. He might have his own reasons for keeping hidden or he might simply have come to see things from an Indian point of view, regarding all strange whites as possible enemies. The presence of these two meant that Hardeman was close to finding Sun Horse, no matter what Lisa Putnam decided to do.

He relaxed even more when he saw a smile on Johnny's face; it was a smile he bestowed only on a friend.

"It's all right," Bat said to Lisa, his attention on the youth. "Hears Twice says there ain't no danger from these two."

The Indian was aware of nothing except the presence of the young man by the stove. He shuffled across the room, looking Johnny up and down with growing delight. He made a few tentative signs, forming the hand movements more broadly than usual, as he would for a child or another who might be ignorant of the sign talk. Johnny responded with a few signs of his own, quick and sure.

Bat pulled a chair out from the table and sat down hard. "It can't be," he said softly.

Hears Twice was smiling broadly. *"Oyate Tokcha Ichokab' Najin,"* he said. He Stands Between the Worlds. And Bat saw it was true.

"It can't be," he said again.

"Uncle Bat?" Lisa looked from Johnny to the Indian to her uncle, seeking some explanation.

"The boy is Sun Horse's grandson," Bat said.

Hears Twice made a single sign, moving his forefinger out from beneath his chin, showing that the words came straight from the heart and tongue—*It is true*.

For a time the measured ticking of the Waltham wall clock was the only sound in the kitchen. Beneath the stove, Rufus stepped back into his basket, curled up, and closed his eyes.

Ling Wo had listened with interest as the identity of the strange boy was revealed, but now she turned back to the stove where she checked the fire, then opened the oven and set the three risen pans of bread dough on the rack before gently closing the door. With the dinner dishes done, it was time for her to start thinking of supper, and she could not allow herself to be distracted for long, no matter what mysteries presented themselves in her kitchen.

"Hmp." Julius broke the silence. "He looks mighty white to me."

"His grandson?" Lisa shook her head. "I don't understand. How could he—"

Bat chuckled as he rose from his seat. "I don't understand it all neither, child, but I'm thinkin' we'll hear about it soon enough." He turned to Julius. "He looks pretty white to you, does he? You got a point there. Yessir, you got a point." He could scarcely contain his glee. "And you're just the feller to know if a man's got a touch of the tarbrush, now, ain't you? Or the Indian paintbrush? Well, he is white, as a fool can see, but that don't change the fact. Old Sun Horse is this boy's grandpap, and that's truth. Was took off a wagon train and raised up by Sun Horse's first boy, White Smoke. That was afore your time, I reckon." He stuck out his hand to Johnny Smoker. "How ye be, boy? You're lookin' right pert for a dead man."

"I'm all right," Johnny said, still smiling. "Glad to see my uncle Lodgepole again. Sorry I didn't get here in time to meet your brother."

Bat nodded. "He'd of took a shine to you, I'm thinkin'. You recollect this old coot." He motioned to Hears Twice.

Johnny made signs to say *I am glad to see you again, Uncle,* and he shook Hears Twice's hand.

The Indian touched his left breast, then raised a crooked forefinger in imitation of the rising sun and the warmth it cast into his heart.

Forgotten by the others, Hardeman tipped his chair back against the wall and rested a boot against the edge of the table, the cup of whiskey in his hand. The bottle was almost empty. The whiskey warmth had risen to his head and he no longer fought it off, allowing himself to give in at last to the bone-weariness that had accumulated on the long journey from Kansas like some slow-acting opiate. What was it about a man who drank too much? People thought he was weak, and they dropped their guard. The trick had worked for him more than once, but it had almost failed him today.

"I still don't understand," Lisa was saying. "I'm sure I have never seen him before."

"Of course you ain't," Bat said, still chuckling at the confusion around him. His high spirits were beginning to infect the others, tempered only by their impatience at his slowness in unraveling the youth's kinship to Sun Horse. Bat turned to Hardeman, noting the solid build and the beard cut neat the way a city man would do, but neither the hands nor the eyes belonged to a city man. The eyes met his own steadily, as Hardeman idly stroked a small scar on his cheek with the fingers of one hand, and Bat saw something familiar in the look the man gave him. What was it? The eyes were the window to the soul, it was said. Bat felt a small shock of surprise as he recognized a soul that was kin to his own.

He took the whiskey bottle from the table and raised it to regard the small amount remaining. He gave Hardeman a nod and a wink.

"You play yer cards pretty close. Well, I'll drink to that." He put the bottle to his lips and drained it in an instant.

"Wagh!" he exclaimed, savoring the harsh bite of the whiskey. He wiped his mouth on his buckskin sleeve and turned back to Lisa. "Well now, you recollect White Smoke, the one married a Cheyenne woman and went to live with her folks? Could be you don't. You was just twelve or so when he went south to get hitched, I make it." But Lisa remembered Sun Horse's eldest son, and she nodded. "They lived with Black Kettle's bunch down south. White Smoke, he brought the boy and his ma to see Sun Horse just one time. We was in summer camp on the Little Horn. Sun Horse took to the boy like he was blood kin, and maybe something more besides." He glanced at Johnny. "That was in '64 they come visitin'. Four years later we heard he was dead at the Washita, killed when Long Hair Custer hit Black Kettle's village, may I get that murderin' son of a bitch in my sights just once afore I go under, beggin' your pardon, Lisa honey. Anyways, the boy's folks was killed, White Smoke and Grass Woman both, and the boy plumb disappeared. The Cheyenne figgered he was burned in a tipi. They found some bodies, after, a few the right size; 'course they was burned pretty bad. Sun Horse took the news hard. . . ." He let his voice trail away, looking at Johnny.

"Chris found me in one of the lodges," he said. "I was shot in the leg. I couldn't walk. He took me away from the fight. We've been together since then."

Bat suspected that those few words were the bare bones of a story that could be fleshed out all night over a warm fire in a winter lodge, a story he would dearly like to know, but he would let it pass for now. With the remarkable fact of Johnny's kinship to Sun Horse told in a few words, Bat remained silent, trying to work out what the boy's presence would mean to Sun Horse and the band, coupled as it was with the news of soldiers coming into the country to make war.

Hardeman was looking at Julius. "You were a soldier once yourself."

Julius straightened in his chair. "Regimental sergeant major, Ninth Cavalry. You?"

Hardeman shook his head. "Civilian scout." He sipped his coffee, hoarding it now that the whiskey was gone. The Chinese cook cracked open the oven and peered in quickly, and the comforting smell of baking bread filled the kitchen.

"Then you were one of the men who led General
Custer to Black Kettle's village," Lisa said.

Hardeman nodded. It was not an action he would
defend. He saw the disapproval plain on her face, but
no similar reaction from the others. If anything, the
knowledge of Hardeman's scouting seemed to reduce
Julius Ingram's suspicions. As a soldier, he knew the
scouts for what they were, frontiersmen of one stripe
or another, good men and bad, but men who knew
the country and the Indians. As for Bat Putnam, he
had the greatest reason to be hostile to a man who
had led soldiers to a sleeping village of Cheyenne,
but his expression revealed no judgment. Most of his
attention was still on Johnny.

The young man shifted from one foot to the other,
glancing first at Bat and then at Hardeman. "I'll unsaddle the horses," he announced, and moved for the
door to the saloon. That was his way, deciding to do
something and setting out to do it all in a moment,
the way he had decided to come here to see Sun
Horse.

Hardeman got to his feet and drained the last of the
spiritous coffee from the cup. "We've got the better
part of a deer we took this morning down below the
canyon. Might be you folks would like some deer
meat for supper." He moved to follow Johnny and as
he passed through the saloon door he heard Lisa
Putnam call after him.

"You'll find grain in a bin by the horse stalls."

On the porch Johnny was waiting. The snow had
stopped and to the north the sky was clearing. Judging by the light, the unseen sun had already gone
below the western ridge. The air had lightened and it
acted like a tonic on Hardeman, washing away the

dullness caused by the whiskey. "It could be we'll see a blue sky tomorrow," he said, and Johnny smiled.

"I can take care of the horses, if you like."

Hardeman shook his head. "We'll do it together." Each cared for his own horse and his own belongings; they treated each another as equals, as much as possible given the difference in age and experience, and Hardeman was not about to change that now after seven years.

He unwrapped his reins from the hitching rail and led his horse toward the barn, enjoying once again the feel of the settlement nestled so snugly at the head of the valley. Back in the kitchen they would have plenty to say right now, about Sun Horse's grandson returned from the dead and the former army scout who rode with him. They could think what they liked. He had quit scouting to care for the boy, that much they could gather from what Johnny had told them, and the rest of the story no one knew, not even Johnny. It was his own affair and none of theirs.

He had signed on with the army during the War Between the States, for the sake of the Union. And he had found himself helping to hold the western mountains not only against the threat of Rebel incursions from the south, but also against the Indians who sortied from every point of the compass, constantly testing the bluecoats, whose reserves were drained off by the white man's war between brothers. Hardeman knew the Indians and their ways, he respected them as warriors and as men, and from time to time he was able to smooth over a misunderstanding and keep the peace. But no quiet words of reason could quell the wave of hostilities that had swept the

Colorado border after an incident that took place in
November of 1864 on Sand Creek. There a peaceful
encampment of southern Cheyenne under Black Kettle was struck and decimated by a ragtag assortment
of volunteer militia led by Colonel John M. Chivington,
a former preacher. Black Kettle was renowned throughout the Cheyenne nation as a great leader whose
efforts to make peace with the whites had been un-
ceasing. Outraged by the unprovoked attack, the Cheyenne sent the war pipe to their allies, the Sioux and
Arapaho, and more than a thousand warriors took to
the trails, launching a year of unprecedented raiding
across the central plains, even as the surrenders of
Lee and Johnston brought the white man's fratricide
to an end.

With the Rebellion over, the Army of the Plains
was strengthened and Hardeman stayed on, offering
his knowledge of the aborigines in the hope that the
bloodshed here could be brought to an end as well.
Unlike most of the men whom he led, Hardeman had
known the frontier before the mutual suspicions between red men and white erupted into open conflict.
He knew that the Indian leaders were reasonable
men, for the most part, willing to talk, even willing
to share the land, which they did not imagine they
owned, not as a white man understood the notion.
But the white man's notion was spreading fast, and
in the years immediately following the war, the violence rose to new heights. Goaded by the Homestead
Act's offer of free land and the release of thousands
of men from the Northern and Southern armies, new
settlements spread rapidly from the major rivers in
Kansas and Nebraska, and the tribes accustomed to

hunt on the central plains reacted by striking at settlers, emigrants and troops whenever the chance arose.

The army officers, fresh from victories in a very different kind of war, were used to set-piece battles and a foe that would stand and fight, but the Indians fought by different rules. They would fade away in the face of a superior force, only to reappear nearby to attack a supply train or steal the soldiers' horses. Time and again the frustrated officers failed to inflict lasting harm on the tribesmen, and in the parleys and councils they did no better. They were impatient with the Indian custom of eating and smoking before important talk; they broke etiquette by interrupting the Indian orators in council; they ordered the proud warriors about and insisted on bringing troops near their villages when they came to parley. On one such occasion, some Sioux and Cheyenne camped on the Pawnee Fork of the Arkansas fled from their lodges, fearing a repetition of the Sand Creek massacre. General Winfield Hancock, then the commander of the Division of the Missouri, felt that he had been tricked, and reacted imprudently. He ordered the village burned, further convincing the Indians that the whites could not be trusted.

Hardeman had quit the government's service in disgust over the incident. It seemed to him that the whites did not want peace at all. They provoked the Indians at every opportunity and seemed determined to push the tribesmen off every decent patch of land on the frontier, or perhaps to exterminate them altogether, and he would have no part of such an undertaking. For a time he sought other scouting jobs but found nothing much to his liking, and in the fall of 1868 he stopped at Fort Lyon, Colorado Territory, to see James Hickok, an old friend who was scouting for the Tenth Cavalry, one of the two Negro cavalry regiments. "Wild Bill," the newspapers had christened Hickok, one of the most famous scouts on the frontier, but he and Hardeman had scouted together for General Smith the year before and had always called each other by their Christian names.

"Christopher," Hickok said, when they had exchanged recent news, "you could do me a good turn, if you were so inclined. General Sully wants me to scout for him down toward the Indian Territory. It's to be a winter campaign, Phil Sheridan's idea. Figgers he might catch hold of the Indians in winter." Hickok had chuckled and Hardeman smiled. The army's inability to come to grips with the Indians was a standing joke among the old hands in the scouting corps. "Now I'll tell you what," Hickok continued. "The army picked the cream of the crop when they chose officers for these darky regiments; they're good fellers, all of 'em. They're quick, and they'll listen what a man tells 'em. The Tenth is goin' on patrol in Kansas while Sully goes south, and I've no mind to leave 'em now."

He had brushed aside the hairs of his moustache with the knuckle of his index finger before he went on, a habitual gesture Hardeman knew well.

"You're the old man in this business," Hickok said, grinning. Hardeman was the older of the two, although by just four years, and Hickok delighted in exaggerating the difference until it seemed to be one of generations. But he turned serious then. "You know Black Kettle from the Medicine Lodge treaty council. Talk is he's been over to Fort Cobb not long ago to find a safe place for his people. Wynkoop was off somewhere, but he'll be back right quick." Edward Wynkoop was a former army officer, now Indian agent for the southern Cheyenne. He had roundly condemned Chivington's attack at Sand Creek and ever since had worked hard to diminish the ill will the massacre had engendered among the Cheyenne. "You go on with Sully. Tell him I sent you. See if you can't set him down with Black Kettle and Wynkoop and pull a treaty out of all this hooraw."

"All this hooraw" was the then-present state of military affairs on the plains. In the north, Red Cloud's War had just been brought to a conclusion with the signing of the new Laramie treaty, while on the central plains the army had suffered two signal defeats in recent months. Sully himself had blundered about the Indian Territory in September, accomplishing little but to convince the warriors there that they could meet and beat him on their own ground, while Major George Forsyth's much-heralded band of frontier scouts had been soundly whipped on their first outing in Kansas, in the fight called the Battle of Beecher's Island.

"There'll be some hotheads want revenge for Beecher's Island before they make peace with the Cheyenne," Hardeman observed.

Hickok nodded. "Sully's no hothead. He ain't Ulysses Grant, neither, but he'll seddown and listen to sense if you make him."

Now, in Lisa Putnam's barn, Hardeman pondered the fateful meeting. Hickok's request had sent him on his way to the Washita and had changed his life.

"There's grain in that bin," he said to Johnny. The three horses were in adjoining stalls, saddles and packs removed, their halter ropes dropped loose through the rings at the feed troughs. Johnny walked to the grain bin and returned with a tinful of oats, then went back for another. Sometimes you hardly noticed the limp, unless you watched for it. Hardeman rolled his shoulder and felt the reminder of the bullet wound there. But for the meeting with Hickok his shoulder might be as good as new. But Johnny would most likely be dead.

On the day when Hardeman and Hickok had talked, Sully's command had already left Fort Dodge and gone south to establish a supply base on the Beaver River. Hardeman had found them there, at the new post they had dubbed Camp Supply, and the state of affairs had not been at all as advertised. Phil Sheridan, eager to observe the progress of the winter campaign, was on hand. He had sent General Sully back to his district headquarters and had given command of the expedition to Brevet Major General George A. Custer of the Seventh Cavalry. Custer had been court-martialed the previous autumn and sentenced to a year's suspension of rank and command over the shooting of some deserters and absenting himself from his command without proper authority. Word had it he had gone to visit his beautiful wife. But Custer was Phil Sheridan's fair-haired boy, and at Sheridan's request the sentence had been remitted by General William Tecumseh Sherman and Custer was returned to his regiment in time to join the winter campaign. When he learned that Hardeman had been sent by Wild Bill Hickok, Custer gladly took him on, and on the morning of November 23 the column left Camp Supply. Hardeman rode at the head of the line with California Joe and the other scouts, full of misgivings. It seemed to him that the

Boy General was eager for action and would not listen kindly to suggestions of peacemaking.

For four days the column marched south in half a foot of new snow without finding any trails. As they struck the South Canadian River, Hardeman suggested a turn toward the southeast and Fort Cobb, where the command might refresh their supplies and discover what the men at Cobb knew of the Indians. Privately, he hoped that Agent Wynkoop would be on hand and might know the whereabouts of Black Kettle.

Custer agreed to the suggestion, but even as the last of the supply wagons forded the river, the advance scouts sent word that they had found what appeared to be the trail of a large war party heading south toward the Antelope Hills. Custer took the scent like a hound with his blood up and for the rest of the day the column pressed close on the heels of the scouts. After a short stop for supper, the pursuit continued into the night, and it was nearing midnight when the foremost scouts returned to say that they had found a village close by, on the south side of an oxbow bend in the Washita River.

Custer began immediate preparations for an attack at dawn. He detailed Hardeman to lead Major Elliott and his three companies around to the northeast, to a position across the river from the village. Hardeman protested that the trail the command had been following had been lost in the dark, hours before, and that it was not certain the war party was in the village or even what tribe of Indians was camped there.

"Oh, we shall see them well enough at first light, Mr. Hardeman," Custer said, and he turned away to give further orders to his troop commanders.

The night was cold, fires were forbidden, and sleep was impossible. Before the first glimmer of dawn, Hardeman slipped away from Elliott's position and made his way cautiously down the east side of the river. As the first glow in the east revealed the countryside around him, he discovered a trail made the day before, leading away from the sleeping village. The war party—if in fact it was a war party— had passed through the village but was no longer there. To the west, stars were still visible. He dared to follow the trail a short distance to the southeast, and as he crested a rise he was greeted with the sight of another large village farther down the stream, and thin columns of smoke rising from beyond the next low hills, visible against the growing light of dawn, where yet another village lay hidden. Obviously there were many hundreds, if not thousands, of Indians, probably from several tribes, comfortably settled in winter camps along a short stretch of the Washita. Any one of the villages could have been the war party's home.

Hardeman spurred his horse back toward the command, urging the tired animal into a slow gallop. From more than a mile away he saw that Elliott's men were preparing to cross the river. He stopped against the skyline and raised his arm in a broad wave, not daring to shout or fire a shot. He was heartened to see an answering wave from the command, but even as he whipped his horse in a circle and pointed to show that he had found the enemy downstream, a rifle shot sounded from the village, followed by a bugle calling the attack, and then it was too late.

When Hardeman reached the village, all three ele-

ments of Custer's force were among the tipis, and the
Indians—Cheyenne, Hardeman saw now—were running for cover in the brush along the river and in the
rough ground to the south and west, where they set
up an angry fire at the soldiers. His face tight with
rage, Hardeman had ridden through the battle, looking for someone who could turn back the clock a
quarter of an hour and stop the slaughter. Through
the dust and smoke he saw a man lead a woman from
a lodge and untie two horses tethered there, and as
the man mounted with a nimbleness that belied his
years, Hardeman recognized the Cheyenne headman
Black Kettle. If he could reach the chief and take him
to Custer, there might be a chance. But Black Kettle
was wasting no time; waiting only long enough to be
sure his wife had mounted, he led off at a dead run
for the river, with Hardeman pounding after them,
shouting uselessly against the din of battle.

Black Kettle had almost gained the river when a
bullet struck him in the back. He fell from his horse
into the water at the edge of the stream and lay there,
face down. The woman turned back to go to her
husband's aid. She saw Hardeman racing toward her
but she disregarded the danger, and she had just
dismounted when she too was hit and fell dead in the
water.

In that part of the country the Washita cut its
channel in a dark reddish soil; where it had been
stirred up by the soldiers' crossing and the splashing
of escaping Cheyenne, the river ran blood-red.

Later, the Kiowas claimed that the war party Custer had trailed was one of their own, returning from a
raid against the Utes in Colorado. They said it had

merely passed through Black Kettle's camp on its way home.

Hardeman came out of his reverie suddenly, wondering what was wrong. Something in the barn had changed—a sound . . . He relaxed and felt a little foolish when he realized it was only the horses. They were done with their grain and had stopped chewing.

Johnny was leaning against the wall of the stall, waiting patiently.

Hardeman put a hand on the youth's shoulder. "We'll turn 'em out now, I guess."

They removed the halters, slapped the horses on the rump and chased them out the back door. Hardeman threw his saddlebags over one shoulder and the deer carcass over the other and waited in front of the barn as Johnny pulled the doors closed behind them. He looked about at the peaceful valley. The sky was clearing quickly now and the cold was growing strong. The lampglow from the windows of the house looked warm and inviting.

In the blood and thunder of the Washita battle, he had managed to save one boy. He had turned from the scene of Black Kettle's death, intending to leave the village, but before he was beyond its confines he had cause to enter a lodge that was as yet untouched by the torch, and there he found a youth of perhaps twelve or thirteen years huddled over a dead man and woman, and despite the boy's Cheyenne garments and his apparent lack of any knowledge of the English tongue, Hardeman had perceived that the boy was white. Over the years he had restored to the boy some of the choices that were taken away on that cold November morning by the soldiers who had killed his adopted parents and scattered his people.

Johnny was a reminder of his failure and a measure of his atonement, and now, at Johnny's behest, they had come here.

Once more Hardeman came as a peacemaker. Once more he came to stop a winter campaign, and this time he would not fail. He would do it without Jed Putnam's help, without the help of Jed's daughter Lisa, if it came to that. This time there would be no sleeping village wakened by the sound of gunfire and bugles. He had come to make peace and peace there would be, no matter the cost.

CHAPTER SIX

The next day was clear and very bright. The morning warmed quickly, the temperature rising to the freezing point and beyond before the riders were out of sight of Putnam's Park. They were five, Hardeman and Johnny Smoker, Bat and Lisa Putnam, and Hears Twice, who had accepted the hospitality of Bat's lodge overnight. In the open, the new snow was soft and damp above an old crust, while in the shade of the trees it remained dry and powdery. From time to time a clump of snow on the branch of an evergreen would let go and fall, knocking more snow from the lower branches, occasionally spooking a horse or bathing one of the riders in a sparkling cascade of white. They rode mostly in single file, taking turns breaking a path. Where the creek bottom widened they rode abreast, the order of march changing as the trail narrowed again and forced the horses to fall in one behind the other.

As they reached a rocky defile where the trail curved away from the creek and rose steeply among large boulders to pass by a small waterfall, Lisa dropped back and allowed Hardeman to go ahead of her. She had felt his eyes on her all morning and she let him take the lead now gladly. Over the years she had grown accustomed to the surprise and frequent glances she had received from men and women who were shocked to see a woman riding astride and dressed like a man, but she had become uncomfortable under Hardeman's gaze.

She wore her short coat of mountain goatskin and a gray stockman's hat of five-X beaver. Her riding pants were buckskin, cut close to give her a sure seat in the saddle. Her hair was loose, gathered at the nape of the neck with a dark blue ribbon. Fur-lined moccasins came up to her knees, in the mountain man's style. The trappers had adopted the Indians' winter moccasins, made from buffalo hide. They had thick rawhide soles, and rabbit fur sewn around the foot, and they were comfortable at forty degrees below zero. For ranch work, Lisa wore boots, but on the trail she reverted to trappers' footwear, a custom she had kept since childhood. It was a practical outfit, suited to the requirements of her surroundings, but even on the frontier few white women dared such unconventional attire and the army wives in the western garrisons still clung to their awkward sidesaddles. Victorian habits and manners were as strong among ''proper'' gentlemen and ladies in the new territories of the American West, seven thousand miles from

Victoria's throne, as they were back in the States and among European gentry around the world, where these attitudes were the ramparts that protected European civilization against the barbarism it encountered on all sides as its empires expanded. Lisa's parents had explained these prejudices to her when she was old enough to understand them, but her father had laughed at such foolishness. He had had no use for customs or behavior that went against common sense, and as a child Lisa had learned to ride astride as a matter of course. When she had returned from four years of finishing school in the East, Jed had been more than a little taken aback to see that his daughter had become a young woman of beauty and considerable refinement. "I always thought a woman sitting on a sidesaddle looked foolish and out of place," he had said, unsure of what to expect from this self-assured stranger. "You do as you please in civilized diggin's, but up here you'd best ride in a sensible manner unless you're plumb set against it." He had never forgotten the bad fall his wife had taken while riding sidesaddle in Putnam's Park, and he had put it partly to blame for Eleanor's early death. His wish had suited Lisa perfectly, for she had felt very foolish and quite out of place whenever she had ridden sidesaddle in the company of her eastern relatives. Her first ride after her return to Putnam's Park had been bareback and astride, full gallop the length of the valley, just as she had ridden to greet incoming wagons when she was a child. As ranch work became part of her life once more, it confirmed her in the habit of wearing men's clothing out of doors. Skirts were a preposterous encumbrance when working with horses or cattle.

Her horse stumbled in the soft snow and she gave him his head. He leaped forward onto firmer footing, crowding Hardeman's mount and causing Hardeman to glance back. He saw how easily she sat, allowing the horse to find its own way, quickly dropping back and falling into step behind his own. She rides as well as a man, he thought.

He committed the land to memory as he rode, noting the lay of the mostly wooded slopes that rose on either side, the evergreens forcing out the aspens more and more as the creek trail climbed higher into the hills, but a part of his mind was still on the night before. "All right," Lisa had finally said. "I'll go with you to see Sun Horse. I won't promise more just now, but I'll go with you." He had expected nothing more. It would take time for her to decide where she stood on the future of the Sioux, but she would come around. Meanwhile, her presence, and Johnny's, would lend weight to what he had to tell Sun Horse.

Hardeman had stayed out of the evening's talk. There were ten of them in the kitchen once the boy Hutch and the Chinese blacksmith came in from their chores and Bat Putnam's Sioux wife joined them for supper. Ling Wo cut steaks from the deer and pan-fried them with onions, and the settlement folk kept up enough idle chatter to be polite, but none of them was the sort to press a stranger to talk when he didn't want to. Then, over a new pot of coffee and the remains of an apple pie, Bat Putnam had found a way to turn the talk to Johnny Smoker again by telling of a summer when there had been heavy traffic on the emigrant trails, and little game, and a white child had been found in an abandoned wagon by a Cheyenne hunting party.

"Them wagons put a fright on everything with four legs for a day's ride either side of the trail," Bat said. "White Smoke and some Cheyenne boys, they come on a handful of wagons herdin' some beef cattle, so naturally they allowed as how they'd take it kindly if those folks would give 'em a steer by way of sayin' thanks for safe passage 'cross Cheyenne lands, you might say. I weren't there, o' course, but I got this from White Smoke hisself when he brung the boy to visit, but I'm gettin' to that. The way he told it, them white folks wasn't much for palaver. Never said a word, nary one o' them. Just leveled on the Injuns and let fly, dropped one young feller in his tracks, name of Dog Runs or some such. Well sir, that set the badger loose. White Smoke and the boys, they lit into them wagons and burned a couple, even lifted a little hair. They figgered to teach them folks some manners if it killed 'em, and it did that for a couple. The rest put out for the tall grass right smart, left this youngun by his lonesome." Here Bat had looked at Johnny for the first time. "White Smoke, him and Grass Woman never did have no offspring, so he took the boy and raised him like his own."

Hardeman had wondered if Johnny knew it all—about the Cheyenne killing whites in the wagon train, maybe killing Johnny's real parents. And for the first time he had wondered what else the boy might not know, or might have kept to himself about his childhood, the way he had kept Sun Horse to himself until two weeks ago.

Bat had passed along then to the summer a few years later when White Smoke and his wife had brought Johnny to the Sioux summer encampment, and Bat had glanced frequently at Johnny, as if hop-

ing to draw some response from the silent boy. And
then to Hardeman's surprise, Johnny had begun to
talk, directing himself to Bat, telling what he remembered of that summer, how the size of the Sioux
camp had impressed him, the young friends he had
made, and how his grandfather, Sun Horse, had taught
him the sign language. Lisa Putnam had seemed
fascinated and young Hutch had hung on every word.
Hardeman had listened closely, but he had concealed
his interest.

Why had Johnny spoken so rarely of his Indian
childhood, if, as it now seemed, he remembered
those years fondly and in such detail? Hardeman had
never inquired overmuch about Johnny's time among
the Cheyenne, which he had thought of at first as a
long captivity, but later came to see was a way of life
the boy had accepted quickly enough, with the adapt-
ability of youth. Johnny scarcely ever mentioned those
years, and instead of asking a lot of questions
Hardeman had sought to ease the boy's way back
into the white world, expecting that his Indian memories would die out in time. But last night, seeing
Johnny's eyes bright as he spoke of his childhood,
hearing the excitement in his quiet voice as he told of
memories he had never revealed before, Hardeman
had wanted to get the boy off alone, to discover why
those memories had burst forth now, so full of life,
and what lay behind the silence Johnny had worn all
day like a cloak. But his head ached from the whiskey and he was groggy with fatigue, and when they
had finally been alone in a back room with two
bunks, made warm and friendly by the fire the
Chinawoman had built in the little stove, he had had
strength only to roll his blankets out on the bare

mattress before falling into bed fully clothed and sleeping like a dead man until an hour after cockcrow.

He urged his horse forward now to overtake Johnny.

"You all right?" he asked as he drew even with the young man. Johnny had hardly spoken a word all morning.

"I'm all right." Johnny's faint smile told him nothing, but the boy spoke again. "I wish there was another way. For Sun Horse, I mean. So he wouldn't have to surrender."

Hardeman's expression was grim. "Burned-out lodges and death scaffolds on the ridgetops, that's the other way."

Johnny made no reply and he kept his thoughts to himself for the rest of the journey, although he remained close to Hardeman.

The riders passed over a divide and began to descend again, soon joining the course of a creek that flowed into a long, narrow valley, whose elevation, Hardeman judged, was probably somewhat lower than Putnam's Park. It was closer to the foothills but well protected nevertheless, walled off on the eastern side by a ridge so sharp and steep it might have been hewn by some giant's axe. The nearer end of the valley was hidden behind a wooded rise; at the far end Hardeman could make out a small lake, frozen and snow-covered. The air was calm here, and warm, as if the valley gathered the sun, and he smelled the scent of the pines on the hillsides.

He wished he and Johnny were alone, riding into the mountains for a day of hunting before moving on to try their luck in the next town or the next territory.

As the small band reached the flat, where the creek curved around the end of the wooded rise and reached the valley floor, Hardeman heard a horse neigh in the distance. He turned his head to locate the sound, seeing at the same time the faint white plumes of smoke rising into the endless blue sky. The Sioux village lay beyond the next grove of trees and still the riders had not been seen. After today, the scouts would guard the approaches better. He cast his mind over the rugged trail from Putnam's Park. Cavalry could follow it easily, but a handful of warriors could hold it against a regiment, and even without opposition it would be hard going for infantry and impossible for wagons. He hoped there was another approach to the Indian camp.

He had left both his rifles in Putnam's Park and now he patted his pistol where it rested in his waistband. Being without the rifles made him uncomfortable; he didn't like leaving his belongings here and there; what he owned he carried with him, ready to move on at any time, but today it was more important to show his peaceful intentions. His slicker was tied behind his saddle and his buckskin jacket hung open in the warmth of the day; he buttoned it now to cover the revolver. He had brought the Colt more out of habit than from any expectation that he might need it. Even if danger threatened, it didn't do to pull a gun in the red man's camp. Grattan had learned that the hard way back in '54. Hardeman had seen the graves.

"We best go first," Bat said as he and Hears Twice moved past Hardeman and Johnny. Bat had noticed how Hardeman caught the sound of the horses before he himself had been able to make it out over the noise of the stream, gushing now in the warm sun. Gettin' deef, he thought. At least I ain't goin' blind. He still had the eyes of a young man, for the long distances.

He glanced at Johnny as he passed by and received a small smile in return. Although the youth had been lively for a time the night before, he was silent today. Bat had a hard time reconciling this thoughtful young man with the cheerful boy he remembered from twelve years before. But that was before the Washita. The White Boy of the Cheyenne the Lakota had called him then, before they saw the way the power moved with him; before he was called Empty Hand and He Stands Between the Worlds.

The riders were in the woods now. There were children playing near the creek and they spied the horsemen first. Two of the older boys ran forth to greet Bat, whom they called by his Lakota name, Lodgepole, as Johnny Smoker had done the day before. Through the trees, Bat could see the village, set back from the creek on a flat expanse of higher ground, away from the cold river air. The twenty-four tipis were pitched in the old way of the Lakota, forming a circle with an opening to the east, whence came the first light of day.

Bat leaned down and sent one of the boys to find old Dust, the camp crier, who in turn would tell Sun Horse that visitors came to see him. Nothing more, for there was no way to prepare him for the news these visitors carried, or the sight of Johnny Smoker.

Bat looked at the camp circle as he drew nearer, noticing how the clear day and bright sunshine made even the patched skins of the poorest lodges appear fresher. Many of the people were about, men sitting on robes in front of their lodges, smoking, and children playing in the sun. Here and there a woman

scraped at an animal skin stretched tight on a frame
of sticks, but he saw nothing larger than a badger and
no meat on the drying racks. In summer the long
poles on their forked uprights were laden with strips
of buffalo meat drying quickly in the sun over smoky
fires that kept the flies away. There were feasts after
a successful hunt, but the Sun Band had not feasted
since autumn. The hunting had been bad all winter
and was no better now, with spring on the way. The
dogs that came trotting to investigate the newcomers
were thin, their noses constantly searching the ground
for some scrap that might have been overlooked.
Even the ponies moved listlessly within the herd,
which had been twice as large twenty years before.
The Sun Band was in no condition to fight horse
soldiers.

Near the stream an old man sat cross-legged on a
rock, facing the sun, which was now at its peak. His
eyes were closed and he sang in a thin voice:

> *Le anpetu kin washtéyelo*
> *le anpetu kin washtéyelo*
> *le anpetu kin washtéyelo*
> *le anpetu kin washtéyelo*

This day is good. This day is good. This day is
good. Over and over he sang, the simple melody
repeating after the fourth time. Bat breathed deeply.
The air was cool and absolutely clean and yet it still
carried all the smells of the evergreens and the creek
and the village so close at hand. He could smell the
horse herd beyond the camp, and the smoke of the
lodge fires, and a mixture of new and old hides from
the lodges. It was a good day, that was true, but he

was nagged by a worry deep within him, a fear that before long he would have to leave the people with whom he had lived since the dying days of the fur trade.

Bat had not greeted the decline of the trade with the same quiet acceptance displayed by his brother Jed. That a change in the preferred style of gentlemen's hats could bring to a halt the way of life most perfectly suited to the exercise of a man's free spirit had seemed to Bat an obscenity. How could a London toff prefer a hat made by a worm to one made from as wily and clever an animal as a beaver? It went against common sense. But then common sense was in short supply wherever white men lived in large numbers. There was nothing like the daily threat of starvation or a sudden and violent end to make a man call forth his full measure of common sense; that was the life Bat had found in the mountains and that was the way he intended to live for the rest of his days. He had never considered any alternative for long. When he finally admitted to himself that beaver would not rise again, he too had left the heart of the beaver kingdom, turning his horse eastward toward the Black Hills. It had not escaped his notice that among the horseback Indians the individual and his right of free choice were as inviolate as among the trappers; a man lived as he wished and followed the leaders he chose. If Bat was to be denied the company of his brother mountain men, most of whom had already trickled out of the mountains to east and west, following the watercourses that they themselves had trapped bare, then he would live with the Indians.

Why he chose the Sioux he had never answered to his own satisfaction. During his trapping years he had had more intercourse with the Shoshoni and the Bannock, but something drew him east across the Divide to the most numerous people of all, who were then still moving gradually westward and adapting themselves to the higher elevations, where they acquired a fondness for wooded slopes and snowy peaks and the buttes where the eagles nested. Perhaps he chose them because they, like the white men, were a people on the move, or because their women were often tall and slender, or because, like the trappers, they were unrelenting foes of the Blackfeet.

At first he had only meant to visit some friends, a small band of Lakota who had come to the Rendezvous on the Popo Agie in '38. He had found them near Bear Butte, a handful of tipis following the aging warrior Branched Horn. Branched Horn's son Stands Alone, later named Sun Horse, was a few years older than Bat; the two had fallen in together at the Rendezvous and now they renewed their friendship. Bat was invited to travel with the band as a guest and he accepted. He observed the Lakota customs, he was a good hunter, he fought the Crows and Blackfeet; he proved himself in the eyes of the people. The visit grew long, covering the passing of the moons, and then a second snow. Stands Alone had a daughter called Otter Skin, and although she was not tall and slender like some of the other women, she found her way into the heart of the gaunt white man her brother Standing Eagle called Lodgepole.

Bat knew what was expected. One day he left camp alone and was seen by no one for ten days. When he returned he had six horses with him, slipped from a Crow pony herd in the cold quiet before dawn. He offered the horses to Stands Alone, and they were accepted.

And then something had happened that made Bat feel at once a fool and a very fortunate man. Like the other trappers, he had always accepted the simple notion that among the Indians a man bought a wife the way he might buy a sack of flour in the settlements. But as Otter Skin was putting up their lodge, the lodgeskins a gift from Branched Horn's wife and the lodgepoles a gift from Stands Alone, Bat saw the horses he had paid to Stands Alone given away to the poor members of the band in Bat's name. From Otter Skin's relatives and other members of the band came more gifts then, backrests and robes and horn bowls and spoons, and porcupine quills and beads and dyes, which Otter Skin would use to decorate shirts and leggings and robes for her husband. And Bat saw that the six horses had started a flow of giving that before long had touched nearly every member of the band either as giver or receiver, and that the "price" he had paid for his wife had been returned to him many times over. As the years went by he observed among the Lakota a continuity of giving that sustained the whole band in times of plenty as well as times of need, and he saw across the gulf that separated these tribal people from the white man; he came to realize that perhaps this life he had chosen was not a poor cousin to his days as a free trapper, that it might contain all the freedom of the mountain men and something more as well, a brotherhood even the mountain men had never known.

As the years became decades he had never found cause to regret his choice, or any cause, until recently, to suspect that he would not live out his days among the Lakota and in the end be wrapped in robes and hoisted on a burial scaffold on some windswept mountainside, there to be taken back to the earth and the elements like any other member of the tribe. But as the hostilities between the plains people and the advancing white men steadily increased, Bat had finally confronted the fact that a time might come when he would have to fight his own kind or return to live among them. As the tribes of the central plains and then even some bands of Sioux were forced onto reservations, Bat heard tales of life in those places and he went to see for himself. He saw the bleakness and broken spirits there, and he resolved that Penelope should never know such a life. When the day of judgment came for the Sioux, he would take her to the settlements, and there, among the people of her husband's race, she would live out her days.

Some trappers had left their Indian wives behind with no more regret than they felt at leaving a pair of worn-out moccasins, but Bat had never considered such a course for a moment. In his marriage robes he had found a comfort and a sharing as profound as that between Jed and Eleanor, if altogether different in substance, and Penelope had proved herself as faithful and true as a woman of any other race or time, even when others whispered that her husband had abandoned her. In the winter of '48, Joe Meek had passed through the mountains. He and his Shoshoni wife, Virginia, lived in the Oregon country then, and Joe was on his way to beg help for the Oregon settlers from the government in Washington City, following the massacre of some white missionaries by the Cayuse Indians. He asked his old companion Bat Putnam to accompany him on the journey, and Bat agreed. He was gone for ten long months. "Your husband will never return," the other women told Otter Skin. "He is a whiteman, and by now he has married a whitewoman." But Otter Skin made no reply to such accusations. She went about her daily tasks, caring for the children, two boys and a girl, and often she sat in front of the lodge, beading a pair of leggings she would give her husband on his return. Young men stopped to speak with her, but she turned them away. When summer died and the snow fell again, her father told her in private that she might consider herself a free woman simply by putting her husband's things outside the lodge. "If he has not returned when the leggings are finished, I will do so," Otter Skin said. But the beadwork grew more and more elaborate until it covered nearly every inch of the leggings, and only when her husband sat in his place at the back of the lodge once more did she declare them finished. It was then that Bat had christened her Penelope, for she had proved herself as constant as Penelope of old.

Bat's daughter had died of an illness before reaching womanhood, and his sons had married girls from other bands. One had been killed by Blackfeet and the other lived with Sitting Bull's Hunkpapas. But he still had Penelope, alone now in their lodge back in Putnam's Park. She had never lived away from the circle of her people before and he wondered if he had done wrong by staying all winter in the settlement. You're a fool, he told himself. When your folks need you, you go. Lisa had needed him, but now her need was ending, and Bat suddenly wished he had thought to pack up the lodge and bring Penelope along with him today. They should return to the Sun Band, to their own people, for whatever time remained.

At the entrance to the circle of lodges—the "horns"

of the camp—the riders were greeted by Dust, the crier. He was a spare, wiry man of more than seventy winters, and it was one of his functions to conduct visitors to the headman of the band. He led off to the left, moving around the circle in the formal manner, and a few passers-by stopped to watch. Riders entering in the ceremonial manner meant important visitors or important news, or both. From around the camp many eyes followed the riders' progress.

Halfway around the circle, opposite the opening, Dust halted in front of a tipi whose lodgeskins were bare of any ornamentation save for a single yellow disk, no larger than a man's head, painted near the entrance flap; overlapping the disk, as if riding out of the circle, was the figure of a horse, blue-black with white markings. The other lodges were decorated, some extensively, with symbols depicting the deeds of the owners, and in some cases showing their special relationship with the spirit powers. A lodge's position in the circle bespoke the honor a man had earned, public trust bestowed by the band and its leaders, membership in warrior societies, and more, but the place of greatest honor was occupied by this simple lodge with its lone emblem.

A tall man peered out of a nearby lodge, then stepped out and approached, and Bat hid his displeasure as he climbed down from his saddle. He had hoped it would be possible to meet first with Sun Horse before Standing Eagle made an appearance, but his brother-in-law was war leader and had a right to be there. "How're ye feelin', Eagle?" he said.

"This child's plumb froze fer 'baccy. You bring some?"

"Nope. Plumb forgot."

"Poor doin's."

Bat's annoyance was banished by the surprise he saw on Hardeman's face. He had forgotten the astonishment that could be occasioned in white men by Standing Eagle's notion of what passed for the American language. The Lakota had learned the tongue from the Putnam brothers, and it stood to reason that they had made sure he would speak it like a true man, not some medicine-show Indian or Bible-thumping preacher. He grinned at his brother-in-law. "By God, Eagle, you look like something the dog dragged in. You feelin' poorly, are you?"

Standing Eagle's eyes were red-rimmed and swollen. Probably he had been hunting in recent days and had kept to the dark of his lodge today to recover from a touch of snowblindness.

"Been sleepin'," said the Indian. "Ain't got much to eat, cain't raise no sign. This coon figgers to catch some rest while he can." He gathered his blanket more tightly about him and drew himself up, trying unsuccessfully to make up for the hair that was not combed and the tattered moccasins on his feet, a pair he no longer wore anywhere except in his lodge.

"You're a wuthless dunghead, and that's truth!" Bat exclaimed. "Never could make a raise with a fat cow breathin' down yer neck." He jerked his thumb at Hardeman and Johnny Smoker. "These boys made meat down below the park yestiddy. A nigger's willin' to shake his bones, 'stead o' lyin' all day abed, he'll make 'em come."

"Wagh!" Standing Eagle coughed, and fell silent. Among the Lakota the relationship between brothers-in-law was unrestrained, permitting practical jokes and teasing without any loss of dignity, but Standing Eagle was the one member of the band who had never fully accepted the white man who had married his sister, and he suffered Bat's insults grudgingly at best.

All the riders had dismounted, and still there was no sign of life from the headman's lodge. Within the camp circle the coming and going that had taken place since the horsemen entered—men and women passing close for a look at the strangers—became now a general gathering as the people came to see their leader greet the whites. From here and there about the camp, groups of men and women approached, led by the older men, the band's councillors. One young boy entered the camp circle at a run and darted among the grown-ups, arriving breathless at Standing Eagle's side.

"Hello, Uncle," he greeted Bat in Lakota. He was Blackbird, Standing Eagle's son, a lad of sixteen or thereabouts; the Lakota placed little importance on birthdays, reckoning a man's age instead by how many winters he had lived through. Blackbird was in his sixteenth winter. Like the rest of the Sun Band, he knew Lisa Putnam by sight. He received a few signs of greeting from Hears Twice, but most of his attention was on Hardeman and Johnny Smoker.

Standing Eagle had glanced at both of the strangers in turn and his eyes had moved on without recognition. Bat smiled inwardly and thought to say something that would whet the war leader's curiosity without giving away the secret, but he held his tongue when he saw the entrance flap of Sun Horse's lodge pulled aside from within.

The first to emerge were the headman's wives, Elk

Calf Woman, white-haired, as old as Sun Horse himself, and Sings His Daughter, young and comely, a Crow captive who had been adopted into the band. Bat winked at Sings His Daughter and she repressed a soft giggle. The two women turned, and when Sun Horse appeared, they took him by the arms and assisted him as he stepped through the low entryway. They released him then and moved to one side, joining the other women as the councillors gathered around Sun Horse.

Hardeman needed no one to tell him that this was the headman. He took in the worn buffalo robe held loosely about the almost frail body, the unadorned gray hair combed straight and long, and he felt the man's power.

What was it about some men that commanded such attention? It was in the eyes, he thought. Among white men they reflected the assurance of being obeyed, the knowledge that a man's position guaranteed authority. He had seen more than enough of that look among whites. But some men revealed something more. William Tecumseh Sherman, for a fact, and Ulysses Grant in a different way. And then there were Black Kettle and Roman Nose and Tall Bull of the Cheyenne who came to mind; Satanta of the Kiowa and Ten Bears of the Comanche, and the great Sioux chief Conquering Bear, who had still been alive when Hardeman made his first trip west on the Oregon Trail. Conquering Bear was gone now, and all three of the Cheyenne. Great men led lives of constant danger. And now here was the same look in the eyes of Sun Horse. It was something far removed from the smug self-assurance of high position. It was the look of a man who carried a burden but saw no way to set it down. Perhaps it was no more than doubt, and a willingness to lead on despite the uncertainties that life heaped on all who held the fate of others in their hands.

Hardeman met Sun Horse's gaze and was careful to reveal nothing. The Indians admired self-control above all other qualities. Sun Horse stepped forward now and it seemed to Hardeman that even his shambling gait displayed a contained self-confidence. In Fort Laramie or D. A. Russell, wrapped in his moth-eaten robe, he would have been indistinguishable from any of the old Indians who lived near the forts, giving in to whiskey and despair, but Hardeman had learned long ago to be wary of judging any man by the finery he might or might not have about his person. Even among the proud Sioux, whose great warriors sported eagle-feather bonnets and finely beaded clothing and who judged a man by the size of his horse herd and his lodge, there were men who shunned these things and yet stood above all others in honor and respect. It was said that Crazy Horse, the young warrior whose name struck such fear into the miners in the Black Hills, went into battle with no paint and no feathers and was always retiring among his people.

Hardeman knew how the reception would go: first welcome the visitors into camp, feed them and smoke with them, then listen to what they have to say; always the formalities were observed. If a man brought news of the end of the world in fire and destruction, it would be the same. A white man would just state his business the minute he got within speaking distance, but an Indian didn't work that way.

"Hau, tunkanshi." Bat addressed Sun Horse for-

mally, as the occasion demanded. Greetings, father-in-law.

Sun Horse replied with equal formality and shook Bat's hand. He turned then to Lisa. "Lisaputnam." He said it as one word, holding out his hands and clasping both of hers, smiling broadly. He had seen her only once since her father died.

"I am glad to see my uncle looking so well," Lisa said in fluent Lakota. There was no blood relationship between them, but among the Lakota, relationship was not defined by blood alone, and Jed Putnam had been like a brother to Sun Horse. The word Lisa used was *até*, which meant "father," but was applied to paternal uncles as well. She swallowed against a lump in her throat and was glad she had come. How can I help him? she wondered. Let me find a way.

"You savvy Lakota?" Bat asked Hardeman, and Hardeman shook his head. He did not have the gift of foreign tongues the way Johnny did, and Lisa Putnam too, it seemed.

"This white man is called Christopher Hardeman," Bat said in English. "He brings a message from the soldier chief Crook, the man we call Three Stars."

Standing Eagle had moved close to his father; he talked softly in Sun Horse's ear even as Bat spoke. The translation was a smooth process, perfected by years of practice. It neither slowed nor interrupted Bat's speech. At the mention of Crook's name, Standing Eagle frowned, but he finished what Bat had said, adding nothing. At the same time, Hears Twice had put the few English words into signs, and so even as Bat fell silent, all those present knew what had been said. A murmur of concern moved around the circle.

Bat switched to Lakota then, and he spoke to Sun Horse for a minute or two, gesturing once at Hardeman. When he was done he turned to the scout. "I told him you rode with Jed back in '51. Said you missed meetin' me and Sun Horse both, down at Laramie. We come down for the treaty council, but you and Jed was already gone on to Californy. Sun Horse, him and Jed got along. Knowin' you was Jed's friend puts you up a step or two in his eyes."

Sun Horse spoke to Hardeman, regarding the white man with new interest, and when he was done, Bat conveyed his message. "He says you're welcome. 'A friend of the Truthful Whiteman'—that's what they called Jed—'A friend of the Truthful Whiteman is welcome in this village' was the way he put it. He says he hopes you'll be a friend to the Sun Band, like Jed was. He invites us to eat in his lodge before the council meets to hear the message. He says the huntin' ain't been good, but what the Sun Band has, it will always share with its guests."

Hardeman saw the councillors nod their approval and guessed that he had been honored by the warmth of the headman's greeting.

"Tell him I thank him for his welcome," he said to Bat. "And tell him I hope we will be friends. Tell him Johnny and I come with a message of peace for the Sun Band."

Standing Eagle translated Hardeman's words for his father as the white man spoke, and as Bat gave the scout's response formally in Lakota for the benefit of the others, Sun Horse turned to the young man standing beside Hardeman.

Bat gestured to Johnny as he concluded, and for Hardeman's benefit he added, "I told him the boy's got a special reason for comin', sump'n besides the message.''

Sun Horse waited for some further explanation, but none was offered. He looked at Lisaputnam. She glanced at the young man, then back at Sun Horse, and she smiled. The man called Hardeman was watching the youth too, as a father might watch a son. Sun Horse wished to know more about this bearded whiteman who seemed so sure of himself. He noted the man's eyes, set so deep beneath the brows. They were farseeing eyes, the eyes of a scout; this was a man with the vision to lead his people. There was something odd in his expression now, as if he expected something to happen. The young whiteman was looking at Sun Horse, and he too seemed to be waiting—

The sounds of the village grew suddenly faint around Sun Horse as all his attention was brought to bear on the young man. He saw something in the youth's eyes that awakened an image long in disuse, a memory placed carefully in that deep recess of the mind where he stored remembrances of beloved ones who had gone on to the spirit world. He felt a chill despite the warm sunshine, and the fear of death, and the heightened awareness of life that he always felt when the unseen forces of spirit power moved near him.

The young man touched his breast and made a few signs. *My heart is glad to see you, Grandfather.*

''*Hunhé!*'' Sun Horse's astonishment escaped him against his will as the young man's signs asked him to believe the impossible. Many called him Grandfather, children of his children and countless more, for it was a term of respect used by children and adults alike, but no whites called him that. There had been one once, a boy now dead . . .

How is it that a whiteman calls me Grandfather? He made the signs too rapidly for any but an experienced sign talker to follow.

Just as quickly the answer came: *It is true I am a whiteman, but I was raised a son of the Cheyenne.* The hands paused, and then they added, *My father was White Smoke.*

Tears sprang to Sun Horse's eyes. As much as the message they conveyed, the hands themselves had confirmed the identity of the young man who stood before him, as they danced in the air with a life of their own. None spoke the language of the hands with that special grace Sun Horse remembered so well, none but the white grandson he himself had instructed in the sign talk one summer long ago.

From the crowd there were murmurs of surprise, and the older ones explained to those who had joined the band in recent years, and others too young to remember, about the baby White Smoke had adopted, and the belief that the boy had perished with his father at the Washita.

Have you come from the spirit world? Sun Horse asked half seriously and half in jest. He felt light-headed and foolish.

Smiling, Johnny shook his head. *I am a man of flesh and blood, as you are, Grandfather. I did not die at the Washita.*

Wordlessly, the old man stepped forward and placed his hands on Johnny's shoulders, content for the moment not to wonder how this thing came to be, simply glad that it was. After a time he brushed a tear from his cheek and smiled. He made more questioning signs, and gestured in Hardeman's direction. Johnny replied with the sign for *friends* and followed with more, telling only that he and Chris had traveled together since the Washita, where Chris had saved his life.

Sun Horse nodded, satisfied to learn the heart of the youth's story now. Later there would be time to hear it all. He turned to Standing Eagle and spoke a few words.

"Sun Horse asks Standing Eagle how come he don't say howdy to his nephew," Bat translated for Hardeman.

Standing Eagle did not hide the hostility in his voice when he replied.

"He says, 'Your grandson comes to us dressed like a whiteman, bringing word from a white soldier chief. I will hear the message before I welcome him.' " This time Bat translated while Standing Eagle was talking, and Hardeman noticed that the mountain mannerisms disappeared from Bat's speech as he gave the running translation with practiced ease. "Standing Eagle's Sun Horse's boy," Bat added, loud enough for his brother-in-law to overhear. "He's war leader of the band. Not much of a one for polite chitchat."

Standing Eagle's words had caused Sun Horse to grow more serious. Would the gift of his grandson's return be taken from him even before he could fully grasp it? Still, the question must be asked. When he spoke now, it was in Cheyenne.

"Have you come, then, only to carry a message?"

Johnny replied in the same language, his use of it uncertain after seven years, but he looked Sun Horse in the eye and his words brought joy to the old man's heart. "I have come to see my grandfather, as he told me I should in the year of my dream."

CHAPTER SEVEN

"My brother Jed spoke of you a time or two," Bat said as Hears Twice's daughter Mist passed more of the steaming soup to Hardeman, who sat across the fire next to Lisa. "You the one picked up a gimpy-leg Dutchman on foot in the Humboldt, ain't you? Summer of '52?"

Hardeman nodded. "We called him Dutch John."

They were in the lodge of Little Hand, Hears Twice's son-in-law, and the sun had fallen halfway to the snowbound ridges since the short council session had ended. The band's advisers had met just long enough to hear Hardeman's news and Crook's message before returning to their own lodges to talk over what they had heard. That evening they would meet again to decide what to do. Hears Twice had invited the whites to eat in his daughter's lodge, but Johnny Smoker had remained with Sun Horse at the old man's request, and since then there had been no word from the headman's tipi.

Little Hand was a short man with a pinched face who sat in the back of the lodge beside Hears Twice. He had not spoken to the whites since his initial greeting, which was so curt it had bordered on being impolite. Hears Twice's three grandchildren, two girls and a boy, had sat wide-eyed for a time, staring at the visitors, but they had quickly grown used to the

184

presence of the whites and they had been sent outside when they grew restless. They returned from time to time to peer into the entrance and giggle, covering their mouths with their hands.

"We called him Good Leg John in the mountains," Bat said. "Was a Gros Ventre arrow pulled him up lame and I'm the fella cut it out of him. Son of a bitch never had a grain of sense in his whole family. He stayed in the mountains long after the trade give out, huntin' beaver. And I'll give it to him, he could raise beaver from a dry crick, but he never got more'n powder money for the plews. Finally give it up. Lit out in the dead o' winter. Said he had a mind to see Californy 'fore he went under. I told him that mule of his had died long since and just didn't have the natural sense to lay down and quit, but he slung aboard and that's the last I seen of him. Glad the coon made it even if the mule didn't." The story came easily to him and required little effort in the telling, but he took no pleasure in it. He had spent half the afternoon trying to loosen Hardeman's tongue with gab, to no avail. Get a man talking and sooner or later he'd show how his stick floated, but it would take a stout pole and a good place to pry to get ten words in a row out of Hardeman today. He was drawn up tighter than a Mormon's purse strings, holding himself way off somewhere out of reach, and Bat gave up the effort now, falling into a moody silence, nagged by the persistent feeling that the scout was holding out on him.

Bat had searched his memory long and hard to find the "time or two" Jed had spoken of a young lad he took on as apprentice scout in the summer of 1851. He had found the right tale, and the handful of words

Jed had applied to Chris Hardeman, but they bore a significance beyond their number. "I liked the cut of the boy's jib," Jed had told it. "He'd come from Philadelphia—city boy like us—made it clear to Missouri by his lonesome. Threw him on a paint horse that could smell Injun from a mile off and knew solid bottom from quicksand in the middle of the nighttime, dark of the moon. The boy learned quick, 'n' he was as good as his word."

He was as good as his word. If Jed said it, it was true, but Bat still couldn't shake a suspicion that Hardeman was holding something back. Like Stone Bull, he thought, remembering the scalp that had fluttered from his rifle until it had grown so ratty that it offended him and he had thrown it away. He and a few companions had come on Stone Bull up on the brakes of the Gros Ventre; the Crow warrior had been alone, standing over a fresh-killed moose, and my, wasn't he friendly. "Seddown," he says, "heap plenty meat." Crows were always friendly when they were outnumbered. He had fallen all over himself to welcome the little party of trappers into his camp and see that they got fed. But he was forthright, and had a sense of humor that tickled Bat's funny bone, and Bat had found himself liking a man that all experience taught him to regard as his enemy. Sure enough, when a dozen other Crows showed up the next day, Stone Bull and his friends had tried to lift the trappers' hair. "He'd tried it 'fore breakfast, he might be carryin' my topknot today," Bat had later told the story. "But me'n Old Webb, we slept sound and et the rest of that moose for breakfast, and we was up to Crow that day." At this point in the tale he would bring out Stone Bull's scalp to show how the fight

had ended. Old Stone Bull, he was a good enough
sort, but he held out. He knew them other boys was
comin' along and he kept shut. What was Hardeman
holding out? Bat had taken a liking to the man, but
he wouldn't let that put him off his guard.

Hardeman knew a thing or two about dealing with
Indians, that much was plain from the way he had
spoken to Sun Horse and the other councillors. He
had relayed Crook's message simply and directly,
adding his own promise to see that the Sun Band was
given all that Crook had agreed to, which was a
smart move on his part. The councillors naturally put
more faith in the word of a man who sat with them
and smoked the pipe than in some soldier chief they
had never seen. Hardeman had handled the long-
stemmed ceremonial pipe well too, one hand cradling
the dark red pipestone bowl while the other grasped
the stem as he offered it to the four cardinal points
and the sky and the earth. He handled it with respect,
and the councillors had noticed. And Bat had been
interested to see how calmly he had filled his belly,
first in Sun Horse's lodge before the council and now
here. It was poor doin's to serve dog to white folks,
Bat thought, but Hardeman pitched in like dog soup
was about the slickest doin's he could imagine. He
knew a thing or two about Indians, all right.

Bat was proud that Lisa had been included in the
brief council out of respect for her father and because
she was now in charge of the settlement in Putnam's
Park. She had sat quietly, saying nothing, and had
borne the initial surprise that a woman should be
asked to sit in council without showing it. She too
had eaten well. Jed had taught her to be grateful for
what there was and not to be bound by conventions

that stood in the way of getting fed. She'd had dog soup before.

Little Hand belched loudly and set his wooden bowl aside face down to show that he wanted no more. He turned to Bat and asked in Lakota what he knew of Hardeman, referring to him only as the *washíchun* scout. *Washíchun* was the Lakota term for white man, but it was also the name given to the ceremonial bundle a Lakota wore about his neck, which often contained some small symbol of a man's spirit power. The word meant something that bore spirit power within itself, and at first the Lakota had applied it only to the *shiná sapa*, the black-robe missionaries who were among the first white men they had seen, the ones who spoke of *God* and wanted to hear nothing from the Lakota holy men in return. Before long, all white men came to be called *washíchun*, and the name conveyed, to those who understood its true meaning, a sense of the strange and unpredictable power within the whites. Little Hand spoke the word as if it made a bad taste in his mouth.

Bat told Little Hand what he knew about Hardeman, and how the scout had cared for Johnny since the Washita battle. Little Hand asked more questions then, and when Bat had answered as best he could, Little Hand gave a noncommittal grunt, looked almost contemptuously at Hardeman, rose, and left the lodge.

"Wanted to know all about how Johnny came to stay with a white scout after the Washita fight," Bat told Hardeman. "I said you was like the boy's *hunká*-father. There's no word for it in English, nothing just like it in a white man's life. Means 'relative-by-

choice' in Lakota. A *hunká*-father takes over some of
the work of a real father in raisin' a boy; teaches him
things, tells him stories of the people. But it's a heap
more—it keeps the boy from stayin' too long in his
mother's tipi, gets him out into the world, teaches
him to trust another man like a father, helps him to
see he's gotta choose his own way, 'stead o' just
followin' in his pa's footsteps. You might say when a
boy's with his *hunká*-father he's halfway to bein' on
his own. Seems to me that's pretty near what you
done for Johnny, ain't it?''

"You could say that,'' Hardeman replied after a
moment, surprised to learn that the Sioux had a word
for a relationship he had thought unique. "Little
Hand didn't seem any too pleased with the idea.''

"Oh, he don't reckon whites know about *hunká*-
relatives and such, but don't mind him. He don't
unbend much any time when it comes to white folks.
Him and Standing Eagle, they're the ones who'll
speak for war.'' He hadn't meant to say it, but it had
been on his mind. He wasn't used to watching his
words here in camp. The steady stream of talk he had
kept up since the council ended had relaxed him after
a silent morning in the saddle. It didn't do to talk
when it wasn't necessary on the trail. You travel in
silence, you'll see your enemy before he sees you, if
you're lucky. Years of habit had taught Bat to curb
his naturally loquacious tongue beyond the camp circle, but now he would have to watch what he said
even here, and remember that neither Hardeman's
ears nor Johnny Smoker's were sure to be friendly.
In the council the youth had spoken in support of
Hardeman, a little reluctantly, perhaps, but he said
he could see no way for the Sun Band to survive but

by surrender, and that put him across the fence from
Bat Putnam, who didn't want to see the free life of
the Lakota come to an end.

"Tell me, Mr. Hardeman," Lisa said suddenly,
"when you and Johnny were in Texas you must have
seen a good deal of the new methods for raising
beef."

"Some," Hardeman replied, trying to imagine how
Lisa Putnam knew that he and Johnny had been in
Texas, until he remembered that Johnny had told her
last night, there in the kitchen, when he learned that
Julius Ingram had spent time on the cattle trails.

"Are many of the stockmen there experimenting
with the new breeds?" Lisa wanted to take Hardeman's
mind off what Bat had said, and the chance that the
Sun Band would decide to fight rather than surrender.

"Some," Hardeman said again. "There's a lot of
them think that the Longhorn is God's gift to the
cattleman and shouldn't be tampered with. But there
are others who look up to Kansas and see rails moving south. First they were in Abilene, now they're in
Dodge and Wichita. Some say before long they'll
build across the Indian Territory into Texas, and then
there will be no need for a beef as tough as the
Longhorn just to get to market."

Lisa nodded. "We used to take our cattle to Cheyenne, but since they built the stockyards at Rawlins,
we only have to drive them a hundred miles. My
father said a dairy cow could walk a hundred miles."

The talk of beef raising held little interest for Bat
and he let his attention wander. The sun filtering
through the hides of the tipi cover suffused the interior with a warm and gentle light. The fire in the
central pit was small, scarcely needed on the sunny

afternoon. He leaned against his backrest and stretched his feet out to the fire, glad of a chance to unbend his legs. The rheumatism was paining him today, a result of years spent setting traps in ice-cold streams, but he suffered the discomfort without resentment; it was a small misery and far less than he was willing to pay for the joy the trapping years had given him.

Outside, the camp was quiet, but it was not a peaceful calm. The news brought by the two *washíchun* had traveled quickly and was now being discussed intently in the tipis of the warrior fraternities. To-night, when the council met again, the lines would be drawn; they would turn to Bat, the white brother they called Lodgepole, both those who favored surrender and those like Little Hand who wanted to fight the soldiers. What will the whites do if we fight? What will the whites do if we surrender? What does Lodgepole advise?

How could he answer? Could he tell them that before he would take Penelope to live on a reserva-tion he would leave them and go back to his own kind?

Hears Twice began slowly to stoke a pipe. The reddish bowl shone from years of handling and found its way in the old man's palms as if alive. When the pipe was lit and going, Hears Twice handed it to Bat and made signs that said *It is good to smoke with friends*. He always did that, making signs or on rare occasions speaking the words, as if it were part of his medicine to smoke with friends and let them know he thought it was a good thing. Bat nodded, the way he always did, and inhaled deeply, letting the smoke burn his lungs and make him giddy before he blew out slowly, savoring again the tang of the willow bark that was mixed with the shredded trade tobacco. He wondered where among the whites he would ever find for Penelope the hospitality and welcome to match those he had received for thirty years among the Lakota.

Bat didn't like changes, especially those that forced him to give up something he cherished. Where had Jed got the ability to move on from one thing to another over the years with his spirits always high?

The talk of cattle and different breeds and how fast they grew had come to an end and neither Hardeman nor Lisa had found anything new to talk about. Bat turned to Lisa now as if what he had to say were no more than part of an ongoing conversation. "He was smiling at the end? You sure of that?"

"What? I'm sorry, I was thinking."

"I asked about Jed, there at the end. You said he was smiling."

Lisa nodded. "He was smiling, Uncle Bat. There was no pain at the end."

But pain wasn't what worried Bat. He saw something else in that ghost of a smile. The thing had haunted him all through the winter months like some puzzle from his childhood—seemingly simple, but the solution so hard to find. The thought of that dying grin on his brother's face gave him pause. How could a man who had taken such joy in life smile at the loss of it? Right through the fur trade and the road ranching and on into his first efforts at raising cattle, Jed had found an unending kind of glory-be wonder in the simplest things, a wonder that had stayed with him right to the end. That final smile went against nature! Jed should have been battling the shadow of Death with the last breath in his body.

But Bat knew that nothing truly went against nature, and all winter he had been trying to shake the suspicion that Jed had learned some secret about life that he himself didn't know, something he would do well to learn before he approached his own end of the trail. He would like to know it now. He had no heart for the life he and Penelope would lead once they left the camp circle of the Sun Band. If only he could divine Jed's secret, it might help him to make the transition with a better will.

He realized that the pipe lay dead in his hand and he passed it back to Hears Twice, who scraped the ashes carefully into the fire and refilled the bowl, lighting it before passing it to Hardeman. It was a social smoke, not ceremonial, all part of an informal ritual that helped to pass the better part of winter in the Lakota lodges, as long as the smoking mixture lasted. It was an accompaniment to the winter tales and the visiting from lodge to lodge, a way to break a silence or prolong it, depending on the moment. Silences were comforting among a people who felt no need to speak when they had nothing to say.

Bat tried to quiet his own thoughts, but the silence here was tense with waiting and he himself broke it again.

"You want to get home by dark, you might think about startin' out pretty soon, Lisa honey," he said. "I'll stay the night, what with the council and all."

"There's a bit of a moon tonight," she said. "We can find our way in the dark if we have to." She hoped for a chance to speak to Sun Horse alone before leaving the Lakota camp. She turned to Hardeman. "Mr. Hardeman?"

"Johnny hasn't seen Sun Horse in a long time.

There's no need to rush him. We'll wait a while longer, if you don't mind.''

The fact was, now that they were here and Crook's message delivered, Hardeman was in no hurry to leave. It had been a long time since he had sat in an ordinary Indian lodge as a guest. Taking such opportunities when they came along was a lesson Lisa's father had taught him, so many years ago. "What you see in council, that's only one side of an Injun," the mountain man had said. "Injuns got a peculiar notion about a man who leads the people. They figger he oughta be serious where the lives of the people are at stake. So in council, a man sits sober and listens close when another feller speaks his mind. He speaks his own in turn, sober and serious. And that's where a white man's likely to see his first Injun, sittin' down to palaver. So the white feller goes home and he says, 'Boy, them Injuns sure is serious folks,' and that's where the mischief gets started.'' The mischief Jed had in mind was the mistaken notion that formal speaking was the normal Indian manner. It had led in turn to the equally incorrect idea that all Indians were solemn and emotionless and somewhat methodical not only in their manner of speech but in their manner of thinking as well, and these errors had played their part in preventing a better understanding between the races. It was good to be reminded that the Indians were men and women not so different from white people in many ways; they had children who grew hungry when there was not enough food, and within a small band like this there were men as dissimilar as Bat Putnam and Little Hand. Hardeman trusted Bat, but he wouldn't turn his back on Little Hand. *Him and*

Standing Eagle, they're the ones who'll speak for war, Bat had said, and Hardeman remembered now that Little Hand had sat next to Standing Eagle in council and seemed to side with the war leader in everything he said.

It was not necessary for a white man to offer the pipe to the sacred directions in council, but Hardeman had held the stem toward the west, north, east and south before he touched it to his lips, moving it around the horizon as the Sioux prayed and as Jed Putnam had taught him twenty-five years before, when they had sat down to parley with a scouting party of Minneconjou. The pipe swore him to tell the truth, and his display had been calculated to demonstrate to the council that he was aware of the obligation. The smoke rose to the sky, alerting the spirits to the words that followed. The councillors had watched him closely as he smoked, and Johnny had watched too, for he had never before seen Hardeman among Indians. When the pipe had completed its rounds, Hardeman had conveyed General Crook's message, saying that the government's order must be obeyed, the Sioux must go to Dakota, but because Sun Horse was a peace man, Crook would give him an escort, and beef and blankets for his people, if he would go in peacefully. But before Hardeman had finished telling all that Crook would promise, Standing Eagle had interrupted him loudly, his voice full of anger. The war leader had retired to his own lodge to dress for the council while Sun Horse fed the guests; he had reappeared with eagle feathers bound in his hair, which he had combed and braided, and he was togged out in all the finery he could muster. His shirt and leggings were finely beaded and he carried a new trade blanket, brightly striped in red and blue. He wore earrings of silver and bits of feather, and necklaces of shell and bear claws. Even among the other councillors, some of whom wore the feathered headdresses for which the Sioux were famous, with tails that touched the ground, Standing Eagle was an impressive figure.

Throughout the proceedings, Bat had translated for Hardeman, talking softly in his ear, conveying word for word what was said, but he listened to Standing Eagle's outburst in its entirety before turning to the scout. "He says he don't need no promises from a white soldier chief. He don't need no meat from the white man's spotted buffalo neither. He says he'll fight Three Stars if'n he comes near to the Sun Band."

It seemed to Hardeman that there was scorn in Bat's voice for the war leader's lack of good manners.

As soon as Standing Eagle fell silent, Sun Horse rebuked his son sharply. The headman was dressed just as he had been when the whites first arrived, in his worn robe, with no feathers or ornaments in his hair, but his voice carried an authority that sent Standing Eagle back to his seat, his face dark with embarrassment at being scolded before the council.

"He put ol' Eagle in his place, right enough," Bat murmured. "Reminded him that in council each man speaks until he's done. It's time to listen now, he says. The council's gonna meet again tonight, and then Eagle can speak his mind. Now it's time to listen."

Hardeman had continued then, directing himself to Sun Horse. "The Sioux can't win this war," he said. "The whites will send one army after another until you surrender. It's time for the peace men to act for peace. Say you will go in, and I'll bring Three Stars here. Sit down and talk with him and you will see that he is not like some of the other officers. He fights to make peace, not to conquer, and he keeps his promises.'' Here he made a sign, bringing a forefinger out from beneath his chin to show that the soldier chief's words were straight. ''When the soldiers have helped your people safely to Dakota,'' he went on, ''then perhaps Sun Horse will do his part to stop this war. Send your men to Sitting Bull and the other headmen. Tell them that Three Stars is an honest man who can be trusted; tell them to make peace while there is still time. Do this, and Three Stars will let you keep your horses, and some guns for hunting.''

When Hardeman was done, Sun Horse had asked a single question. ''What will Three Stars do if we will not go in?''

''Three Stars is coming here to find the Sioux. When he finds a band, he'll give them a chance to surrender. If they won't surrender, he will fight.'' Hardeman put it bluntly to emphasize the danger. Sun Horse had merely nodded, but he kept his eyes on Hardeman for what seemed like a long time, as if searching for something else behind the white man's words. At last he had moved his gaze to Johnny Smoker. Hardeman had felt lightheaded, as if a weight had been suddenly removed from him, and only then had he realized that Sun Horse had responded directly to his words. Standing Eagle, silenced by his father's rebuke, had ceased his translating. Sun Horse understood English. Then why did the war leader translate for the old man at all? Hardeman wondered.

Probably to give him more time to consider what he had heard and prepare his reply. The old fox was too clever by half.

"I don't mean to pry, Mr. Hardeman," Lisa said now, "but I have wondered why Johnny waited so long to find Sun Horse. Even to let him know that he was alive would have saved an old man some unnecessary suffering."

Hardeman handed the pipe back to Hears Twice before answering. "The boy never wanted to come before, or I would have brought him." His tone was meant to discourage further talk on the subject, but the woman wouldn't take the hint.

"They seem to think a great deal of each other," she said. "What was it that Johnny said about coming here because of a dream?"

I have come to see my grandfather, as he told me I should in the year of my dream, Johnny had said. He had spoken in Cheyenne, but evidently old Hears Twice understood Cheyenne, for he had translated Sun Horse's question and Johnny's answer in signs for the Sioux, and Hardeman could read the sign talk better than most white men. It appeared that Lisa Putnam could read signs too. She seemed to know a good deal about Indians, and missed very little that went on around her. Well, if she wouldn't let it alone, he would tell her enough to satisfy her curiosity and silence the questions that way.

"When Johnny was with the Cheyenne, he had a dream," he said. "It wasn't a dream like white people get; more like one of those special Indian dreams. A spirit dream, he called it. It said he would return to the whites one day, and when he was about to become a man he would choose whether to live with the whites or go back to the Indians. It was the summer Johnny and his folks were visiting Sun Horse.'' He saw that Bat was listening now. The mountain man nodded as if he were well acquainted with that summer, and the dream. ''The old man told Johnny that when he was ready to choose he should come see him. He's ready to choose. He picked the white world, so he came to tell Sun Horse.''

''Powerful dream,'' Bat said more to himself than the others. ''Come true too.''

It was clear from Lisa's expression that the unexpected revelation had given her more than enough to think about for a while, but Hardeman wished the matter were as cut-and-dried as he had told it. Ever since the moment in front of Sun Horse's tipi when Johnny had told Sun Horse why he had come, the old man had taken on the air of someone whose fondest wish in life had come true. Once he heard the boy's words, he seemed to attach to Johnny's return an importance out of all proportion to what Hardeman had expected.

What more could there be to the dream, beyond what Johnny had told him all those years ago back in Utah?

Shortly after the Washita battle, Hardeman had found the boy a home with an army officer's brother, a St. Louis merchant. The man and his wife were childless, and they had taken Johnny in willingly when Hardeman delivered him there shortly before Christmas. The boy showed none of the wildness sometimes evidenced by other white boys who had lived for a time with the Indians. Those who had grown to manhood among the savages sometimes rejected their white relations completely, slipping away at the first opportunity to rejoin their wild adopted kin. But other children taken by Indians and recovered while still young had reverted to white ways without protest; Johnny's case was not so unusual.

Early in the new year, Hardeman had left St. Louis, thinking to return in a year or two and see how the boy was getting on. He took a job with the Union Pacific, hunting meat for the crews, and as the spring warmed and sent the snowmelt rushing down the rivers and streams, the rails had leaped westward like a quick-growing vine, sometimes advancing fifteen, seventeen, almost twenty miles in one day, in the final sprint to meet the tracks of the Central Pacific, which were rushing eastward across the Utah desert. And there in Utah, two weeks before the golden spike was driven at Promontory, Johnny had found him.

The boy rode up on the same Indian pony Hardeman had picked for him from the captured herd after the battle. He was dressed like a St. Louis schoolboy, with the rest of his belongings tied in a sack behind his saddle. The merchant and his wife had treated him well, he said—his English had improved greatly during the winter—but he had had enough of cities. He would stay with Hardeman, if the scout would have him. It had been so simply put, with Johnny's eyes looking straight at him, that Hardeman had been unable to refuse.

The boy had spoken of the dream for the first time there by the U. P. tracks. Once Hardeman had said that Johnny could ride with him and promised he wouldn't send him back to St. Louis, Johnny had sat the two of them down right on the track and, like a couple of men entering a business arrangement together, they had discussed the terms of their partnership. As they talked, they could feel in their rumps the hammer blows from a quarter mile up the track, where the crew was spiking down a new section of rail.

"I am going to work my own way," Johnny had proclaimed, all of thirteen, maybe, but tall for his age. "I had a talk with the crew boss here. He said I could be water boy. It ain't a job I want to do for long."

"Well, now," Hardeman had said, trying to come to grips with the new self-assured manner of this boy who only a few months before had been wearing Cheyenne clothes and paint, "it's not a job that'll last too long. Rails figure to join up in a few weeks, and that's that."

"What do you reckon to do next?" Johnny had asked, all serious.

"Why, I'm not exactly sure. I never saw Santa Fe and that country down there. I had a thought I might head that way. Maybe drive some freight. Seems like it might be a way to see the Santa Fe Trail."

"That suits me," Johnny had said, and surprised Hardeman by adding, "I can do most anything with horses or mules. I can learn to drive a team quick enough."

"All right then, we'll try her," Hardeman had said. "As a matter of fact, I'll tell you what. Let's say we stay on at one place or one kind of work just as long as we're both satisfied. When one of us wants to put out for someplace else, we go."

Johnny had stuck out his hand and they had shaken on the deal then and there, and they had kept to it ever since.

"There's one thing I ought to say," Johnny had added. "A few years back I had a dream. A spirit dream, the Indians called it. It said I would come back to my own people and live with them for a time. But I don't really belong to this world. Not to the Indians, neither. When I come to be a man, I got to choose. Dunno if you put stock in such things."

"I do if you do" was all Hardeman could say, and Johnny had nodded.

"It said I stand between the worlds, and on account of that I shouldn't fight any man, white or Indian. I don't carry a gun or knife." When Hardeman made no objection to that, he went on. "I reckon I should see as much of the white man's world as I can, so I'll know how to choose when the time comes. Only thing is, how will I know when it's time?"

"You'll know," Hardeman had said then. "You'll feel the need to step out on your own, and you won't need me anymore."

Since then Hardeman had all but forgotten the dream. They had watched the cheering crowds at Promontory Point and seen the two steam engines head to head, all polished and shining, and the high mucky-mucks of the Union Pacific and Central Pacific talking about what the rails meant to the nation, and then Hardeman and Johnny had gone south, but they hadn't stayed long on the Santa Fe Trail. One trip was all it took to convince them that watching the back end of a string of mules was no way to see the country, and before the year had come to an end, Johnny remarked that he'd like to see the Longhorn cattle over in Texas, and the cattle ranges had kept them busy for the better part of six years. Through all that time, Johnny had never mentioned the dream again. But he had never carried a gun, and although he took to carrying a pocketknife he had used it only as a tool; it never seemed to enter his mind that it might be a weapon. Hardeman had looked out for Johnny when trouble threatened, but the boy didn't rub people the wrong way and more often than not it had been Johnny who helped Hardeman out of a touchy situation by watching his back and keeping an eye out for unexpected threats. More than once in the Kansas saloons and bordellos during the winter just past, Johnny had been there when Hardeman needed him.

And then two weeks ago, back in Ellsworth, Johnny had said out of the blue, "I guess it's time."

"Time for what?" Hardeman had asked. They were in the boarding house where they shared a room. Like most trail hands, their jobs had ended in the fall when the cattle were delivered to the rail-head. There had been no jobs in Dodge, so they had moved up the U. P. rails until they found work in Ellsworth. Hardeman had passed the winter as a deputy city marshal, and Johnny had worked in a stable, where he had trained and cared for the horses of the town's best citizens.

"Time to choose," Johnny had answered. He was lying on his bed, with his feet propped up on the steel frame that was painted white.

"Choose?"

"Choose between the worlds." Johnny sat up then, grinning. "I'm a white man, I guess, and I reckon to give the white man's world a go." He had seemed pretty pleased with himself. "Like you said," he went on, as if the conversation had been just the other day, instead of nearly seven years before, "I got the notion to put out on my own. Course, there's nothing to say we couldn't get back together in a year or two, like equal partners, so to speak."

"We've always been pretty equal," Hardeman said.

"That's true enough," Johnny agreed. "But I guess we might be even more equal after I've been off on my own, like you've been." He was still smiling to show he meant it all for the best.

"Might be," Hardeman had conceded, a little taken aback by the whole thing. That was Johnny's way, thinking something over on his own and only saying it when he had it all worked out. Johnny must have seen something in his expression, like disappointment, or maybe just surprise at the suddenness of his announcement.

"Oh, I'm not fixing to run off just yet. I've got something to do first, and I'll need your help. It'll mean leaving Ellsworth."

Hardeman hadn't objected. A winter of lawing had been enough to convince him he wasn't suited for the job, although he had earned the respect of both the rougher elements and the gentry, such as it was. But he had never stopped in a town for so long, and he had been ready to move on. Now that he was back in the mountains, he understood the feeling better. As a scout, he led by persuasion; if other men granted him authority it was because they believed in his leadership, not because they feared his badge or his gun. Unlike some men he did not like being feared, or making others do things against their will.

"Where are we headed?" he had asked Johnny then.

"I don't exactly know," the youth had admitted.

"I've got to find a Sioux Indian called Sun Horse. He's my grandfather."

"Your grandfather?" This revelation had shocked Hardeman only a little less than hearing Sun Horse's name from Johnny's lips. "You say his name is Sun Horse?"

Johnny had nodded. "He's a peace chief. He's got his own band. They winter somewhere in the Big Horns. The Valley of Flowers, he called it, but I guess that's just an Indian name."

These few words had been enough to convince Hardeman that Johnny was talking of the same Sun Horse who had given Jed Putnam the land for his road ranch, and he had marveled at how the lives of a few men could cross and recross in a land as vast as the western territories. How different his own life would have been if he had never met Jed Putnam, or Hickok, or Johnny, he had thought. It seemed that Sun Horse was destined to join that company.

"It might be I know where to find Sun Horse," he had said, surprising Johnny in turn, and the boy had told him the rest of it then, about how his Cheyenne father wasn't Cheyenne at all, but Sioux, firstborn son of Sun Horse, and how he had met his grandfather at the summer camp of the Sioux nation.

They had left Ellsworth the next day.

Two weeks had passed quickly since then, and it seemed to Hardeman now that Ellsworth was as far away as Philadelphia, and as long ago.

Footsteps approached the lodge and a soft cough announced someone waiting outside.

"That'll be Sun Horse, I'm thinkin'," Bat said, rising stiffly to his feet, but Hardeman was already halfway to the entrance.

Outside, Sun Horse stood next to Johnny, his weathered face struck full on by the afternoon sunshine. Hardeman looked from one to the other and saw that whatever had passed between the old man and the youth over the past few hours had brought them even closer together.

"I'll be staying here," Johnny said, as Lisa and Bat emerged from the lodge. "I'll come down with Sun Horse when he brings word what the council decides. Tomorrow, most likely."

Hardeman nodded. He had expected that Johnny would want more time with Sun Horse, now or later. If the boy handled himself right, he could do much to persuade the old man to surrender.

"I'll fetch the horses," he said to Lisa, and he went to where the animals had been picketed beyond Sun Horse's lodge. As he tightened the girths of his own saddle and Lisa's, he looked back across the camp circle and saw that she had drawn Sun Horse aside. They were walking slowly, her arm linked in his, and she was talking earnestly for his ears alone. But it didn't matter what she said to him; nothing could change how things stood. Sun Horse would see that. He had to think of the women and children. "The helpless ones," the Indians called the women and the young, and the old men who couldn't pull back a bowstring any longer. The first thought of a chief was always for the helpless ones, and there was only one way to protect them now. Hardeman had come to show him the way.

Back in Ellsworth, Hardeman had been astonished to learn that by a roundabout circle that passed through Putnam's Park, Jed's dream had come true in the Big Horns, Johnny and he were both connected to an old

Sioux he had never met. It had seemed fateful, somehow, and yet as they left Kansas, Hardeman had had no more in mind than to accompany Johnny on his quest. When the boy had found Sun Horse and told him of his choice and had bid the old man farewell for a last time, Hardeman would return with Johnny to the settlements and there see him off on his own, and he would know that the obligation he had undertaken back at the Washita had been honorably discharged.

But they had stopped in Cheyenne to buy a few supplies, and they had seen the swarms of miners and the new houses and other buildings springing up everywhere, and heard the talk on every lip about the Black Hills and the Powder River country and how the whole territory would open up for gold and settlement and the fulfillment of any man's dreams once the savages had been pushed out of the way by the military force that was even then gathering at Fort Fetterman. Hardeman had seen at once that the Sioux were doomed, their fate sealed beyond recall; they would be confined where the white government wished them to be confined, or they would be attacked and punished until they bowed to the inevitable. He had felt a new urgency then to find Sun Horse and, with Johnny's help, persuade the peace chief to take his people to the reservation, to safety, before it was too late.

They had bought their supplies and mounted up and started out of town, bundled up against falling temperatures and a strengthening wind, when Hardeman had spied a familiar figure moving along the boardwalk, a man that stood a head above the rest of the crowd, dressed like Sunday-go-to-meeting in a starched collar and frock coat, his long hair oiled and combed. "James!" Hardeman had shouted.

Hickok had turned and peered about with eyes that seemed not to see so well any longer, and only when Hardeman rode over and dismounted did he exclaim, "Why, Christopher, old boy! It's been years! Damned if you don't look the same. And Johnny Smoker too, grown up like a sapling."

Hardeman and Johnny had seen Hickok a few times over the years, first at Fort Hays, Kansas, just a week or two after the Washita fight. It had been Hickok who gave Johnny his name. "What do you call the boy?" he had wanted to know, and Hardeman had shrugged. "He remembers his name's Johnny, but that's all. He doesn't know his family name." But then Johnny had spoken up, the first time he had talked to any white man other than Hardeman. "My father White Smoke!" he had announced, and Hickok had laughed at the boy's proud tone. "Why that'll do, won't it? We'll call him Johnny Smoker!" And the name had stuck.

In the following year Hickok had been badly wounded by some Cheyenne that caught him alone near Fort Lyon and since then he had aged beyond his years. There in Cheyenne, Hardeman had felt that he was looking at an older man.

Hickok had insisted on buying the two of them a beer and they had been unable to refuse.

"Christopher, you old rascal," Hickok had said, wiping the foam from his mustache with the knuckle of his index finger. "You can't fool me. I know what brings you here. You couldn't pass up the chance to get in on one last campaign. You've come to see George Crook."

"Crook?" Hardeman was puzzled. He knew Crook had been given command of the Department of the Platte the year before, but had no idea that Crook was anywhere near Cheyenne.

"He's here, old boy! Don't tell me you didn't know? He's across the street in that very hotel." Hickok pointed out the window of the saloon to a three-story brick building with a false front. "He'll take on another scout. You go find him and see if he won't. One thing for certain, Christopher, the army won't take no for an answer this time. They're going to finish the job, good and proper. There won't be any more scouting for the army in this neck of the woods, not after this. Take the chance while it's there."

"What about you, James?" Hardeman asked, feeling the beginnings of an idea he couldn't quite seem to grasp.

Hickok looked suddenly very tired. "Oh, I've done my scouting. Times aren't what they were, at least not for me. Besides, I'm getting married in a week or two! Going to take the wife to Cincinnati to see her folks. It's past time I settled down. You and I, Christopher, we've done our part."

Hardeman had scarcely heard his old friend's reply, for in that moment all the pieces of the plan had fallen into place as comfortably as hot beans in a hungry man's belly and he saw it whole in an instant. It was work of a master craftsman, all the makings set up one by one over the years and brought together in a single sweep by the hand of luck. If he hadn't known Jed Putnam and heard the story of Sun Horse giving him the little valley in the mountains, if fate hadn't put Johnny Smoker in the hands of Sun Horse's eldest son, if Hardeman hadn't stopped to visit Hickok in the fall of '68 and gone off to scout for General Sully, and—most improbable of all—if he hadn't been the one to enter the tipi in Black Kettle's village on the Washita and find Johnny still alive . . . And now here was Hickok again, to provide the final piece of the puzzle: the presence of George Crook in Cheyenne as Hardeman and Johnny passed through. Here all the chance encounters over the years were suddenly combined to show Hardeman a way not only to save Sun Horse but perhaps to end the new campaign before it started, and bring to an end twenty years of fighting between the Sioux and the white man.

If only Crook would agree.

Hardeman had left Johnny with Hickok and he crossed the street to the hotel, where he found Crook in the lobby, surrounded by a group of officers and newspapermen. Hardeman identified himself as an army scout, mentioning Hickok and Generals Sully, Custer and Smith all in one breath, and said he wished to speak to General Crook privately. To his surprise, Crook agreed after only a moment's hesitation, and they retired to the dining room, then deserted at mid-morning. There Hardeman had set forth the plan. If he could find the Sioux peace chief Sun Horse and persuade him to go voluntarily to the Dakota reservation with his people, would Crook provide an escort, and beef and blankets for the women and children? Would Crook send riders from the reservation to the other hostile headmen, saying that the peace man Sun Horse had gone in willingly, to see if such news might not bring in the others? Hearing that the soldiers had helped the Sun Band to make the journey safely would surely persuade some bands to surrender, and those in turn might persuade others until the remaining hostiles were so few that they would see no hope in further resistance. He told Crook that he had with him a boy related to Sun Horse, a white youth who had lived with the Indians, and he knew a former mountain man who was friendly with the peace chief. He believed that with the help of these two he could influence Sun Horse to trust General Crook's word.

Crook stroked first one fork of his beard and then the other. "And if Sun Horse will not agree, what then, Mr. Hardeman?" the general wished to know.

Hardeman answered without hesitation, for that eventuality too was part of the plan and even then there was a way to make a peace that would bring the hostiles to Dakota.

Crook had asked more questions then, and Hardeman had answered him, and when there was no more to say, Crook had thought in silence for less than a minute before he agreed the idea was worth a try, and gave it his blessing.

"But understand me well, Mr. Hardeman," Crook had said. "I cannot delay this campaign. You must reach Sun Horse and bring me his reply as quickly as you can. If I come upon one of the war leaders first, there may be no way to prevent fighting."

Within an hour of leaving Crook, Hardeman and Johnny had bid farewell to Hickok and left Cheyenne behind them. As they made their way toward the Big Horns, Hardeman had told Johnny what he hoped to do, and asked him for all he knew about Sun Horse, wanting to learn anything that might be useful in dealing with the peace man. Johnny had been a boy of just eight winters or so when he met his grandfather and he didn't remember much, but he did remember that Sun Horse was Sitting Bull's cousin; the Hunkpapa holy man had been in the Sioux camp that same summer and Sun Horse had talked with Sitting Bull about Johnny's dream. Hardeman seized on the relationship as a sign that his hopes were justified, that the plan might really work, and it was then that he had conceived the notion of asking Sun Horse to send word directly to the hostile bands, to plead with them to make peace and go in. The promise that the Sun Band could keep their horses and guns had come from Hardeman, not Crook, but if Sun Horse would take this step for peace, Crook would surely grant him any favor within reason. The horses and guns were a gift from Hardeman to Sun Horse, as the peace man's help would be a gift to Crook. The plan had assumed a life of its own, and Hardeman was the only one who knew the whole of it; by keeping it to himself and offering such unexpected gifts as these at the right moments, he might maneuver them all, red and white alike, into positions from which fighting would be impossible, and with luck the Indian wars on the north plains could be ended forever before the Sioux and Cheyenne ponies had time to grow sleek on the new grass of spring.

Across the camp, Lisa and Sun Horse turned back toward Little Hand's lodge, where Johnny and Bat Putnam were waiting. At even a short distance, Lisa might be taken for a man, another scout perhaps, in buckskin pants and trappers' winter moccasins, come to bring a message to the Indian chief. What had she told him? And how much influence did she have with Sun Horse now that her father was dead? As the old man rejoined Johnny and Bat, Hardeman saw how Johnny positioned himself beside Sun Horse, as if he belonged there.

In that moment he suddenly realized, not as a worry or a suspicion but as an inescapable truth, that he had made a fundamental miscalculation. He had intended Johnny's return to be an unexpected gift too, one that might have a powerful effect on Sun Horse, making him more likely to take Hardeman's advice and join him as a peacemaker, but he had never for a moment considered what effect seeing Sun Horse again might have on Johnny, nor what feelings might arise in the boy when he found himself once more among the Indians. He understood now the doubts he had felt the morning before, down below Putnam's Park, when he saw Johnny building a sweat lodge; even then the boy had seemed to be loosening his hold on white man's ways and remembering the Indian customs he had left behind seven years before. And now, having seen the bond between Sun Horse and Johnny, having heard the talk of the dream, Hardeman knew in his bones that something more was taking place here than a simple reunion between an old Indian and a long-lost grandson. It was as if a promise had been fulfilled.

An Indian had a dream and it changed his life. It gave him strange notions and made him do stranger things. What would Johnny's dream make him do now? Since the Washita, Johnny had moved through the white man's world without objection, regarding it curiously on occasion but never showing a desire to return to the Indians. He could read and write and name the eighteen Presidents of the United States in order. He could eat with a knife and fork and converse with a mule skinner or a banker's wife, and his recent decision to remain permanently in the white world had seemed heartfelt and genuine. But that was back in Kansas, and Kansas was far away. What if he changed his mind and stayed with the Sioux?

And what if the Sun Band would not surrender? Hardeman was prepared for that event, but not for the possibility that Johnny might cast his lot with theirs, nor had he told the boy that part of the plan.

A wolf howled in the timber far away. Much nearer, kiotes on the other side of the village answered, the eerie warbling song of the pack rising and falling and echoing from the hills before dying out. The day was getting on when the kiotes sang for their supper. Time to be getting back to Putnam's Park. He held an arm straight out and measured the height of the sun. The width of two palms separated the blinding disk from the western ridge. Two hours until sunset, three until dark. Above him the sky was still unblemished. The air, which should already have been taking a chill that would deepen quickly as night fell, remained strangely warm. A change was coming, and it could only be a change for the worse after a day like this one. He took a deep breath and wished he could drink in the whole sky.

The next move was up to Sun Horse and the council. Until they gave their answer Hardeman could only wait, but no matter what they decided there could be no turning back now.

He swept his eyes around the narrow valley for a final time to set the picture in his mind. When he first arrived, he had noticed the trail that went away to the north, leaving the valley beyond the little lake at the far end. That would be a better way for the cavalry to approach, so they need not pass through Putnam's Park. If Sun Horse would not surrender, Hardeman would slip away alone to intercept Crook on his march up the old Bozeman road and he would bring the soldiers here to surround the village in the dark of night and capture the horse herd without a shot while the warriors were still groggy with sleep. Sun Horse and his people would be taken to the Red Cloud Agency under guard, and word would be sent to the hostile bands that the great man was on his way to the reservation after a peaceful surrender in which not a man had been harmed. With the right words of persuasion, at least some of the hostiles would go in, and by the time they learned that Sun Horse had been taken by surprise it would be too late for further resistance.

Crook was the key to the plan. Without him the risk would be far too great. He had no love of senseless bloodshed and his reputation was that of a man who made and kept the peace, not one who sought his own glory in battle. In Arizona he had sent riders dashing throughout the department to call an immediate halt to further military actions the instant the proud Apache headmen said they would sit down and talk peace. He knew how to talk to Indians and he had pacified the most feared corner of the Southwest with straight talk and a conviction that if Indians were treated fairly they would come to see the fruits of living in tranquillity side by side with the white men. With Crook in command and Hardeman to lead him, for once there would be a bloodless surrender.

He started across the camp with the two horses, and then he saw the smoke.

From the ridge that formed the eastern boundary of the valley, a column of smoke rose straight into the air, lit by the golden glow of the lowering sun, a white pillar against the spotless blue, growing taller by the moment. Now the smoke was interrupted, and Hardeman made out a figure on the ridge. The man moved, a blanket or robe flying in his hands, and again the smoke puffed up, the signal visible as far as the eye could see.

CHAPTER EIGHT

Sun Horse stepped out of his lodge into the dark and walked beyond the camp circle to relieve himself. The snow did not squeak beneath his moccasins as it had the night before. The air was damp; perhaps it would snow tomorrow. He was grateful for the relative warmth of the evening; he was in his sixty-ninth winter and no longer shook off the cold as a young man might. He opened his robe and pulled aside his loincloth to urinate in the snow.

To the west the crescent moon lowered its slender blade into a bank of clouds that breathed and moved closer as he watched. This was the Moon of Sore Eyes, the Snowblind Moon, when the sun rose higher each day to shine off the lingering snows and a man's eyes became red and painful from long days spent hunting far from camp.

Delay.

The feeling came over Sun Horse suddenly. Delay. The people and the horses were not strong enough to fight Three Stars' soldiers, but neither were they strong enough to flee to the larger encampments of Crazy Horse and Sitting Bull, nestled somewhere in the river bottoms near the Yellowstone. That afternoon, Sun Horse had directed that a signal should be sent, in the hope that it might be seen and relayed, so the people there should know that soldiers were coming soon. For a moment he had wished that he and his people were with the northern bands, but even with strong horses such a journey would be dangerous now. In the Snowblind Moon the weather changed suddenly and often; a village on the move, lulled into carelessness by springlike warmth, could find itself suddenly enveloped in stinging snow that seemed to leap out of the ground itself, obscuring everything in the space of a few breaths. It was not safe to travel in the Snowblind Moon.

Delay.

Lisaputnam had advised the same thing that afternoon. "Find a way to put Crook off," she had said, her voice full of urgency. "Tell him you will come to the agency in the spring. Tell him anything, but don't leave this country now or you will never get it back!" He could hear her voice still, feel the touch of her hand on his arm, and the strength of this white woman who stood alone, leaning on no man. "Stay here for one more year without fighting the soldiers and there will be a new government in Washington—a new President and men with new ideas. They will have a new Indian policy, I am sure of it."

"And will they leave us in peace?" Sun Horse had asked in English, although she had spoken in Lakota.

He had learned the whiteman's tongue long ago, so as to understand them in council and speak to them there. In his own village he used English rarely; it was not a language well suited to expressing Lakota thoughts. But he had used it without thinking, speaking of the *washíchun,* and Lisaputnam had replied in the same tongue.

"My father believed that if the Lakotas could keep this land until President Grant left office, there might be a chance to keep the Powder River country forever."

If a whiteman like her father were the Great Father in *Washing-ton,* then perhaps . . . But Sun Horse knew the futility of trusting one *washíchun* to right the wrongs done by another. Had not this man Grant proclaimed his respect for the red men when he was raised to power? "The Indians have a right to live," he had said. But his promises had not brought peace to the Lakota, nor the certainty that they would be able to continue living in the way of their grandfathers. Sun Horse had spent much time learning what he could of the whites, and still he understood so little. Only that over the years there was little difference between one President and his successor, or between the men who made up one council of government and the next. In the end they acted as whitemen always acted, like the thunderclouds that roamed the mountains in summer—inconsistent, unpredictable, striking out without warning.

Delay. It was the first certain feeling he had had since hearing Three Stars' message; but as soon as it came, the sureness gave way to questions. How to delay? And to what end?

The winter moons were usually the most contented

of the year, women happy because the men were in the lodges instead of off hunting or at war. Winter was a time for storytelling and quiet talk over the shared smoking of a pipe as the men visited from lodge to lodge. But this winter there had been little peaceful talk. There was too much concern for the sacred Black Hills—the *Paha Sapa*—and the thieves' road that the bluecoat chief Long Hair had made two summers before, now crowded with men rushing into the hills to dig for the yellow metal that made whitemen crazy. And there was worry of a more immediate kind, for the children and the old ones, in whose eyes the beginnings of hunger could be seen. The supply of dried meat from the fall hunt had been small, the hunt not very successful, and the meat was almost gone. Daily the hunters went out, but they brought in little meat. Even during the thaw, the buffalo and elk and deer—the four-legged brothers that provided the Lakota with all their needs—had been absent from their accustomed feeding grounds.

The talk in the lodges touched often on these misfortunes and the threat of war with the whites, and the people turned to Sun Horse for counsel and leadership.

But Sun Horse had been silent.

"The Great Mystery perhaps turns away from the Sun Band," Sees Beyond had suggested, but he had spoken the thought softly to Sun Horse, not openly to the people. Like Sun Horse himself, Sees Beyond was a *wichasha wakán,* a man who sought to understand the spirit world, that realm of powers, great and small, that lay all around and within the visible world of living creatures. The younger *wichasha wakán* was a mystic, often retreating to the high places where a man could feel the strength of the earth and sky most strongly. Sees Beyond took no part in the affairs of the band, the decisions about when to move and where to go or what course to take.

"We live as the Lakota have always lived," Sun Horse had answered. "There is no game because there is no game. In some seasons the four-leggeds are not so numerous." Sun Horse had trained Sees Beyond, whose power now grew so different from his own. The younger man seemed almost to dwell in the spirit world, while Sun Horse used all his abilities to guide the people through this life, in harmony with the powers that touched the lives of men. Sees Beyond had surpassed him in some ways, he knew, and he had felt the beginnings of uncertainty about the true reasons for the Sun Band's misfortunes. Perhaps it was true, perhaps *Wakán Tanka*, the Great Mystery at the center of all things, had turned away from the band, but Sun Horse could offer no course that would bring meat to the lodge, not until the snows melted and the new grass was up and the horses grew strong again.

And now came word that a white soldier chief would give meat to the Sun Band if they would go to the Dakota reservation. Soon the council would meet to decide. War or surrender, or hopeless flight. The councillors would speak and express their anger, and they would turn to Sun Horse for guidance.

Perhaps the headmen who had long since gone to the agencies were right. There was no way to fight the overwhelming power of the whites, they said. Red Cloud himself was there now, at the agency that bore his name. He had been twice to *Washing-ton*, traveling the iron road, and it seemed he had become like a whiteman himself. Little Wound was there, and Spotted Tail, the uncle of Crazy Horse. Even Man Afraid of His Horses had gone. He was Oglala of the Hunkpátila band, like Crazy Horse, and once he had been a great leader in peace and war. Make the best bargain with the whitemen, these leaders said, and work hard to see that the whites keep their word.

But how to be sure a whiteman would keep his word? Some were honorable, to be trusted as one might trust a Lakota who gave his promise. But the others . . . There was a saying among the Lakota: "The promises of the *washíchun* are like the wind in the buffalo grass."

Over the years Sun Horse had watched the advance of the whites, keeping his people removed from the spreading conflict. Like a war leader, he had watched the battle from afar, so as to see all its parts. But now the battle drew near and he could no longer remain aloof.

He straightened his breechcloth. The last fragment of the moon sank into the approaching clouds and the air turned cooler, as if the tiny fingernail of a moon had provided the warmth that Sun Horse had found so pleasant only a moment before.

He turned to look at the camp, taking pleasure in the glow from each tipi, the quiet and the calm. A village at peace. He stretched out his arms to encircle the lodges, seeking to protect them. More than anything else he wanted to preserve the peace he felt in this place. But how? The chill of his indecision was more discomforting than the dank night air. For years he had been preparing himself for this moment, following the power of his vision, and now his power seemed to have left him, leaving him alone, not knowing which way to turn. He was like a tree in a dead calm, seeking any hint of a breeze to sway him one way or another.

Twenty-five snows had fallen since the summer of his vision. It was a warm summer; his name was Stands Alone then, and his father, Branched Horn, was still alive. Branched Horn had led his band of Hunkpapa to the fort called Laramie for a great council with the whites, and there Stands Alone had seen for the first time the stream of whites flowing westward in their wagons, the dust constantly drifting this way and that on the summer breezes. He had been fascinated by this endless journeying, all in one direction. In less time than it took for one moon to grow fat he had seen more whites pass westward before his eyes than all the Lakota who lived in all the lodges of all the bands, and he felt a growing certainty that his destiny was linked to these pale strangers from the east. One day, without telling anyone, he made *inipi*, the cleansing ritual that preceded all ceremonies, and then he went to a little hill overlooking the wagon road to seek a vision. *Hanbléchiyapi*—they cry for a vision—the Lakota called this quest, and it was usually performed when a youth became a man. A young man went alone to some high place for days and nights without food, praying for a promise of power. If the Great Mystery heard, the reply might be borne in a hundred forms, by a cloud or a puff of wind, by an insect, a bird or an animal, some creature that in the years that followed would be a special helper to the man. Stands Alone had performed the ceremony in his sixteenth year, but he had seen nothing; after five nights alone on a rocky butte in the Black Hills he had finally returned to his people weak and ashamed, with no vision to tell. Even so, he had become *pezhuta wichasha*, a man who cured sickness with roots and herbs, and later *wapíye*, a healer. His lack of a vision seemed less important then, for practicing these callings would have been impossible without the favor of the spirits, who were all but separate aspects of the One Spirit at the center of everything—*Wakán Tanka*. Branched Horn was *wichasha wakań*, a holy man, and he gladly instructed his son in matters of the spirit world; he encouraged the young man and urged him to make the vision-quest again when he felt that the time was right.

There at Fort Laramie Stands Alone had been certain that the time for his vision had come. Sitting naked atop the small hill he had prayed continuously to the four quarters, to *Wakán Tanka* above and the earth below, asking for the vision that had been denied him in his youth. And on the morning of the fourth day it had come to him, the horse from which he took his new name, running to him out of the sun, bearing a promise of power. He had followed the vision to this valley where he and his people had wintered for twenty-five years. The band had become his on the day following his vision, as he had become Sun Horse, for on that same day his father had passed the leadership to him. Over the years the band had been strengthened by lodges from other bands, men and women who had heard of Sun Horse's vision and wished to live under his leadership, and for twenty-five years he had brought them to spend each winter here, beyond the corrupting influence of the whites, beyond the reach of their whiskey and diseases, yet close enough to learn their ways with the help of Jed Putnam, a truthful whiteman.

Even before he had walked down off the hilltop to tell his vision to Branched Horn, Sun Horse had understood its meaning. His power was to understand the true nature of the whites, and to lead his people to live in peace with them. Since that day his understanding had increased steadily and his people had remained at peace. Yet now a *washíchun* soldier chief demanded that Sun Horse surrender or prepare to fight, and he could see no other choice before him.

The night had darkened as the moon set. The chill of the snow penetrated to Sun Horse's feet even through the fur-lined moccasins he wore. The clouds were advancing rapidly and only a few stars remained in view above the eastern ridges. Sun Horse gathered his robe tightly about him and made his way back to his lodge.

Inside the tipi a fire burned brightly. Sun Horse's elder wife, Elk Calf Woman, had built it up, knowing he would need to warm himself when he returned. Even as he entered, she was adding more wood, kneeling beside Johnny Smoker where he sat looking into the flames. At the rear of the lodge the younger wife, Sings His Daughter, was working a piece of mountain goatskin between her hands, softening it. She had saved it for more than a year, until Sun Horse should need a pair of summer moccasins that would resist the brambles and thorns when he walked alone on the mountainsides, as he liked to do. Sings His Daughter smiled shyly at her husband, still modest about showing affection in the presence of others.

Sun Horse looked at her kindly, and once again he

congratulated himself on his good fortune. With Elk Calf he had enjoyed almost fifty years of contentment, despite their occasional differences, and now that she was getting old he had taken a second wife to help her with the work. Standing Eagle had captured Sings His Daughter from the Crows two years ago, in the autumn, thinking to make her his second wife, but Willow Woman, Blackbird's mother, would have none of it. Standing Eagle had brought the young captive into his lodge, although not into his sleeping robes, but when it became clear that Willow Woman's jealousy would not subside, Sun Horse had arranged to marry the girl to preserve peace within his family and within the band. Sings His Daughter was young and strong, and she was very pretty. The enthusiasm she displayed in the privacy of her sleeping robes and the pleasure she gave Sun Horse were unexpected gifts she had brought to his life.

"You should not stay out so long," Elk Calf chided him, frowning.

"I like to look at the village at night," Sun Horse said, a little petulantly. He would not be scolded in front of his grandson. "It is quiet outside. I can think better there, away from all your talking."

"My talking! Hmp. I have hardly spoken since you returned from the council."

It was true. Elk Calf knew that Sun Horse was concerned about the message from Three Stars, and the second gathering of the council that would begin in a short while. She had motioned to Sings His Daughter to keep quiet as Sun Horse and his white grandson talked through the afternoon and into the evening, and between them the two women had spoken only a handful of words.

"I see the fires in the lodges and I know my people are warm," Sun Horse said, moving his elkhorn backrest a little closer to the fire. He sat back against the robe that covered the horn frame and he reached for his smoking pipe.

"They are warm, but they are hungry," Elk Calf said, taking her place at his left hand. She said it gently. She picked up the legging she was repairing with a new piece of deerskin. Sun Horse would not wear new leggings until his old ones were in tatters.

Sun Horse made no reply. This was his wife's way, reminding him, with a few well-chosen words, that all was not well with the band. Reminding him of his duty. *Let none grow hungry through the actions of a leader.* The Ancient Ones, the wisest Lakotas of past generations, had said this, the wisdom handed down over the years.

Elsewhere around the camp circle other wives were making their concerns known at this very moment. It was the men who met in council, but when they gathered in the council lodge the opinions of the women would be represented there, and no course would be adopted of which the women did not approve.

Sun Horse's people were hungry, and now they were threatened by war. How could he lead them away from both dangers? What would the council decide to do? What should he advise?

He filled his pipe carefully with a mixture of trade tobacco and red willow bark and lit it with a small stick from the fire. He smoked without ceremony, wishing only to calm himself, and while the pipe was still burning he passed it to the youth beside him.

Johnny Smoker was the source of his hope. Hand in hand with the soldier chief's message had come the miraculous return of Sun Horse's grandson, so long given up for dead, and what was more, his coming had been foretold.

Two nights before, Hears Twice had coughed softly outside Sun Horse's lodge. When he was invited in, he had sat quietly for a time, as if listening. Then, in signs, he had told Sun Horse what he heard. *Something comes,* he said. *A power is coming. It is very strong. It can help the Sun Band or destroy us. It grows from the meeting of two people.* That, and no more. This afternoon, at the moment when he had recognized his grandson, Sun Horse had felt sure that the young man was one of those the prophet had heard. But who was the other? Hears Twice did not know. Nor did Sun Horse, but he sensed a hidden power in the return of his grandson, something as yet formless, undirected.

Taku shkanshkan, the wise ones said. Something is moving. Something not of the world of men, and yet a part of it. Something unseen and unseeable, yet it could be felt. Sun Horse felt it now, as if the force that animated all living things had recently grown stronger.

The youth passed the pipe back now and Sun Horse set it aside to cool. He did not know what to call this grandson, even in his thoughts. To all appearances he was a whiteman, a stranger. Yet within him there were the memories of a boy who had lived with the people called *Shahíyela,* a boy Sun Horse had once known. Johnny Smoker, the whites called him, but other names demanded to be heard, names that recalled a young boy's dream, and a promise of power.

That afternoon, Sun Horse had drawn the young

man out, seeking to know what he had become in his years among the whites. Johnny had told of the places he had been and the things he had seen, speaking in English at Sun Horse's urging, using the whiteman's language to describe his life in the whiteman's world. His tales had confirmed much of what Sun Horse already knew—the limitless numbers of the *washíchun*, each one alone, without tribe or band, often without even a family, moving from one place to another for no reason that Sun Horse could understand. And although the youth placed no emphasis on such things, Sun Horse saw too the endless cleverness of the whites, and many examples of their power. Through it all, the young man's words revealed the constant presence of the man called Hardeman, guiding him and teaching him, showing him the way in a strange world, but leaving Johnny free to form his own opinions about the whites and their customs. He was fortunate to have had such a teacher.

At length, Sun Horse had turned Johnny's thoughts to his childhood, asking to hear about the years between the young boy's visit with his parents to the Lakota summer camp and Long Hair Custer's attack on Black Kettle's village at the Washita.

"I was proud to be *Tsistsístas*," Johnny had begun. The Cheyenne name for themselves meant the One People, the Real People, the word carrying a meaning that set them apart from other men. *Shahíyela*, the Lakota said, people who speak another tongue. The white name came from the Santee Lakota, who said *Shahíyena*.

"When I was a boy," Johnny said, "I was *Tsistsístas*, and I wished to be nothing else." He fell silent then, making an effort to remember, choosing his words with care, and when he spoke again it was in the Shahíyela language. The words came haltingly at first, and then more freely, the speech and images flowing from the same world. Occasionally he used a word of English or Lakota, or a few signs, when the Shahíyela words failed him.

It had been in the year the whites called 1864 when Johnny and his parents had summered with Sun Horse, and they had stayed on through the autumn, accompanying the band on the fall hunt. At last, late in the Moon of Falling Leaves, when the Sun Band had set out for their wintering place in the Big Horns, White Smoke and Grass Woman had taken their son and returned to Colorado to join the village of their people at Sand Creek.

There they found tragedy. Black Kettle's camp had been attacked by territorial militia and many were dead. Outraged by the attack, the *Tsistsístas* were preparing to take up arms against the whites throughout the eastern part of Colorado Territory, accompanied by their allies the Arapaho and the southern bands of Lakota. But Black Kettle would not fight. His first responsibility as a chief was to keep the peace, no matter what the provocation. He took his band away from the troubles, and in the years that followed, he remained at peace with the whites. White Smoke stood by Black Kettle's side and helped him calm the angry howls of the young men. In the autumn of 1868, Black Kettle and White Smoke went to Fort Cobb, in the Indian Territory, to seek the protection of the army, for there was new trouble following some raiding along the Solomon and the Saline. General Hazen, the officer in charge, denied

sanctuary to the Cheyenne, but Black Kettle understood that if he remained south of the Arkansas, he
would be safe from the bluecoats' punitive expeditions. He went into winter camp on the Washita,
close by the camps of Kiowa and Apache, Comanche
and Arapaho, and there Long Hair's soldiers found
him on a wintry morning in late November.

Here Johnny had paused, not sure he should continue, but Sun Horse had nodded to encourage him.
"I would hear how my son died," the old man had
said. Until now there had been none to tell him.
Others had been able to say only that the one called
White Smoke was gone, not the manner of his going.
And so Johnny had told him of the battle.

"The Lakota message-carrier Man Who Rides had
come to us that day, bringing word that the war in
the Powder River country was over and a new treaty
had been signed at Fort Laramie. We were glad that
the Lakota and *Tsistsístas* had won the war and the
whites had been made to leave our country there. I
think even my father was glad that we had won,
although he was a man of peace." Throughout the
telling, Johnny never spoke his father's name, for it
was not good to speak the names of the dead.

"There was a feast that night, and dancing, and
while we were dancing, a war party of Kiowas came
through the camp and told us they had been raiding
against the Utes. They had seen the tracks of many
soldiers not far away, but we were south of the
Arkansas and we were at peace, and we thought we
had nothing to fear.

"In the morning I was still in my robes when I
heard a shot. I thought one of the horse guards must
have shot a deer by the river, but then I heard many

horses approaching camp and someone shouted that soldiers were coming, and then I heard the bugles. My father and I jumped up and ran outside, and we saw soldiers crossing the river and others coming from another side. I saw the horses' breaths make steam in the cold air. 'My friends, do not fight them,' my father called out. 'We are at peace,' he said, but already the fighting was starting, and no one heard him. My father and I were both barefoot and we were hopping from one foot to the other to keep our feet from freezing, and I laughed because we looked foolish, but he told me to be quiet.

"Before long the soldiers were in the village and my father said, 'We must take your mother away where she will be safe.' So we brought my mother out of the lodge and started away to the south, but while we were still among the lodges we saw Black Kettle and his wife come out of their lodge and mount their horses, and we watched, hoping they would get away. But when they reached the river, Black Kettle was shot and his wife was killed when she went to help him. This made my father very angry. 'Now I must fight!' he said, and he ran into a lodge to find a weapon. My mother and I ran in after him. I wanted to fight too. There was no one in the lodge, but there were some weapons there and my father took a rifle and began to load it. I saw a bow and some arrows and I took them, but my father grabbed them from my hands. 'You must not fight,' he said. 'Remember your dream!' 'I am *Tsistsístas!*' I said. 'I will fight to protect the helpless ones!' But he would not let me go, and before I could say anything more there was shooting outside and bullets came into the lodge and struck both my father and my mother. I wanted to fight more than ever then, for my mother was dead and my father was dying, but still he would not let me go. 'Remember your dream,' he told me again, and then he died.''

Johnny had fallen silent then and the lodge was very quiet as Sun Horse and the two women had waited for the youth to continue.

After a time he said, ''When I saw him die, something inside me changed, and I did not want to fight anymore. I stayed with the bodies of my parents to protect them from the soldiers. When the soldiers attacked the village four winters before, on Sand Creek, they had cut the bodies of the dead, I was told, even the private parts of the women, and I would not let that happen to my parents. I was holding my mother's body when more bullets came into the lodge and struck me in the leg. Then a whiteman came through the entrance with a pistol in one hand and a knife in the other. He was not a soldier. He was dressed in buckskins and I knew he was one of the scouts who had led the soldiers to our camp. I thought he would kill me, but he looked at my mother and father and he saw the wound in my leg, and the fight went out of his eyes. He said something I didn't understand, for I had forgotten the English I knew as a child. Then he made signs, asking if I was white. I wanted to say I was *Tsistsístas*, but I remembered my father's words and I remembered my dream. I signed to him 'yes.' He picked me up and took me out of the lodge, into the whiteman's world.''

Again the boy had fallen silent, but then he had looked at Sun Horse, and Sun Horse saw the trouble in his eyes. ''My father died because of me,'' Johnny had said. "If he had not stopped to talk to me he might have gone outside and lived."

Sun Horse had shaken his head. "And he might have died there, fighting the soldiers." He had waited for more than seven years to hear this tale, and the strength of his son as a peace man gave him joy. "Your father was angry when he saw his friend shot down," he had said. "A great peace man dead at the soldiers' hands. But when he saw you prepare to fight he forgot his anger and he reminded you of your dream. And so he died as a man of peace must die, trying to stop fighting with his last breath."

Sun Horse had risen then and suggested to his grandson that he remain for the night, and together they had gone off to Hears Twice's lodge to send Lisaputnam and Hardeman on their way, Sun Horse smiling and enjoying the warmth of the afternoon, keeping to himself the stunning effect of the boy's tale.

It was the manner of telling, rather than the story itself, that gave Sun Horse pause. At first, Johnny had spoken as a whiteman might, making no distinction between things that he knew from his own experience and things he had heard or been told. But soon there had come a change in the way he spoke, and by the time he related the battle and the death of his father, he told the tale exactly as a Lakota or Shahíyela might have done. Both peoples had strict customs that governed how a man conveyed something he knew whenever he spoke of matters that were important to the people, for such events became part of the history of the bands. A man told only what he knew from his personal knowledge, and no more. If possible, one or more witnesses stood by to correct any errors in the telling and to prevent boastful embellishments. For eight winters the youth who was now called Johnny Smoker had been among the whites, speaking only English and hearing only the careless way of talk that was the white custom, yet here in a single afternoon he had fallen naturally into a manner of storytelling that was careful and correct in the Lakota manner, and wherever he had touched on matters Sun Horse had heard told by others, every detail was exact.

Now, sitting beside his grandson once more in the warm lodge, Sun Horse reached again for his pipe. While his hands were busy with the familiar task of filling the bowl with the smoking mixture, he turned to the youth and spoke in Shahíyela.

"Your friend the whiteman. Why has he come here?"

"He came because I asked him to come," Johnny replied. "It was he who went to Three Stars and asked that you be given a chance to surrender. He hopes the other headmen may surrender too when they hear what you have done and know you were not harmed by the soldiers. He came because I asked him to come, but he has also come to make peace."

Sun Horse pondered this for a time, and then he said, "And you. You have come because of your dream?"

Johnny nodded. Except to mention it in telling of his father's death, he had said nothing of his dream, or why he had come.

"I am an old man," Sun Horse said, lighting the pipe. "I do not remember so well anymore. Tell me again of your dream, whatever you remember."

The truth was that Sun Horse remembered his

grandson's dream very well. It loomed in his memory as sharp and clear as his own vision from the hill overlooking the Laramie fort. All afternoon he had circled around and around, approaching this thing; above all he wished to hear how well the youth remembered the dream, and what it meant to him.

As he had done that afternoon, Johnny gathered himself for a time, preparing himself to speak. "It was in the summer when we visited the Lakota," he said at last. "We arrived in the Moon of Ripe Cherries, when the young moon still had horns." He located the story in time, as a Lakota would always do when speaking of events long past. "We had been in the camp for four nights, and on the morning of the fifth day I awoke before my parents and I did not know where I was for a little while because I had had a strange dream. I dreamed I was standing alone in the middle of a plain. To one side, at a great distance, stood all the Real People and Lakota, all the men and women of both nations, and they were calling out to me, but I could not understand the words. To the other side, also at a great distance, stood white men and women covering the land as far as I could see. They too were calling to me, but I could not understand the words. Then from far away on the plain, something approached me, walking between the two peoples. As it came near, I saw that it was a white buffalo cow. She spoke to me so that I heard the words not with my ears but only in my thoughts, and she said, 'You are standing between the worlds. You live with the Real People now, but in time you will return to live among the whites. When you are about to become a man you will decide to which people you belong, and until then you shall fight no man, red or white, lest you kill your brother.' I looked to either side and I saw that all the people had disappeared, and when I looked back at the buffalo cow I saw a beautiful young woman standing there. She smiled at me and turned to walk away and then she became a buffalo again and walked until I could see her no more.''

Sun Horse was shocked to the center of his being, and it took all of his control to remain calm. A leader of the people must be calm. Only in calm could a leader decide what was best for the people.

The words were the same. The dream had been told now just as the young boy had told it twelve years before. Only the voice had changed, that of a man replacing the voice of a boy, and within the words Sun Horse heard the voice of Little Warrior, the White Boy of the Shahíyela, speak again. Word for word the two tellings were the same.

"Have you lived as the dream said you should?" Sun Horse asked, his voice calm.

"I returned to the white world when my mother and father were killed at the Washita, and since then I have carried no weapons nor fought any man."

Sun Horse nodded calmly, as if this were no more than he expected, but his thoughts were anything but calm. From the dream the boy had been given two names: He Stands Between the Worlds, to remind both peoples, Lakota and Shahíyela, that he did not truly belong to them, and he was also called Empty Hand, so all should know he would fight no man. I gave him names, Sun Horse reminded himself, not one but two, passing on to him the custom of my family that each man shall take a name from his vision-dream if it has sufficient power. But I did not truly believe in the power of this dream. No white child could dream of *Ptésanwin*, the White Buffalo Cow Woman, who brought the sacred pipe to the Lakota and showed us how to use it. *Ptésanwin*, the greatest figure from the old tales, could not come to a white child in a dream. So I believed in my heart.

Why?

Only because the boy was white, and that is why I am a fool. Who is to say that a boy born white shall not have a dream of power if he is raised among the Lakota or Shahíyela, or even among the Pawnee or Crow or Blackfeet? Lakota children raised by the whites do not have dreams of power. They lose touch with the spirit world and become almost like whitemen. Shall a white child living among the Shahíyela or Lakota retain only the powers of a white child? Power is in the life we live.

But I doubted the dream when the boy told it to me, and when I heard he had died, I believed it to be so and I forgot the dream.

There in the Lakota encampment, that summer when the boy was young, Sun Horse had been so moved by the dream that he had gone to tell it to his cousin Sitting Buffalo Bull, himself a spiritual man who dreamed often of what was to be.

"If he has truly dreamed this," Sitting Bull had said, "he is Buffalo Dreamer."

Sun Horse had nodded. Already the boy was called by so many names. Little Warrior and White Boy of the Shahíyela, and now Empty Hand and He Stands Between the Worlds. Buffalo Dreamer was not a name, but it was an obligation, more than it seemed a boy of eight winters should have to bear.

"He is white, yet he is Shahíyela," Sitting Bull

had continued, very serious. "But if his dream of *Ptésanwin* leads him in time to give up the white world, it will not be to the Shahíyela that he returns. *Ptésanwin* is Lakota. She brought us the pipe and taught us how to live. If the boy chooses to return he will live among the Lakota, and he will bring the power of *Ptésanwin* to help the people."

Sun Horse had told the boy none of what Sitting Bull had said. They had decided this between them, the two holy men. If the boy chose the Lakota world, he would be told then, so he would understand his responsibility to use his power for the good of the people, but first he must make his choice freely, unburdened by any sense of obligation.

In the Moon of Falling Leaves, before White Smoke and Grass Woman and their son had gone off to the south, Sun Horse had made the boy promise to return to see him when it came time for him to choose between the worlds. "I will come, Grandfather," the boy had promised solemnly.

And now he had returned. The prophecy of *Ptésanwin* had come to pass. Which world would the young man choose?

As soon as he asked himself the question, Sun Horse knew that Johnny had already made his choice, and he knew that he had chosen the white world. Surely if he had decided to live with the Lakota he would have said something before now. But he had said nothing of his dream until Sun Horse brought it up, and yet he remembered it perfectly. And Sun Horse recalled now a certain reserve in the young man, an occasional unwillingness to meet his grandfather's eyes, as if he were embarrassed or ashamed. So he had chosen the white world. And he had no

reason to be ashamed; he had been among the whites
for seven years, while his Shahíyela childhood was
far behind him. But even so, Hears Twice had pre-
dicted power in the boy's coming! *It is very strong. It
grows from the meeting of two people.* . . . Was he,
Sun Horse, the one who would join with the young
man? Sun Horse the Lakota meeting the One Who
Stands Between the Worlds, even though the youth
had chosen to remain white? If the power of the
Lakota could be joined with that of the *washíchun*,
what might then be accomplished? Anything at all . . . !

But Sun Horse felt certain that he was not the one.
He sensed no new power in himself, nothing to
match that brought by the young man. Who was it
then? And would the power from this meeting help
Sun Horse's people or destroy them? Could he have a
hand in determining that, at least?

For a moment he wished he knew what the future
would bring. But it was not his power to foresee
what was yet to come. The spirits knew all that had
been done and all that would be done, the Ancient
Ones said. It was given to some men to hear what the
spirits had to tell about events yet to come. Hears
Twice was one of these, and Sitting Bull foresaw the
future in dreams. But Sun Horse dealt with events of
the past and present, with what he knew and what he
saw before him, and in this lay his strength as a
leader.

He wished his cousin Sitting Bull were nearby
now, so they could visit and talk again of the boy's
dream. But the Hunkpapa was far to the north, many
days' travel, too dangerous in the Snowblind Moon
with soldiers riding down the Powder. If Three Stars
found Sitting Bull's camp, the soldier chief would

attack and Sitting Bull would fight. Perhaps it would be easier that way, not knowing of the approach of the horse soldiers, simply to spring from the lodges and fight, perhaps to die in defense of the camp. It was good to die for the people, the Ancient Ones had said so.

If he were not attacked, Sitting Bull would still choose war. He was of the bands that had fought the whites at every turn, driving them from the soldier forts on the Bozeman road, harassing them along the Yellowstone three summers ago when they came there to mark the ground for an iron road like the one in the south, going in recent moons with Crazy Horse, the strange man of the Oglala, to fight the miners who dug in the sacred *Paha Sapa*. Sitting Bull's young men would demand to fight once they knew that soldiers were coming to the Powder River country. Perhaps they already knew, if the riders from the agencies had found Sitting Bull's camp in the Moon of Popping Trees. A rider had reached Sun Horse's village, but many had believed the message ordering the Lakota to the agencies was false, sent by white traders in the hope that more bands would come to trade for iron pots and colored cloth and *mni wakán*, the burning water that took a man's mind for a time and left him weak and easy to anger.

Now Sun Horse knew the message was true. The hunting bands had not gone in and the soldiers were coming, and so he had ordered the signal sent from the ridgetop to warn others of the bluecoats' approach. Perhaps even now Sitting Bull was preparing to trap them in some wooded draw on the Tongue or on the creeks of the Rosebud. Sooner or later, Sitting Bull would fight, Sun Horse was sure, and he was just as sure that to fight the whites was to fight the whirlwind.

A turning point had been reached and a choice was demanded. What was the power his grandson brought? How could it be used for the good of the people? To these questions Sun Horse could give no answers. Still his only certainty was the need for delay.

The fire fell in on itself, one log rolling up against the ring of stones that lined the pit. Sun Horse prodded it back onto the coals and added more wood. For some time he had been aware of sounds coming from outside the lodge, men moving about the camp, and he had recognized the voices of the principal men as they moved towards the council lodge. Now the camp was quiet. The council awaited him.

He put the clamor of his unresolved thoughts suddenly to rest and rose to his feet. He went quickly around the fire, then bent low and stepped out of the lodge, closing the entrance flap carefully behind him.

CHAPTER NINE

Elk Calf Woman rose as Sun Horse left the lodge. Sings His Daughter had already gone to her sleeping robes and the old woman moved to her own pallet now, smiling at Johnny as he glanced at her. Elk Calf's hair was white and her skin was as brown and wrinkled as her husband's. Johnny wished he could speak to her, but she understood no Cheyenne and he remembered little of the Lakota he had learned as a youth.

He had almost called out as Sun Horse left, to make the old man stop and hear what he had to say. Half a dozen times during the afternoon and evening he had tried to tell why he had come, and each time his tongue had failed him. I have chosen the white world, he had wanted to say. It was simple enough, but for the past few days it seemed he couldn't find the words to talk to anyone about what was on his mind, not to Chris, not to his grandfather, the old man he remembered and yet did not know.

This morning, when he and Chris had arrived in the Lakota camp, the decision had seemed right enough. He had seen the hungry dogs and the weakness of the people, and everything so unexpectedly primitive. The tipis that had been spacious for a young boy seemed smaller now, and unpleasantly smoky on such a calm day. Most of all, Sun Horse was not as Johnny had remembered him. Throughout the afternoon he had struggled without success to associate the old man who sat beside him in the lodge with the imposing figure he had approached with such awe as a young boy. He had been about to tell the old man of his choice then, when he judged that enough time had passed for him to tell his true reason for coming, but then a horse had neighed softly somewhere beyond the edge of camp.

The sound had awakened in Johnny's memory a sharp image of his boyhood, from the day when he and his parents had drawn near the great Lakota gathering where he had met his grandfather for the first time. White Smoke had given him his first horse for the trip north and he had ridden it proudly, ranging out in front of his father and mother like a scout, but always keeping within their sight. When he topped a rise and saw the peaks of the Lakota tipis in the river plain below, set among the dense cottonwoods, his pony had neighed, catching the scent of the Lakota horse herds, and he had reined in, awestruck by the size of the encampment. It was not a gathering of all the Lakota bands, but the Cheyenne were few compared with the Lakota and their camps not so large, even in summer. Johnny had kicked his pony's ribs and galloped down the grassy slope; even then he was a better horseman than most boys his age and he was proud of his skill, so highly prized among the Cheyenne. He swung down to peer from beneath his horse's neck, imagining that he was charging on a camp of Crows or Snakes. An *akíchita* rode out to meet him, one of the marshals that guarded the camp. Seeing that the attacking rider was only a boy, the man allowed him to enter the encampment at the run, whooping with glee. The *akíchita* laughed, and called out, "Look, the Shahíyela send their warriors to make war on the Lakota." A few lodges of Real People were with the Lakota and they took the boy for one of their own. He was tanned from years in the sun and covered with dust from the journey. One man had recognized him, but he said only, "This is the son of White Smoke and Grass Woman. He is called Little Warrior," and Johnny had been proud to be a Real Person and a boy who was growing up fast. He had joined the other boys in their rough games and he had held his own, despite his slight build. Even as a small boy he had displayed the same temperament, his father said, always ready to stand up to any challenge. On the day the Cheyenne war-

riors found him, in a wagon abandoned by the fleeing
emigrants, he had pointed his hand at the Indians like
a make-believe pistol, and he had shouted "Bam!
Bam!" "He is a brave little warrior," White Smoke
had observed, and so the boy had received his childhood name.

But within a few days of arriving at the Lakota
summer camp, Johnny had given up his childhood
name and his life had been changed forever by a
dream.

This afternoon the call of a Lakota pony had brought
back these memories. The gentle light of the sun
filtering through the lodgeskins had become suddenly
familiar then, and Johnny had felt a comfort he had
not known for a long time.

Now, as he listened to the soft breathing of the two
sleeping women and the gentle hiss of a damp log in
the fire, the feeling returned as if he had summoned
it, familiar and comforting. But as soon as it returned, the sense of belonging abandoned him, leaving him alone once more, and he did not seek to
recapture it.

He had not come here to recall his boyhood or to
regain a feeling of being at home among the Sioux.
Since leaving Kansas he and Chris had talked a great
deal about what lay ahead for the Sioux, and Johnny
could see no way out for Sun Horse and the hostiles;
they would have to go in now, or lose everything if
they fought the army. He had told the council as
much, reluctantly, wishing he and Chris could have
brought some other message. But there was no escaping it. One way or another, the Sioux would all be
living on the Dakota reservation before long, with no
pleasant wooded camping places and no quiet springs

where the buffalo came to drink. By the look of things, there might soon be no buffalo left at all in Dakota or anywhere else. The northern herds were being thinned out fast by the hide hunters, Chris said, and down in Indian Territory you could go from one season to the next without seeing fresh tracks. With the buffalo gone, the life Johnny had known in his childhood would disappear. He had cast his lot with his own race, whose future seemed bright, but the confidence he had felt in his decision back in Kansas eluded him now.

It had all been so clear to him in Ellsworth. He had made up his mind and set out to tell the grandfather he had not seen in twelve years that he had chosen to remain in the white world, where a man could go where he wanted and do as he wished, where Johnny had come to understand what the whites meant when they spoke of freedom and a man's right to choose his own way. He had come to say that he valued that freedom as his own now and could never give it up. It was something that had been growing in him, becoming a part of him, ever since he got his first job breaking horses for a white man.

He and Chris had been together for a year and a half when Chris took a job with a former Confederate major who was about to set out for Abilene with three thousand Texas Longhorns. At first the major hadn't wanted to take Johnny along. The boy wasn't strong like some of the youths he had accepted for the drive, the major said; he was still a tad young for drover's work. Instead the major offered to let Johnny do odd jobs around the ranch until he and Chris Hardeman returned from Kansas.

In a corral nearby, three men were breaking horses

that would go into the remuda; the major had the most cattle in the herd and it was up to him to provide the cow horses that all the drovers would ride. The horses in the corral had been halfway broken by the simple methods used by men who had little time to accomplish a job that should have taken months of steady work, but they were sturdy animals and showed promise, Johnny thought. The wranglers were fighting a stubborn horse that had picked today to refuse the saddle or even the blanket, while the major's young son watched from atop the fence. Johnny had walked to the corral and asked, "You mind if I try?"

The wranglers had got a good laugh out of that, but when they saw that Chris Hardeman's quiet young companion was serious they had agreed quickly enough. They didn't mind a chance to sit on the fence and be entertained by this kid who thought he could do a man's job, not if the boss was willing. Johnny had taken the reins and talked softly to the animal in Cheyenne for a time, too softly to be overheard by the others. Then he had led the animal to the gate.

"Don't turn him loose!" one of the wranglers cried out. "He's rope shy! It'll take us all day to fetch him back!"

Johnny paid no attention, opening the gate against the man's protests, leading the horse away from the noise and scents of the corrals, away from the other penned horses stamping nervously, and then he had mounted the animal bareback and ridden him at a gallop around the house and corrals and bunkhouse, slowing him to a lope and finally a trot before coming to a stop by the corral again, where he had saddled him and handed the reins to one of the speechless men.

"All right, son, you've a way with horses," the major had said. "Tell me what you think of that animal there." He pointed to a small corral where two horses were penned apart from the others. The horse in question had one front foot resting toe-down on the ground.

"He's got a bruised bone," Johnny said after examining the animal's leg and hoof. "I don't know what it's called. This one here."

"The pastern."

"If you say so. He'll be all right if you don't let anyone ride him for a while. Say eight or ten days."

"What about the other one?"

"You give him to your boy there. He'll be all right around the ranch. No good for long drives. Too narrow in the chest."

"You're a Yankee, I believe. No offense," the major said. "I happened to notice an accent in your speech. It's New England, am I right? Vermont, I'll wager."

"New Hampshire," Chris said, stonefaced, imagining what the major would have said if he had known that Johnny was still more at home speaking Cheyenne.

"Well, no matter if you're both Yankees," the major said. "By God, Hardeman, you must have raised the boy in a stable. He has surely got a way with horses." Chris had said nothing. "Damn it all, man, I can't put the boy in charge of the whole damn cavvyard!" the major had exclaimed, and Chris had grinned. Cavvyard was what Texans called the remuda, which was what the Spaniards called a bunch

of horses. The profusion of tongues among the whites
had not surprised Johnny, not after living with the
Cheyenne and Sioux and Arapaho.

"Just let me work with the horses," Johnny had
said, and the major had agreed. From Texas to Kansas five years running, working with horses had been
Johnny's doorway into the white world. Wherever he
and Chris had gone, there were always horses, draft
horses and cattle horses, horses for work of many
kinds, and even on the frontier they were sometimes
kept purely for pleasure, and a young man who could
gentle and train them quicker than most, with no
harsh words or brutality, was always in demand.
Johnny had marveled that a skill he took for granted
was so valued by the whites, and over the years he
had come to see that his way with horses could take
him wherever he wanted to go. He could stay in any
place as long as he liked, and when he wanted to
move on he could pack up and leave, sure of finding
work in the next place that struck his fancy, and in
the end it was this sense of being his own man that
had made him choose to remain among the people of
his birth, living as one of them.

There had been no single moment when Johnny
had made his decision. Rather it was as if it had been
made for him some time back and left for him to
discover. He had discovered it two weeks ago in
Ellsworth and he had told Chris about it the same
day. That morning, at the stables where he worked, a
cattle buyer from Chicago had offered him a job. The
man was raising racehorses and he wanted Johnny to
come and work for him as a trainer. Johnny had said
he would have to think on it, and as he pondered the
offer that afternoon, it struck him that there was no

reason he should not take the job. Chris would want nothing to do with a place like Chicago, but Johnny had never seen a big city. Why not go by himself? He had found the thought exhilarating. He could get the feeling of standing on his own two feet with no one to look out for him, and after a time he and Chris could hook up again as equal partners, man to man.

With that realization, he had become a free man. The understanding of his independence was simple and strong, like something he should have known long before. "How will I know when it's time?" he had asked Chris when they were first together, and Chris had said, "You'll know. And then you won't need me anymore." He hadn't really intended to say anything to Chris about his new feeling, not until he had more time to be sure of it, but in the evening after supper the words had just come out of him as if they were said by someone else, and the minute they were out, Johnny had felt proud of himself.

But before he could accept a job in Chicago or anywhere else he had an obligation to fulfill, and so he had turned the cattle buyer down and he and Chris had set out for the Big Horns to find Sun Horse. He had thought at first to come alone, but the truth was, he had been a little afraid of that notion. One white man riding by himself into the heart of the Sioux hunting grounds might not get a chance to say who he was or why he had come, if he were taken by surprise. Two men would have a better chance, he had reasoned. Chris was a scout and he knew how to deal with the Indians, and so Johnny had asked him to come along, glad of the chance to make this last journey with his partner before setting out on his own.

And then yesterday morning down in the willows below Putnam's Park, he had awakened with a strong desire for a sweat bath, although he had not had one for more than seven years. The urge had not struck him as strange. It was the simplest ritual of the plains people, practiced in a like manner by the Sioux and Cheyenne and many other tribes as well, a cleansing made in preparation for other ceremonies, before hunting, before any serious undertaking, and Johnny had performed it as a fitting preliminary to seeing his Sioux grandfather again. It had taken him only a short time to build the small structure and warm the rocks on the fire, and when he emerged from the heat and the steam he had felt renewed, ready to confront Sun Horse, ready for whatever might come. But it seemed to him now that he had washed away not only the stink of the towns and saloons but his deeper attachments to the white world as well, leaving himself cut adrift, his confidence in why he had come shaken and his memories of the Kansas town he had left only two weeks before unaccountably remote.

Elk Calf Woman stirred in her sleep. She rolled onto her back and began to snore softly. The wind shook the smoke flaps and blew the rising smoke back into the lodge. Johnny got up quietly and stepped outside to adjust the flaps. It was beginning to snow. Beyond the camp circle, the horses had turned their tails into the wind. To the east a few stars were visible, but the clouds were sending probing fingers out toward the plains, settling lower and snuffing out the stars one by one. It was not a true storm, Johnny knew. The clouds had formed around the mountain peaks in late afternoon and descended to the foothills as night fell. Tomorrow might dawn as clear as today, or the clouds might linger on for a day or two and drop a few inches of new snow on the mountains. Mountain squalls could be severe, even dangerous, while fifty miles away on the plains the sun shone brightly.

As he settled himself by the fire again, Johnny welcomed the warmth and the shelter. Once more the tipi and the fire and the sleeping women were all that was real, and it seemed to him that something deeper inside him than the thoughts a man turned over in his mind had pushed him to make the jump across the gulf that separated whites and Indians so he could feel comfortable once more in a smoky lodge, if only for a few fleeting moments. What was it that could push him so, almost against his will? It was a force beyond his control, something that moved him toward events he couldn't see on his own, something like the spirit power his grandfather had told him about all those years ago on the morning of his dream. "You have been given a promise," Sun Horse had said. "If you remain true to your dream, in time the power will touch you."

Could it be that such things were real after all? Hadn't the dream said he would leave the Cheyenne? And hadn't he left them at the Washita, feeling so rootless and alone at first, just the way he felt now. . . .

It was true! What he felt now was the same thing he had felt seven years ago as Chris Hardeman carried him from the lodge where his parents lay dead and away from the burning ruins of Black Kettle's village! . . . But he had overcome it then, and he had found a place for himself among the whites. Why did he have to bear it a second time? . . . Because his

grandfather had seen to it that he would come back!
"When it comes your time to choose between the
worlds, come to see me," Sun Horse had said, making him promise, knowing that to keep his promise
he would have to leave the white settlements behind
and return to the Lakotas, where all his old memories
would be awakened!

He had come back as he had promised, and now
he truly stood between the worlds.

In his own lodge Hears Twice sat quietly in his
accustomed place, facing the entrance across the fire.
It was called *chatkú*, the seat of honor, sometimes
given to a guest of high standing, usually occupied
by the man of the lodge. It had been offered with
unexpected deference to Hears Twice two winters
before, a few days after the old man had heard his
son-in-law complaining in the night to Mist that her
father was worthless. Hears Twice knew that his
daughter had demanded this concession in some way
Little Hand could not refuse, as a means of asserting
her father's place in the lodge. Usually he took pleasure and amusement at Little Hand's continued discomfort in this matter—the warrior was too proud,
and devoid of humor—but this evening Hears Twice
was as oblivious to such things as he was to the small
movements in the lodge as Mist prepared the sleeping
robes for her husband's return from the council. In
warmer weather Hears Twice would have sat outside
the camp circle, free from all distractions, as he did
when he listened to those special sounds only he
could hear—the sounds of what was to come—but
tonight even in the tipi he could sense the approach
of something he had first heard before his trip to the

white settlement, before the arrival of Sun Horse's grandson and the *washíchun* scout. The meeting he heard had not taken place yet, but it would happen soon, and what was still unseen drew steadily nearer.

CHAPTER TEN

The raiders struck in the dead of night when everyone in the camp was asleep, save for the herders and pickets. It was the second night of the march and the expedition was camped on the Dry Fork of the Cheyenne River, less than thirty miles from Fort Fetterman. The beef herder saw the horsemen first and he cried an alarm twice before a shot caught him square in the chest and hurled him from his horse.

Whitcomb was awakened by the herder's warning cries and when the first shots sounded he was already slipping into his buffalo greatcoat. It seemed to him that only moments had passed since he had been lying in his bedroll looking up at the fat crescent moon, which hung in the sky like something almost artificial. It was like a clever creation for a night scene on a theater stage, he had thought, a man-made moon lit from within by a coal-oil lamp. But no lamp ever burned as clear and bright. He realized that he must have dropped off to sleep soon after thinking those whimsical thoughts, for the moon was nearly touching the horizon now, its light silhouetting the fringe of pines on a low ridge ten miles west of the encampment.

Just after dark he had taken a last turn around the
E Troop bivouac to see that the horses were picketed
properly and the men had their "A" or dog tents set
up and sufficient bedding from the wagons. As long
as the column was in company with the supply wagons, the men would sleep in tents and there would be
extra blankets and robes and even crushed-cork mat-
tresses for some, but Whitcomb had decided to sleep
from the start as he would sleep throughout the campaign. Satisfied that everything was in order, he had
spread his bedroll out on the ground beyond the
company's twin rows of tents as he had done the
night before. The canvas strip in which his buffalo
robe was wrapped was laid down first, then a double
poncho of India rubber to ward off the dampness,
and then the robe itself, in which Whitcomb wrapped
himself thoroughly. After the trip from Fort Laramie,
when he had only the robe, his new accommodations
seemed the height of luxury. When the attack came
he discovered that there was an important advantage
to sleeping under the stars: he was the first man on
his feet, his new Army Colt in his hand, ready to
repel the attackers, while the rest of the company
struggled to escape the confines of their tents.

A shape loomed up beside him. "Report, Mr.
Whitcomb?"

He recognized Lieutenant Corwin in the dim moonlight. Corwin was in his field blouse and he too had a
pistol in his hand.

"Sorry, sir. I have no idea what caused the alarm."

"What in hell's going on?" came a shout from
across the camp.

"Indians!" someone answered.

"Where'd they go?"

"This way," came a cry from the left, and then, "Over here!" from the right.

First Lieutenant Francis Corwin, brevet major, had reddish-brown hair and tired eyes that sparked now with sudden life as the camp erupted in confusion around him. "Find Sergeant Dupré," he said calmly. "Tell him to get eight men mounted up and wait for my orders by the picket line. Tell Polachek to hold the rest of the men in a defensive perimeter and for Christ's sake not to shoot unless they have a clear target. When you've done that, report back to me."

"Yes, sir!" Whitcomb made as if to doff his cap in the traditional salute to a superior officer, but his Colt was in his right hand and he realized that the salute, which was a custom of the service, not a regulation, was a waste of time in battle. He ended the motion awkwardly, embarrassed by his own stupidity, then turned and set off down the tent line at a trot, determined to carry out his first order under fire in record time. He and Corwin had got off on the wrong foot and he was anxious to repair the damage as soon as possible.

Two days ago he had met Corwin in the officers' mess at Fetterman, already eating. "See me in my quarters after dinner," Corwin had said, and an hour later Whitcomb had reported to a tiny room in the Bachelor Officers' Quarters. Three iron bunks had been fitted into the small space in the effort to accommodate Crook's command on the post. The extra beds had displaced the usual folding and rawhide chairs, leaving as additional amenities only a pine washstand, a greenish looking-glass, a chromolithograph of the coast of Maine, and two chintz curtains. When Whitcomb appeared, Corwin had been forced to sit on his own bunk to receive his new subaltern after first pushing aside some books and his folded dress uniform.

"So you're the Rebel cadet," had been his opening words. Whitcomb had heard the hostility in his tone and his heart had fallen.

"Yes, sir," he had replied.

"If I had my way," Corwin had said, looking him in the eye, "no offspring of Rebel officers would be at West Point and sure as hell none would serve in this army. But then I don't have my way, do I?"

Whitcomb had ventured no answer to that question and after a moment Corwin had waved at the opposite bunk. "Sit down, Mr. Reb. Has anyone told you about the situation in this troop?"

Whitcomb nodded. On first hearing of "Major" Corwin from Lieutenant Bourke, Crook's aide, he had assumed that Corwin was E Troop's commander, but as he left the mess hall after the noon meal he had been intercepted by Bourke, who had taken him aside and informed him that Corwin was actually the troop's first lieutenant, although he had been brevetted a major during the war and had commanded a battalion at the time. It seemed that Company E's true commander, one Captain Alexander Sutorius, was under arrest at Fort D. A. Russell, the troop's permanent post, for chronic drunkenness, leaving Corwin in temporary command for the duration of the present campaign.

"Most officers make a great to-do about their brevet ranks," Bourke had said, "but not Boots Corwin. He won't insist you call him Major. I observe the courtesies and refer to him that way in General Crook's presence. I thought you should know what was what before you met him."

"I appreciate your taking the trouble to tell me, Mr. Bourke," Whitcomb had replied, genuinely grateful. Remaining ignorant of Corwin's position could easily have led him to put his foot in his mouth, and once he was there in the tiny room with Corwin he had been careful to give his superior no further cause for annoyance. Corwin seemed to find the mere fact of his Southern birth quite sufficient.

"We're on our own, Mr. Reb, just the two of us," Corwin had said. "But this troop is going to perform as if we had a full complement of officers. You may be a Rebel, but you're my Rebel now, so hear me well. We have good non-coms. First Sergeant Dupré and Sergeant Polachek and Corporal McCaslin are the backbone and the rest are good enough. They're all veterans. When you don't know what to do, and that will be most of the time, ask me or ask one of them. They may be wearing stripes, but they know a hell of a lot more than you do, and don't forget it. I will expect you to think for yourself when you have to, but when you're within reach of my orders you will follow them without question. I want that to be as clear as spring water. Understood?"

"Yes, sir," Whitcomb said again. Corwin had asked him a few questions then, about his duties since leaving West Point and why he wished to be a cavalryman, and finally he had dismissed him brusquely, leaving Whitcomb feeling that he had a black mark on his record before he even began, through no fault of his own.

He came upon a knot of men and made out Sergeant Polachek, the senior line sergeant, in their midst.

"Polachek!" he called out, lowering his voice as

he reached the man's side. "Form the men in a defensive line on the camp perimeter and tell them to hold their fire unless they have a definite target. Quick now."

"Yes, Leftenant. I haff already given such orders." Polachek had learned his English in England and his Middle-European accent was strangely tinged with British mannerisms.

"Where is First Sergeant Dupré?" Whitcomb demanded. "I have an order for him from Major Corwin."

The spare form of Corporal McCaslin appeared at his side. "He's took two men and gone to see after the horses, sorr. Just to be certain there's nothin' amiss there."

"Good. You take four more men and bring them to the picket line. You're to get them mounted and await the major's orders. I'll inform Sergeant Dupré."

Without waiting for a reply, Whitcomb turned and started off at a trot toward where the troop's horses were picketed. Each company's mounts covered a fair expanse of ground at the edge of camp. When the column halted for the night, each trooper rushed to stake his horse in the best grass available; planting a picket pin established his claim, which extended the length of a lariat in all directions, and woe to the trooper that staked an overlapping claim. In hostile country the mounts were usually hobbled on picket lines at dark, but no one had expected an attack this close to the Platte.

The camp was growing quiet as officers took control of their men. The campfires had been quickly smothered and the only light on the scene was supplied by the setting moon. Soft calls from one point to the next revealed that no one knew where the shots had come from, and on every side men looked fearfully about with guns held ready.

As Whitcomb approached E Troop's horses he could make out the beef herd beyond. The steers were bawling anxiously and milling about; from somewhere in the darkness came the sound of a man moaning softly. Whitcomb spied the stout form of Sergeant Dupré talking to the horse guards and he quickly conveyed Corwin's instructions. With his orders carried out, he started back for the company's tent line, moving along the edge of camp, when a shift in the breeze brought him the faint sound of hoofbeats and he made out two horsemen streaking for the beef herd. The Indians were clinging low to the necks of their mounts, riding straight for the camp.

"There they are!" he shouted, and even as the warning left his lips he was cocking the Colt, which he had held in his hand all the while. He squeezed off a shot and he knew he would remember the moment forever—the first shot he had fired in anger. But it wasn't anger, or the chaos of battle his father had described. The scene was unnaturally quiet, broken only by the mooing of the frightened steers, and the emotion he felt was little more than a childlike excitement.

The Colt bucked again, brought to bear and fired almost without his conscious effort; he had been taught familiarity with hand and shoulder arms since early boyhood and the actions came automatically to him. There were other shots now, the booming of Springfield rifles from Major Coates's infantry pickets and the crack of a Winchester. The Indians whooped and urged their ponies ahead, darting among the cattle, which scattered at their approach.

Whitcomb lowered his gun and hesitated, uncertain which way to go. He was ordered back to Lieutenant Corwin but the attackers were in the other direction. He saw motion near the horses and made out Corporal McCaslin and his men arriving to join the horse guards, who were gathering mounts from the picket ground. Sergeant Dupré already had one horse saddled. Beyond the horses, steers were bolting in every direction from the herd, and the milling in the center of the bunch revealed the progress of the Indians, who were hidden in the rising dust. The steers running toward the camp found themselves confronted by men afoot, wagging their hands and shouting, and the frightened animals shied away, turning back into the herd and past it, and from these the leaders took their direction. In the blink of an eye the bunch had form and purpose, stringing out away from the camp, wheeling to the south. Full of all the fear that the uncertain smells of a strange landscape and sudden noises in the night had awakened in them, they turned toward the trail by which they had come to this place, perhaps lured by some dim memory of Fort Fetterman, where they had grazed peacefully for more than a week before being prodded northward against their will. The edge of the herd passed among E Troop's horses, spooking those closest to the frightened steers. Sergeant Dupré's horse shied and broke away from him, cantering off in a snaking path that brought it near Whitcomb, some fifty paces distant.

"Whoa, now," Whitcomb said in a gentling voice that carried through the din of rushing hooves and

bawling steers. He held out a hand to the animal. Its
eyes were wide, the whites showing; faced with panicked cattle on one side and a man on the other it
chose the man, slowing to a walk and allowing him
to take the reins. Whitcomb reached his decision
almost without thinking. He swung up the on-side
stirrup and cinched the girth in a single motion, too
fast for the horse to inhale if it were a bloater. With
the girth made fast, Whitcomb was in the saddle in
an instant and off in pursuit of the herd, which was
even then vanishing into the darkness. He was beyond
the reach of Corwin's orders and opportunity had
presented itself. It was a chance to show his superior
what he was made of. "Follow me!" he called out,
and then he gave his attention to the rough terrain,
keeping an eye on the cattle as they arced in a long
curve around the encampment.

There was no sign of the Indian raiders as he
gained on the tail end of the stampeding herd. The
cattle raised dust on each stretch of bare ground and
bawled as they ran, never swerving from the course
they had chosen once they completed their sweep
around the camp and found the smells of the trail
back to the fort.

Behind him, already faint in the distance, he heard
the call to boots and saddles from at least one bugle.
There would be help on the way soon. Meanwhile he
would do what he could. Ahead of him the steers
flowed down into a ravine and up the other side with
barely any loss of speed. One animal bellowed hid-
eously as it snapped a leg and fell. Whitcomb's horse
stumbled once but caught itself, and it struck him
that if he were unhorsed out here he would have a
long walk back to camp in the dark.

In that moment, with the realization that his life was truly in peril, the campaign became real for him. Until now it had been little more than the fulfillment of a boyhood dream, full of romance and devoid of danger, although since his arrival at Fort Fetterman most of his ideas about what life with the frontier army would be like had been rudely shattered, commencing with the image he had of himself riding to battle in a column of smartly uniformed men. He had greeted with stunned disbelief the garments urged on him by the post trader, to whom Lieutenant Corwin had sent him in response to his embarrassed question about what General Crook might have meant by "proper clothing." Many of the items were unfamiliar to him and he hesitated to don them, but when the expedition had formed up the following morning, he saw that all notions of regulation dress had been thrown to the winds as the command clothed itself for the campaign. Uniforms, what few items a man deigned to keep from his standard issue, were buried under buffalo and bear greatcoats and overblouses of Minnesota blanket. Field boots were discarded in favor of high buckskin moccasins worn over two pairs of heavy woolen stockings and then themselves stuffed into buffalo overboots almost too cumbersome to fit a stirrup. Similarly discarded were the officers' sabers, which were heartily denounced as a "clattering nuisance" in the field. Emblems of rank were dispensed with as well, although General Crook wore a black Kossuth hat with the insignia attached and had replaced his bearskin hunting coat with an army overcoat trimmed with a high collar of wolf fur that came, Whitcomb was assured by Corporal Stiegler, from a wolf Crook himself had shot with a pistol while on foot. Apart from the general and a few others who kept the Kossuth hats, the common headgear was a woolen campaign hat with fur borders that pulled down over the ears. Those who could afford them wore green Arizona goggles as well, so called because they had first been used to protect the eyes in the desert Southwest, where the sun was intense, before being drafted into service for winter campaigns. The post trader had included a pair of the goggles in Whitcomb's kit. Once on the march it had struck Whitcomb that the cavalry bore more resemblance to a raiding party of Cossacks or the Mongol hordes of Genghis Khan than a force of the United States Army, save for the Springfield carbines, which were hung from the shoulder by a sling and rested muzzle down in a socket on the off-side of the saddle, and the coloring of the horses by troop, which was visible from a great distance. This was a custom originated at the instigation of General Custer shortly after the war, whereby all the bay horses were assigned to a single company, all the blacks to the next, and chestnuts, grays, sorrels and the other colors all similarly assigned; the roans, piebalds and other leftovers went to Company M, the last in the military alphabet, giving rise to its designation as the Brindle Troop. Depending on the horses available, a regiment might have two or more troops with mounts of the same color. General Crook's command contained elements of both the Second and Third Cavalry Regiments, and as it happened, there were two bay troops in the column, of which Whitcomb's company was one. At Fetterman he had reluctantly given up the sorrel gelding that had carried him safely from Cheyenne in exchange for a mount of the proper color.

To Whitcomb's surprise, General Crook himself rode not a horse but a mule that had carried him through all his Arizona campaigns, a sturdy specimen called Apache.

Behind the ten companies of cavalry, the men all clothed in motley anonymity and the horses wearing their different colors with pride, came the two companies of infantry, followed by the ambulances, supply wagons, pack train and beef herd. There were eighty-six wagons, four hundred mules and sixty steers. It was an imposing force, and before long Whitcomb had begun to take a perverse pride in the rough appearance of the men. The frontier Cavalry was already an uncommonly hirsute military force, with individually tailored sideburns, mustaches and chin whiskers everywhere in evidence; once on the march the differences began to pale as most of the men allowed their facial hair to grow unhindered as protection against the weather. Within just two days, most visages were darkened by the beginnings of full beards, increasing the column's resemblance to a band of brigands.

From the start, Whitcomb had been impatient with the pace of the march. On the first day the column had gone into camp at one o'clock, after covering just twelve miles. On the second day, sixteen was sufficient. Neither officers nor men seemed put off by the slow progress, but Whitcomb was champing at the bit. The country north of Fetterman was gently rolling, sparsely covered with bunchgrass and small clumps of sagebrush, and it seemed to go on forever. Because of the undulations of the land the command could never see more than a mile or two in any direction, and when some distant landmark, such as the four squat forms of Pumpkin Buttes off to the northeast, was seen first from one rise and then another, it never seemed to grow nearer. It had occurred to Whitcomb that in such country a body of armed men, friendly or hostile, could approach close to the column without being detected, and he had placed this lesson in his memory, but until the moment of the attack it had been widely assumed that the hostiles were far to the north. This impression had been reinforced on the first day of march, when the command had encountered a band of Arapaho moving toward the agencies. "Heap plenty Minneconjou," they had told the scouts, pointing north and describing a distance the scouts had interpreted as being about seventy miles or more. Crazy Horse was reported to be up there, and within half an hour his name had been spoken up and down the length of the column.

Now, alone on the prairie, chasing pell-mell through the dark after the fleeing cattle, Whitcomb wondered if the hostiles might not have been watching Fetterman all the time, just waiting for Crook to venture out. The column had marched under a brilliant sun despite Crook's hope for bad weather. It had snowed the night before they left the fort, confirming the scouts' predictions, but since then the entire countryside had been clear, save for the distant Big Horns, which had remained hidden under a low bank of clouds that clung to the mountains like a winter cape. Had the command been shadowed every step of the way? Whitcomb felt a chill, as if someone were watching him from behind.

The Longhorns had found their stride now and even stretched low over his horse's neck he could

gain no ground on the herd. He knew next to nothing
of beef cattle, but he saw their steady run and fear-
driven determination and in a moment of unpleasant
comprehension he knew that he had no hope of turning them without help. He looked back over his
shoulder. Off to his right the last sliver of the moon
was sinking below the horizon. If a party of troopers
had been sent out, chances of overtaking the cattle in
the thickening gloom were next to nothing. Simply
following the trail would be difficult enough. He was
on a fool's errand.

As soon as the realization came to him, he acted to
correct his mistake, slowing his mount to a canter
and reining him back in a tight turn. The quick
response of the horse to the command of the reins
saved Whitcomb's life.

A shot came from very close at hand and a ball
tugged at his shoulder, jerking him around in the
saddle. Even as he kicked his horse into a gallop
once more, he looked about and gasped to see an
Indian horseman almost upon him. The sound of the
unshod Indian pony had been hidden by the rumbling
hooves of the cattle, now rapidly fading into the distance. The Indian fired again and Whitcomb saw that
the man was shooting a pistol.

He urged his horse into a flat-out run, but even so
the brave drew alongside of him, his arm holding the
pistol straight out. There was a loud click as the
weapon misfired, clearly audible across the short
distance, and Whitcomb thanked a kind Providence
for the cap that had fallen off or the powder that had
fouled or the brave's carelessness in checking his
loads. He drew his own pistol and threw a shot at the
Indian, who shied off and lost a little ground but kept

coming. Whitcomb leaned low in the saddle, concentrating on goading the horse onward. He wished he had reloaded the Colt back in camp. How many shots had he fired? Two in camp and one now. He had had only five to begin with because the hammer rested on an empty chamber for safety's sake, so he had two left. He had better not waste them.

At home in Virginia, Whitcomb had ridden to hounds and taken part in steeplechases and he prayed now that his unfamiliar mount would prove up to the race. The cavalry horse plunged into the ravine he had crossed with the cattle only moments before and surged up the far side without breaking stride. Whitcomb no longer looked back, concentrating instead on spurring the animal on, signaling in every way he knew that the utmost speed was needed.

And then suddenly he saw a fire in front of him and the tents of the encampment in their neat rows. He cast a look over his shoulder but the Indian was nowhere to be seen.

Ahead of him a frightened trooper raised a rifle. "Hold your fire!" Whitcomb shouted and he reined in his horse as he passed through the sentries. Armed troopers were spaced evenly around the perimeter of the camp and the fires were being rekindled. He kept away from the light, hoping against hope that his absence might not have been noticed and his re-entry into the camp might miraculously go unremarked, but even as he dismounted, Lieutenant Corwin walked through the light of the nearest fire and approached him.

"Are you a born fool, Mr. Reb?" Corwin's voice was heavy with sarcasm.

"The beef herd was getting away, sir. I tried to stop it. I assumed some help would be sent along."

"No help was sent because no one knew you were gone. And we sure as hell wouldn't risk the men just to chase cattle halfway through the night. Can you think hard and tell me why not?" Whitcomb said nothing and after a moment Corwin supplied the answer. "General Crook would prefer not to have the next Captain Fetterman come from his command. Now do you understand?"

"Yes, sir." Whitcomb understood. Corwin was referring to the darkest chapter in the annals of the Indian wars. In December of 1866, during Red Cloud's War, Captain William Fetterman had left Fort Phil Kearny with eighty-one men to pursue a small party of Sioux. He had been under strict orders not to go beyond a ridge within sight of the fort, but his column had followed the taunting raiders over the ridgeline and not a man had come back alive. The raiders had been decoys and Fetterman had followed blindly into the trap.

"We heard shots. Were you attacked?"

"Yes, sir." Only now did Whitcomb remember the tug at his shoulder from the Indian's first shot. He felt no trace of a wound. He reached up and found a hole in the buffalo coat where the Indian's ball had torn the leather.

"How many savages were there?"

"Just one, sir. That is, I only saw one."

"I don't imagine you brought him down?"

"No, sir."

"Then it seems you have nothing to redeem your escapade. Now I will say this just once. During this campaign you will be put at risk often enough by the orders of your superior officers. Wait for those orders and don't set out to be a hero."

By the look on Whitcomb's face the young officer had learned his lesson. Corwin hoped it was so, and he hoped that his first impression of Hamilton Whitcomb was not wrong.

Corwin was still angry with himself for revealing to Whitcomb the bitterness that had lingered in him since the end of the Rebellion. Back in his cramped billet at Fetterman he had set a bad example by letting his personal feelings show, and he had sought to cover his mistake by trying to learn a little about his new second-in-command. He had looked at Whitcomb's papers and was surprised to discover that Whitcomb had graduated twelfth in his class.

"You had a good record at the Point," Corwin had remarked. "Good enough to have chosen the artillery or the engineers." Those branches of the army were customarily the first choices of the top graduates of West Point, but Whitcomb had requested duty with the cavalry.

"My people are cavalrymen, sir," Whitcomb had replied stiffly.

Attached to Whitcomb's record was a list of his male relatives who at one time had served in the United States Army. His father and an uncle were both graduates of the military academy, and after each name Corwin had noted the letters C.S.A. appended. Seeing that, his anger had risen again. He had spent two long years in a Rebel prison and he was lucky to have survived. Many of his friends had died of starvation or disease, but he had seen Rebels starving too, after the war, and he had recognized the bitterness of jealousy in his resentment of Whitcomb. In the young officer before him, he had seen someone who might succeed where he had failed.

Boots Corwin was a veteran of fifteen years in the army and his career had nowhere to go. Brevet major was almost certainly the highest rank he would ever attain, and even that was just a vanity with no substance. Brevet ranks were temporary, conferred for heroic service. During the heady days of the Civil War, when mounted officers had been felled like stalks of wheat, and men were promoted in uncounted numbers to meet the needs of command, hundreds of men had risen from the ranks, Corwin among them, and brevet promotions had been doled out freely, enabling junior officers to serve in positions of command higher than that to which their regular ranks entitled them. Before his capture and imprisonment Corwin had commanded a battalion of cavalry, exercising the full authority of a major. But after the war Congress had quickly reduced the army to fifty-four thousand men, then to forty-two thousand, leaving the service overloaded with officers, most of them veterans of the war who were entitled to be addressed by their brevet ranks and to wear the corresponding insignia but reduced again to command positions commensurate with their permanent ranks. To thin the top-heavy officer corps, service records were given a thorough going over by boards of review, which were quickly dubbed "Benzine Boards," after the harsh and ever-present cleanser. Between 1869 and 1872, seven hundred officers with less than commendable records were washed from the service, which still left more than enough men in command after Congress reduced the army in 1874 to a total of twenty-five thousand men.

Boots Corwin had survived the Benzine Boards, and being demoted from commander of a battalion back down to second-in-command of a single company had been no more than he expected. His imprisonment had crippled his career in mid-stride, just when he had become convinced that he was destined for higher things. While the war lasted he had hoped to be exchanged, in order that he might take part in the fighting again and prove that his early recognition was deserved. But when he had finally been exchanged it was in order that he not die in Rebel hands; by the time his unexpected recovery was complete, the war was over. He had applied at once for duty on the frontier, for it was clear even then that the Indians were not going to accept the advance of civilization without complaint, and where there was battle there was the chance of promotion. The only alternative was to take part in the social climbing and politicking that accompanied the quest for permanent promotion in every army post east of the Missouri, and Corwin had no taste for such pastimes, where he felt at a disadvantage to the well-bred and socially polished West Point officers. On the frontier posts the natural aversion between the West Pointers and the Volunteer officers, many of whom had risen from the ranks as Corwin had done, was held in check by the presence of a common enemy and the opportunities every man had to prove his individual worth in demanding circumstances. But promotions were painfully slow and men grew old in the lower grades. Corwin was thirty-five and he had remained a first lieutenant for thirteen years. He no longer wore the insignia of a major and he did not insist that he be addressed as one, unlike some peacocks whose pride was greater than their hopes of advancement. Corwin wanted an honest promotion won on merit, gained in battle, and he had sensed his chances ebbing away as the years passed; the Indian wars could not last much longer.

There in his quarters at Fetterman, in the eyes of the fuzz-faced youth who had not a scratch on his gold class ring, Boots Corwin had seen the same anticipation of glory and excitement that he himself had felt when he first enlisted, and Whitcomb's hopeful countenance had fanned the awareness of his own failed dreams. But he knew it was done without malice, without awareness.

He had given Whitcomb the customary warning about obeying orders without question, and in the youth's simple "Yes, sir," Corwin had detected no resentment or reservation. It had occurred to him then that perhaps Whitcomb was one of the rare ones, an officer still prepared to learn. If he was, Corwin would take him under his wing and bring him along. Such an officer could reflect credit on his immediate superior, and Corwin had high hopes for the present campaign. Suddenly, unexpectedly, his opportunity had come. With Sutorius under post arrest and himself in command of the company, outstanding conduct during the next few weeks could tip the balance in his favor. But he would need some exploit beyond the ordinary to gain the attention of Colonel Reynolds, the expedition's commander, or perhaps even of General Crook himself. He would need a stroke of luck, and all the help he could get.

Whitcomb had done an idiotic thing in chasing after the beef herd, but he hadn't made excuses. He had taken the blame and stood ready to take his medicine if punishment were given out, but Corwin decided to withhold the sting of the lash.

"All right, Mr. Whitcomb. If you're done with your evening constitutional, perhaps you'll resume your duties. We'll keep a double guard for the rest of the night. Reveille is at five o'clock. See that the men get what rest they can."

"Yes, sir." Whitcomb saluted and he watched Corwin walk away, leaving him alone with his shame and embarrassment. He realized now that he was trembling slightly in all his limbs. He shook himself as if to ward off a chill and looked around. Beyond the nearest fire he caught sight of a face he knew, the forked beard stirred by the light breeze, the level eyes looking at him for an instant before the figure turned away and vanished in the darkness that was now complete. His spirits sank even lower, knowing that General Crook had witnessed his dressing down.

"It is not so bad, sair," a voice said, and Whitcomb saw First Sergeant Dupré and Corporal McCaslin standing nearby.

"What did you say, Sergeant?"

The two non-commissioned officers stepped nearer. "It is not so bad, I think," Dupré said in a confidential tone. "You 'ave made a shavetail's mistake. So? You are a shavetail. With respect, sair, Major Corwin, he knows that."

Dupré's *r*'s rolled softly in his throat. His hair was black and his mustache was waxed and curled upward into two precise points. He looked more Latin than Whitcomb supposed was common in most Frenchmen. Perhaps in his blood he carried a reminder of Caesar's legions—a moment's dalliance with some fetching Gallic lass two millennia in the past.

Whitcomb smiled ruefully. Dupré's offer of comfort, however small, was welcome. "I hope so, Sergeant. I feel the perfect fool. You'll see to the horses, will you? Make sure the picket line is in order? If you'd take this animal along and unsaddle him, I'd be grateful. I'll see Sergeant Polachek about the guard."

Dupré took the reins and set off, not a man for extra words.

"Beggin' yer pahrdon, sorr. Moight I address the lieutenant confidentially?" Corporal McCaslin stood at parade rest, his eyes looking off into the dark, or not on Whitcomb in any event. His brogue was thick enough to cut with a saber and Whitcomb was hard put not to grin whenever he heard it. Just hearing it now improved his spirits. It reminded him of the appalling Irish accents put on by his classmates at the Point in the impromptu skits that had oftentimes convulsed the barracks, with their barbs equally divided between pompous officers and broadly drawn enlisted men. Whitcomb had half expected to find his entire troop composed of strapping Irishmen who burst into song at the slightest opportunity and were forever drunk or sleeping it off in the guardhouse. Here in Crook's command he had found that the skits struck surprisingly true to the mark, although the officers were a far cry from the stuffy martinets satirized by the cadets; but here he had met for the first time the immigrant soldiers of every nationality whom he had seen depicted in caricature back at West Point. There were Frenchmen and Englishmen and Italians and Germans, the latter seemingly doing their best to live up to the common notion, often found in any duty that required a precise mind and strict devotion to the letter of an order. E Troop had

more than its share of the immigrants; in the Third
Regiment it was known as the "Foreign Legion," for
it possessed not a single non-commissioned officer of
American birth. Nearly a third of the company was
Irish, and although they had no opportunity to drink
once the fort was left behind, they enjoyed a few
songs around the evening campfires. The sons of
Erin loved horses and fighting and they had flocked
to the cavalry in great numbers after the completion
of the transcontinental railroad, the work that had
first brought many of them out of the teeming eastern
cities. Whitcomb had been relieved to find that Corporal McCaslin was a dour man of slight build who
neither drank nor cursed and had no voice for sing-
ing. His chisel face seemed unacquainted with any
type of a smile and he rarely spoke unless addressed,
but he was steady, and devoted to the army, Corwin
had said. He was formal and correct in his dealings
with all officers, and in that respect reminded
Whitcomb of his father's colored majordomo. His
request to speak confidentially now came as a surprise.

"What is it, Corporal?"

"Well, sorr, in the cavalry there's an auld sayin'
—'Either the captain or the first sahrgint is a son of a
bitch, or yez don't have a throop.' Beggin' yer
pahrdon, sorr, but that's the words they use. Well, as
yez can see, sorr, First Sahrgint Dupree is a kind
man, a natural-born gentleman, yez moight say. And
Captain Sutorius is not with us but we've still got a
throop, yez can bet yer pay on that. I'll leave yez to
make yer own conclusions."

"I won't hear any disrespect for Major Corwin,
Corporal."

"Och! Meanin' no disrespect atall, sorr!" McCaslin

was genuinely shocked at the thought. "The lieutenant is an officer and a gentleman, sorr, wid more
years in this army than I have. He'll take the E
Throop to the gates of Perdition and I'll be marchin'
alongside him, 'cause I know he'll be comin' back
directly after thrashin' the Divil. Himself is a *foine*
son of a bitch, sorr, that was what I meant to say.
Well, good night, sorr."

With that McCaslin saluted and left him. After he
had found Sergeant Polachek and inspected the guards
along E Troop's section of the perimeter, Whitcomb
continued on around the camp, strolling within the
outer cordon of pickets. He was certain he would not
be able to sleep again tonight, so he used the time to
ponder what McCaslin had said. Perhaps there was
some truth in the corporal's words. Corwin had been
harsh with him from the start and he seemed to have
no great love for Southerners, but he had done nothing that was outright unfair. Perhaps if Whitcomb
obeyed orders and stayed on his best behavior, Corwin
would warm to him. They were the only two officers
in the company, and the better the relations between
them, the better the campaign would go.

"Duty first, then initiative," his father had often
instructed him in days gone by. He would remember
that maxim in the days to come. His father had said
something else, though, as well: "It is far better to
err by doing than by not doing," by which Cleland
Whitcomb meant that an officer who arrived ahead of
the rest and acted on his own initiative suffered less
for his mistakes than one who obeyed only the letter
of his instructions and attempted nothing more. Ham
now had the opportunity to learn if that were true.

He nearly stumbled over a figure seated on a low
rock. The figure started, and asked, "Who's there?"

"It's Lieutenant Whitcomb, E Troop. Who are you? Oh, excuse me, General, I'm sorry I disturbed you." He felt himself blush and was glad of the dark. Crook was the last man he wanted to see just now, with his humiliation fresh in his mind.

"That's all right, Mr. Whitcomb. I couldn't sleep either. It's something I associate with the start of a campaign. After I have seen action I find that I sleep very well. Perhaps action has the opposite effect on you."

"Yes, sir, perhaps it does."

" 'In the intoxication of enthusiasm, to fall upon the enemy at the charge,' eh? It stays with you for a time, especially the first time."

"Sir?"

"Pity the warrior, indeed, Mr. Whitcomb, who never knows that intoxication. Just don't let it overcome your judgment."

Whitcomb blushed again to remember himself just two days ago saying "I don't imagine you have read Clausewitz" to the "scout" with whom he had ridden on the road to Fetterman, the same man who now so gently quoted the Prussian strategist back to him. *In the intoxication of enthusiasm, to fall upon the enemy at the charge* . . .

"Yes, sir, it was something like that. I'm afraid I made a fool of myself."

"Oh, not entirely, Mr. Whitcomb. You followed your instincts. At least you saw your mistake and made your way straight back to camp. I was not so lucky a few years after the war, out in the Oregon country. We were returning from an engagement with the local Indians, approaching a campsite I knew well, when I saw some sheep tracks. I left the command and climbed to the top of a butte to follow them. Well, don't you know a fog set in just as I reached the top. By the time I found my way down to flat land again, night had fallen and it began to sleet. Before long I was soaked through and I had no matches. In fact, I had nothing to rely upon but my instincts, and so I followed them. I started off in what I took to be the right direction and along about midnight I sat down on top of a sagebrush and waited. Along about two or three o'clock in the morning the sky cleared and the moon came out and there was our camp, half a mile off.'' Crook paused and stroked first one fork of his beard, then the other. ''We have not been given instincts merely to confuse us, Mr. Whitcomb. Over the years they become tempered with experience, but we should never ignore them entirely.''

''Yes, sir. I understand, sir. Thank you, sir. Good night.''

''Good night, Mr. Whitcomb.'' Crook heard the young officer's footsteps move away and he resumed his seat on the rock. The breeze had freshened from the west. He missed his dog, but two hundred miles of marching over rock and ice would have lacerated the collie's feet and he would not consent to be carried on a pack animal, so the dog had been left at Fetterman to await his master's return.

If young Whitcomb puts himself in harm's way when next we meet the enemy, and is killed, am I to blame? the general wondered. Perhaps. But the boy needed some encouragement, if he was not to lose his spirit. Corwin was wrong; Whitcomb was no Fetterman. He lacked the fatal arrogance of a Fetterman. There was a cautious self-awareness that would hold him in check. With luck and a little urging he might become one of the peacemakers.

Crook's thoughts turned to Hardeman then, and he wondered where the scout was tonight. He had had enough time to reach Sun Horse, if the peace chief was in his accustomed winter camp.

For some reason he felt the cold suddenly and he got to his feet, stamping to bring some warmth to his legs. A sentry turned in his direction, recognized the tall, bearded silhouette, and continued his rounds.

As he made his way toward the headquarters tents, Crook reviewed his conversation with Hardeman. How the scout had found him in Cheyenne he didn't know, but the man had struck him as being straightforward and sincere, and he had decided to trust him. After all, in Arizona the Apaches had been brought to heel by reason, not by the force of arms alone. Might not the same thing be accomplished here? There was everything to gain if Hardeman was successful. A peace that stemmed from Sun Horse's surrender might well be more lasting than one gained on the field of battle, with all the bitterness and lust for revenge that would give rise to among the young men of the Sioux. Somewhere there had to be an end to the cycle of assault and revenge that both sides had perpetuated on the plains for more than twenty years. The end could come in only two ways—in combat, death and blood, or in a peace made quickly and quietly while the bloodhounds on either side were caught napping. If the fighting continued, sooner or later the Sioux would send the war pipe to their allies and then there would be hell to pay. The formal alliance among the Sioux, Cheyenne and Arapaho was believed to be of recent origin, formed after the early hostilities with the whites, and it was unique in the history of the nomadic and fiercely independent western tribes. The three tribes had agreed to come to one another's aid if any one of their many bands were attacked by the soldiers, and the alliance had been invoked only twice, first by the Cheyenne in 1864, after the Sand Creek debacle, and again four years later by the Sioux, in Red Cloud's War in this very country. Each time the three tribes had taken the warpath together the consequences had been dire for the United States. In January of 1865, following Sand Creek, a thousand warriors had attacked Julesburg, Colorado Territory; they had sacked the town, causing few deaths but much damage to property, and then they had carried the war to the surrounding territories. For most of the next year the western trails were all but impassable without armed escort. Red Cloud's War had been worse. The Indians considered it a great victory, and the massacre of Fetterman and his men their greatest triumph. What might be the cost of a new outbreak, with thousands of warriors moving in concert against the much more numerous white settlements that now dotted the frontier states and territories?

The command tent loomed before him and he found his bedroll beside the tent, which he used only as an office. His striker, Andy Peiser, prepared the bed outside except in foul weather. Peiser knew his commander preferred to sleep where he could see the sky and feel a change in the wind.

Once settled comfortably in his robes Crook lay a while on his back, finding the constellations one by one in and around the broad swatch of the Milky Way that arced across the zenith.

Without the hotheads like Fetterman, and Grattan, who had started it all, would there have been the same history of bloodshed and broken promises between the two peoples? Probably. They were too different. One race would have to submit to the ways of the other, and there was no doubt which would ultimately dominate. Only when the Indians surrendered would red man and white live side by side. The question that remained was when the surrender would be obtained, and at what cost.

Crook was glad that Custer had been called to Washington, although the summons boded ill for Custer's career. The quick-tempered Boy General was a paradox. From his headquarters he fired off one salvo after another in defense of the Indians' right to be treated fairly once they had submitted to the white man's will, yet in the field he was careless of which Indians he attacked and merciless in battle. He was like a sputtering fuse attached to a keg of powder, liable to detonate at any time and destroy the best-laid plans of his superiors, oblivious of the cost to the army and the nation. With Custer gone and Terry in command of the Seventh, there was a better chance that the three prongs of the assault on the Powder River country might coordinate their efforts and bring about a swift victory. Only after the victory could there be justice for the Indians.

The fact was, Custer might do more good for the army in Washington City. If his testimony helped to expose the flagrant corruption in the Indian Bureau, Congress might be better disposed to return the control of Indian affairs to the War Department, where it rightfully belonged. But no matter what the effect of his testimony, Custer was sure to suffer for it. His presence at the hearings could only draw more attention to what was already a major embarrassment to the President, and it seemed certain that Grant's wrath would descend on the colorful general. In all probability he could expect no further field command while Grant remained in office. He would most likely become very familiar with some barren desktop in the capital until after the next inauguration. By then, with luck, the Indian wars on the northern plains would be history.

Crook took a last look around the sky. Above him a star lost its moorings in the heavens and fell, flung across the firmament by an invisible hand, streaking to the north where it disappeared in a final winking flash. He sent a prayer for peace after the falling star and dropped at last into a fitful slumber.

CHAPTER ELEVEN

Blackbird moved quickly across the snow in the still brightening light of morning, lifting his snowshoes high, being careful not to catch them on some hidden snag. They were Crow snowshoes, taken by Blackbird's father, Standing Eagle, on a raid he had made against the enemy in the Moon of Falling Leaves, before the first snow. Among the Lakota, it was well known that the *Kanghí oyate*—the Crow people—made the best snowshoes of all.

A sudden squall twisted across the wooded slope,

lifting snow from the branches of the pines and whipping it among the bare aspens, gusting up the soft new flakes that had been falling since before dawn.

The boy paused as the squall overtook him, pressing his cheek against the cape of raccoon fur that lay over his shoulders. For a moment his ear grew warm as he scanned the snow with eyes that were quick and bright beneath a high forehead. Under the cape he wore a trade blanket belted at the waist, two shirts, leggings and winter moccasins. He wished he had brought his buffalo robe, but the clothing he had would be protection enough if he kept moving. As the squall subsided, he started off again.

Here among the trees the trail was easier to see. On the open slope where he had first caught sight of the faint tracks he had not been sure they were recent enough to pursue. They were drifting over rapidly, perhaps made the day before, he had thought, but where the tracks entered the shelter of the trees he had found the droppings, not yet frozen, and had set off in pursuit. Where the wind could blow close to the ground the tracks were sometimes no more than faint whirls in the snow, seen by letting the eyes roam the surface for the telltale pattern of irregularities, but Blackbird already tracked as well as a man and he could tell now that he was gaining rapidly on the deer. He hurried on, careful to look ahead as well as down—a hunter who looked only at tracks would go hungry, for his prey would see him before it was seen and would run; if the prey were a great bear or another man, the hunter might lose his life with his eyes still on the ground before him. The boy knew this so well that he no longer thought of it as something to remember; he tracked without effort, moving

across the snow as naturally as a lynx, and in the
back of his mind it was not meat he tracked, but
man, imagining that it was a Crow or a Blackfoot, or
the hated *washíchun*, who had made these marks in
the snow. And as always he also stalked his manhood, sensing it drawing nearer every day; he longed
to capture this most of all, impatient for the day
when he would be a warrior like his father.

But that day might never come. He came to a halt,
losing interest in the tracks. Intent upon the chase, he
had forgotten for a time the decision of the council.

Two nights before, the band's councillors had
reached no decision. Yesterday, under skies that were
mostly clear after a dusting of snow in the night, they
had met twice more, once in midday and again in the
evening, and when Standing Eagle had returned to
the lodge at last, his voice had been laden with
disappointment and anger.

"The council will not fight," he had said bitterly
to Blackbird's mother. "The *washíchun* come to steal
our land and we will not fight. The council will
surrender to Three Stars. All we have they will give
to the whites, and our children will grow up as white
children do!"

Blackbird and his sister, Red Fawn, had been sent
to bed as the council began, but Blackbird had lain
awake waiting for his father to return. Standing Eagle's anger had frightened him.

"What did your father say?" Blackbird's mother
had asked softly, motioning Standing Eagle to speak
quietly so his son and daughter would not be disturbed. But Standing Eagle had seen Blackbird's eyes
reflecting the firelight from deep in his sleeping robes.

"Let my son hear his grandfather's words," he

said. "Sun Horse says the return of his *washíchun* grandson has reminded him of the strength of the warrior who does not fight. Only that and nothing more. After that he sat silent as the council talked, silent as they decided that we shall accept the meat Three Stars offers and go with him to the Dakota reservation!"

"And the family of Standing Eagle, what will they do?" Blackbird's mother had asked. His sister was awake too, and they all had awaited Standing Eagle's next words.

"We will leave the Sun Band. We will go to Sitting Bull, where the Lakota still know how to fight."

Blackbird felt his anger rise now, directed at the strange young man who had been raised among the Shahíyela by White Smoke, the uncle Blackbird was too young to remember. His uncle had been killed by *washíchun* horse soldiers at the Washita River, far to the south, that much Blackbird knew, and he knew he wanted to fight those bluecoat soldiers; he wanted to fight them now to rid himself of his anger against this pale cousin he did not know, against his own grandfather for turning away from him that morning. He had gone to Sun Horse's lodge, needing to tell someone that he was going off to hunt for meat. His father was already up and gone to see how much snow lay on the trail to the north, needing to get away from the village on any pretense. Blackbird had scratched softly at the entrance to his grandfather's tipi and had spoken his name, "Blackbird is here," but instead of the cheerful greeting he usually received, there had been only his grandfather's voice, sounding weary and old, saying, "I am speaking with my grandson. Come back tonight when I have returned from the whiteman's lodge in the valley below.''

Blackbird had told no one where he went then, sneaking away from the village as if it were an enemy camp, angry at the *washíchun* grandson who had taken up all of Sun Horse's time for two days, angry at anyone who threatened to deny him the manhood he wished for so hard. Already he had killed his first buffalo, and in the Moon of Red Plums he had made his vision quest under the guidance of the *wichasha wakán* Sees Beyond, and he had been given his young man's name, Blackbird. He did not like the name. A blackbird was a small thing, clever perhaps, but not strong like *igmú tanka*, the mountain cat that had come to him in his vision together with the blackbird. Following family custom his grandfather had named him, taking the name from the vision. ''Your name is Blackbird,'' he had said, smiling. ''*Igmú tanka* has given you strength to be a hunter, or a warrior if you choose, but the blackbird is wise. Your name will remind you that strength used unwisely is more dangerous than weakness.''

It was just like Sun Horse to give him a name that contained a lesson. The old man was overflowing with lessons. Blackbird liked to sit at his grandfather's feet and listen to stories of the days when Sun Horse was a young man, before the *washíchun* came to the plains, but somehow the stories always contained a lesson about what it meant to be a man among the Lakota. Blackbird was still enough of a boy to hope that growing up meant only more chances to ride with the men on their hunt for deer and elk

and antelope and buffalo, and to fight real enemies
when the time came. But this was not manhood as
his grandfather described it. "Becoming a man means
not only leaving behind the small bow of a child,"
he had said. "It means taking responsibility for the
people. A man of the Lakota thinks always of the
people; he acts always for the good of the people,
and to be a leader among the people is to carry the
heaviest burden of all. We live in troubled times and
the people need wise leaders."

And now Blackbird was not sure he would ever
know what it meant to be a man of the Lakota, let
alone a leader. He would go with his father to Sitting
Bull's camp, making the choice for himself, as a man
should. And if the *washíchun* came, he would fight
them. At least he would know what it was to fight for
the people, perhaps to die for them, as a man of the
Lakota.

Before his eyes the tracks were vanishing, drifting
full and being wiped away by the wind even as he
watched. He raised his face to the clouds and cried
out silently, praying for a warrior's strength to see
him through the storm and a hunter's cunning to find
his prey and bring it home to his family. If he
brought back fresh meat, his going off without per-
mission would be forgiven. The family needed meat
now more than ever, to strengthen them for the trip
north to Sitting Bull.

Blackbird thought suddenly of Yellow Leaf, the
daughter of Hawk Chaser. Beneath his deerskin shirts
he wore an armband of braided leather that Yellow
Leaf had made for him. Would Hawk Chaser follow
Standing Eagle, the war leader, or would he surrender? Hawk Chaser was Blackbird's *hunká-até*, his

father-by-choice, and next to Standing Eagle the boy respected no man more. Was it possible that he would have to leave Hawk Chaser and Yellow Leaf behind?

He took up the pursuit again, moving off as fast as he dared, almost running, as if his haste might help to assure that Hawk Chaser would make the right decision.

The youth was relieved to find the tracks fresh and clear as he passed over the crest of the small ridge he had been climbing, clearer still as he made his way down the more heavily wooded slope on the other side toward a flat bottom where a creek flowed. The snow thickened suddenly around him, obscuring everything until he could see no farther than the distance across the camp circle back at the village, and for a moment he longed for the comfort of his father's lodge and his mother seeing that his bowl was full, if only with dog stew. And then as quickly as it had come the flurry passed and he saw the deer.

It was a doe. She was moving away from him, pausing now to sniff the wind. Satisfied, she moved on and passed behind a cluster of young spruce at the edge of a small clearing. The boy let out the breath he had instinctively held as he froze in position, hoping the deer had not seen him. He moved forward cautiously and drew an arrow from the quiver that hung at his shoulder. With luck he would have a shot from the edge of the clearing.

He crouched low behind the young trees and peered through the branches. The doe was at the far side of the open space, head down, pawing at the base of a tree, seeking a few blades of grass. Blackbird fitted the arrow to the bowstring and arose as Hawk Chaser had taught him, no faster than a shoot of grass arose from the earth on a warm spring day. But now the doe looked up, eyes wide, muscles tensed. Blackbird held himself motionless, his heart pounding. He had done nothing to reveal his presence; he was downwind of the deer and almost completely hidden by the trees, revealing no man-silhouette; he had made no sound that could carry through the storm. The doe looked about, wet black nose sniffing, graceful ears moving. Blackbird waited. He was not yet ready to make his shot, but any further movement might catch her eye. He must do nothing to alarm her.

But it was no action of the boy's that finally released the trembling muscles of the deer. A trumpeting blast of sound broke from near at hand and sent the deer bounding off through the trees in great leaps that carried her out of sight in the space of a few heartbeats. Blackbird spun in the direction of the sound and his jaw dropped, the bow and arrow forgotten in his hands. Not thirty paces away stood a creature for which nothing in his life nor in the tales of his people had prepared him. A hulking gray-brown body, more massive by far than the largest buffalo he had ever seen, was supported by four treelike legs planted firmly in the snow; from the huge head, a snake grew where a nose should be, and two horns many times longer than those of the big-horn sheep sprouted from the bottom of the creature's head and curved up past the snakelike snout, reaching for the sky. Great flaps stood out from the sides of the head, wings perhaps, to carry the beast aloft so it could swoop down like an eagle to rend its prey with its impossible upside-down horns. The flaps waved back and forth now as the creature raised its head and gave forth once again with the noise that had sent the deer fleeing in terror. As it roared, it lumbered forward a few steps, shaking its head from side to side.

Tasting fear strong in his mouth, Blackbird forced his legs to move. He stepped backward, but at once the tail of the snowshoe caught in the snow and he fought to keep his balance. Turning carefully, he started away through the trees, looking back over his shoulder, praying that the thing would be content to let him go. He broke into a shuffling run.

The eyes spaced far apart in the massive head watched him go, keeping him in sight until his small figure disappeared among the trees. Alone now on the windswept mountainside, the elephant raised his trunk and trumpeted again into the blowing snow.

LISA PUTNAM'S JOURNAL

Friday, March 3rd. 5:50 a.m.

Yesterday, as I glanced often at the trail from Sun Horse's village, I grew increasingly angry at the injustice of his threatened removal from this land. Today I awoke early, and in the moments of my waking I realized that my anger on his behalf is partly a lie. It has not been easy for me to admit this, but I must be completely honest in the days that lie ahead. If I should lose all that my father worked to build, I would want my descendants to know how this came about and to judge if any of the fault may have been my own.

In truth, much of my anger is directed at myself,

for failing to see until confronted by this new threat to my home just how much it means to me, and how much I long to remain here and continue in the life my father built; I am angry that Julius and I may not have the chance to succeed or fail here on our own, to see if we are up to the work.

I see too that I have blamed Mr. Hardeman unfairly; he has only brought word of events set in motion through no fault of his own. I should be angry at President Grant and his cronies instead of Mr. Hardeman, but he is here and they are not. I thought myself very clever to tell him of the deed, and my fear of losing Putnam's Park, convincing myself that this was merely a ruse to distract him from my real intention—to help Sun Horse. But my fear for the ranch is very real, and now I am angry with myself for letting selfishness cloud my judgment.

These thoughts come tumbling out, and I am not setting them down very clearly. I hope this process may help to calm me, for from this moment forward, the course of events may depend in part on my actions. Until now I do not believe I could have done anything to change what has come about. I cannot sway the President and the Congress by myself. But now that the danger is at our doorstep I will have a hand in determining the outcome, both for Putnam's Park and, if I can find a way, for Sun Horse. I have no parent to turn to for guidance any longer, but they did not rear me to run from danger. (I do not feel nearly as brave as this sounds. I write it to remind myself of my duty to uphold not only the example set by my father, but that of my mother as well.)

On Tuesday I took a look at my father's life; today I will say a few words about my mother and her *family, for she too has lessons to offer. Her decision to marry my father, and, even more shocking, to follow him to this wild place, came as a complete surprise to her relatives. The Emersons tend toward intellectual pursuits and look askance at merchants. They pointed at my father's long stay in the western regions and his failure to assume the running of Putnam & Sons on his return as clear evidence of lack of discipline, a failing they scorn above all else. They knew nothing of the disciplines he mastered in order to survive all those years beyond the limiting conventions of proper society. They arrived early in New England and settled down firmly; the land suited them as did the civilization that arose there, and they made a place for themselves. Unlike the more recent immigrants, or those less fortunate than themselves, who saw the opening West as a place in which to escape old troubles and limitations, the Emersons had no need to escape, and they experienced few limitations on their settled lives. They educated themselves, including the women in the family (I must give credit where it is due), and became professionals, although rarely in professions that earned a great deal of money. For the most part, they scorned wealth. Yet daughters were expected to stay close to their native hearths and to bring new blood, and money, into the family. But within my mother's breast there lived a spirit of adventure undreamt of by her closest kinfolk, and a matching strength of will. My father, of course, perceived this. Her relations did not, until she left them. Even then they expected her imminent return, and only after years of receiving cheerful letters from Putnam's Park did they realize that the family tree had sprouted a branch of pioneers. Then,* of course, they took full credit for her decision, and accepted it as proof that the Emersons bred hardy stock. When I went east to school they received me graciously and inquired with genuine interest about every aspect of our life here. They are intelligent people, and always willing to learn. She had those qualities, and an exceptional measure of courage.

Most of these perceptions I gathered from my father, for my mother told her story simply. "I wanted a change," she said, and in those few words she explained her willingness to go beyond the settled life in search of a different achievement and perhaps a deeper contentment. Putnam's Park is as much her creation as my father's, for he would not have remained without her. I will keep their examples before me through whatever comes.

We have no idea why Sun Horse did not come yesterday to convey his decision. "It takes Indians some time to talk things over," Mr. Hardeman said, and his simple acceptance of their differences from ourselves reminded me of my father. Mr. Hardeman is about forty-five, I should say, and bears himself well. He has had much experience on the frontier and has that force of character one expects in men who succeed in making their way out here. He knew my father many years ago, and although he does not say so, I believe my father thought highly of him. I have always found my father's judgment of character to be close to the mark, but I feel some caution where Mr. Hardeman is concerned and I will reserve my own judgment for now. He seems to have a genuine concern for Sun Horse's welfare inasmuch as he is Johnny Smoker's grandfather, but he persists in the belief that surrender is the Sun Band's only course. I *see surrender as their last resort and cannot believe things have come to that pass.*

As for Johnny Smoker, how I wish I could ask him a thousand questions and hear the entire story of his life, most of all his years among the Cheyenne. Certainly the astonishing fact of his relationship with Sun Horse, and Uncle Bat's evident fondness for him, played a part in my decision to lead him and Mr. Hardeman to the Sun Band's valley, but it did not prepare me for the welcome he received. I have never seen Sun Horse so moved as at the moment he recognized the grandson he believed to have been dead for seven years. And from that moment Sun Horse was not himself. He seemed lost in thought and scarcely aware of the immediate danger to his people. He was attentive when I spoke with him before I left the village, and I hope he heeds my advice, but I fear he did not put much faith in my hopes for a new Indian policy.

Johnny, in what little time I saw him, was mostly silent. He is well spoken and polite when he does speak, and he appears to have good intelligence. Yet there is something about him that makes him seem not quite a part of what is taking place around him. I would not be surprised if he was permanently scarred in some way other than his physical wound by the manner in which he lost his Indian parents and was returned to civilization. I find myself strangely touched by the boy and his story.

Can he truly want his grandfather to surrender and lose everything?

CHAPTER TWELVE

Hardeman looked out the kitchen window at the snow that now floated down in a dead calm. All morning the mercury in the big thermometer on the back stoop had hovered near the freezing point while the weather had changed in some way every time he had peered out a window or stepped outside to feel the air. He had been up before dawn, stalking the blue-gray darkness of the empty saloon, pacing off the limits of his patience, wishing for a life in which he would never again have to wait for another man to make up his mind. The snow had been falling then, whirling this way and that in the uncertain gusts, and while he roamed the hallways and public rooms of the sleeping house the wind had risen and brought a moan from the flue of the big saloon stove and a chattering in the strongest gusts from a loose storm shutter somewhere upstairs. As the people had stirred and come to breakfast wrapped in thoughts no one wanted to speak out, the flakes had grown smaller and flew across the yard between house and barn without falling at all toward the earth, and then in the time it took a person to drink half a cup of coffee the wind had dropped to nothing; it was resting, in the way of a spring storm, but it would come back and blow again from the other side before long.

The smell of bacon still hung in the close air of the

kitchen. Outside by the barn, Hutch buckled the last strap on the team's harness and swung aboard the empty sled where Julius was waiting for him. The sled moved off quickly down the packed trail that sloped away from the barn and was gone from sight.

The day before, Hardeman had passed the morning by staying restlessly on the move about the settlement. Before breakfast he had helped Harry Wo with the milking and later he had ridden with Lisa almost the whole length of the valley to look at the cattle. They had both kept watch on the creek trail, but neither had spoken of Sun Horse or the Indians. During the noon meal, Hardeman had looked often out the kitchen window and afterward he had stood for a time on the kitchen stoop, waiting, but even then he had known Sun Horse would not come. To decide such an important matter, the Sun Band councillors would talk, and talk, then adjourn to go to their lodges and think, and meet to talk some more. Indians preferred to take the time needed to reach a unanimity of opinion rather than risk a majority ruling that would leave a division in the band, which might weaken it at a crucial moment. They might be talking still, but soon the talking would end.

Today Hardeman was a scout once more, dressed in the scout's uniform of the northern territories. He had worn the buckskin shirt and pants occasionally on the Texas trails but they were unsuited to the respectability of the Kansas towns, and they had spent the winter deep in his saddlebags. It had seemed only natural to don them here. He was too hot in the warm kitchen and longed to get out of doors where a man could breathe, but he had no wish to weary himself by pointless wandering. He would wait here.

Yesterday he had gone to his room and slept the afternoon away, rising for supper, then going back to sleep again until just before dawn. He was thoroughly rested now and ready for what was to come.

"It will come back around from the other side," he said.

Lisa spooned a last measure of coffee into the enameled pot and set it on the stove to boil. She wore a gray dress of homespun today, one that had belonged to her mother. Her hair was once more piled atop her head; a loose strand hung in her eyes and she brushed at it absently from time to time. "What will?" she asked.

They were alone in the kitchen. Ling had not felt well at breakfast and she had finally consented to rest a while and leave the work to Lisa.

"The wind. It will come back and blow again from the other side before it quits. It always does that on this side of the mountains."

Lisa had noticed when she was a child the way the wind backed in the middle of a snowstorm, but it displeased her that Hardeman should know this secret. It was as if he knew which boards in the upstairs hallway creaked, or how to lift the handle of her bedroom door so it would swing open without a sound.

From close outside the back door she could hear the sound of Harry Wo's axe as he split stovewood. Julius and Harry shared the wood-splitting by mutual consent, not as a way of dividing unpleasant labor but because it was work both men enjoyed, and today was Harry's turn. *Chop*, and then a pause as Harry set another log on the block. *Chop*. Like the ticking of a clock that had lost its momentum and might drag to a halt before Sun Horse brought his answer. *Chop*.

The coffeepot began to hiss within itself. Lisa washed a dish idly, irritated by Hardeman's presence. She did not want to make polite conversation. Each word they had spoken seemed stilted and irrelevant. She wanted to be alone, to recapture for a moment the peaceful solitude she had enjoyed so ungratefully just three days earlier, before the strangers came, before the threat to her home. But Harde-‧man had shown no sign of leaving when breakfast was done, and she had offered to make another pot of coffee as she cleaned up the dishes.

He had found her early that morning in the library, as she was putting the journal away in the drawer of the mahogany secretary where she sat to write. His breath had smelled of whiskey, and she had found it difficult to maintain the dispassion she had achieved while alone with her journal. But her father had always made the library available to guests and so she had let the scout intrude in what had become her private reserve since her father's death. It was her winter retreat, and Hardeman was the first to broach its sanctuary. She had left him there with scarcely a word and had gone outside in the slowly brightening gloom to climb the rise behind the Big House and stand by the graves of her parents, to be alone and think. The handful of others who had died in Putnam's Park over the years were buried in a small plot down beside the wagon road, sheltered by the clump of pines; for twelve years Eleanor Putnam had lain in solitary rest where now she was joined by her husband.

It was from this spot that Jed had first seen the valley that became his home. Lisa had climbed the knoll frequently over the years to tend the flowers on her mother's grave, but only in recent months had she taken the habit of going there to think, standing between the graves, rarely glancing at the two wooden markers, one weathered and the other so new; she knew the names and dates by heart and had no need to refresh her memory.

Today the hillock was almost bare, swept clean by the morning winds, and the stalks of last season's flowers stood bent and broken above the thin layer of snow, marking a rectangle around the edge of each mound. Lisa had looked down the valley, not seeing the house and barn and sheds and the twin ruts of the wagon road, but seeing it instead as it had first appeared to her father, remembering his tale of discovery.

When he left the dying fur trade behind him, Jed Putnam had returned to Massachusetts and his family's shipping business. He made a voyage to the Orient to protect the firm's interests against a threatened British monopoly of the China trade and was gone two years; shorter voyages took him to London and the Caribbean. Between these travels he found time to court and marry Eleanor Emerson, a younger cousin of the well-known lecturer and essayist. Their child Elizabeth was born a year later and Jed settled his wife and child on a farm in Lexington, twenty miles from Boston. He took pleasure in his family, but even they failed to quell his restlessness. The politicking of the seafaring merchant trade held no lasting interest for him and the smoky air and rabbit-warren congestion of Boston oppressed him, and while the Massachusetts countryside was pleasant and serene, it lacked the ruggedness and the untamed nature he had become accustomed to in the western mountains.

His pulse quickened whenever he heard news of the West. He whooped with delight and startled the cook half out of her wits when a letter arrived in the spring of '48 from his brother Bat, saying that he had come along with their old friend Joe Meek, who had crossed the continent to plead for making Oregon a territory. They would be in Washington City on such and such a date Bat guessed. By the time the letter arrived, the date was at hand. Jed was on the next train.

"What's a coon like you do fer fun up Boston way?" Joe Meek greeted him, once he and Bat were through pounding Jed on the back and cursing, to show their delight at seeing him. "Not much," Jed was forced to admit. "I been to China, though. London too. Got myself a farm." "Hell's full o' farmers," Meek said, and ordered brandy all around. To console themselves once more over the passing of the beaver trade and to commemorate bygone friends, the three former mountain men got moderately drunk and managed to astound or terrify almost all the guests in Coleman's Hotel before the night was over.

And then, not long after this joyous reunion, came the word, moving across the land like lightning, that bright flakes of gold had been found in the tailrace of Johann Sutter's sawmill in the foothills of California.

As soon as it was clear that the strike at Sutter's Mill was something more than a flash in the pan, Jed made up his mind. If the country's westward progress had been slow and steady in recent years, it would be hell-for-leather now, and Jed Putnam did not intend to be left behind. He yielded his interest in

J. Putnam & Sons to his brother Jacob in exchange for a fixed amount to be paid over a period of twenty years in installments that would not cut deeply into the firm's capital reserves; he made the same arrangement on behalf of his brother Bat, and in the spring of '49, Jed crossed the Missouri for the last time.

He knew what he was looking for and it was not the ephemeral El Dorado that drew thousands of argonauts along the trails to the Pacific coast. He wanted a home in the mountains, a place to put down roots deep enough to sustain those of his descendants and kin who might want to remain in the place he chose long after his own mortal remains had been turned under its soil.

He signed on with a wagon company in St. Joseph and guided the emigrants to Sacramento, crossing the Divide at South Pass, the same spot where he had said goodbye to the mountains twelve years before; the gateway to the fur kingdom had become the gateway to the West. Jed reveled in the hardships of the journey, confident that he would find what he was looking for if he was patient. One look at the teeming settlements of California convinced him that his future did not lie in that place, already as noisy and crowded and beset by greed and contention as the states back east. But he continued to guide wagons west each summer, and on the return trip he would ride alone or with a companion, revisiting his old haunts and exploring familiar byways, trusting his instincts to tell him when he had found his home. Here and there he encountered an old friend—Jim Bridger at his road ranch on Black's Fork, Tom Fitzpatrick at Fort Laramie, where he was Indian

agent to the Sioux. In the fall of 1852 he found his
brother Bat on the Tongue River, traveling with Sun
Horse's band of Hunkpapa and Oglala, and on the
spur of the moment he accepted an invitation to
winter with them in the new wintering place the band
had adopted just the year before, a secluded valley in
the Big Horns. "Shinin' country," Bat said, and Jed
agreed when he saw it. The big treaty council of '51
had given the Big Horns to the Crows, but Sun
Horse's valley was far in the southern end of the
range, and Crows rarely came that far south anymore, choosing instead to yield the ground to their
numerous enemy the Sioux.

Jed said nothing of his quest until a time when the
snow was deep outside the lodges and there was little
to do but smoke the pipe and talk. Then he chanced
to remark one evening that perhaps Bat and Sun
Horse knew of a place where a man might build a
house. Bat looked at Sun Horse and after a time Sun
Horse had nodded and smiled.

The next day the three of them put on snowshoes
and walked over the southern ridge to a small mountain park that Jed had never seen. They came out of
the woods on a low rise that commanded a view of
the entire valley and in the space of a deep breath Jed
knew that he was looking at his home. But he didn't
let his excitement show, not yet. He had to be sure.

For days he tramped the mountain heights on snowshoes with Bat as his guide, exploring the two nearby
passes by which generations of Indians had crossed
the mountains in summer. One was accessible from
the valley by the gentle course of a stream. And then
for additional days he rode down to the eastern plains
and back until he found a way to the park by a grade

gentle enough for wagons to ascend. And only then
did he return to Sun Horse's lodge and tell the headman what he had in mind. He had a white wife and
daughter and he intended to live like a white man, in
a proper house, Jed explained. Wagons would come
to the valley, and men who were foolish in the ways
of the mountains. But Sun Horse brushed these things
aside. It did not matter, he said; in winter there
would be no wagons, and winter was when Sun
Horse and his people were nearby; in summer they
moved north to the Powder and the Tongue and the
Greasy Grass to hunt buffalo and camp in the circle
of the nation. Jed was welcome in this place. He
could trade with the wagons in the summer, and in
winter he could visit with his brother Bat and the
people of the Sun Band. It was good for the whiteman
and the Lakota to live side by side in this place, the
headman said.

The fact was, Sun Horse seemed downright anxious that Jed should agree, as if he might have had
just such a thing in mind from the start. For Jed's
part, he had hoped to live where he might have some
peaceful contact with the aborigines, and so to experience once again that part of his mountain life. The
arrangement was perfect. When Sun Horse filled a
ceremonial pipe and passed it around to seal the
bargain, Jed solemnly offered it to the four directions
and smoked. He had found what he was looking for.

This morning, as she stood beside her father's
grave, Lisa had stood in his moccasins, feeling Sun
Horse and Bat by her side, seeing the snow of the
valley unmarked except for the feed runs of the
moose, which had been more numerous then and
were now retreating to the higher valleys west of the

Divide. And she had felt a tug deep within her, a contraction of the spirit before a swelling that threatened to burst her heart. The only father she had known was the man who had lived here, at home in the country he loved; she had not known the wandering years of the fur trade or the restless exile on New England shores and far-flung seas. Here Jed had transmitted his love of the land to her and a respect that approached that of the Lakota themselves, who called the earth Grandmother and Mother because it brought forth every generation of man and nurtured each one at its breast. Within Lisa, the love of this land, enclosed and sheltered by the arms of the mountains, was almost painful.

Her father had told her the story of his quest for a home, and of his first view of this valley, on the day she turned twenty-one, not asking that she feel the same thing for Putnam's Park, only wanting her to know what it meant to him. On that same day he had given her a small volume of Thoreau, with a stalk of timothy grass marking a particular page:

> *Of thee, O earth,*
> *are my bone and sinew made;*
> *To thee, O sun, I am*
>   *brother*
> *Here I have my habitat.*
> *I am of thee.*

How could a man like Hardeman understand a tie to the land, a sense of what this home meant to her? He could not. She had seen how he came alive on the trail. It was being on the move that he loved. She had seen it—the eyes always roving, the alertness beneath the outward calm, the body so relaxed in the saddle except for the way he occasionally rolled his right shoulder as if to relieve an almost forgotten pain.

She observed him now as she went about her kitchen chores, not giving him cause to notice that she watched. He sat back in his chair—her father's chair—with his feet on the seat of another, staring out the window at nothing. When he looked in her direction his deep-set eyes were impenetrable, revealing nothing. He seemed to belong here now, clad in his leather shirt and pants; he was no longer the stranger from the settlements who had sat at the table drinking whiskey only three days before. He could have been from another time, a friend from the fur trade come to visit her father or her uncle Bat. It would be easier then to admit to herself that she found him attractive, easier to get him talking, easier to discover what sort of a man there was beneath that guarded look. . . . But he was a scout, not a mountain man; he had led General Custer to the Washita and he came here now at another general's bidding. . . . How could he wait so calmly?!

"Is there a chance the storm will slow down General Crook's march?" she asked, grasping at straws.

Hardeman shook his head, his attention returning from far away. "It's the cold that slows down the army. That and all the fool gear they carry. Crook's done away with most of that. He knows how to cover ground." Nothing short of a blizzard would stop him, and this snowfall was just a half-grown mountain storm that probably wouldn't shed a drop of moisture on the Bozeman road.

"What will Sun Horse and his people do?"

"We'll know soon enough."

"What would you do, if you were Sun Horse?"

"I'm not Sun Horse."

Her patience broke. "Is it that easy to send other men to prison?" Suddenly she wanted to loose all her anger on this man who sat so calmly in her father's chair. "That's what the reservation will be for these people, you know. There are no trees, no game, no camping places that aren't fouled—"

She bit off her words and held the anger in. I need it, she thought. I need it to give me strength. I will fight for Sun Horse and when that is done I will fight to save my home.

But how will I fight? Without an answer to that question her resolve seemed impotent and she felt her courage dissolving. If only she could sway Hardeman to her side. If he were her ally . . .

She poured a cup of coffee from the pot. "I owe you an apology," she said. "I have been blaming you for bringing bad news, but you are not to blame. I'm sorry."

"There's no need to apologize. We weren't invited. You have been kind, under the circumstances." Hardeman had not meant to make her angry; he welcomed the conversation and wished it to continue, both to keep his mind off the waiting and in the hope of bringing Lisa Putnam around to his point of view. He had provoked her carelessly and he sought a way to placate her now. As Lisa leaned across the table and set the steaming cup before him, he caught a delicate odor he had thought was part of the room, coming perhaps from the woodwork of the cabinets or an unfamiliar herb in the dried bouquets hanging by the sideboard, from which the Chinawoman took a small pinch now and then as she cooked. He realized that it came from Lisa herself, from her hair or a scent she used, or just from her skin.

"Wasn't there a king who killed the messenger because he brought bad news?" he said. He blew on the coffee, regarding her through the rising steam.

"Yes. I can't recall his name right now. Was it Solomon?" she smiled. "No, he was too wise."

Hardeman smiled, and Lisa felt better.

"Maybe it was Lear, on one of his darker days," he suggested.

"You seem to have read a good deal." She took a dish towel from the bar on the oven door and began to dry the dishes.

"More than you expected in a man like me?" Hardeman asked, but he smiled to show that he took no offense. "It was your own father who got me in the habit, and mine, before that. It wasn't something I expected to keep up on the western trails, but Jed was always lending me books that year we rode together. He kept them in his saddlebags, more books than you could imagine. I remember when we got to Sacramento there was a mail package waiting for him, full of books. He sent the old ones off."

"We used to send them from home," said Lisa, delighted by the memory. "First to St. Louis or Independence, then to Sacramento. Twice a year he got new books from the library at home. Tell me which were your favorites."

"Dickens," Hardeman replied without hesitation. "And any man who could tell a good story. Scott. And Shakespeare. Jed said that Bill Shakespeare was the best storyteller in the fur trade, and he had plenty of competition. Your father had this little set of all

the plays, each one small enough to put in your shirt
pocket, and I carried one of them more than once. I
found the whole set there in the library this morning.
It was like seeing an old friend.''

Lisa pulled out a chair opposite him and sat down.
She leaned across the table, the dish towel held in
both her hands, and he caught her scent again, more
subtle than any perfume. ''Sun Horse was my father's friend, Mr. Hardeman, just as you were. He is
truly a good man; you must have seen that. He has
wintered here in peace since before my father came
to this valley. A vision brought him here, to avoid the
hostilities. His power is to understand the white men
and make a lasting peace, my father said.'' She was
twisting the towel unconsciously, as though wrestling
with it. ''Don't you see? If Sun Horse could just hold
on for one more year, it could make all the difference. President Grant will be gone and there will be
a new Indian policy . . .'' She let her voice trail off.
Her slim hopes seemed too fragile.

''A year's too long. It will be over by then.''

''It doesn't have to be. Not if you help him. He's
Johnny's grandfather.''

''We helped him all we could by coming here,
Miss Putnam. We gave him time.'' Too damn much
time and too many uncertainties to take a hand in
things. Too much time to think, and who knows what
goes on in that old man's mind. Why did she have to
spoil the moment by bringing up visions, and Johnny,
and his kinship to Sun Horse?

Doubts about Johnny and his dream and what
changes might come over the boy up there in the
Indian village had wakened Hardeman that morning,
making him rise and dress and sending him out to

prowl the house to escape them. He had gone to the kitchen in the hope that Ling Wo might have a fire going, but the stove was cold and the room dark. By the light of a candle he had found a full jug of whiskey in a cabinet and he drank from the jug, lighting a fire within himself to ward off the predawn chill. Then to distract himself he had searched the dim rooms, seeking anything that might make immediate and real the late Jedediah Putnam, the boisterous teacher and companion he had known so briefly, so long ago.

In vacant bedrooms built for people who were long gone and would never come again he had found only the influence of Jed's Boston wife, seeing her hand in the curtains hung at each window—some no longer bright and new but always clean and ironed—the washstands and bedspreads and looking glasses in each room, the framed prints of eastern cities and landscapes and ships traversing the high seas under full sail.

In the downstairs hallway he had encountered the house cat, Rufus, prowling silently, but the cat's search, like Hardeman's, seemed to be fruitless.

Then, rounding a corner, Hardeman had seen light beneath a door, and Lisa Putnam's voice had answered "Yes?" at his knock.

There was no welcome in her eyes when he opened the door, but she had left before he could withdraw, and by the light of two brightly polished brass lamps, their green glass shades and yellow light giving a soothing warmth to the cold light of a stormy morning, he had discovered the library, and it was there that he found what he sought.

In his library Jed Putnam had tucked away that

portion of his heritage that did not lend itself to the
tall tales, the rough-and-tumble, the outrageous hooraw
and brag talk of the leather-clad mountain man he
had become by choice. There, enclosed by walls that
were lined to the ceiling with books, permeated by
the aroma of good leather, from both the upholstery
of the matched armchairs beneath the reading lamps
and the bindings of the volumes set cheek by jowl
around the room, another man lived. Mixed with the
odor of leather was the scent of paper, old and new,
overlaid with a hint of ink and a coating of dust and
the quiet calm that pervades rooms where people
come to read. It might have been the reading room of
the cattlemen's club in Denver, but no cattlemen's
club was ever arranged to suit the taste of the Yankee
trader who looked down from the portrait above the
fireplace, where Lisa's fire had subsided into a pile
of glowing coals. It took Hardeman a moment to
realize that the sober gentleman in his frock coat and
neatly knotted cravat was Jed Putnam. The hair was
combed, the beard and mustache trimmed and tamed.
As background, the artist had painted the pilings of a
wharf and beyond them the sea, with a single clipper
ship in the distance. But in the eyes of the subject
Hardeman had found his old friend; the painter had
captured the trace of humor in Jed's appraising gaze.
They were the same eyes that had looked down on
young Chris Hardeman all those years ago, and they
said the same thing now as then: "All right, friend,
let's see if you measure up."

They seemed to ask questions too, about what had
brought Hardeman here after so many years, and
why he was still a man on the loose, with no home of
his own. "Wanderfoot's a young man's disease,"

Jed had said when he spoke of leaving the emigrant roads and finding a home. "Most fellers get cured of it without any doctoring. Me, I aim to set a spell when I find the right spot. You'll do the same when your time comes, if you got good sense. A young man roams about to see the world, find out what suits him; but there's more to bein' a free man than always movin' on from one place to the next. You pick the life you want and a place to live it, there ain't a man in the world can stand taller'n you. Mark my words, Christopher. Get yourself a grubstake and set it by. When it comes your time to stop, you'll know."

Hardeman had never forgotten Jed's advice. In the years just before the Rebellion, he had scouted twice for government survey parties, which were then trekking everywhere across the western lands with devices that measured the heights of mountains and the distances between points, searching out routes for trails and railroads and mapping the land to make it known. They had paid well; so well that an experienced scout like Hardeman had made more in one day with the government parties than most men earned in a month. He had had no need for such money then, but neither had he frittered it away at gambling or reckless pursuits. Remembering Jed's words he had placed his earnings in a St. Louis bank, and there they remained. He had not yet found the place to call home.

In the library this morning he had answered Jed's questions as best he could, telling him of the money he had set by against the time when he might stop his roaming, and why he had come here now. He told him what he would do if Sun Horse agreed to go in, and what if he did not, and why he was bound to go through with it no matter what Jed might think, and he had asked Jed for his blessing. But he got no answer from the painting, so he raised the bottle and drank to their friendship, and then he turned down the wicks of the lamps and snuffed the flames and saw that the screen was set in front of the fireplace before he left Jed to his books and went off to the kitchen, where breakfast was already on the stove and Julius and Hutch and Harry were sitting down at the table, each of them as close-mouthed as Jed himself, as if they followed his example.

Now, Lisa rose to return to her task and Hardeman watched her as she worked the handle of the iron pump at the sink and filled the huge tinned kettle that lived on the back of the stove. Her Yankee backbone was stiff and straight and the light from the window caught the wisp of loose hair that hung over her forehead and made it shine.

He drank off the rest of his coffee and set the cup on the table. He had made his plans as best he could and nothing remained but to get on with it. He silently cursed the uselessness of his feelings for this woman, the need to help her and the wanting that was stronger than it had been for any woman in a long time.

That was the way of things, to want what you couldn't have. When it was all over and done, he would do what he could to help her and maybe she would keep her valley and her home, but he knew that no matter which way things went for Sun Horse, Lisa would see his part in the old man's fate and she would hold it against him.

He looked out the window and saw that the wind was rising again as he had known it would. Close beside the house, Harry Wo was still splitting wood, untroubled by the gusts that sometimes blew over the logs before his axe could rise and fall. A stubborn log bound together with knots had resisted his first blow. He replaced it on the block, moving with patient deliberateness. He stepped back and swung the double-bitted axe in a full circle, down and around and up and over, with enough force to challenge the chopping block itself. The blade entered precisely in the old cut and cleaved the log cleanly in two, and Hardeman wished that his own doubts could be cut asunder as neatly.

CHAPTER THIRTEEN

''That's about the last of it,'' Julius said as he tossed the final straws to the feeding cattle, and Hutch breathed an almost audible sigh of relief. They were the first words Julius had said all morning, apart from what was strictly necessary for getting the work done, and that was precious little. Hutch had been more than a bit concerned about the colored man's silence, for although Julius was sometimes serious he was not given to brooding. But ever since Hardeman and Johnny Smoker had ridden in three days before, things had changed in Putnam's Park. The little group of friends Hutch had taken such pleasure in had broken up and gone their separate ways, at least in their own thoughts. Yesterday, scarcely a word had been said at mealtimes. Hutch couldn't understand it. To him, the strangers were a welcome sight and he hoped he'd get a chance to ask one of them how things were back in Kansas, where they'd been until recently. Just knowing what sort of a winter it had been would make him feel closer to his ma and pa.

"You reckon you could handle this team for a bit?"

"Sure!" Hutch exclaimed, taking the reins Julius offered.

Julius had seen the worry in Hutch's face and he realized he had been off in his own thoughts all morning. The boy needed some cheering up. It had been a hard morning on the sled. The falling snow made for slippery work, trying to handle a fork and keep your footing, and twice they had had to unhitch the team from the sled and ride the doubletree to break a new trail where the wind had drifted in the old one. Julius was angry with himself for not hitching up all four horses today; he'd decided not to take the extra time, and his laziness had cost more time in the end. Through it all, Hutch had kept at his work without complaint, but every boy needed some encouragement now and again. Julius had got his share when he was Hutch's age, from his father and the other men.

He had thought a time or two this morning about saying what was on his mind just for the sake of getting it out and said, and maybe then he wouldn't think on it so much. But how could he tell Hutch what worried him? I'm too old to start over, he would say, and the boy would think, hell, I just started out on my own and it ain't such a big thing. How could he tell a boy who packed a sack and slung it over some mule and lit out with his pap's blessing, more than likely, what it meant to be Julius Ingram? He would have liked to take out like that when he was seventeen, all right, but he had seen what they did to runaway slaves.

I'm too old to start over, he thought again. I was old the first time and I got lucky. I won't find that kind of luck again.

He had come a long way since Georgia. A long way. How do you tell a boy who's just rid out from Kansas because he felt like it what it meant to be a slave for thirty-nine years and have a Union major tell you you're free on a sunny afternoon while the plantation burned to the ground around you? Thirty-nine was a late start at being free. Two days after the major set fire to the big house at the head of the lawn back up from the Altamaha River, Julius had enlisted in the army for the first time. He had served for a year, first as a hospital orderly and then as an infantry soldier, before being mustered out at the end of the war. And when the four black regiments were formed in 1866, he had enlisted again, and spent three more years in uniform in the Southwest. But he had quit the army in '69 because it was still a white man's army and would be for all time, and he had gone as high as a colored man could go: regimental sergeant major; and every man, black or white, knew he was the best soldier in the regiment. But he wasn't through yet finding out what he could make of himself, and so after three years with the Ninth Cavalry, some of the time spent in Texas, where he had seen the huge herds of Longhorns, he had joined the other freed men who were working with the cattle, and he had become a top hand. He already knew horses and he had learned quick about cows, but before very long he had seen the limits to what a hired man could do. All the drovers, black and white alike, talked at one time or another about owning a spread of their own, but it took money to get enough land to run livestock and not just a cowhand's end-of-the-trail money; it was eastern money and English money buying up the range, and bookkeepers running the business end of a cattle outfit. Julius had seen it all in his time on the trails and he didn't see himself getting any closer to what he really wanted, some place of his own, something that belonged to him that no other man could take away. "Forty acres and a mule" was the dream of many a freed man, but Julius wanted something more. He couldn't see himself going back to tilling the soil; he had been a field hand in Georgia.

"You like it here, boy?" he asked Hutch.

"Sure enough," Hutch said, all serious now and feeling important with the Belgians answering the reins in his hands, plodding steadily toward the clump of tall pines, the only landmark that could be seen in the swirling white. "Get on, Zeke," he said, just to let the lead horse know he was being watched. "It's a good place to winter, all right."

"You reckon you'll move on come summer?"

"Oh, I might."

"Well, I don't blame you, being young and all. You've got a lot to see, I reckon."

"Seen a right smart lot just getting here," Hutch said, and he grinned. " 'Bout the time I set eyes on the Big House for the first time, I was seein' Injuns behind every tree and glad for a place to hide. I like to took you for one when you opened the door."

"Took me for an Injun?" Julius chuckled. "There's some get pretty dark, boy, but not as dark as a Georgia nigger." He leaned on the front of the sled to rest the strain in his back and looked for a glimpse of the house through the snow. Hutch was following the tracks they had made that morning coming out from the first crib.

"I imagine there'd be a place here for you, if you had a mind to stay. You might think on it. There's a trip to Rawlins for supplies. More hands hired on come haying. It gets downright lively then." Julius wouldn't blame the boy if he went on. That's what he would have done, kept moving on, if he hadn't met up with Jed Putnam. You couldn't tell a boy that age to pick some place and stick with it. Besides, he wasn't even sure there would be a ranch come haying this year, but there was no sense burdening the boy with that. By August they might all be gone, or dead in an Indian war. Maybe he had best start toting a pistol when he was out away from the house.

"I'll think on it," Hutch said, and he looked to his driving as the heavy sled coasted past the first crib, the one nearest the settlement, and made the turn for home. The hay from the crib had been fed early in the winter and the square log structure stood empty now. It looked like a cabin started by some faint-hearted homesteader, abandoned even before he put on the roof.

"I ever tell you how I met Jed Putnam?"

"A time or two. Abilene, you said."

"Yeah, I guess, I did. Seventy-one, it was, late summer. There was half a million beeves drove to Abilene in '71, and that was a sight to see. Grand ideas folks had about raisin' cattle, and they still

got 'em. But there'll be a change. Old Jed saw it
coming." He turned to look at Hutch. "Folks used to
raise cattle for hide 'n' tallow, you know that?"
Hutch nodded. "Reason was, there wasn't no way to
ship live cattle, no way to ship the meat without it'd
spoil. So folks raised hogs and ate hog meat. Then
here comes the railroad. Now they haul cattle live,
butcher 'em where they please, so folks eat beef."
He looked back at the cattle, still snuffling in the
snow for the last of the hay, and he grew more
serious.

"The railroad put an end to Jed's road ranching,
good and proper. But Jed, he always looked ahead,
and he seen a way to get some good out of the
railroad. He went to raising cattle. But not thousands
of head all turned out to hell and gone like the big
outfits. Just a handful, five hundred or so when we
build the herd up. Few enough we can keep 'em in
the park in wintertime and feed 'em when they need
it. Old Jed, he seen forty winters in the mountains.
Some of 'em all right for a tame critter, he says.
Some not. He reckoned to keep his cattle where he
could keep an eye on 'em."

He fell silent. There he went setting out all of
Jed's ideas about why the herd should be small as if
it were gospel, and he himself had often argued that
the ideas were wrong. Build up the herd, Julius had
said. Turn 'em out down below the park, raise as
many as we can while we can. When the homesteaders come, that's time enough to think small. Just
the other morning he had been planning on how to
persuade Lisa that his ideas were right, and he had
believed he had all the time in the world. It would
take some years to build up the herd until the park

wouldn't hold any more, and over the years Julius had figured to bring Lisa over to his way of thinking. In time he had thought the Sioux might be pushed farther to the north, and then the homesteaders would come, but he had imagined that time to be far in the future.

A lot had changed in three days. Now it was a matter of keep the park or lose it all.

"Old Jed, he seen the changes coming," Julius mused, "but he didn't see this."

"What's that?" Hutch wanted to know.

Julius smiled at the boy. "He was a wild one when I first set eyes on him. Could drink his weight in corn liquor. You ever been to Abilene?"

"I seen it onct. My pa took me to buy a milk cow. Our spread is on the Smoky Hill up above Salina."

Julius wondered how big the boy's pa's "spread" was. A quarter section in that country. They'd let you take a half section out where it was poor land or dry. But a quarter section was a quarter section more than Julius's own pa had ever owned.

"Abilene was good'n lively back in '71. Took a heap o' hands to drive half a million beeves north. Bill Hickok was marshal then. Might be still, for all I know."

Again Julius fell silent. If the supply of Longhorns driven up the Texas trails in '71 hadn't outstripped the need for beef, and if he hadn't run into a lean and gray-haired frontiersman in an Abilene saloon, he wouldn't have a half interest in Putnam's Park today. It was strange how choosing one saloon over another could change a man's life.

Julius had been out of a job, fresh out, when he met Jed Putnam. The half million Longhorns had

caused such a glut on the market that the price had
gone lower than ever before. Julius's boss, a canny
man who was experimenting with a Longhorn-Durham
crossbreed, had been forced to hold his herd outside
town like many another stockman, waiting for the
price to rise. As the weeks passed, he had let most of
his men go, paid off at half wages with money he
borrowed against the herd. In time, prices rose all
right. An early blizzard rolled down out of Canada
and froze nearly two hundred thousand head of cattle
to death. The price for the surviving animals went
sky-high, but by the time the blizzard hit, Julius's
former boss was already bankrupt and Julius and Jed
Putnam were long gone from Abilene.

He had spotted Jed right off for a frontiersman,
taking him at first for a buffalo skinner, one of the
hide men who were even then picking the southern
plains of the last great herds. The Texas drovers
could always tell when the hide men were working
upwind. Sometimes it took half a day to ride clear of
the stench. Jed had looked restless and edgy, like a
Longhorn put in a pen for the first time. He was
moving among the rowdy drovers, stopping here and
there to listen to the talk and maybe buy a man a
drink. He was talking cattle, and Julius learned quick
enough that he was no hide man. "Jersey and Guern-
sey, Holstein, Hereford, Brahma, Longhorn, Angus
and Durham, I've had 'em all," he told Julius over
the first of several drinks he bought for the tall
colored trail hand who seemed to know a thing or
two about a cow.

Jed had recently culled his herd and driven all but
a handful to Nebraska, where he sold the animals to
the army at the Red Cloud Agency before heading

south to Kansas with the proceeds in his pocket. He was looking for advice and help, and he limbered Julius up with whiskey and told him what he planned to do. For fifteen years he had traded animals with the emigrants who passed through Putnam's Park, as all the road ranchers on the western trails had done. He had taken a sick or exhausted animal in trade for something an emigrant needed, and when the animal was well and strong again and in fit condition to go on, he would exchange the animal for two more that were worn out. The profits in such a trade were quick, when a man knew animals as well as Jed Putnam, but he was not in the trade just for profit. He was looking for breeds that would thrive in his mountain home. From time to time he would go down to the ranches along the main trail and do some trading there, and for horses he traded with Indians as well as the whites.

Julius smiled, remembering how Jed had loved to barter. He was a fair man, but he had cut his trading teeth on the fur trade in its heyday, and he could spot the gleam of greed in a fool's eye at a quarter mile. Over the years he had kept back the beasts he liked best, stocking Putnam's Park with work and saddle horses, milk cows, chickens and pigs, and a flock of geese, mostly because he liked their ornery and rambunctious nature but also because he was fond of roast goose for Christmas dinner. He couldn't abide goats, and kept none, but he had cared for and doctored just about every breed of cattle known to man. "I've wintered 'em all," he had told Julius in the Abilene saloon, then growing crowded as dusk fell, "and I'll tell you what: with a little care a nigger could raise some beef up my way. No offense. Now

I'm thinkin' beef, not legs and bones.'' He had no
great love for Longhorns, but he knew their virtues.
''All hoot 'n' holler 'n' bones,'' he said, but even
though he reckoned to feed his cattle in winter, he
knew they would need some endurance and something more than the stubby legs of the English breeds
to get them to the Union Pacific stockyards at Rawlins, and so for the time being he had settled on half
Longhorn blood, maybe to be bred down to a quarter
or less later on. He listened with growing interest as
Julius told him about the speed with which the newer
strains grew to market weight, compared with the
four years it took a Longhorn steer to mature, and as
the evening wore on and the level in the bottle he had
bought ebbed steadily, Jed grew fond of his newfound
companion. ''Here's a nigger knows poor bull from
fat cow!'' he whooped, and a dozen colored trail
hands had turned in his direction with fire in their
eyes, but Julius waved them off and poured the last
of the whiskey.

The next day the two men rode out of town to the
grasslands the vast herds were grazing down to stubble. Among the Texas cattle were cows and calves as
well as steers, breeding stock for the northern plains.
Jed bought sixty pair from a man who could afford to
wait no longer, and gave him a better price than he
would have got elsewhere on that day, and then they
went to the stockyards. In a pen by the railroad siding
were three Durham bulls ordered by a man who
couldn't afford to pay for them until he sold his herd.
''I don't like to take advantage of another feller's
hard times,'' Jed said, but the man said, ''You'll be
doing me a favor. I'll have to stick to Longhorns this
year to cut my losses.'' And so when Jed and Julius

set off the next day for Wyoming Territory with their little herd, the shorthorn Durhams grumbled along behind.

"One thing you never said," Hutch interrupted Julius's thoughts.

"What's that? About what?"

"You never told me you killed them fellers."

Julius looked at him sharply. "Where'd you hear a thing like that?"

"Miss Lisa. I asked her a week or two back how you come to be a partner. I sure didn't mean to pry. You never told me that part. Is it true?"

"Anything Lisa said, you got the truth of it. You know that." The boy knew it all now. Julius had never told him about Buck and Sweeny because he wasn't one to take pride in killing a man, even if the two of them put together didn't amount to half of Jed Putnam. Even before they crossed from the Solomon to the Republican, Jed had dropped back from where he was riding point to ride beside Julius for a while and tell him to keep an eye on Buck and Sweeny, two of the hands he had hired to move his herd all the way to the Wyoming mountains. "Here's a child as wouldn't want to cut trail in Blackfoot country with them two" was the way he put it.

Three weeks later, when they were pushing the herd across the Platte, a cow had balked in midstream and Jed's horse had lost its footing when he tried to get a rope over the cow's head. The commotion spooked the other animals and before the cattle were all safe on the far bank one had run over Jed in the water and broken his leg. Once Jed was dried out and laid next to the fire and the cattle were settled down, Buck and Sweeny presented Julius with a deal

that pleased them both quite a lot. Old Putnam had
the papers for the herd on him and there were half a
dozen outfits within a hundred miles where a bunch
like that could be sold and the sellers disappear back
to Kansas or Texas with no one the wiser. Jed Putnam would be just another grave beside the Platte
and there were plenty of those already. Julius said the
idea didn't seem entirely fair to Jed Putnam, but
perhaps because he was a quiet man or perhaps just
because he was black, Buck and Sweeny had shrugged
and made a move to put Julius out of the way along
with Jed, figuring that Spooner, the other hand and a
man who never in his life made up his own mind
about a thing, would fall right in line behind them.
As things turned out, Spooner was more than willing
to help Julius bury Buck and Sweeny and help get the
herd moving again, with Jed Putnam carried on a
drag behind one of the horses, his leg set and splinted
by the tall Negro.

Julius had thought no more about the incident. He
had acted according to his own instincts of what was
right and had dispatched Buck and Sweeny with his
Starr Army .44 only when there didn't seem to be
any other way to convince them. But Jed was inclined to be more generous. Julius had been hired on
to trail the cattle to Putnam's Park, and before the
incident at the Platte he and Jed had already found
that they got along sober as well as drunk and Jed
had offered him a job as foreman of the Putnam Land
and Livestock Company, a creation that existed only
on the bill of sale for the sixty pair and in Jed's
imagination. Julius had said he would think about it.
He wanted to see Putnam's outfit first. When he
finally rode up the wagon road into the little valley

and saw the hillsides painted in the aspen yellows and pine green and golden grass of early autumn he had been about to take the job when Jed brought out a new offer, one he had been mulling over as he jounced along on his pony drag. He offered the colored man a partnership down the middle, and held up a hand to stop the protests that rose to Julius's lips. It wasn't as if the business was already a going concern, he said; it was nothing more than the two of them would build together. "I'm pert, and that's truth, but I ain't no cub. You'll do half the work and more."

"Well sir, there we are." Hutch reined the team to a halt in front of the barn, pleased with himself.

"You done her slick," Julius said as he swung off to the ground. "Reckon I'll take it easy from now on."

"About them fellers, did they have the drop on you?"

"Not quite."

Hutch hoped for more and got nothing, so he began to unharness the team, his spirits damped down.

Julius hadn't meant to cut the boy off, but he knew he could tell him the whole story from beginning to end, go over it up, down, and sideways, and it wouldn't matter. He could tell him about each day of his life from the time he was born and there was still no way a boy who had just lit out on his own and took his freedom for granted like the hair on his head could ever see what Julius's stake in Putnam's Park meant to him, or what it was that had been bothering him for three days now. The threat was there, plain enough, although it hadn't been said in so many words: help Hardeman find Sun Horse, help him persuade the old Sioux to take his people to Dakota, and the scout would do what he could to see that Lisa and Julius kept Putnam's Park when the country was opened up for settlement. Sit back and do nothing, or worse yet, side with the Indians, and lose everything for sure.

Lisa had taken Hardeman to see Sun Horse, but had she told him to surrender? Had she gone against her true feelings and turned her back on thirty years of friendship between the Putnams and Sun Horse's band? Julius knew better than to think that. And he knew that even Lisa could not put herself in his boots and feel what he felt for Putnam's Park. If she lost her home she could still start over someplace else, but a colored man's opportunity was a different kettle of fish. For Julius, Putnam's Park was a dream come true, and such good fortune did not fall into a colored man's lap twice in the same lifetime.

Bat Putnam's dog got up from where it had been lying in front of the tipi by the woods and trotted down the path to sniff at the team and the two men.

"Hello, dog," Hutch said, scratching the mongrel's ears. "What in hell is this dog's name, anyway?"

"Ain't never heard him called a name." Julius was working at the harness on the other side of the team. "Leastways not in English. They call him *shunká* in Sioux. Just means dog."

The dog seemed to lose interest in Hutch suddenly. Its ears went up and it turned to look down the valley, a low growl rising in its throat. It rarely barked. Sioux dogs learned to be quiet or they went swiftly to the stewpot.

Julius stopped work and turned to follow the dog's

steady gaze. The wind was blowing up the valley toward the settlement, but he heard nothing and the snow was falling thickly still, blocking the road from sight. "You hear anything?"

Hutch listened. "I don't hear nothing."

Julius lifted Zeke's collar off. The dog growled again, never taking its eyes from the valley road. Then for a moment the wind shifted, the snow thinned, and Julius could see to the notch where the wagon road passed through the hills. Emerging from the dark of the cut was a line of moving dots—ten, twelve, more still coming—all gone in an instant as the snow dropped again like a curtain.

CHAPTER FOURTEEN

"Can't see a thing." Hardeman peered down the wagon road, but the snow continued thick and heavy. He stepped off the saloon porch and walked down the steps to the hitching rail, as if that advantage would make it possible for his eyes to pierce the dense flurries.

Harry Wo approached from the blacksmith shed, his hammer in his hand; Ling was watching wide-eyed from a window of the saloon. Hutch came running from the barn where he had finished turning out the horses and putting away the harness alone while Julius went to alert the settlement to the coming of wagons.

Julius pointed to a long-handled shovel leaning by the saloon door. ''Get the porch cleared off, if you would.'' Hutch was not sure what this chore had to do with the arrival of wagons in the park, but he set to it with a will, glad to have his part in preparing for company. In the last few days, life in Putnam's Park had become halfway exciting.

Lisa glanced at Julius. ''Are you sure?'' Her mountain goatskin riding coat was thrown over her shoulders and she had donned her hat to protect her hair from the snow. She had slipped her feet into a pair of gum-rubber boots, which appeared incongruous beneath her gray woolen dress.

''I'm sure.''

Hardeman held up a hand for silence, but he could hear nothing over the wind, see nothing but the snow that now hid even the clump of tall pines where the road turned for the settlement.

And then he made out the first sounds, carried on a backrush of air that brought the snow straight in his face—whispered memories of his days as a young scout: the soft creaking of wagon wheels. Then, as if they materialized out of the snow itself, riderless horses appeared, walking and trotting, driven by three riders. In the trail broken by the horses came the wagons. They were like small houses on wheels, enclosed with boarded sides and gabled roofs, drawn by teams of oxen and mules and draft horses.

The snowfall thinned suddenly, the gusting wind dropped, and the full length of the strange caravan was revealed. There were twenty-four wagons in a row, and the first impression of tiny houses was confirmed down to the windows in the sides and the tin chimneys protruding from the roofs. The wagons were brightly painted with decorations of wild animals and gilt lettering on each wagon that said *Tatum's Combined Shows*. The unmistakable growl of a large cat came from one of several flat-topped wagons whose sides were covered by lashed-down tarpaulins.

In the pasture by the barn, the draft horses took fright and galloped to the farthest corner of the fence; in their own enclosure, the bulls pawed the snow. Two geese were walking on the bank of the spring pond; they took to the water now, and there were a few honks of alarm from the flock. The group in front of the saloon stood transfixed, none moving or saying a word.

At the head of the caravan rode a large man on a white stallion that stood seventeen hands at the shoulder. Throwing back his full cloak of royal blue, the rider raised a hand in command. As one, the wagons stopped and the draft animals stood still in the traces, clouds of steam puffing from their nostrils.

From the top of his silk hat to the polished tips of the high black boots into which his tight broadcloth riding trousers were tucked, the man bore his tailored finery as if it were the only fitting dress for a solitary mountain fastness. His eyes were wide-set and alert, the tips of his mustache waxed, his muttonchop whiskers neatly trimmed. His hair was dark and his complexion was ruddy from the cold. Without yet acknowledging the people in front of him, he made a slight motion with one hand.

A small figure jumped from the lead wagon and bounded forward, turning cartwheels and somersaults in the snow, bouncing to a stop in front of the hitching rail where Hardeman stood. The settlement group could hardly have been more surprised if Ulysses S. Grant himself had appeared before them in a clap of thunder, dressed up like a cowtown whore. The small figure was garbed in a loose white blouse, multicolored baggy knee-pants and white stockings, red shoes like bedroom slippers and a conical red hat with a blue tassel. The face was painted and powdered a solid white, save for the sharp black star-points radiating out from the eyes that were wide with excitement.

It was a clown.

He smiled at his dumb-struck audience and passed a hand down in front of his face, wiping away the smile and replacing it with the doleful mask of tragedy. Up went the hand and back came the smile. The figure winked at Hardeman, bowed, and swept a hand toward the man on the white horse. With a spring of his legs, the clown turned a backflip and bounded away towards the wagons as the rider cantered forward, the horse prancing with feet lifted high, coming to an abrupt stop twenty feet away. Then, to the amazement of those in front of the saloon, the horse bent delicately to one knee and bowed his head before rising again to stand before them. The rider swept the silk hat off his head and bowed low in the saddle.

"Madam and gentlemen," he said with all the formality of a ringmaster addressing an audience of city gentry, "I am Hachaliah Tatum, proprietor of Tatum's Combined Equestrian and Animal Shows. Our feats have delighted and astonished young and old alike from Philadelphia and Boston to the Black Hills of Dakota; our next intended venue, the mining establishments of Montana Territory. But I fear we have lost our way. May I inquire as to our whereabouts?'' His pale blue eyes paused on each person before him, seeking the one whose authority most nearly approached his own.

Julius was the first to recover his voice. ''You're in Putnam's Park. The lady is Miss Lisa Putnam. My name is Ingram.''

Tatum smiled and bowed to Lisa, ignoring the Negro completely. ''Miss Putnam.''

Hardeman moved a little to one side so he could see past Tatum to the full length of the caravan, every man of the circus within his view. Two riders had moved away from the wagons and were drawing nearer. They stopped halfway between the wagons and the Big House. One was of middling height, with a full black beard and mustache. Sharp eyes peered from beneath a derby hat. He wore a buffalo coat and carried a rifle across his lap, the barrel cut short at the end of the forestock. The man's high-strung horse shifted about nervously, prancing this way and that. The animal shied at an imagined something in the snow and turned halfway around, and Hardeman saw that the left sleeve of the buffalo coat hung empty; the rider had only one arm. The other man was shorter. He wore a slouch hat and an angry scowl, and Hardeman guessed he was the guide who had blundered off the main trail.

''Hey, mister,'' Hutch called out from where he leaned on his shovel. ''Is that a sure-enough circus show you got here?''

Tatum smiled his thin smile. ''We are a troupe of professionals, young man, bringing entertainment to the hinterland.'' He shifted his gaze to take in all of them. ''We encompass the riding of Astley, the clowning of Grimaldi, the talents of a dozen foreign lands making an unparalleled tour of the western provinces before our much heralded appearance at the centennial celebrations this summer in San Francisco. We carry in our ears the applause of all the great eastern cities, the booming metropolis of Chicago, the teeming polyglot of St. Louis. We are the first to pioneer such a spectacle in the wild territories of Dakota, Wyoming and Montana, and we shall give a week of performances for the Mormons in the Salt Lake valley before boarding the train for the golden shores of California.''

"I imagine you're looking for the Bridger road," Lisa offered dryly. "You will have to go back the way you came and around the southern end of the mountains."

"I been through here in summer, years back," the rider in the slouch hat called out. "There's a trail out to the west."

"There is, in summertime." Lisa returned her attention to Tatum. "The West Pass won't be open until May or June. This has been a bad winter."

"I see." Beneath his calm exterior, Hachaliah Tatum was containing a growing rage. It had been clear for some time now that the man called Fisk was no scout, despite his boastful claims, but to mistake this goat path for the wagon road to Montana was more than Tatum would bear. It would take a week or more to backtrack, precious time that could not be regained. He would settle with Fisk later, but now he must put his best foot forward, to encourage hospitality and whatever help might be needed to get the circus safely on its way once more. Assuming the proper facade was the essence of showmanship.

"At the moment I am afraid we appear somewhat the worse for our travels. If we might encamp for the night or perhaps—" He had spied the sign that creaked softly above the main doors of the Big House and now he read it aloud. " 'Putnam House.' Is this by chance a public inn?"

"Yes, it is." Lisa felt an almost forgotten excitement. "My father built it in the fifties for the emigrants."

"You have accommodations then?"

"My goodness. We only have a few rooms, but—"

Tatum held up a hand, refusing any apology. "Only a few of us will need to sleep indoors. The rest will be quite at home in the wagons. We will be on our way in the morning, weather permitting." He threw a cold glance at Fisk.

Lisa's excitement was growing. She found herself calculating how many meals would have to be cooked—she and Ling would need the help of the circus's cook and supplies for that—and how long it would take Julius and Hutch to get the wagons and stock settled while she and Ling made the beds and prepared the saloon as a dining room. These were more wagons than had been in the park for ten years or longer, more than might ever arrive again at one time, and she felt like celebrating. It occurred to her that it might be a celebration to mark the end of her father's dreams, but she refused to let the thought dampen her good spirits. Even if just for one last night, she would welcome her guests in a style her father would have approved. "We will do everything we can to make you comfortable." She favored Tatum with her most hospitable smile. "It will take us a while to warm the rooms and make things ready, but

I imagine you will need some time to get your people settled." The circus master returned her smile and she noticed the even white rows of his teeth. He was rather a handsome man.

"You are very kind," Tatum said. "If your man will show us where to make camp?" He glanced at Julius.

"I'm nobody's man, Tatum." Julius felt the blood rush to his face.

"Mr. Ingram is my partner, Mr. Tatum," Lisa explained quickly. She had heard the underlying threat in Julius's tone and she wanted nothing to spoil the occasion.

"Your partner. Indeed. I stand corrected."

Julius imagined that he heard carefully veiled condescension in Tatum's tone, but it appeared that Lisa hadn't noticed it. Ignoring Tatum he turned to Hutch, who had rejoined the others; half the porch was cleared and the way to the saloon doors was shoveled clean. "We'll put 'em out by the barn. Show the wranglers where the hay is at and put the stock west of the fence. See what they need for—"

He was interrupted by a distant sound so alien that it sent a chill through his body. With everyone else he turned to look down the valley in the direction of the sound and for the second time that morning the inhabitants of Putnam's Park were struck speechless by what they saw. Half a mile away, coming up the wagon road at a lumbering run, was an African elephant bull, his trunk raised before him. He trumpeted again as he ran.

The people of the circus poured from the wagons, talking and shouting to one another in a handful of languages as they greeted the astonishing sight with obvious delight.

"Rama!" Tatum exclaimed. He wheeled his horse about and called out, "Chatur!"

"Tatum, *sahib!*" A dark-skinned man with his head encased in a tightly wound white turban was running toward Tatum, baggy white pants flapping beneath his heavy overcoat. He carried a long staff in one hand. "It is Rama coming, *sahib!* Did I not say he would be finding us?" The man pronounced the Hindi honorific as a single syllable: *sa'b*. He was grinning jubilantly.

"Stop him, Chatur! Get him calmed down before you bring him in!"

"Excellent, *sahib!* I am doing so!" Chatur changed course and ran off toward the elephant, stumbling often in the snow, which came halfway to his knees.

On the porch, Hutch managed to find his voice. "What in creation is that critter?"

"It's an elephant," Hardeman answered from the hitching rail. He wished he could have a few moments for his understanding to catch up with the events taking place around him, which seemed to have gotten out of hand.

The elephant stopped as Chatur drew near. The onlookers could see the small turbaned figure gesturing and addressing the beast, looking for all the world like an outraged father lecturing a child who had misbehaved. Suddenly the long trunk snaked out and grasped the little man, raising him into the air and provoking a gasp from Lisa, but in a moment Chatur was deposited gently on the beast's shoulders where he seated himself nimbly and touched the elephant with his staff, turning him toward the settlement at a placid walk.

"I'll be . . ." Hutch could think of nothing more to say.

Tatum turned the stallion back to the porch, obviously pleased. "Don't be alarmed. Our elephant broke loose last night. I was certain we had lost him for good, but—" He was interrupted by cries of surprise and horror from the crowd of circus people who had gathered beyond the wagons. Riding into sight atop a low rise at the edge of the meadow, midway between the settlement and the approaching elephant, were a dozen mounted Indians accompanied by two white men. The Indians carried lances and bows and a handful of rifles, and even over the distance it was possible to make out paint on some of their faces.

A hush fell on the settlement. It was the turn of the circus crowd to stare dumbstruck at the newest arrivals. The snow had thinned to nearly nothing and the wind had dropped, leaving the valley quiet and still beneath a tightly bound covering of clouds that hung motionless, close to the ground.

"Great God in Heaven!" Tatum breathed.

"They're on the warpath, sure!" Hutch's voice trembled with excitement.

"Hush, boy," Julius calmed him. "They're a hunting party."

Hardeman too had seen that the Indians bore none of the round bullhide shields they carried to war, the raw buffalo hide so hard and thick it could stop an arrow or a lance and might even deflect a bullet, except at close range. He recognized Johnny and Bat among the riders, flanking the gray-haired figure of Sun Horse, but it was Standing Eagle who stood out, with four eagle feathers bound in his hair and a winter cape of grizzly bear covering his shoulders and back.

Why Sun Horse brought so many men with him to carry the council's reply, Hardeman did not know, but he was sure the Indians intended no harm. Close at hand, the circus whites were backing nervously toward their wagons, all eyes fixed on the Indians.

The elephant had come to a stop facing the horsemen across a hundred yards of snow, the huge ears flapping, the great head swaying from side to side. With unnatural clarity across the distance that separated himself from the Indians, Hardeman heard the startled snorts of their horses as they caught the scent of the strange creature.

Aboard the lead circus wagon the driver glanced anxiously from Fisk to Tatum, looking for a sign, painfully aware of the train's exposed position, but no sign came and now he decided to act on his own. He shook the reins and clucked to the oxen and the wagon began to roll. Behind him the other drivers followed his lead and in a moment the whole caravan was on the move. The people on foot started to edge toward the safety of the settlement, some breaking into a run.

"It's all right! They're friendly!" Lisa called out, but her words were lost among the snap of traces and the creaking of wheels, the snorting of animals and the hubbub of nervous chatter among the circus people. Julius unbuttoned his coat and placed a hand on the butt of his holstered pistol, glad now that he had thought to don the gunbelt before stepping out to await the wagons.

On their small hillock, the Sioux were oblivious to

the commotion in the settlement. All eyes were on the elephant.

Blackbird sat his horse next to his grandfather, intensely glad that they had found the beast that had frightened him so badly. He had returned to the village as quickly as he could from the mountainside where he had spied the monster, afraid to disturb his grandfather again but certain this was something he should tell as a scout would do, saying only what he had seen and what he knew to be true. To his relief, Sun Horse had been more disposed to receive a visitor then, and had listened patiently. A hunting party had been mounted, led by Sun Horse and Standing Eagle. Let the hunters find this beast, Sun Horse had said, and then we will go to the white settlement to say what the Sun Band has decided. Blackbird's father had not wished to go but Sun Horse had insisted. We will go together, he said, Sun Horse and Standing Eagle, peace man and war leader, to say that the Sun Band agrees to Three Stars' request and will peacefully await his coming.

Sun Horse too was glad they had found the creature his grandson had seen, glad his words were true. The beast was yet another mystery produced by whitemen, another sign of their unpredictable power. "What is this thing?" he asked Bat Putnam.

Bat was looking at the unexpected crowd of strangers in the settlement, hiding so fearfully behind the wagons that were tightly bunched in the yard. Before he could form a reply, Blackbird suddenly put his heels to his horse and charged down the gentle slope straight for the elephant.

"That'll set the badger loose or I'm a nigger," Bat

muttered, but neither he nor any of the Lakota moved to stop the boy.

Astride Rama's neck, Chatur awaited the attack nervously. He knew that Rama could not outpace the swifter horse, and he resolved that if these were to be his last moments he would die as a true mahout, defending his elephant with every means at his command. Although Rama was African, chosen by Hachaliah Tatum for the imposing spectacle of his gigantic tusks and ears, Chatur had taught him all the maneuvers of an Indian fighting elephant, and now, with signals from his feet and his wooden staff, he readied the leviathan for battle. But the young rider on his fleet pony was too quick.

Blackbird had planned his move before launching his horse off the knoll and it worked as he had hoped. With all his attention fixed on the huge creature before him, he guided the horse effortlessly, using his knees and the single rein of braided buffalo hide that was looped around the pony's lower jaw. Feinting to the right he drew the beast-rider's attention in that direction, but as the giant head began to swing to meet the challenge, Blackbird swerved the pony quickly to the left, darting past the creature's flank, where he turned to the right again, cutting within an arm's length of the hindquarters and striking them sharply with his bow as he passed. The elephant wheeled to his mahout's command, but boy and pony were safely away and the Indian youth turned for the settlement, bow held high, shouting his excitement and his pride. He had avenged himself on the monster that had sent him running for his life that morning and once more he felt himself on the verge of manhood.

Seeing his triumph, the Lakota whooped their approval and rose to follow him. They gave the elephant a wide berth and formed into a line abreast, charging toward the buildings and the milling people, firing their new rifles into the air.

"Hooraw fer the mountains!" Bat cried out, loosing his own shot. With the wind in his face and the scent of gunpowder sharp in his nostrils before it was snatched away by the breeze, he felt more alive than he had all winter.

On the porch, Julius was enjoying the spectacle when the frightened cries of the circus people awoke him to the danger. "They don't know what it means!" he said, and he looked about for the first sign of trouble.

Beyond the hitching rail, Hardeman turned at the sound of Julius's warning. He had let Blackbird's charge distract him, and now, even as he turned back to the circus folk, a shot sounded close at hand. Seeing the Indian boy come within range, Hachaliah Tatum had drawn a nickel-plated Colt and fired, and was now aiming for a second shot. Hardeman's right hand moved to his belt, but Julius had his gun already out and swinging to bear on Tatum.

"Tatum! You leave it be!"

Tatum turned to look down the barrel of Julius's Starr .44, and in a single motion he returned his own revolver to its elaborately tooled holster, but already another shot boomed out nearby, from the short-barrel Winchester in the hand of the rider in the derby hat.

To Hardeman, his own movements seemed slow and leaden as his hand found the grip of his pistol and his eyes took in everything before him in a rush of fragments, like bits of rock hurled outward from a blast of powder set to break up a boulder. He saw the fluid ease with which Tatum handled his weapon and he noted the fancy twirl the unthinking hand gave the gun before returning it to the holster. On the fringes of his vision he took in the chaos of movement from the circus crowd, all running hither and yon, looking for any cover that would hide them from the Indians, who now scattered prudently in all directions and rode back out of range, those with guns beginning to reload them. He saw Blackbird bent in the saddle, gripping his upper arm, and he prayed that the boy was not seriously wounded. Through it all, most of his attention was on the Winchester in the hand of the one-armed rider. The weapon lurched in a short arc as the man cocked it for another shot, then leaped up to the rider's shoulder.

"Hold your fire!" Hardeman shouted, but as the pistol left his belt he saw the barrel of the Winchester start to swing in his direction, the sharp black eyes finding him in the middle of the confusion, and he saw in the rider's eyes an expression he had seen before, the look of a man caught up in a sudden outbreak of gunplay, ready to strike out at any danger, real or imagined.

Every particle of Hardeman's awareness held on the horseback man before him and the feel of the gun in his hand, his thumb pulling back the hammer, the other hand coming up to steady the shot as his body dropped into a slight crouch. It took forever before the hammer fell and the gun bucked in his hands.

The Winchester went off as Hardeman's bullet smashed into the stock. The force of the blow hurled the one-armed man from his saddle, and as the sound

of the two shots echoed off the far wall of the valley
and came rolling back again, a third shot sounded, a
booming explosion from the porch, where Lisa Putnam stood holding a shotgun aimed just over the
heads of the men below her. Smoke curled from the
black mouth of one barrel as the muzzle swung slowly
around to stare at each person in the yard in turn.
Beside her, Julius held his pistol high, his eyes never
stopping, searching for any sign of movement.

"The next man that moves gets the other barrel!"
Lisa warned in a voice that cut across the yard and
silenced the murmurings of the circus crowd.

Hardeman didn't doubt that she meant it, but he
turned back deliberately, slowly, to look at the one-
armed man, who now struggled to a sitting position
in the snow, blood dripping from a cut in his wrist
where a splinter from the shattered Winchester had
pierced him. Beyond the fallen rider a dozen men
from the circus were frozen in the act of bringing
their own weapons into play, pistols mostly, drawn
in panicked fear of the Indians. Lisa's warning had
come just in time to prevent a ragged broadside.

Hardeman kept his gun in his hand and his thumb
on the hammer, ready to support Lisa and Julius if
any of the men thought to follow up his original
intention.

"I will have no more fighting on my place!" Lisa
ordered. "Not between the two of you"—she gestured with the shotgun at Hardeman and the one-
armed man—"not with those Indians." She fixed her
gaze on Tatum. "You don't know our customs, Mr.
Tatum, but you had better learn. We are all here on
the sufferance of the Indians. They are my friends
and I will insist that they be treated accordingly."

She felt light-headed and curiously elated. With a
gun in her hands all her doubts of the past three days
had vanished and she knew she had made the only
possible choice: take a stand and fight.

"Your friends have a peculiar way of making us
welcome." Tatum fought to hold his temper in check.
He had no wish to antagonize this woman despite her
incomprehensible behavior in defending the savages
who had threatened the pride and joy of Tatum's
Combined Shows.

His words brought a murmur of angry agreement
from the crowd, and one man called out, "They shot
at us! You call that friendly?"

"They shot in the air!" Lisa snapped. "It means
they are coming into camp with empty guns. Those
are one-shot muzzle-loaders! It's a peace sign!"

The circus men lowered their weapons, the first to
draw them now the first to melt back into the crowd
once the rashness of their impulse was made clear.

"You won't deny that the boy attacked my elephant?" Tatum said with some heat. Rama had cost
him five thousand dollars in gold.

Bat Putnam had left the Indians in the meadow and
had ridden forward alone. He was near enough to
hear Tatum's last remark. "He didn't attack your
elephant, y' idjit!" he told the circus man. "He was
countin' coup!"

"Counting what?"

"Countin' coup! You touch your enemy with a
stick, you get much honor. Takes a brave man to do
it. The boy run into that critter this morning and it
give him a fright like to turned his hair. Now he's got
his honor back, good and proper!" Grinning, he
turned to Lisa and Julius, and gave Hutch a wink.

"That boy's gonna be famous, and that's truth. By Christ, this nigger'll give a pony to honor what he done. I'll give two!" A cackle of laughter rose in his throat. "Only man in the whole Sioux nation to count coup on a elephant! That's *some*, now!" With a fling of his left arm he threw the barrel of his Leman rifle into the air without warning and let fly. "Ooeee! Won't he stand tall!" The laughter burst forth in a long peal that echoed hand in hand with the booming report.

On the porch, Julius chuckled softly, amused as much by the mountain man's good humor as the notion of the boy who had counted coup on an elephant. Even Lisa softened her expression and lowered the shotgun.

Hutch found himself laughing. He wasn't certain what was so funny, but since the appearance of the elephant he had watched the unfolding events almost gleefully, as if it were all part of some kind of show put on for his particular enjoyment. The notion that he might be in some personal danger didn't occur to him until the sudden gunplay was over, and even then he had felt certain that Julius and Miss Lisa would protect him from harm. The way Miss Lisa had run into the saloon and returned in an instant with the shotgun, even before Hutch knew why she was alarmed, confirmed this feeling. Hardeman too had taken a stand to protect the settlement and the Indians from the stupidity of the circus greenhorns, and even Harry Wo had raised his hammer threateningly, as if he might crack the skull of anyone who dared to approach the porch where Hutch stood all the while, grinning like a fool. By the look of him, the circus boss Tatum figured the whole shebang might have been put on simply to get his goat.

Bat reveled in the uncomprehending annoyance on Tatum's face. He laughed so hard that he doubled over in the saddle, tears streaming down his cheeks. It delighted him beyond words so utterly to bewilder a man who wore a silk hat.

Hardeman stood apart from the others and felt none of their mirth. He returned his gun to his waistband, struggling to control a slight trembling in his hands. He sucked in a deep breath and held it as he looked off down the valley to where the Sioux had regrouped. They were waiting to see how the action in the settlement would be resolved. He could make out Johnny Smoker in their midst and saw the young man move one hand in a sign that told of no trouble from that quarter. Standing Eagle examined Blackbird's arm and dismissed it with a nod; the wound was not serious. Led by Sun Horse the Indians started forward now, keeping a wary eye on the crowd near the circus wagons.

Hardeman let the breath out slowly and began to relax. He spat in the snow, wanting to rid himself of the bitter taste that was the willingness to kill.

He had taken part in the quick gunplay instinctively, siding with Lisa and Julius because they were right and the circus men were fools, and because he could not afford to have the Sioux enraged by some unthinking offense on the part of ignorant whites. Soon he would hear what Sun Horse had to say and the waiting would be over. He felt the lingering anger and heightened awareness the gunplay had brought out in him and he realized that it didn't really matter which answer the old man brought, so long as the last doubts could be laid to rest and things could move forward in a rush that would keep both sides off-balance, for it was then that he would triumph, when events were moving fast and decisions had to be made in an instant, not after days of thought and misgivings.

He remembered the unspoken oath he had made when he smoked the pipe in Sun Horse's council. The smoke bound the one offering the pipe to speak the truth not just in what he said but all the truth he might know about the matter at hand, and while Hardeman had not told the councillors every detail of his plan, he was at peace with his oath. To him, the whole truth was that the Sun Band must submit. If they yielded to the inevitable, that could be the first step to a broader peace.

It struck him then that what he was trying to do was neither more nor less than to make a piece of history single-handed. There was an army marching up-country to impose a peace by different means. But he had seen his chance and he had taken it, and the truth was, he was not trying to oppose the inexorable forces descending on the Sioux, which would be a fool's errand for certain, but only to slip through the gate and change the outcome a little before the gate slammed closed and another section of the past was penned in for good, immutable and permanent. If he succeeded, and no one saw the mark of a former army scout on the final peace, that would suit Chris Hardeman, for he would have paid his debt all the same and he could go to his grave knowing that but for him the terror and killing of the Washita might have been repeated here, among Johnny's last living relatives.

He watched Johnny riding among the Indians, approaching in a walk, his horse next to Sun Horse's, and he saw once again how at home the boy seemed to be with his grandfather. And he forced himself to remember then that Johnny was a boy no longer. If his dream were to be believed, he would cross the threshold to manhood by his own deliberate choice, and once he 'had chosen between the worlds for good and certain, he would be free of the dream and he could fight if he wanted to. What if he changed his mind and picked the red man's world? The doubt resurfaced in Hardeman's mind. He had not protected Johnny for seven years just to see him go back to the Indians and maybe die in a winter campaign like the one in '68. Meeting Sun Horse and seeing how much he meant to Johnny had given Hardeman pause; now more than ever he had no wish for harm to come to Sun Horse or his people, yet now more than ever he saw that his way was the only way. Willingly or at the point of cavalry carbines, Sun Horse and his people would go in, and then Johnny would see that the free ways of his Cheyenne childhood were gone forever. Faced with life on the reservation if he stayed with the Indians, he would surely keep to his first choice and remain in the white man's world.

Sun Horse and his warriors had reached Bat now, twenty paces beyond the hitching rail, and they gathered around the mountain man. Johnny caught Hardeman's eye and gave him a short nod, but he made no move to leave the Indians and join his companion.

Hardeman's feet were cold. He turned back to the porch and when he reached the top of the steps, where the boards were shoveled clear, he stamped his boots to shake off the snow. He would wait for

Johnny here. The youth would come in good time, and Sun Horse would come too. They had no other course.

Surrounded by the Indians, Bat spoke to them in Lakota, gesturing at the elephant and explaining that the fearsome creature came from halfway around the world; "many moons across the great water, brought on a boat blown by the wind" was the way he put it. He added that in their native land, elephants were greatly respected and often used in war, knowing this could only add to Blackbird's glory. When they heard this, the warriors voiced their praise once more, and Blackbird tried to bear his pride with suitable dignity.

The circus crowd was moving closer now, drawn by interest in the Indians. Some paused to welcome Rama's return as Chatur stopped the beast by the wagons, but most were driven by a stronger curiosity; they had never seen wild Indians before and these horseback warriors were a far cry from the drunken beggars they had seen at Fort Laramie, offering their women to passers-by for a drink of firewater. But there was danger mixed with the curiosity, and hands resting near the butts of pistols that were stuffed in pockets and belts. The wagon drivers had been recruited in the Black Hills to replace men who had contacted sudden bouts of gold fever and deserted for the diggings with Hachaliah Tatum's curses ringing in their ears. The replacements had lost their own lust for gold after hard months in the frigid creekbeds, where arrows and gunshots had come often from the nearest timber. They had eagerly accepted Tatum's offer of work that would take them out of the Black Hills, but their memories of Indians were fresh and vivid and their hostility was obvious to the Sioux, who moved their horses to form a line facing the oncoming crowd.

Between the Indians and the men and women of the circus was the mounted figure of Hachaliah Tatum, one hand resting on a hip. He waited until the crowd drew near him, then touched his heels lightly to the stallion's flanks and rode in front of his people, becoming their leader.

On the porch Lisa grew apprehensive and raised her shotgun once more, but before she could issue a new warning, a chorus of titters arose from the crowd and one man gave out a loud guffaw. Puzzled, Tatum looked around to see that the clown was close behind him, mimicking his posture and bearing, one hand on a hip and the other holding invisible reins, the head held high and the haughty expression matching perfectly. Caught in the act, the clown dropped his pose and scurried into the crowd, provoking new laughter as he hid behind a huge man in a purple cape. The man stood head and shoulders above everyone else. Beneath the cape he wore a red shirt and brown wool trousers tucked into floppy boots. He wore no hat, and his flaxen hair hung to his shoulders, moving now as a breeze stirred it. The imposing giant remained silent and solemn, apparently oblivious to the clown, who peered from behind the safety of the cape. Tatum smiled tolerantly, not seeming to mind being the butt of this joke. At once the clown lost interest in the circus master and pretended to see the mounted Indians for the first time. His eyes sprang wide open and his jaw dropped as he ducked back behind the giant, but soon his curiosity drew him out and he darted forward, using the men and women of the circus as cover, finally daring to emerge from the crowd and approach the Indians on tiptoe, as if they might not notice him if only he were quiet.

The warriors watched this new figure with growing fascination. One man tightened his grip on his lance, but Sun Horse put out a restraining hand as the clown broke into a make-believe Indian war dance for a moment and then drew an imaginary arrow and fitted it to an invisible bowstring, which he drew back, releasing the arrow high into the air. With a hand to his brow he watched its flight, growing concerned as it soared directly overhead. He ran about in panic to avoid its fall, then suddenly clutched his breast and fell dead at the feet of the horses. The Indians burst out laughing, joined by the crowd of whites.

Johnny Smoker could scarcely believe his eyes. He was captivated, smiling broadly and laughing along with the rest.

Now the clown sprang to his feet as a gunfighter, his eyes on Julius, who still held his forgotten pistol in his hand. The clown approached the porch, his hand poised over an unseen holster. Julius hesitated, not sure what was expected of him, and then he entered into the spirit of make-believe. He replaced the pistol in its holster and dropped his hand to his side, waiting. At once the clown's face dissolved into abject terror. He backed away, then turned and ran toward the Indians, where he fell on his knees in front of Sun Horse, his hands clasped in supplication. The crowd roared.

Sun Horse smiled, charmed by the small figure. Like the other Lakota, he had been astonished to learn so unexpectedly that the whitemen too had clowns. *Heyoka*, the sacred clowns of the Lakota, wore tattered skins and robes, not brightly colored clothing, and they decorated their faces and bodies with the jagged lightning symbol to show their sacred relationship with the thunder beings from the west. Their power was based on doing everything backward. They said "no" when they meant "yes," they walked backward, they laughed to show sorrow and cried to express joy. They held special ceremonies and sang many songs, and in neither actions nor appearance did they resemble this whitefaced creature, but there was no mistaking the purpose held in common by the *heyoka* and the small figure kneeling before Sun Horse: each sought to bring happiness to people who were troubled or downhearted or angry. Only moments before, the whites from the painted wagons had approached the Lakota as enemies, the hostility on some of their faces plain to see; now the men and women moved closer in ones and twos, unafraid. The white clown had delighted the hearts of everyone present; he had brought two peoples close enough together to share the warmth of laughter. Sun Horse felt a lessening of the gloom that had enveloped him ever since the council meetings, and something akin to hope.

Finding no help from the old Indian, the clown got to his feet, but he slipped in the snow and teetered sideways, grabbing Johnny Smoker's leg with one hand to keep from falling. Johnny reached down and took hold of the clown's arm—too late. The clown's feet shot out from under him and he threw up his free hand in a futile effort to regain his balance, knocking off his tall red cap. A piled mass of long brown hair fell down about the clown's shoulders.

Sun Horse drew in a short breath of surprise. He saw at once that the small features now framed by the soft hair belonged to a girl. The *heyoka washíchun* a young woman? Was there no end to the surprises of the whites? The Lakotas murmured in astonishment.

On the porch, Hutch said, "I'll be . . ." and once again ran out of words.

Johnny still had the girl by the arm, holding her up until she could regain her footing. He was aware only of her, nothing else.

"Thank you," she said, looking up at him for the first time. He loosened his grasp and her arm slipped through his until their hands touched. She held the contact for a moment, clasping his hand in thanks before finally breaking the grip.

The crowd began to disperse now, sensing that the performance was at an end.

"We best get these folks settled," Julius said to Hutch. The two of them descended from the porch and started off toward the wagons, finding the guide Fisk in the crowd and taking him with them.

From the west, beyond the low-hanging clouds, came a soft roll of thunder. Sun Horse felt a chill sweep through his body like the shock of entering a winter stream. Was it real? The sound had been so faint that he wondered if anyone else had heard it, and then he saw that the other Lakota were looking nervously at one another and glancing at the skies. Thunder in winter was a dangerous power, to be pacified by the ceremonies of the *heyoka*.

Had the clown girl heard the voice of *Wakinyan*, the thunder being? Most of the whites were moving off towards the painted wagons now, the clown girl among them. She was walking beside the man on the tall white stallion. She gave no sign of sensing anything out of the ordinary.

Lisaputnam had gone inside the house. Only Hardeman remained on the porch. He was watching Sun Horse, waiting to hear what the council had decided. Johnny Smoker rode towards the house now to join his friend.

Again came the rumbling from far away, fainter still, and again Sun Horse felt the chill of power.

"*Taku shkan*," he murmured. Something is moving. Something *wakán*. He felt his power rising strong within him, comforting and familiar. Why did it return to him now?

He reined his horse around and rode a short distance beyond the wagon road, facing the stream and the valley. There he opened himself completely to what moved about him.

The *heyoka* girl made the people laugh and thunder came to her. Why?

He looked at the sky and saw that the clouds had risen to the ridgetops. Fine flakes still fell, scarcely enough to see, making the air shimmer. A soft breeze blew from the river and still the power moved around him and he felt calm and balanced, as if he touched the spirit world with one hand and the world of men with the other, receiving the strength of each one. Why?

The power came from the west, he was certain. *Heyoka* were of the west, and the thunder beings dwelt there. So rare to hear thunder in winter. . . . Even in summer the power of the west was not completely benign; it was the power to make things live but also the power to destroy; rain, the symbol of the lifegiving force; lightning, the power to destroy.

A power is coming. It is very strong. It can help the band or destroy us. . . .

This was what Hears Twice had heard! The unpredictable strength of the west brought here now, to help the people or to destroy them! . . . In spring and summer the rains came from the west, and the snows in winter, the water entering the ground to feed the grass, to feed the buffalo, to feed the people, the life-giving chain flowing from the west. . . .

It grows from the meeting of two people. . . .

Sun Horse shivered violently, so strong was the feeling that coursed through him. He had witnessed that meeting! As soon as the thought came to him he was sure. There was no trace of doubt. Here with his own eyes he had seen the coming together, the touching of the *heyoka* girl and his white grandson, and he had felt the power!

The hope rose quickly in him now, but he quieted his rushing thoughts and calmed himself to listen. He must be sure. Again he looked at the sky, the clouds hanging soft above him, enclosing the valley, turning each sound back on itself so it stood out sharp and distinct, carrying undiminished in the cool air. He heard the grunt of a bear from the painted wagons, the snort of a horse in answer, the beating of his own heart, which surely echoed throughout the valley to be heard by all; and then, carried on the breeze, came the short cry of an eagle.

His eyes searched the valley, never pausing, seeking motion.

There. He saw it coasting low above the willow marsh and the winding river, a young golden eagle, the undersides of its wings still flecked with white. It was the bird the Lakota called *wamblí gleshka*, the spotted eagle, the one that flies highest of all living things, closest to *Wakán Tanka*, the Great Mystery.

The bird soared on motionless wings far down the valley, now banking, now twisting, following the river towards the cut in the hills. And now the wings moved and *wamblí* rose into a sweeping spiral that grew wider and higher until the bird grew small and vanished into the clouds.

Sun Horse did not search the grayness for the moving speck—*wamblí* had given a sign and would not return. Something in motion here, something felt but unseen, something truly *wakán; wamblí gleshka* had said so, rising into the sky with the same sign that a Lakota made with his hand to indicate whatever was *wakán*, a mystery.

Wakán Tanka, I am sending a voice, he sang softly, the words said within his heart. Hear me, Great Mystery, I am sending a voice. A two-legged is sending a voice. In a sacred manner I call. In a sacred manner a nation is calling. Hear me, Great Mystery, I am sending a voice. . . .

He felt his own power stronger than ever before and he raised his eyes to the spot where *wamblí* had disappeared.

For the people I sing! In a sacred manner I sing. . . . Four times he hummed the chant and he had to restrain the laughter that rose to his lips, joy in the return of his power.

Delay! The thought returned with new force, and now he was prepared to speak to the council. Delay, that what comes together here today may grow. . . . Here in this valley that has never known war, a power begins. . . .

Delay.

And now a pathway opened before him and he saw the means to delay.

Send a pipe to Three Stars. A pipe of peace from a man of peace. Send a pipe so Three Stars will know our intention is peaceful. Say the Sun Band will not fight. Ask him to leave our country in peace. Say that in summertime Sun Horse will speak to the hostiles, and he will speak for peace. *With hope we can live until summer*. Our ponies are too weak to travel now. . . .

Send Standing Eagle! Send the war leader to bear a pipe of peace to the soldier chief! *With hope the people can live*. Send a pipe to Three Stars.

But also, now while the snows linger around the villages of the Lakota, send another pipe. Send a pipe to Sitting Bull and through him to all the bands. Ask them to remain at peace. Even if Three Stars will not hear the plea of Sun Horse, let the bands avoid fighting now; if the soldiers come near, let the people move away. Soon the bluecoats will tire of fighting *Waziya*, the winter power, and they will go home. In the summer, when the grass is tall, let the bands meet along the Tongue or Rosebud. Let word go to the agencies and call for relatives to slip away and come to this gathering. Let the great hoop of the Lakota nation be raised in the Moon when Buffalo Calves Grow Fat, and there let the people decide if they will go to the Dakota reservation and leave behind forever the grassy streams and wooded hunting grounds of the Powder River country. There in the great circle of the nation, Sun Horse would speak for peace.

Surely all the Lakota gathered together are strong enough to make a peace with the whites, a peace that might include some of the country here?

That was not for Sun Horse to say. Let the people decide, together.

Once more the Sun Band's council would meet, soon, tonight or tomorrow, but now Sun Horse would speak to them. With their leader strong and confident again, the councillors would agree to send the pipes. They would agree to this delay in order to give Sun Horse time to discover the true nature of the power he had seen joined here today, the power that brought him so much joy.

With a gentle pull on the single rein, he turned his horse to face the settlement. The last flakes of snow had ceased to fall and the air was turning cold. The clouds had risen and thinned. From the west came a shaft of sunlight that bathed the buildings and the snowy hillside in a reddish glow, like the light from a fire. The painted wagons were gone from the yard and were arrayed beyond the barn, where the figures of many whites moved this way and that. The Lakota horsemen, all but Lodgepole and Standing Eagle, were moving toward the wagons, a few whites walking beside them, looking curiously at the Indians. Men were rolling up the tarpaulins that covered the flat-topped wagons and Sun Horse could see in one of them the bear he had heard a short time ago. The animal was pacing back and forth in his cage.

On the porch, Hardeman was speaking with Johnny Smoker. They fell silent and looked in Sun Horse's direction when they saw that he was watching them.

What would Hardeman be prepared to do when he heard that the Sun Band would not surrender? Sun Horse could not guess, but he was certain that the white scout had planned for such an event. He would have to be outwitted, and that would be difficult. He must believe there was a better chance for peace with the sending of the pipes, and he could not be left to stand idly about. . . .

Send Hardeman with Standing Eagle! The war leader to bear the pipe and the white scout to carry the message for Three Stars! And send Lodgepole as well! Lodgepole would speak for the Lakota and Hardeman would speak for the *washíchun*, and together they would show Three Stars a way to make peace without more fighting! "Take your soldiers and leave the country so there will be no fighting now; in the summer Sun Horse will speak to the war leaders of the hostile bands, and he will speak for peace."

The message would be true. Hardeman would believe it, and he would not see the true reason for delay.

Sun Horse felt a deep contentment. With his mind composed and his face betraying no trace of emotion, as befitted a headman of the Lakota, he rode forward alone to surround his enemy.

THE SNOWBLIND MOON

PART TWO:
THE PIPE CARRIERS

is coming from Tor Books
in August

What lies ahead . . .

Once again the pipe carriers examined a place where the cavalry had spent this night, this one on the Clear Fork of the Powder. The morning was not yet half gone and they had already come ten miles since dawn. It was their fifth day on the trail and the third day of the storm, which was blowing still as if it meant to blow forever. By Hardeman's calculation it was the tenth of March, and with every hour that Crook moved northward the risk of war increased.

There were growths of cottonwood and willow along the course of the stream, the first trees the pipe carriers had seen since the Big Horn foothills and the first willow brush since Crazy Woman's Fork. As they moved north the land was becoming less arid. The river bottom was grassy, and Blackbird permitted the horses to crop what they might while the men examined the bluecoats' camp for signs.

Hardeman had looked at the campsite only briefly. He stood now with Blackbird and the horses, waiting for the others to satisfy themselves. As he waited he worked out times and distances, trying to force the cavalry closer by willpower. The signs said the cavalry had been here longer ago than one night. If they were ahead of the pipe carriers by two days, it might as well be two weeks. Crook was moving his troops up-country with a speed Hardeman would not have believed possible under such trying conditions; if he kept up the pace, the pipe carriers would never catch him. Unless Hardeman pushed on alone while his roan was still strong.

"Let's get moving," he said curtly, and the other men paused in their searching to look at him. "They were here and now they're gone. What else do you need to know?" He climbed aboard his horse. "The trail goes downstream." He started off without waiting to see if they would come now or waste more time.

The soldiers' trail was easy to follow in the relative shelter of the river bottom, and in what seemed to Hardeman an impossibly short time, certainly it was less than two hours, he came upon a small cove where there were many fire pits and evidence of some cooking.

"They laid over," he said to Bat as he dismounted. He led his horse down the bank into the cove and looked about, his spirits rising. "Must have spent all day here, or a long night, waiting out the storm. They might be just a day ahead." He remounted and gave the horse a sharp tap with his bootheels, urging the roan up the bank to where Bat was waiting. The mountain man had not bothered to dismount.

"Could be we're gettin' lucky," Bat said. "We'll press on. Eagle! Quit yer dawdlin' and climb onto that piece o' wolf meat y' call a horse!"

Through the middle part of the day the riders made good time, despite the steady resistance of the storm. The going was hard in the broken country of the divide, but the unshod Indian horses were nimble-footed and Hardeman's roan seemed at home in any terrain; he negotiated ravines and steep hillsides without complaint. The going was easier when the cavalry's trail descended to a stream Bat believed to be Prairie Dog Creek, and at mid-afternoon the pipe carriers found the soldiers' next night camp.

The riders dismounted from their grateful horses, which Blackbird led to a thick patch of grass close at hand. The stalks of last year's growth rose through the thin covering of snow everywhere hereabouts, carpeting the land even far from the watercourses.

The men chewed jerky and *wasná* as they poked about the camp. Here Hardeman dug in one of the fire pits. Six inches down, the earth was still warm. He grinned in triumph, feeling a growing excitement. "Bat!" he called. "They were here last night."

"Still a ways ahead and movin' quick," Bat said, stooping to press his bare hand to the warm earth. "We'll move on a bit, but we best find some shelter and some feed for the ponies afore dark."

Hardeman nodded, knowing Bat was right. The horses had eaten poorly the night before, and the strength they had gained back at Crazy Woman was gone now. Much as he would have liked to forge on through the night, hoping to close on Crook by dawn or soon thereafter, he knew such a course was foolhardy. The trail might easily be lost in the storm, and it was reckless to chance stumbling on the cavalry in the dark, possibly provoking a deadly reaction from the sentries before Hardeman could identify himself. The little band would have to find a good place to camp and start out again at first light. With luck they would catch Crook tomorrow.

"We ain't makin' tracks settin' here," Bat said, rising to his feet and moving toward the horses. In the last two days the mountain man had taken a controlling hand in deciding the pace of the march.

There had been some grumbling from Standing Eagle but no open opposition, and Bat and Hardeman often rode in the lead now.

Bat's horse started and shied sideways as he mounted, throwing her head and rolling her eyes, her nostrils flaring. The mare made a soft *huh-huh-huh* and her ears flicked this way and that. "Grizzly, maybe," Bat said, calming the horse and looking about. "Early yet, less'n he went to bed hungry."

The others mounted up and drew closer together as their eyes looked all about, trying to penetrate the ever-shifting clouds of snow.

"Might be nothin', or could be she seen a spook," Standing Eagle said, but his own eyes kept moving.

"It was sump'n," Bat said. The wind covered all sounds a man could hear, but the other horses showed signs of nervousness now, snorting the air and turning their heads as if they were as anxious as the men to know what lay beyond the obscuring snowfall.

"There," Hardeman said softly.

"I see 'im," said Bat.

A single rider materialized in the snow and drew near, a lance held ready, his mount moving at a cautious walk.

"*Kanghí wichasha,*" hissed Little Hand, and Bat muttered "He's a Crow," to Hardeman. *Absaroka* the Crows called themselves in their own language; they were the Children of the Raven, but the white men came from the east, where crows were more common than ravens, and the mistranslation had stuck.

Blackbird kicked his horse to move closer to his father. He reached for one of his boyish arrows that hung in the quiver at his shoulder, but Standing

Eagle made a curt motion and the boy dropped his hand.

More horsemen appeared now, all in a line abreast, walking slowly. They stopped when they were a dozen paces behind the lone man in the lead. There were eighteen of them all told.

"Here's wet powder and no fire to dry it," Bat said for Hardeman's ears alone, and he withdrew his Leman rifle from the fringed and beaded case that rested in his lap. Still the Lakota sat silently on their horses and still the Crow rider in the center made no motion, spoke no word.

He's sizing us up, Hardeman thought. Doesn't know what to make of Sioux and white men traveling together in these parts. He wondered whether to clear the way to his pistol. It would be pistol against bow and lance at this distance. Bat might get off a shot but there would be no time for reloading, and none of the Lakotas carried firearms. Apart from Blackbird, only Hawk Chaser was armed at all. He had both lance and bow, but the bow was slung across his back with his quiver and he had only the lance in his hand. Christ, Standing Eagle must feel as naked as a babe about now, Hardeman thought. Eighteen against six. This bunch isn't up to a fight with eighteen Crows. He thought of Johnny Smoker, who, like the two men carrying the pipes, did not go armed, and hadn't done for seven years now, and he missed having Johnny to keep an eye on his back when a fight was in the offing.

He unfastened three buttons on the St. Paul coat, moving slowly. Winter was a poor time for fighting; the clothing got in the way.

Now Standing Eagle raised a hand, moving slowly.

He moved the hand in broad sweeps, making the-signs-that-are-seen-across-a-distance, so all the Crows could understand him. *You are far from the camps of the Crow.*

The lone rider responded. *We have come to hunt. The four-leggeds are few in the country of the Crow.*

The four-leggeds have left the Lakota as well, signed Standing Eagle.

You are not hunters, the Crow said.

"And he's a lyin' Injun," Bat said softly. "Ain't no eighteen Crows out huntin' this far south o' the Yellowstone. Them's young bloods out huntin' coup."

I am Standing Eagle, war leader of Sun Horse's band, signed Standing Eagle. *Today I carry a pipe of peace to the white soldier chief Three Stars.*

This statement caused a stir among the other Crows and there was some brief talk among them. The leader listened for a time before returning his attention to the party in front of him. He motioned at the campfires and the tracks leading away to the north. *There have been many horse soldiers here*, he signed.

Standing Eagle nodded. *They are led by Three Stars. We follow their trail.*

The Crow smiled. *The horse soldiers do not come to the land of the Crow. We are at peace with our white brothers.*

Standing Eagle's expression did not change, but his motions became more emphatic. *We will live at peace with the whites when they leave our land and let us live like men!* He made the last motion sharply, the index finger of his right hand thrust erect before him, like the erect organ of a virile man.

The Crow leader's face grew dark at the insult and

from the others there were a few angry words, but the leader cut them off with a quick sign.

Hardeman changed his mind about the pistol. Moving no more purposefully than he might have done to scratch his ear, he slipped the Winchester out of its scabbard and rested it across his lap, in the same position as Bat's muzzle-loader. The pistol would be more use if the Crows decide to fight, but they didn't even know he had a pistol yet, and they feared the reputation of the many-shots-fast lever gun.

The Crow leader noted the motion, and the way the six riders sat quietly before him, their eyes meeting his. *Does it take four Lakota and two whitemen to carry one pipe?* he asked.

We have two pipes, Standing Eagle signed. *This man, Little Hand, carries a pipe to my cousin, who winters nearby.* He did not name Sitting Bull, who was a bitter enemy of the *Kanghí,* but he hoped that the Crow might temper their bravado with caution if they thought there were more Lakota close at hand. *The old whiteman is my brother,* he signed. *The other carries a message for Three Stars from Sun Horse, my father.*

"Old man! I oughta pin yer ears back for ye," Bat muttered. "If'n I live long enough."

There was more talk among the Crows and this time the leader was not quick to end it. Finally he turned back to the Lakotas and whites. *The Crow do not make war on those who carry pipes of peace,* he signed. *We will go now. Another day we will meet again.*

As silently as they had appeared, the Crows turned and rode away, quickly disappearing in the snow.

"I'll be dogged," Bat breathed. "I give it to ye,

Eagle, you done that slicker'n dog shit on a wet rock.''

Standing Eagle grunted and favored his brother-in-law with a rare smile. "Felt nekkid as a child, and that's truth. Figgered us for gone beaver.''

"Oh, I'd of thrown that nigger cold, all right," Bat grinned. "It war the others I worried on. But I reckoned Christopher here and old Hawk and young Blackbird was up to Crow today.''

"I will fight the Crow," Blackbird said, and grinned at Hardeman. "But I would rather fight *washíchun*.''

Hardeman did not entirely conceal his surprise. It seemed every member of Sun Horse's male line had been studying on the English tongue.

"You notice he speaks a mite better'n Eagle here," Bat observed. "I'm teachin' him different. Figger when he's full growed there won't be many left that savvy trapper talk.''

He laughed, joined by Blackbird and Standing Eagle, and Hardeman laughed too, enjoying the high spirits that followed a brush with danger, but he wondered if Blackbird would have time to get full grown. He was Standing Eagle's son, there was no mistaking that. The boy watched his father closely and imitated him in many small mannerisms and gestures. He wanted to be just like his father, and Hardeman wondered how much chance he would have. If war came, Bat had said that Standing Eagle and Little Hand would take their families and join the fighting bands. Blackbird could easily find himself confronting army troops before the month was out. But his initial hostility toward Hardeman had given way in the course of five days together to guarded curiosity. Probably he had never had much chance to see a white man close up over a period of time, except for Bat Putnam, his uncle Lodgepole. Hardeman had noted the respect with which the boy always addressed Bat and the considerate good humor Bat bestowed on Blackbird.

"We better put some country between us and those bucks before they change their minds and decide to raise a little hair after all," Hardeman said.

Bat nodded. "We'll move on till dark. Won't be easy to cut trail tonight. I reckon we'll shake 'em."

But even before nightfall the sky cleared rapidly from the west. As the clouds receded toward the eastern horizon the moon rose above them, its rounded face a welcome sight after so many stormy nights. The air turned frigid and the pipe carriers kept a close watch on their back trail, with an eye always to the front as well, searching there for the glow of camp-fires or a glimpse of moonlight smoke that might betray the presence of the army camp ahead. The valley of the Prairie Dog widened gradually until it grew as large as the Clear Fork had been, where the trail had left that stream. As the moon rose higher its light grew brilliant; the Big Horns, all cloaked in snow, loomed so close in the west that it seemed the men might reach out and touch them. Finally, with no sign of pursuit and the horses breathing hard, unwilling to go faster than a slow trot, the riders stopped in a grove of cottonwoods by the creekbank. They stripped bark from the trees by moonlight and fed it to the horses and tethered them, hobbled, amidst what grass there was, close by the shelter they built for themselves against the numbing cold.

As he drifted toward sleep Hardeman could hear the regular working of the horses' jaws, and he felt pleasantly contented. The rich grass would restore the animals' strength somewhat, and a few hours of sleep would restore the men. Tomorrow they would catch Crook for certain.

He awoke suddenly, with no idea how long he might have slept. It was still night, but from somewhere came enough light for him to make out the painted face of a Crow warrior inches from his own. The man was smiling broadly and Hardeman recognized the leader of the Crow war party.

A knife rested against Hardeman's throat. He could feel the razor-sharp blade and the pounding of his heart. Beneath his blankets his hand closed around the Colt but he dared not cock the weapon for fear the Crow would sense the movement. Ever so slowly, the Crow drew the knife across Hardeman's throat, the touch feather-light. Hardeman felt a drop of blood run down his skin to the collar of his wool shirt. The Crow removed the knife blade and tapped it lightly on Hardeman's forehead, taking his coup gleefully. A man's honor was greatest of all if he moved close among his enemies, to touch them without doing harm and escape with his own life.

Fairly certain now that the Crow did not intend to harm him immediately, Hardeman's awareness expanded. He saw that the lashings holding down the covers of the shelter had been cut, the robes raised on one side, admitting the moonlight. The moon was still high. He heard the stamping of horses and their soft snorting. The sound came from too far away. Blackbird had gone to sleep as he did each night, with his own pony's lead rope tied to his wrist and passing out beneath the coverings of the shelter. As far as Hardeman could tell, the boy and everyone else in the shelter were still asleep. He heard the horses again, still farther away. Most likely that was what the Crows wanted. Steal the horses and count coup on the sleeping men they had left afoot. A good joke on the little party of Sioux and whites.

Because of the encounter with the Crows that day, Hardeman had brought both his rifles into the shelter for the night. They lay beside him now. The Crow picked up the Winchester and admired it briefly, then passed it to a second warrior standing outside the shelter. The leader whispered something to the other man, who nodded and disappeared from sight. The Crow picked up the Sharps then and prodded the sleeping form of Bat Putnam with the muzzle of the buffalo gun. Bat rolled over, his eyes opening. The Crow rested the barrel of the Sharps on Bat's forehead. Bat's eyes widened.

Hardeman waited no longer. With the Colt's trigger pulled back to disengage the hammer from the sear, he thumbed back the hammer and fired from beneath his blankets, hoping the layers of bedding wouldn't deflect the bullet. The two-hundred-grain lead projectile struck the Crow in the side, lifting him from his knees and dropping him dead across Bat Putnam. The muffled roar of the Colt broke the soft night sounds and released a bedlam of reactions within the small shelter.

"Christ almighty, Christopher!"

"He's not alone! They've got the horses!"

Standing Eagle leaped to his feet, stumbled, and fell against the side of the shelter, pulling away the last of the covering and most of the supporting poles. Bat threw off the dead Crow and stood up as Hawk

Chaser and Little Hand struggled to free themselves from their robes.

As Blackbird jerked awake he reached instinctively for his bow even as he pulled on the buffalo-hair rein tied to his wrist. The moccasin carrier was the horse guard, and no duty was more important than that one. To his horror he found that his rein had been cut, leaving only a short piece attached to his arm. The horses were neighing now, somewhere off among the cottonwoods. In an instant, Blackbird was on his feet and running, bow in hand, racing for the trees without stopping to see if anyone followed. The theft of the horses was his fault; he would rather die alone trying to get them back than live with the shame of letting the hated *Kanghí* put the pipe carriers afoot.

He was among the trees now and the sounds of the horses were nearer. If only the other *Kanghí* would wait for their companion!

There! Two men were mounting, trying to control the excited animals. He saw no others. Had there been just three of the enemy? He heard his father call his name from somewhere behind him, but the men would not reach the horses in time. He was closest.

He ran silently, bending low so the *Kanghí* would not see him until he was upon them. The moonlight made it easy to avoid the obstacles in his path. How could they not see him now?

Each of the enemy held four horses. The brazen *Kanghí* had ridden or led their own mounts right up to the pipe carriers' tethered animals! They had them all, even the pack horse. If they got away . . .

One man started off downstream, leading his four horses, but the other was having trouble with Lodgepole's little bay mare. She crossed behind the

Kanghí, pulling him around by the arm that held the lead ropes, twisting him in the saddle. He tried to shift the mare's rope to his other hand, the one that held his own rein, but the mare's rope slipped from his grasp. He grabbed for it, missed, and in that moment Blackbird leaped at the man and knocked him from his horse.

They landed on the ground and rolled apart, but the stocky Crow was quick, already reaching for the lithe boy and seizing him by the ankle, the other hand raising a knife. The Crow's horse reared, whinnying and pawing the air as the two men struggled on the ground at his feet. The Crow looked up and Blackbird struck out wildly with his bow, catching the Crow on the side of the head and stunning him, making him lose his hold. In an instant Blackbird was on his feet. He seized the horse's rein and vaulted into the saddle, urging the frightened animal into flight. Ahead of him, three of the remaining horses were running downstream after the fleeing *Kanghí* and the horses he led, but Lodgepole's mare was circling and slowing. The men would catch her easily enough, and they would deal with the remaining *Kanghí*, who was alone and horseless now. Blackbird was concerned with only one thing, the horses that were getting away. They were gone from sight now around a curve in the riverbed. He leaned low over his mount's neck, using his bow as a quirt, straining to hear any sound beyond the clatter of the horse's hooves on the gravel and ice of the river bottom. What if the rest of the *Kanghí* awaited the horse stealing party nearby? What could one boy do against the entire war party?

He could die.

*   *   *

. . . When the scouts returned, appearing silently out of the misty air, Frank Grouard was grinning.

"Big village, Colonel! Plenty horses! Down in the bottom. We find a way down, one here, one there."

He pointed, and aided by the other scouts, he conveyed what they had learned. Two rocky gorges led down to the river, hundreds of feet below. One emerged south of the village, they believed, and the other to the north. The village was west of the Powder, between the frozen stream and the mesa on which the command now stood. Its location had had to be judged by the situation of the large pony herds on the bottomland, but there was no doubt that a village was there and that it was a large one.

"We shall have to move without delay, gentlemen," Reynolds said after hearing the scouts out, and he gave his orders quickly. Captain Henry Noyes's Third Battalion, composed of his Company I and Egan's K Troop, would descend the southern gorge, led by Big and Little Bat and three other scouts. They would attack from that side as soon as they reached the bottom, with Egan's gray-horse company charging the village while Noyes himself secured the horse herd and drove it away upstream. Capturing the Indian horses and leaving the warriors afoot was a vital part of the scheme. Meanwhile, Captain Moore's Fifth Battalion, after being led to the valley floor by Frank Grouard and Louis Richaud, would advance from the bottom of the northern ravine to prevent escape in that direction; thus Moore would be the anvil against which Egan's hammer would strike. Mills's and Corwin's companies, the First Battalion, were to follow behind Moore and be kept in reserve, to be used as needed as the battle developed. Both of these battalions would lead their horses as far as possible and leave them in a safe location, going the rest of the way on foot. Reynolds was to accompany Moore and Mills; he wished Noyes and Egan Godspeed with a firm handshake to each one.

"Well, Ham old fellow, this is where we part company, I'm afraid," Bourke said to Whitcomb. "Mr. Strahorn, Steward Bryan, I propose we accompany Captain Egan."

"You lucky bastard!" said Whitcomb, but he was grinning and he shook Bourke's hand fervently.

"It's the luck of the Irish, boyo. Happy Saint Paddy's Day!" With a farewell wave, Bourke moved to join Egan, whose soldiers were already starting off behind Noyes's company. With Strahorn and Bryan close on his heels he joined Egan at the head of K Troop and in a short time the other elements of the attack force were left behind.

When the two companies reached the boulder-strewn defile that the guides had chosen for the descent, Bourke was aghast. It seemed impossible that men, let alone horses, could make their way down the eroded gorge, which was cluttered with fallen trees and undergrowth. Leading their mounts, the battalion entered the gorge in single file and immediately their progress was marked by the snapping of twigs and limbs as the guides forced a way through the brush. Saddles creaked in the cold and the men cursed as their horses stumbled repeatedly. Bourke winced at each stone overturned, every clatter of hoof against rock or frozen ground, but he soon ceased worrying about the noise and concentrated instead on getting himself to the bottom in one piece. There were frequent halts as one horse at a time was helped past the worst obstacles, and when the column emerged at last into a gentle vale that sloped away to the valley floor, the sky was bright overhead. The descent had taken more than an hour.

The vale was bordered on the left by an uneven ridge that intruded into the valley like an arm. Ahead, in the narrow width of valley bottom that was all they could see, there was no sign either of an Indian village or of the expected horse herd.

"Is this where we're supposed to be?" Noyes wondered aloud. Neither four years at West Point nor fifteen years of army service since then had erased his strong Maine accent.

Egan nodded to Big and Little Bat. "You boys have a look-see over that ridge."

The two scouts mounted their horses and raced off to a low saddle that was fringed with pines. They were out of sight for only a few moments and when they returned they brought shocking news. "We ain't nowhere close to the village, Cap'n," Big Bat said to Noyes. "You best see for yourself. We can cross the ridge up yonder."

The battalion mounted, and followed the scouts over the saddle and into the much broader valley beyond, where they halted again. To their right was the Powder. Ahead of them lay a wide benchland divided roughly in two by a small creek that flowed from the west. Beyond the benchland, over a mile away, where the river swept close to steep, rugged bluffs that overlooked the valley, the peaks of many tipis were visible in a sizable stand of cottonwoods. Nearer at hand in the valley bottom, which was ten or twenty feet lower than the edge of the benchland, hundreds of ponies were grazing in plain view.

"My God, we've botched it!" Noyes exclaimed.

"Couldn't be helped, Cap'n," Big Bat said. "Frank, he reckoned the village was down about there." He pointed to the foot of the ridge behind them. "It was there, we'd be sittin' pretty."

"Look!" cried Bourke, pointing across the benchland. There, on the southern end of the bluffs, was a line of men on foot advancing toward the slopes overlooking the village. Below and behind these small figures was another group, probably Mills's command, descending the edge of the benchland beyond the creek. Noyes's battalion, which had confidently expected to be the first into battle, was in danger now of being the last.

"That must be Moore up on the bluff," Egan said. "It looks like he's trying to work his way along to the north end of the village. He might still cut off their retreat."

"But the Indians will see him!" Strahorn objected.

"They can't yet but they will soon enough," said Egan. "The quicker we get into the village, the better." This last remark was directed at Noyes.

"You don't think the mix-up calls for any change of plan?" Noyes seemed perplexed by the discovery that Reynolds' plan of attack could not be executed as originally given.

"Good God, Henry!" Egan exploded. "We're the only ones who still have a chance to do what we're supposed to! Let's get on with it!'' He yanked his horse around and started off with his troop following behind, placing Noyes in the awkward position of hastening to overtake his nominal subordinate.

"These animals don't have much spunk left," Egan said to Bourke, reining in from a trot to a fast walk. "Damn the luck, anyway! I just pray to God we get close to that village before some young buck decides it's time for a look around the countryside."

In a double column the battalion crossed the benchland. Once down off the low ridge they were out of sight of the village, and the danger of sudden discovery lessened for a time. As they crossed the little creek they saw Mills's battalion emerge from a gully not far ahead, and Egan sent one of the scouts to tell Mills to hold back until the attack began, then to come in and support him from behind.

"I can't see Moore," said Bourke, searching the bluff that now rose close above them.

"I hope to hell he keeps out of sight until we get into the village," Egan muttered. "If the Indians see us now and set up a defense, we'll be in hot water."

The battalion was approaching the northern edge of the benchland, and once more the peaks of tipis could be seen among the cottonwoods on the river plain below. The scouts, who had been moving ahead of the column to watch for gullies that might impede its advance, now returned.

"Injuns wakin' up, Cap'n," said Little Bat. "Boys 're takin' the horses to water."

"Better yet," said Egan, pleased. "The ponies will be that much farther from the village. Where do we get down off this bench?"

"Go down here," Little Bat replied, gesturing to a

gully nearby. "Ain't many trails good for horses up ahead."

"Dismount. Pass it back," Noyes called out in a soft voice as he swung out of his own saddle.

Like dominoes toppling in a row, the mounted men leaned over one by one and stepped to the ground. Overhead, two ravens floated on motionless wings and one of the birds croaked twice; otherwise the valley was silent but for the soft rush of the wind and the small stampings and whuffings of the horses.

Egan glanced at Noyes, who nodded. "You go ahead, Teddy. We'll follow you. I'll separate to the right when you form into line."

Egan moved partway down the short column of troopers and addressed his company in a tone just loud enough for all to hear. "Once we're down below, mount up when I do. Forward by twos and left front into line on my signal. Trot until we're seen. Buglers will then sound the charge, and forward at the gallop." He grinned. "From then on it's Murphy's saloon, boys. Don't be afraid to let them hear you coming."

As they descended the gully the soldiers were hidden from the village and when they gathered on the bottomland only a few tipis were visible at the edge of the cottonwoods. There was no movement there.

The scouts drew aside as the soldiers formed up by company. The attack was up to the troopers. For now, the scouts' job was done. Together with the men who had guided the other companies to the valley floor, they would join Colonels Stanton and Reynolds, to be reassigned as needed during the fighting.

"Good luck, John," Egan said to Bourke as he set his foot in his stirrup. As one the troop mounted behind him and the riders moved out two by two, straight toward the river. Bourke rode beside Egan, with Strahorn and Bryan right behind. When the company was formed in a straight column, Egan raised his arm and swung it to the left. In the space of a few heartbeats the troop had executed a letter-perfect left front into line, and the forty-seven horses and riders advanced in a company front, breaking into a trot. Behind them, Noyes's black-horse troop moved away from the gully in a column and swung off to the right, toward the pony herd. K Troop's grays strutted as they advanced, sensing the repressed excitement of their riders, but the line remained as straight as if they were on parade, and still, ahead of them, the village was silent.

ACKNOWLEDGMENTS

I am indebted to the following people, who generously contributed their time and expertise and thereby did much to assure the historical accuracy of *The Snowblind Moon*: Marie T. Capps, Map and Manuscript Librarian at the United States Military Academy Library, West Point, New York; Catherine T. Engel, Reference Librarian, Colorado Historical Society, Denver, Colorado; Neil Mangum, Historian, Custer Battlefield National Monument, Montana. Special thanks are due to B. Byron Price, Director of the Panhandle-Plains Historical Museum, Canyon, Texas, who read the sections concerning the frontier army and made many valuable suggestions, and to my friends John and Elaine Barlow and Melody Harding of the Bar Cross Ranch, Cora, Wyoming, and Pete and Holly Cameron of Game Hill Ranch, Bondurant, Wyoming, without whose kindness and hospitality I would know even less about the care and raising of beef cattle.

I am particularly grateful to Dr. Bernard A. Hoehner of San Francisco State University, San Francisco, California, for his invaluable advice in matters pertaining to Lakota language and culture as they appear in the novel. (A *Sihásapa*-Lakota, Dr. Hoehner was given the named Jerked With Arrow in his youth, and is now also known as Grass among his people.)

In including some Lakota words and phrases in a work intended for a general readership I have chosen to disregard certain conventions commonly employed in writing Lakota; I have used no linguistic symbols other than the acute accent and have adopted spellings intended to make something close to proper pronunciation as easy as possible for those with no previous knowledge of the language. These decisions were mine alone. I hope persons familiar with Lakota will forgive these simplifications.

Naturally, any remaining historical errors in *The Snowblind Moon*, whether of fact or interpretation, are my sole responsibility.

John Byrne Cooke
Jackson Hole, Wyoming

ABOUT THE AUTHOR

John Byrne ·Cooke was born in New York City in 1940. He was graduated from Harvard College and has worked as a musician, filmmaker, rock and roll road-manager, screenwriter and amateur cowboy. He has lived on both the East and West coasts and now resides in Jackson Hole, Wyoming. *The Snowblind Moon* is his first novel.